PLACES IN WRATH OF THE PICTS

Alt Clota – Strathclyde, home to the Damnonii people
Caer Ebbas – Ebchester, County Durham
Celefyn – the River Kelvin, Glasgow
Dun Breatann – Dumbarton Rock, West Dunbartonshire
Dun Edin – Edinburgh, home to the Votadini people
Dunnottar – Dunnottar, fortress of the Picts, Aberdeenshire
Kinneil – Kinneil, Falkirk
Medio Nemeton – Bar Hill, East Dunbartonshire
Mucrois – St. Andrews
Nant Beac – Bexwell, site of battle in *Bear of Britain*
Shirva – Twechar, East Dunbartonshire
Veluniate – Bo'Ness, Falkirk

WRATH OF THE PICTS

by

Steven A. McKay

Book 5 in the

WARRIOR DRUID OF BRITAIN

CHRONICLES

Copyright © 2022

All rights reserved. No part of this book may be reproduced, in whole or in part, without prior written permission from the copyright holder.

PROLOGUE

Lancelot was tired. Not the kind of tiredness one feels after a good day's work in the fields or mending broken fences after a winter storm, no, this was a terrible bone-weariness that most people were quite unused to. Even after a battle his body hadn't felt like this – used-up and utterly spent. Fighting was often a pleasure, as it stirred the blood and made one truly happy to still be alive once it was all over, and there would usually be good food and drink to enjoy afterwards. A chance to restore the energy spent during the battle.

Lancelot wished he could fight right now. Lift a sword, and take it to his enemies, cut every last one of them down and make them regret ever crossing him. He snorted with bitter amusement, knowing that, even if someone were to hand him a weapon at that moment, he'd be unable to wield it with the skill he was renowned for. By Taranis, he'd hardly be able to lift it off the deck of the ship, never mind attack his captors with it. The day had been spent rowing until his hands were blistered and every muscle ached, and whenever the Saxons thought he was slacking, he got the lash.

It had been a hellish day.

And tomorrow he would get to do it all over again.

The Saxon jarl, Leofdaeg stood over them, face twisted in a cruel smile. "All right, you lazy pigs," he said. "Feeding time."

To his shame, Lancelot leaned forward along with the rest of the slaves chained at the oars of the longship, desperate for the meagre fare that kept them alive, if still perpetually hungry. It wasn't always Leofdaeg who dished out the food, but the jarl enjoyed the task for he hated the slaves, all of whom were Britons, or *Waelisc* as the Saxons insultingly called them. And, of them all, Leofdaeg despised Lancelot the most.

The food – bread mainly, with the occasional lucky recipient also receiving a little cheese – was handed out, the slaves eagerly snatching it from their Saxon owner. Lancelot was, as ever, left until last.

"Hungry, pretty boy?" Leofdaeg asked, lip curling cruelly. He didn't bother waiting for a reply, simply lifted the chunk of bread that was left for the Briton and spat onto it before tossing it to Lancelot with a laugh.

Despite the spittle soaking the food Lancelot didn't hesitate to bite some off and begin chewing. Gone were the days when he would throw away the disgusting rations – it hadn't taken him long to realise he would get nothing else to eat until the next 'meal'. Being forced to row for hours at a time on a completely empty stomach was a horrible experience. Light-headedness sometimes even gave way to hallucinations and those scared Lancelot more than the Saxon whips.

So, he swallowed the bread despite its vileness, desperate to keep his strength up that he might, somehow, eventually kill Leofdaeg one day. There could be no chance of escape, no way to return to his old life as the warlord Arthur's right-hand man and champion, but if he could just find a way to watch the light of life fade from Leofdaeg's eyes, Lancelot would gladly consign himself to a watery grave.

He'd been captured when he led his warband to the Saxon stronghold at Garrianum, hoping to take advantage of the fact that most of the enemy were miles away, fighting the rest of Arthur's army. Yet, despite disguising themselves in Saxon armour Lancelot's raiders had quickly been discovered and brutally wiped out. Leofdaeg was in charge of the Saxons in Garrianum that day, and he'd gloried in the slaughter of the Britons, until a hammer thrown by Lancelot had shattered the jarl's forearm. For that, Lancelot was savagely beaten and now forced to serve as the Saxon's slave, ultimately ending up here, rowing this ship day after day, subject to Leofdaeg's insults and indignities.

In truth, the rest of the Saxon sailors were nothing like as vindictive as Leofdaeg. Most did not seem interested in the slaves who rowed the ship from place to place. On this journey there was a second nobleman, another jarl who seemed to somehow outrank Leofdaeg, judging by the interactions Lancelot had noticed between the pair. Sigarr was the second jarl's name, an unimpressive-looking little man who appeared clever and confident despite his lack of physical stature. Sigarr never handed out the slaves' food, and his frown suggested he disapproved of Leofdaeg's treatment of them, although not enough to ever say anything about it. From bits of conversation Lancelot overheard it seemed Sigarr was cousin to the powerful Saxon warleaders, Hengist and Horsa, which explained why he outranked Leofdaeg.

Lancelot thought about all this as he ate, glad to rest his aching muscles which, despite the heavy physical labour of recent weeks, had not grown much. The lack of food saw to that. It had also dulled the lustre of his once sleek blond hair, although he did not know it himself since slaves had, obviously, no access to a mirror and no opportunity to gaze into the waters around the ship.

If Arthur, or Bedwyr, or any of his other old companions, could see him now they would have wept, for Lancelot was a shadow of the man he'd been just a few months ago. For a warrior who'd prided himself on his appearance, the wiry, lank-haired, sunken-eyed slave who sat chained to the Saxon ship now would have been quite a shock for his friends to look upon.

Yet, despite his appearance, Arthur's fallen champion's spirit had not been broken. Perhaps it would be eventually – Leofdaeg had not beaten him too badly after all, not since that first day when the Briton had been captured. Now that had been a beating, and had left Lancelot unconscious for quite some time, bruised and terribly battered, but the jarl clearly valued his prize and wanted to prolong Lancelot's suffering rather than letting him escape his life as a slave with an early death.

Sigarr had noticed the oarsman's gaze and he said to Leofdaeg now, loudly enough that Lancelot heard, "You should really ransom him to the *Waelisc* warlord. He'd fetch you a hoard of treasure."

Leofdaeg smiled grimly and glared at the blond slave who looked back dully. "Maybe I will. Eventually. But just now I'm enjoying myself too much watching him suffer. Perhaps, when he's half-dead and of little use to me, I'll send him back to Arthur. With no hands, maybe. Or no nose. Or perhaps I'll take his eyes."

Sigarr did not reply. Such boasts and threats were commonplace amongst warriors of course and *something* was needed to pass the time on trading journeys such as this one.

"Right, you lazy bastards," shouted another of the Saxons, cracking a whip over the slaves, who by now had finished their frugal meal and were doing their utmost to rest. "There's no wind, so take up your oars and pull, or we'll never reach our destination!"

Without needing to be told twice, Lancelot dutifully set to work again, his eyes still fixed on Leofdaeg. The jarl could spit on his food, wipe his nose with it, even shit on it if it meant Lancelot kept his strength up just enough that one day he might slaughter the whoreson.

As the ship picked up speed again, slicing nimbly through the rolling, dark waves, and the rowers settled into the familiar, steady rhythm, Lancelot's mind drifted off as it often did these days. Sometimes he would recall that fateful day when he'd been captured. Others, he would imagine killing his Saxon masters, or being with a beautiful girl in a field bursting with summer flowers, or with Arthur and his other companions by a roaring fire with fine meat and drink...

Now, Lancelot thought of the giant druid from the northern lands, Bellicus of Dun Breatann. The pair had become friends the previous winter when they'd crept into a Saxon encampment and killed the jarl there, a vicious man called Saewine. Leofdaeg had also been there that day and watched impotently as the two Britons made their escape, swearing to pay them back one day, for Saewine was his father.

Idly, Lancelot imagined what it would like to be a druid himself and have mystical powers of his own. Powers to make Leofdaeg's cock swell with black pus and burst in a miasma of filth, or powers to make a bolt of lightning strike the jarl where he stood, or...

His thoughts drifted again and he wondered where Bellicus was at that moment. Hopefully the druid was safe with his people, enjoying his freedom, and faring much better than Lancelot...

CHAPTER ONE

"D'you think Catia is safe?" It was the question the travellers were all desperate to know the answer to, since the moment the messenger brought them the news of the princess's disappearance. The rider had come all the way from Alt Clota to Nant Beac, where Arthur's Britons had finally engaged – and defeated – Hengist's Saxon army in battle, to tell Bellicus what had happened. A journey of around four-hundred miles, yet the messenger could not explain why, or how, an eleven-year-old girl had left a fortress like Dun Breatann without anyone noticing. And in the company, apparently, of an enemy hostage who also happened to be a princess?

It was all very strange, as Bellicus had noted more than once during this journey, but he nodded in response to Duro's question.

"Aye," the young druid said firmly. "I think she's safe enough, for now. Aife would not harm her, I'm certain of that."

Duro, a former Roman centurion who although now into middle age was still a fearsome warrior, accepted his friend's assertion without question. In the years since he'd known Bellicus he'd come to see the druid as a great judge of character. Besides, Duro had met the Pictish Princess, Aife, himself and been impressed by her. She was not much like her father, King Drest, a man Duro despised. He tried not to think of the dark days he and Bellicus had spent as prisoners in Dunnottar's cells, beaten and tortured, culminating in Drest cutting off two of the centurion's fingers before they'd finally managed to escape with the help of Ria, the Picts' druidess. He clenched his fist and looked forward to the day when he would have revenge on Drest, and the Saxon jarl, Horsa, who'd killed the centurion's wife, Alatucca.

Life had certainly not been boring since Duro had met Bellicus, that was certain. Painful at times, but never boring.

A twig cracked in their campfire, jolting the centurion from his dark reverie, and he turned to look into the dancing orange flames, knowing it would not help to dwell on the past.

"So, where the hell are they then?" Eburus, the third member of the little group spoke up, rather too loudly as usual. "And why did they bugger off without telling anyone where they were going?"

Duro had found Eburus, champion of the Votadini tribe, incredibly irritating for a long time after they'd met, since the young red-headed warrior had seemed arrogant, bullish and, frankly, an arsehole, but the three men had slowly become firm friends. Still, certain aspects of Eburus's character rubbed the centurion the wrong way.

"Keep your voice down, by Mithras!" Duro hissed, shaking his head as if scolding a naughty child. "There could be Saxons, or Dalriadans, or the gods-know-what lurking in those trees behind us."

"Aye," Eburus snorted. "And they'd not have noticed the light, or smoke, from our fire by now, eh, centurion? Sometimes I wonder how you got that promotion in the legions."

Bellicus smiled in the shadows at the playful barb, and even more so when Duro retorted, "And sometimes I wonder how you're still alive, when you're so damn annoying!"

"Because no-one can beat me in a fight," Eburus responded instantly, but his triumphant grin quickly fell away as he remembered his first meeting with Bellicus, who had broken his nose with the butt of his staff. He nodded somewhat sheepishly at the massive druid and admitted, "Well, apart from him, maybe."

They fell into a companionable silence then, listening to the crackle of the small fire and the occasional cry of a nocturnal animal, stalking the darkness nearby. Eventually, Cai, Bellicus's massive dog, wandered out of the circle of light and emptied his bladder before they heard his tongue lapping thirstily at the little stream they'd chosen to camp beside. Even soldiers used to sleeping outside in the open, as they were, found it reassuring to have the finely-honed senses, and fearsome jaws, of a mastiff guarding their camp.

Eburus stood up, stretching stiffly to his full height before taking a piece of meat which was slowly roasting over the fire. He blew on it until it was cool enough to eat and then tore some off with his teeth, revelling in the tasty juices that filled his mouth.

"Could the girls' disappearance have anything to do with your prince?" Duro asked him, and Eburus frowned.

"Ysfael? Why would he be involved?"

Duro shrugged. "I'm not sure. Something about him annoys me."

"Everyone seems to annoy you, centurion," Eburus noted with a smile.

"You know what I mean," Duro said seriously.

Bellicus muttered agreement, coming forward himself to take some of the meat. "Ysfael is like a lot of young noblemen," he said, selecting a choice piece while also lifting some of the gristlier cuts for Cai. "Arrogant and entitled. I never spent much time around him, but I didn't think much of the man. It sticks in my craw that he's now married to Queen Narina."

Duro knew that Narina and Bellicus had been close – indeed there were rumours that the pair were lovers, and a suggestion that Catia was actually the druid's daughter – but that had not coloured Duro's view of Ysfael. He was simply not a likeable young man, hence Duro and Bellicus's misgivings.

Could the Votadini prince, and new husband of the Damnonii queen, have harmed Catia and Aife?

Eburus finished his food, wiped his beard, and belched loudly before shaking his head. "Ysfael is arrogant, and he looked down on everyone, even me although I was – am – the Votadini champion. I don't think he'd murder girls though. Why would he? What could he gain from it?"

No-one had an answer for that. They simply did not have enough information on what had been going on in Alt Clota. Ysfael's marriage to Narina added a whole new dynamic to the already tangled relationships within the kingdom, however.

The queen's previous husband, King Coroticus, had ended up a drunken sot who'd grown paranoid and dangerous to himself and his people before Bellicus was forced to kill him in a duel. After that, Narina's marriage to Ysfael had been seen as a shrewd political move, to join the two tribes – Damnonii and Votadini – together. Surely Narina hadn't just swapped one bad spouse for another?

"We'll rise as early as possible," Bellicus said, placing more wood on the fire before lying down and pulling his woollen blanket over himself. "I want to get home as fast as we can and find out exactly what's been going on while we've been in the south fighting beside Arthur."

Without another word, the three men closed their eyes and went to sleep, setting no watch for they were in safe lands and Cai would certainly hear any enemy's approach, as would the three horses which were happily dozing nearby.

As he drifted off, Duro thought of all the various kings, warlords, and peoples vying for supremacy or just survival in Britain. Arthur, Drest, Horsa and Hengist, Dalriadans, Saxons, Picts, Damnonii, Dumnonii…By Mithras, would there ever truly be peace in this great land that even the Romans couldn't quite bring to heel?

CHAPTER TWO

"If only Bel and Duro were with us," said Catia fearfully as they sat shivering in the dark, wishing they could risk a fire to stave off some of the chill.

"The Roman?" asked Aife. "I can understand you missing the druid – his powers would be reassuring right now. But the old centurion?"

Catia frowned, apparently annoyed by her companion's words. "Duro's a great warrior," she said waspishly. "He'd even give you a good fight. And he makes me feel calm. Nothing ever seems to frighten him or worry him." She stared out in the night, as if wondering where her one-time protectors were at that moment. "I mean, he *does* get scared, and nervous sometimes, but he can control it well. You don't see it, and that makes everyone around him feel more confident. If he and Bel were here, I'd not be worried about falling asleep at all. They'd protect us, from enemy soldiers, or outlaws, or…spirits."

Aife felt a pang of guilt at bringing the young princess with her on this dangerous journey, and not for the first time. Aife and a few other high-ranking Pictish nobles had been taken as hostages by the Damnonii after a failed invasion of Dun Breatann, while King Drest agreed not to attack Narina's lands again and the rest of the survivors in his beaten army were allowed to go home.

Had Aife been rash, to climb down the towering rock and escape her life as a political prisoner? No, she felt she had no choice. But bringing Catia along was undoubtedly selfish. She thought back to the events that had led them here.

For weeks, Prince Ysfael had been showing more and more interest in her. Watching her whenever she walked past on her daily exercise about the fortress. Then little compliments. He even followed her once and, when they were on the far side of the rock, out of sight of any guards, he'd kissed her. It had been so unexpected that she'd reciprocated at first – he was quite handsome after all, and Aife was very lonely in Dun Breatann. Soon enough, though, she'd come to her senses and broken his embrace. Queen Narina already disliked her, it would only make her life in the Damnonii fortress worse if she found out Ysfael and Aife were having some kind of relationship.

Besides, he was an arrogant young man who felt entitled to take anything, or anyone, he desired, as Aife found out. He was no longer complimentary towards her after that day, instead eyeing her menacingly. If she'd not been an accomplished warrior she would have been quite frightened of him, yet, even with her skill as a fighter, she soon dreaded seeing him around. She feared he might try to force himself on her eventually, and slept with her dagger beside her at all times, just in case.

And then, after a feast in the hall one evening, when most of the revellers had fallen asleep or departed, Aife had heard Ysfael talking with some of his Votadini companions. She had not been able to make out exactly what they were saying, just a snatch of conversation that had made no sense to her, but Ysfael noticed her in the corner and immediately fell silent. His expression had not just been one of dislike or even hatred, there had been distrust and fear in it too, as if the prince thought Aife had overheard some terrible, dark secret.

She wished she had, for it might have given her some power over him. Instead, she'd become aware of Ysfael's men regularly hanging around her dwelling, watching her. Aife was not yet twenty summers old, but she was a warrior and a commander in the Pictish army, and she knew when her life was in danger. The Votadini men lurking about, touching the hilts of their swords and scowling whenever they saw her, were just waiting for an opportunity to harm her without being seen, she was sure of it.

If the druid, Bellicus, had been around she might have gone to him with her concerns, for she believed him to be trustworthy, but he was far in the south with Arthur's army of Britons, fighting the Saxons. Her only other friend in Dun Breatann was Catia, and Aife did not want to trouble the child with her fears, especially when they were based merely on instinct rather than any real proof. The idea of approaching Narina was ludicrous, for the queen would naturally support her husband, even if she didn't already dislike Aife. And the Damnonii guard captain, Gavo, although undoubtedly a good man, was completely loyal to the queen so…

Aife had decided to escape from Dun Breatann before Ysfael and his men came for her. She'd prepared herself and even managed to hide a length of rope which she'd stolen from some workers near the little house she'd been living in. But she'd wanted to say goodbye to Catia and, when she did, the afternoon before she climbed over the fortress's wall, the young princess had said she'd come with her.

Of course, Aife vehemently argued against that, but Catia was having none of it.

"If you go alone our hunters will shoot you down," she'd argued. "But if I come with you, they'll have to be careful in case their arrows hit me."

That reasoning hadn't entirely convinced Aife but eventually Catia threatened to tell Queen Narina about the escape plan and so, not entirely unhappily, the Pictish princess agreed to take the younger girl along and they'd left Dun Breatann that night.

Now, many days and miles later, they were close to their destination and, thank the gods, it seemed everything would work out well.

"Do you think—"

"Hush!" Aife's long arm swept out, signalling for silence, and Catia immediately complied. They listened, hearing nothing at first, but then the unmistakeable sound of someone walking along the trail behind them could be heard. Whoever it was moved quietly, as if trained in tracking and hunting, but at this time of night, with the insects and birds silent, even a quiet movement carried through the sparse trees along the track that had brought them to their camp site.

Aife was on her feet now, the tall, well-built young woman moving gracefully, drawn sword in her hand. Catia followed her friend's lead, also getting up and moving to stand behind the thick trunk of an old ash tree. She too pulled her sword silently from its sheath and leaned against the rough bark as they waited for whoever was coming towards them. Both princesses were clad in dark, forest colours, making them hard to spot, and Aife had a short-sleeved chainmail shirt beneath her green checked tunic. They remained as still as the trees that were hiding them, occasionally meeting one another's gaze, eyes showing white in the gloom as they prepared to fight, or run if there was no other choice.

For days they'd been walking, and their ultimate destination was clear: Dunnottar, fortress of the Picts, and Aife's home. But they hadn't simply taken the busiest roads and tracks there, for there would be pursuit, and the first place searched would obviously be the main routes leading northeast. So, for a time they'd simply camped wherever they could, travelling over fields and meadows by night and sleeping during the day, until they'd eventually moved far enough north without being captured that they began to feel safer. That's when they'd started to make more of a concerted effort to aim towards Dunnottar, and not placed so much emphasis on moving by night as they could travel faster by the light of day.

It would be heart-breaking to be so close to their goal – surely they needed just a few days more travelling – only to be taken now by the pursuers from Dun Breatann. Especially if the men trailing them were sent by Ysfael rather than Narina…

Aife stood, heart pounding in her chest, waiting for whoever was coming. She forced herself to be calm and focused on the sword in her hand and the forest ahead. Although she was young, she'd been through a lot in her life, seen men and women fight and die, and learned how to defend herself as well as any man. And there was Catia to protect, standing tense and pale in the shadows.

Aife would not let their pursuers take them easily, that was certain.

"Someone's passed this way recently." A voice filtered through the trees, low yet clear enough, and Aife felt as if her heart had jumped into her mouth. There could be no doubt now, it wasn't a fox or wolf stalking the land behind them, it was men and, from the accent, Aife knew they were of the Votadini – Ysfael's soldiers.

Oh well, thought the princess, perhaps that was for the best. If it had been trackers from Catia's Damnonii tribe she would have been loath to attack them. She had no such qualms about the Votadini prince's lackeys.

"I can smell them," the voice came again, closer now. There was a sound of sniffing, and the man made a crude remark about how much he enjoyed the scent of a sweating woman and how it made him feel, and then Aife saw him, stepping out of the trees and into the clearing as he followed the path.

He was a small man in a green tunic, wiry and balding, and Aife had, of course, seen him around Dun Breatann. It was a mighty fortress but, after all, not particularly big. One saw the same faces day after day and quickly grew to recognise them all. She thought this man was named Docimedis and knew he was one of Ysfael's inner circle. Watching him sniff the air, the woman could only feel distaste towards him.

A second man appeared behind the first, another of the Votadini, and this one was bigger. He was called Maccis and was another of Ysfael's closest companions. Clad in a brown fur cloak which surely covered armour of some sort, he looked much more of a threat than Docimedis. More soldierly. Although, Aife thought grimly, you could never judge the threat a fighter posed from their size alone – she herself could, and often had, beaten men bigger than herself. Catia could also beat boys older and stronger than her on the sparring field. The men looking for them were not boys, of course, but now that the trackers were upon them, Aife's anxiety faded, replaced by a cold resolve.

"Are you looking for me?"

The bigger of the two hunters cursed and stepped back fearfully as Aife stepped out from behind the tree, her naked, polished blade glinting in the dim light. That had been one benefit of allowing Catia to come with her. The younger girl had been able to bring extra supplies, and even retrieve Aife's own weapons from the armoury and return them to her before they escaped the fortress.

The smaller man did not flinch, instead drawing his own weapon with his right hand but holding out his left palm at the same time, as if trying to push back the Pictish princess.

"Aye," he admitted. "We were sent to track you, my lady. Queen Narina wants you, and the other princess," he glanced about at the other trees and undergrowth but did not spot Catia, "to head back to Dun Breatann. The people are worried about you."

"Well, there's no need," Aife said, and her voice was low, unwavering. "We're quite safe, so you can turn around and leave."

Docimedis smiled but he was frowning at the same time. Aife stared at him, knowing he was wondering how to get out of this unexpected situation. The trackers had obviously expected to steal up on their quarry, and surprise them while they slept – they'd not expected the girls to be ready for them like this. And, since they still hadn't noticed Catia behind her tree, that added another element of uncertainty to the standoff.

"We can't just go back," he said, shrugging, still smiling almost apologetically. "I'm not much of a liar. If I told Prince Ysfael and the queen that we'd not found you, they'd know I wasn't telling the truth." He shook his head, acting as if he were talking to an old friend. "I'm too honest, that's my trouble. Besides, there are other trackers out hunting for you, and they might not be as kindly as us."

"Aye," rumbled the bigger man, who hadn't moved but was obviously watching and listening intently for signs of Catia.

Aife's lip curled disdainfully. "'Kindly'? Well, I'm not unkind myself, so I'll give you another chance to turn and head back the way you came."

Docimedis was losing patience, his smile fading to become more of a grimace. "Lady, like I said, we can't just let you go. You abducted the Damnonii princess, by the gods! We have to return her to her mother." He spun his sword expertly around in his hand, as if showing Aife his skill with the weapon. "Honestly, we were told to bring the girl back safe and well, but you…" He shrugged. "No-one said we had to take *you* back unharmed."

Maccis moved forward to stand in line with him, but with a dozen paces between them, offering two quite separate threats to Aife should she decide to attack.

"Where is the other girl?" asked the big man coldly.

"Long gone," Aife said, and suddenly exploded into motion, drawing a dagger from her belt with her left hand and throwing it at Maccis. At the same time, she ran forward. Her target had been ready for her doing *something*, but he was forced to raise his hands to defend himself from the dagger which, as it happened, flew well wide of him, but Aife's sword did not miss him.

There was a pained cry as the princess's blade pierced his thigh and he fell backwards, placing all his weight on his uninjured leg, teeth bared but afraid to step forward, understanding the agony it would cause.

The smaller hunter had reacted instantly too, but Aife was able to bring her sword around in time to parry his attack. He had not been lying about being willing to harm her, for his swing was intended to kill or maim the princess.

"Fucking Picts," he shouted, swinging his blade again, and again, as she expertly batted his attacks aside. "Useless liars, every one of you. Will you help me kill her, Maccis?" His big companion did now attempt to lumber forward but, the moment he placed more weight onto his right leg he screamed in pain and collapsed onto the grass.

Catia roared then, high-pitched and throaty, charging out from the trees with her own sword held ready. The smaller hunter was forced to turn away from Aife momentarily for he saw Catia in his peripheral vision, saw the blade in her hand and knew that, despite her age, she could kill him quite easily if allowed to plunge that steel into his side.

Aife kicked out, into the back of the man's leg behind his knee, and he stumbled while at the same time parrying Catia's attack.

"Don't kill us!" he cried in terror. "We're not your enemies, we're all on the same side!"

Aife was right behind him now and she lashed out, smashing the pommel of her sword into the back of his head.

"You bitch!" roared the bigger man who had managed to stand up by clumsily using his sword as a crutch and now pointed it at her furiously. "I'll gut you for this! Prince Ysfael will thank me for it."

"Shut up, Maccis," Aife replied in a bored tone. "And sit back down." She watched him warily as she knelt on the back of the smaller man who was lying groaning and unresisting now. Taking his sword from his limp fingers she tossed it far away into the trees and then did the same with a knife she found in his belt, and another that was strapped to his ankle. "You're lucky I didn't kill you both," she said, standing up and moving to the other side of the big man.

He watched her, face a murderous mask as he squeezed his wounded, bleeding thigh.

Catia walked around to take up a position behind him, and then Aife told him to throw his sword into the trees too.

"You'll both live," she said. "As long as you see to that injured leg. Or you can try and kill us, even though you can't walk and I've already proved how easily I can beat you." She jerked her head upwards. "Throw the sword. You can collect it later, once we're gone."

The hunter snarled something incoherent, a threat or an insult it was impossible to know for he was so angry it came out merely as garbled noise. He knew he was beaten, however, so, still muttering oaths, he threw his weapon. It sailed into the gloom and clattered against a tree trunk before falling through rustling leaves and landing with a soft thump.

"Come on, Catia. Let's go."

Without another word to the hunters, Aife waited until the younger princess was safely ahead of her, following the same track they'd been following previously, and then she retrieved her thrown dagger and backed away until they were safely out of sight.

"That was…exciting," Catia said, and, as they met one another's eyes, both started to laugh in wild relief.

"Come on," Aife said again, breaking into a jog. "Those two won't be coming after us for a while, if at all, but their shouting might draw more trackers towards us. We should get well clear of this place before dawn."

And, blood still coursing through their veins from the short but violent confrontation, they ran.

CHAPTER THREE

"I knew we should never have trusted that Pictish woman. She was too proud, and too dangerous, to hold as a hostage." She shook her head, perplexed. "But why would she abduct Catia?" Queen Narina's voice was tight with anxiety and impotent anger. Fear, even. It was possible Catia had not simply been taken by Aife, but harmed. Killed even…It did not bear thinking about.

"Who knows?" Her husband, the Votadini prince, Ysfael, replied in a bored tone. "Does it matter?"

Narina spun to face him, eyes blazing. "Yes, it matters!" she shouted. "She's my daughter, you fool!"

Ysfael waved a hand dismissively. "Calm down, woman. I simply meant it didn't matter *why* the Pict took Catia – what matters is that we bring your daughter home safely."

Narina stared at the young man she'd married for political reasons rather than love, gauging his words. He wasn't looking at her, instead he was gazing out across the wooden wall of Dun Breatann, watching as a cloud passed the sun, drawing a long shadow across the land. Her land.

"My men will find them," he said, eyes drawn upwards by the cry of a wheeling gull. "Or yours will. Two young women, wandering about in the wilderness? It won't be long before they're brought back, Narina, stop worrying. Catia is far more mature than most children her age."

The queen's jaw tightened but she remained silent now. How could Ysfael understand how she felt? He was ten years younger than her at just nineteen years old, childless as far as she knew, and seemed to care little for anyone other than himself, as many young people did. Especially those who'd been born to a life of privilege.

Ysfael was the son of Cunedda, the Votadini king, but he was not the firstborn so not in line for the throne when his father died. As a result he had been allowed to live quite freely, never being forced to learn how to be a good ruler – instead, he'd spent most of his time drinking, gambling, fighting, and wenching. Indeed, now that Narina thought about it, her young husband probably did have children, somewhere.

"You need to stop worrying so much about things," he repeated, turning to look at her with an irritated expression on his face. He had a red beard, but it was wispy, and there was a scar on his jaw which was hairless; he was handsome, but not particularly impressive looking. Especially when he was petulant. "You're the queen, by Taranis! Enjoy it, instead of walking around your fortress as if the sky was about to fall on you."

Again, Narina did not reply, but she did cross to stand beside him and look down at the green fields and wooded hills that lay to the north of Dun Breatann. His criticism of her was not a new one, indeed many of her closest friends and advisors often told her the same thing. Even Catia thought she was overly serious and worried too much about her people while ignoring her own happiness.

Perhaps she would try to enjoy her life a little more, she thought. Once her beloved daughter was safely home.

"Maybe you're right," she said, and Ysfael smiled. "When Catia is back by my side, I'll try to delegate some of my responsibilities a bit more."

"Good idea," Ysfael agreed heartily. "Gavo could do more, for a start. There's no need for him to be riding off with the warband, patrolling the borders all the time. That's something you could do occasionally – let your people see you. Let you see them, and enjoy their food, drink and hospitality."

Narina met his gaze and wondered if he was trying to get rid of her for a while so that he might spend even more time with the young women of Alt Clota. She didn't particularly mind, it was more of a political union than anything else after all and, as long as he didn't publicly make a fool of her, it didn't seem to matter. Still, she stared at him as she replied, "That's a good idea. You should come too."

His sudden look of dismay was almost comical, and he quickly looked away, muttering, "Aye. Maybe."

"Have you heard from any of your trackers?"

He pursed his lips, shaking his head and, for a moment, Narina thought he seemed almost as worried about the princesses' disappearance as she was herself.

"What about you?" Ysfael said, and turned to the east, away from Narina.

"Not since we had word a couple of days ago that their trail had been found, heading north. I expect Aife will be trying to make it home to Dunnottar. Why she took my daughter with her is a mystery, though. A prisoner? As Aife was here?" The queen sighed. "I can't understand it at all."

Ysfael reached out and took her hand in his, an unusually tender gesture from him. "Catia will be fine," he said, although he still didn't meet Narina's eyes. "She can take care of herself. That sword she carries around so often isn't just for decoration. I've seen her fighting."

Narina smiled proudly. "She is good with it. When the Saxons abducted her, she vowed never to be such an easy target again. Her face fell once more. "Hasn't done her much good though, has it?"

Where was Catia? Narina thought about what she knew of the disappearance. She had woken up one morning a few days before the Lughnasadh celebrations and broken her fast, only growing concerned when Catia did not appear. The girl always ate some bread and cheese in the mornings – always – so, when there was no sign of her, Narina had gone into the girl's bedchamber. Catia hadn't been there, and some of her clothes were missing, along with the blanket that had been on her bed, and, naturally, her prized sword.

Soon enough, Aife's guards discovered their charge's quarters – a well-appointed little cottage on the northern side of Dun Breatann's peak – was also empty.

The girls had not exited the fortress through the gates, which had remained barred the entire night, with sentries watching them the whole time. It hadn't taken long to discover the length of rope tied to a section of wall behind Aife's house, however.

Narina pictured her daughter climbing down the side of Dun Breatann, and her stomach lurched. What if the girl had slipped, or her arms weren't strong enough to hold onto the rope? The volcanic rock which the fortress had been built on wasn't incredibly high – 240 feet at the taller, eastern peak – but it was steep, and a fall down it would certainly be fatal.

Yet no bodies were discovered at the bottom of the rope, or anywhere else.

The guard captain, Gavo, Narina's closest advisor besides Bellicus, had done all he could to investigate the disappearance of the girls and, when he was done questioning everyone within the fortress and examining every area of the place, he'd come to a firm conclusion: "Catia wasn't abducted. She went with Aife willingly."

It was the only real explanation. Aife was a strong young woman, a true warrior, but she could not carry an unwilling, or unconscious, Catia down that rope.

Narina simply refused to accept Gavo's suggestion though. If Catia had willingly run off with the Pictish princess, it meant her daughter was content to put Narina through this torture, of not knowing where she was or what had happened to her, *again*. Catia and her mother were very close, and it seemed unthinkable that she might do that to Narina.

So, while Gavo's soldiers, and those of Ysfael's own Votadini guards who were skilled at tracking, scoured the land for the missing girls, Narina tried to understand what really lay behind this mystery.

"Aife is supposed to be her friend," the queen said, half to Ysfael and half to herself. "Maybe Aife just wanted to escape and go home. She's been treated well enough here, but she was still a prisoner. Maybe she threatened to kill me if Catia didn't go with her."

Ysfael said nothing, but Narina went on anyway, speaking her thoughts aloud regardless of her audience's attentiveness.

"The people of Alt Clota know Catia – if she asked them for food, they would gladly give what they could. And, similarly, if Catia, their princess, told them not to tell anyone they'd seen them, well, they'd do as they were commanded. On the other hand, if Aife was alone and tried to get food from some farmer or shepherd, they'd have no reason to give her it. That's why Aife would have found some way to force Catia to go with her." To Narina, this explanation made sense.

It was also rather more frightening than the idea that Catia had run off to Dunnottar of her own accord.

Neither scenario was pleasant, truth be told. And now Narina conceded to herself that she'd not been the best of hosts to Aife. No, she'd not been cruel to the younger woman, but neither had she been friendly. In truth, Catia's blossoming friendship with the Pict had rankled with Narina; she was jealous, she had to admit.

Aife had also been cold towards the queen at first, and that too had driven a wedge between them. They were enemies after all, so it was a difficult relationship from the very beginning, with neither woman trusting the other and, when Narina noticed Ysfael eyeing the Pictish warrior-princess with undisguised admiration, it had only added to her resentment. Yes, Narina could accept her husband sleeping with other women, but seeing Ysfael lusting after the girl who'd also become the closest companion of Catia…

"I'm hungry," said Ysfael abruptly. "Come, you should take something too. You've hardly eaten these past few weeks; you'll make yourself ill."

Narina nodded, wondering if she could finish a bowl of broth and following her husband towards the path that led down to the great hall where they took most of their meals. The smell of roasting meat and simmering broth filtered out through the chimney hole, wafting towards them on the late-summer breeze.

"My lord." A pair of guards stood at the doorway, Votadini soldiers who saluted their prince before opening the door for Ysfael and Narina to pass through. Narina wondered why guards were needed there, so deep inside the fortress, but she didn't care enough to question it.

Inside the hall the smells were even stronger and, despite her worries, Narina's mouth began to water. It was simply a natural physical reaction to the beef roasting over the fire although she didn't think she could eat much. Admitting to herself that she might have been part of the reason why Aife had taken Catia over the wall to the gods knew where had made her feel even worse than before.

"Sit," Ysfael said to her, gesturing at the nearest bench. He sat opposite her and looked up as one of the serving women approached.

"My lord," the servant said, almost fearfully, eyes fixed on the floor as she clasped her hands before her. "Lady."

Narina watched her, wondering at the woman's demeanour.

"Bring us some of that beef," Ysfael commanded, without turning to look at the servant. "And wine."

"I'm not really hungry," Narina said.

"You need to eat," Ysfael said firmly, waving a hand in the air. "I like my women to have some meat on their bones. Well? Hurry up, you, fetch our food," he said, glancing at the servant, a middle-aged, stocky matron who immediately hurried off to do as she was told.

Narina felt slight irritation at her husband's words, but she was in no mood to argue with him. When the food was brought by the nervous servant she forced herself to chew a slice – it was cooked to perfection and, on another day, would have been greedily devoured. But all Narina could think of was her missing daughter and, after that first cut of meat she pushed the rest towards Ysfael. He frowned at her but accepted the food and ate it all in silence, washing it down with a cup of wine as he watched the younger, more attractive serving girls preparing food. One in particular seemed to draw his eye and the queen wondered how many times Ysfael had bedded her. The girl was quite pretty, she had to admit, with a full figure and thick red hair.

Narina almost laughed as she realised she'd conditioned herself to actually approve of her spouse's choice of bed-mate, rather a different reaction to how she'd viewed her previous husband's infidelity. That had been entirely different of course – Narina and Coroticus had truly loved one another and been very close for years, until Catia was abducted by the Saxons and everything had turned rotten.

She looked at Ysfael, who didn't notice her gaze. He was arrogant and overbearing, and didn't seem to have much respect for women, but then again, he didn't respect men he thought were beneath him either. Which was just about all of them.

He was not physically abusive towards Narina though, did not force her to sleep with him if she was not in the mood, and, when he did lie with other women, he usually tried to do it discreetly. As a husband, he was not the worst.

"You sure you won't eat more?" Ysfael asked, finally turning back to look at her.

No, he was not the worst, Narina thought, appreciating again his boyish good looks. Still, the idea of spending the rest of her life with him seemed, at that moment, terribly sad and she desperately wished things in Alt Clota might have turned out differently over the past two or three years.

But she would do her duty, as a queen must. She would take care of her people and support her husband.

Forcing a smile, she stood up. Ysfael made no move to do the same.

"Where are you going?" he asked.

"Back to the wall," she said.

"You won't see her," Ysfael told her as she headed towards the doors. "Not from here."

Maybe not, Narina agreed silently. *But perhaps I'll see Bellicus, coming home at last.*

CHAPTER FOUR

Bellicus had smiled when he saw the towering rock of Dun Breatann on the horizon. The fortress, with its twin peaks and sturdy wooden walls, dominated the skyline and was always a welcome sight for the druid, although his joy was short lived as he thought again of the reason for their hasty return.

"I'll be glad of a decent bed for a change," Eburus said as he looked at their destination, not far off now, across the River Clota. He gazed at the top of the massive rock, seeing the distant plumes of smoke trailing into the air from cooking fires. "And some proper food. A change of clothes too." He rubbed ineffectually at a grubby mark on his red and black checked trousers to punctuate his point.

"We'll not be there long," Duro reminded him, looking idly along the river in both directions. It was a fine view on a dry, warm day like this, and the sight of a fishing boat bobbing on the waters was strangely comforting. "I'm sure Bel will want to head out as soon as possible and help in the search for Princess Catia."

"Of course," the druid agreed, gently guiding his mount, Darac, towards the ford which would allow them to cross the river. "We'll let our horses get a proper rest and rub-down, since we've pushed them hard to get back here. And we can have a good feed and a night in a comfortable bed indoors." He shook his head, realising how long it was since he'd enjoyed a night when he wasn't outside exposed to whatever elements the gods decided to subject them to. By Taranis, it was never fun trying to catch a few hours' rest when a storm was raging all around you! It would be a welcome change to sleep in his own cosy house again, even if just for a single night. "But once we find out what's been happening in Dun Breatann while we've been away, and where to search, I'll be out hunting for Catia."

He didn't bother to suggest his companions could stay and rest in the fortress for longer if they wanted, he knew they would be outraged at the very idea of letting him go out alone. It was a gift to have the friendship of such men, and Bellicus thanked the gods for his good fortune every day.

"What about you, Cai?" he called to the great dog loping easily along beside them, tongue lolling out, occasionally stopping to mark a spot of territory but never falling behind for long. "Would you like to stay in Dun Breatann while the rest of us look for Catia?"

The dog did not reply, obviously, not even a bark. But the baleful look he gave the druid made Eburus and Duro both smile for it truly seemed as if Cai had understood the question and felt as disgusted by it as they would have themselves.

"You've run a long way, old friend," Bellicus said, more to himself than the dog, and it was true. Whenever they met a merchant or some other traveller on the road with a wagon Bellicus would pay them to let Cai ride in it for as long as they were going in the same direction, but, even so, the mastiff had covered a lot of ground in the past few months and the druid was acutely aware of it. He smiled warmly and said, "We're almost home now, though, boy."

They came to the ford and urged the horses into the water. At its deepest point it didn't come much higher than the animals' knees, and Cai followed, unfazed by the soaking. Although the Clota was shallow here, it was much deeper towards the west, where Dun Breatann's docks were located. In Roman times great vessels – military and trade – had come here, and that continued on a smaller scale to this day, as traders sailed to Alt Clota bringing spices, glass, wine, cloth, furs, and all manner of goods, while Queen Narina's ships patrolled the river, protecting the settlements all along it from Dalriadan pirates.

Darac led the way across the river, splashing onto the far side and continuing along the shore without slowing as Duro and Eburus came behind. Cai paused to shake himself vigorously, and nibble the pads on one paw for a moment, before he too resumed the journey.

It wasn't much longer before the pebbled shore brought them to the fortress, and Bellicus felt real delight as he dismounted and walked towards the gatehouse.

"Hold!"

The druid's pleasure quickly flared to irritation as he looked up at the – unfamiliar – face peering down from the crenelated wall above.

"Who are you, and what d'ye want?" the guard demanded. He was dressed in full armour, helmet polished to gleaming perfection, and the tip of his spear towered above him, suggesting he was not a particularly tall man. Or maybe he just favoured a really long spear.

"I'm Bellicus, Druid of Dun Breatann, and I want inside. Who are you?"

The soldier frowned and turned to look at a fellow guard to his left. The other man shrugged.

"Who's that with you?"

"Open the fucking gate," Eburus roared, pointing his finger at the guard. "You know who I am. I'm your bloody champion!"

The guard blanched – clearly, he did recognise the flame-haired Eburus now, and didn't want to get on the wrong side of him. "Sorry, my lord. I was too busy looking at the druid." He turned away and bawled over his shoulder. "Open the gates!"

Beneath, there was a clatter as the massive bar that held the entrance closed was lifted away, and then one of the gates swung open. Another guard Bellicus didn't know looked at them suspiciously, but he stood back and let them walk past, remaining silent as Eburus glared at him, and almost jumping out of his skin as Cai sauntered by.

"Where's the usual gate guards?" Bellicus shouted up to the man on the wall when they were inside. "I don't know any of you."

"They're searching for the princess, my lord," replied the guard, much more deferential now that the enormous druid was on the same side of the wall as him. "We're Prince Ysfael's personal guard."

Bellicus grunted at that, and cast a sidelong glance at Duro who returned the look stonily. It was never a good sign when one's own fortress was being guarded by men from another tribe, even if their prince was wedded to the queen.

"Just doing our duty, my lord," the guard said apologetically, and it was to Eburus he spoke, for the warrior was still glaring at him as if he might run up the stairs to the parapet and punch him. Eburus was young, in his early twenties still, but he was as hard as they came and had earned his place as the Votadini champion by fairly, and brutally, beating the previous title-bearer. The guards did not want to get into a fight with him.

"Come on, we're in now," Duro said, tugging on Eburus's arm as Bellicus headed for the stairs leading up to the main living section of the fortress. "By Mithras, that's your own tribesmen you're growling at, man. Calm down."

Eburus pointed at the guard on the wall again, threateningly, as if saying, "I'll see you later," but, when he started up the stairs behind Bellicus, Duro could see he was smiling.

"No wonder people don't like you," said the centurion, grinning himself now.

"You like me."

Duro just laughed. He did like the big man, as unbelievable as it would have seemed to the centurion given their first few meetings.

Bellicus climbed the stairs two at a time, his long legs easily carrying him up towards the middle area of the fortress where another, smaller, guardhouse was positioned. It was no wonder Dun Breatann had never successfully been taken by an enemy force, thought the druid distractedly.

"Who are you?"

"Oh, not this shit again," Eburus shouted, but Bellicus had already shoved past the guard who stood barring their way. The man tried to stop the druid, but he was much smaller than Bellicus, who brushed off his grasping hand as if he was no more than a child. Before the angry, embarrassed soldier tried to use his spear, Eburus grabbed him.

"Don't be stupid," he said. "The druid will shove his staff up your arse before you even have a chance to try and stick him with that." He flicked his head towards the guard's shelter. "Get back to your post."

"Eburus? I didn't realise they were with you." The man was still frowning, but he didn't look quite so murderous now that he knew the men were accompanied by one of his own Votadini warriors.

"*We* are with *him*?" Bellicus spat, rounding on the guard angrily. "Gods below, what's happening here? Come on, the sooner we see the queen the better."

"You have to see Prince Ysfael first," the guard called after them. "That's the rules."

"I'll damn well see who I like," the druid shouted. "If Ysfael has anything to say about it, he can come looking for me. That's *my* rules." He strode on, muttering under his breath.

Duro hurried after him. "You and Eburus both need to calm down," the centurion said in a hard tone. "Remember, Ysfael is married to the queen now."

"That's as may be," Bellicus admitted sourly, not slowing as he approached the great hall. "But marrying the queen doesn't make him king. Not in Alt Clota. He's merely her consort, he does not wield her power."

"In theory," Duro said. "But it certainly seems as if the Votadini hold *some* power here, going by the number of guards Ysfael has stationed about the place. Be careful, Bel. Remember the last time we came here and the king didn't take too kindly to us."

"I am remembering that," the druid said. "That's why I'm so angry! Surely it's not happening again..."

"Just tread softly," Duro cautioned again as the two guards at the great hall's doors saw them passing and began walking towards them, surprise and caution etched on their features. The queen's house was near the top of the rock, and that's where Bellicus was going first.

The guards ran now, blocking the path upwards as a handful of women who were washing clothes by the well stopped to watch what was going on. At least they recognised the druid, and knew something entertaining might be about to happen.

"Who—"

"I'm Bellicus," the druid said angrily, not slowing as he headed straight towards the guards who did not move as he approached closer and closer. "Ask the women there who I am, if you're interested."

The guard on the left reached out and grasped Bellicus's sleeve, but the druid rolled his arm around, catching the guard's own wrist and twisting it up his back. The second guard cried out in fury and swung his spear but the long weapon was far too slow and unwieldy at such close range, and Bellicus simply shoved the first guard into the second. They both fell back and Cai sprinted forward to stand over them, growling viciously, teeth bared.

"Just stay down, lads," Eburus said, shaking his head ruefully. "Call yourself Votadini warriors? Guards?" He sighed theatrically as Bellicus walked on, calling sharply for Cai to follow.

Duro did not draw his spatha, but he stood with his hand on its hilt, gazing coolly down at the sprawling guards whose faces were flushing red with anger and shame.

"This is the druid's home," Eburus said. "You shouldn't have got in his way, he's in a bad mood."

"Bad mood?" shouted the man whose wrist had been twisted up his back. "Well, so am I now."

"Learn your lesson, soldier," Duro barked, voice harsh but strong, as if he was back on the parade ground with his legion. "The druid isn't a man to get on the wrong side of."

Eburus grinned. "The centurion's right, lads. Go back to the hall and forget your damaged pride – there's no shame in getting put on your backside by Big Bel. He did the same to me too, once, broke my nose an' all! I'll buy you a drink later, all right?"

The guards looked at one another, and at first Duro was sure they'd go after Bellicus, but Eburus stared unblinkingly at them until, at last, they got up and wandered away, down the slope to the doors of the hall, casting sullen glances back at them until they reached the hall and went inside, presumably to report to some superior about what had happened.

"Come on," Duro said, fearing they'd made enemies of Ysfael's men for no better reason than Bellicus's sense of outrage.

The druid and his dog were out of sight as Duro and Eburus jogged up the hill towards the queen's home, which was larger than most other buildings in the fortress but still small in comparison to other royal dwellings in Britain. Dun Breatann was an important fortress, but there wasn't a lot of ground to build upon, thanks to its shape.

"Well," said Eburus with a wry grin as they came to the low house and stopped outside, wondering whether to knock or just let Bellicus be alone with the queen. "At least they're not shouting at one another."

Duro grunted, but he wondered if the silence meant more trouble than an argument might have.

* * *

Narina had given up staring out at the lands surrounding Dun Breatann not long after she'd left Ysfael to eat his meal. She could see her people in the fields below: working busily away to gather in the harvest; herding sheep from one pasture to another with better grass; even a group of soldiers training on horseback. What she could not see was any sign of Catia or her trusted advisor and friend, Bellicus. It was a lonely place without the druid, whose apprentice, Koriosis, was competent enough despite his youth, but nothing like as close to the queen.

She'd walked back to her house and gone inside, no guards to salute here, then sat on the bed and thought wistfully of happier times. She thought of Coroticus and the many enjoyable days they'd spent together in the early years of their marriage, and she thought of Catia when she was just a little thing, toddling about the great hall unsteadily, her smile and sparkling eyes bringing joy to everyone who saw her.

And Narina thought of Catia's conception, and her deception of Bellicus who had no idea it was his friend Coroticus's wife he was bedding. The Damnonii people had been celebrating Beltaine that night, and the young druid had imbibed much drink and certain mushrooms before heading into the hills along with other young men and women of the tribe to properly mark the feast of fertility. Bellicus had waited for the gods to send him a partner, and, in the dark, he'd lain with the slim young woman who'd come, never suspecting who she was, although she'd told him eventually, years later.

Narina still felt guilt over that deceit, but Coroticus had been unable to make her pregnant, and Alt Clota needed, demanded, an heir.

Who better to provide the seed for a royal child than a warrior-druid?

And then, when Coroticus had gone mad, imprisoning Narina and forcing Bellicus into a confrontation that ended with the druid killing him…Narina wished she might have followed her heart and married Bellicus then, but it could never be. There were too many rumours already, too much doubt over everything that had gone on, and besides, taking Prince Ysfael as her new husband bound the eastern Votadini tribe to Narina's Damnonii, strengthening her people's position greatly. An important alliance, given the constant threats of attack and invasion from the Picts in the north and the Dalriadans in the west. Who knew what might come from the south eventually, too, since the Saxons seemed to grow in power with every passing year?

The thoughts of invasion and war made Narina unsettled and, with tears springing to her eyes as they so often had in recent days, she stood up, pacing nervously from one side of the small chamber to another. She felt like a child herself, lost and alone, desperate for a deeper connection than Ysfael would ever offer her...

There was a knock at the door and Narina stopped pacing, wiping her face, not wanting her husband or the guards to see her tears, but then the door opened and a massive dark shape filled the entrance.

"Are you alright, Narina?"

As Bellicus stepped into the room the queen's face lit up in pure joy and, without thinking, she ran to him and threw her arms about his enormous arms, reaching up to pull the back of his shaved head down to hers, and she kissed him almost desperately, as if she could draw his strength and vitality into her.

The tears were flowing again, but they were a sweet release now as Bellicus returned her passionate kiss. She reached down between his legs, need and desire making her reckless, but the druid pushed her hand aside and broke the embrace, stretching up to gaze at her in wonder.

"By Cernunnos," he breathed. "What was that all about?"

They heard footsteps approaching then and Narina sat on her bed, wiping the tears once again, and her moist lips, before placing her hands in her lap and trying to look as demure as possible.

Two faces appeared at the open doorway and Narina laughed, a choking sob of both pleasure and relief, as she recognised Duro and Eburus. They smiled and murmured respectful greetings of their own but neither man entered, just looked at Bellicus whose expression was enough to make them turn away and walk off towards the wall nonchalantly. They would probably not guess what had just transpired, but the atmosphere in the queen's chamber was unmistakably charged with some powerful emotion.

"I'm sorry," said Narina, sighing and turning away so he couldn't see her face. "I've been struggling since Catia went missing again. Seeing you…" She turned back to him, smiling sadly. "Familiar old Bel. It's good to have you back home, Druid. Alt Clota has missed you."

"You're taking Catia's…absence," Bellicus said tactfully, "particularly hard, eh?"

Narina nodded, her face tight with anxiety. "Yes. She's still just a child. My child." She met his eyes. "*Our* child. I'm so worried for her, Bel. After you brought her back from the Saxons I thought I'd never let her out of my sight for the rest of her life! To have this happen again…I'm supposed to be a queen, but I feel utterly useless."

Before they could speak more, they heard voices – angry voices – coming up the slope towards the house. Ysfael and some of his men, from the sound of it.

Bellicus stepped back, as far as possible from Narina without actually going outside and they waited for the Votadini prince. It didn't take him long for the distance from the great hall wasn't great and Ysfael was a fit, young man. He walked into Narina's house as if he owned it, which, she thought, he basically did. She saw Bellicus's frown, however, and knew Ysfael treating Dun Breatann like his own personal fortress was proving hard for the druid to accept.

"What do you think you're doing?" the prince demanded, pointing a finger at Bellicus. "My guards told you to report to me. How dare you ignore my orders?" He was angrier than Narina had ever seen him and she opened her mouth to intervene, but, before she could say a word, Bellicus pushed his shoulders back and seemed, somehow, to grow even bigger, his great bulk filling the room.

"I am Druid of Dun Breatann," Bellicus growled, eyes boring into the much smaller man. "I go where I like in these lands, and no Votadini fool will give me orders." He leaned down, putting his face close to Ysfael's. "Do you understand?"

The men outside gasped audibly, almost theatrically, at the clear challenge in the druid's words and stance, their own faces twisting into angry frowns. Narina felt a sudden thrill of fear – those were Ysfael's guards, and they would follow his orders, not hers. She was sure of that. She could see Duro, looking irritated, behind the Votadini soldiers, and Eburus who seemed to be enjoying the whole spectacle.

Whose side would the red-haired, tall warrior take if a fight broke out, she wondered? He might be friends nowadays with Bel and the centurion, but he was still Votadini, and sworn to defend his king's interests. That must, surely, include the prince?

Ysfael was no fool, though. Even if his men did back him up, everyone knew Bellicus was not someone to get into a fight with in such close quarters. The druid's skills were legendary for good reason, and that wasn't even taking into account the fact he was a representative of the gods. Narina knew Ysfael feared the gods, and he instinctively feared the druids, even the old men and women who served his father in Dun Edin.

Still, he was the queen's husband now, and that made him a powerful man in these lands, whether Bellicus liked it or not.

"I will overlook your behaviour this time," Ysfael said, trying hard to make his own voice as steady and commanding as the druid's but failing spectacularly. "You will be worried about Princess Catia, no doubt, and in a hurry to speak with my wife about everything that's been happening while you were away." He said the last three words with emphasis, as if criticising Bellicus for riding off on adventures while his people were left here in Dun Breatann to deal with whatever troubles the gods decided to heap upon them. Like Catia's disappearance. "In the future I would appreciate it if you'd respect my wishes, Bel. We all have to survive here, together. It would be easier if we got along, eh?"

The druid's mouth curled in the suggestion of a smile, but never quite completed the movement, ending as more of an amused grimace than a genuine show of pleasure or acceptance. But he said, "Aye, Lord Prince. It shall be as you say." He nodded, but offered no apology and that had to be enough for Ysfael, who mirrored Bellicus's nod and then looked away, moving to join Narina on the bed.

"Have you told him what's happened?"

Narina allowed Ysfael to take her hand in his while she shook her head. "No, I didn't have a chance. He'd only just come in before you arrived."

"Sit," Ysfael said to the druid, gesturing towards a stool in the opposite corner. "We'll fill you in. D'you want a drink? Food?

Aye?" He looked through the still-open door to the men framed in the sunshine outside. "One of you run back to the hall and fetch something for the druid. Nothing for me." He glanced at Narina. "Or the queen."

Bellicus raised his head, finding Duro and Eburus still standing behind the other soldiers. "Go with them," he said. "I'll join you later."

"Eburus," Ysfael called, nodding in the manner of a middle-aged commander, glad to see a respected subordinate safely home from battle. "Good to have you back with me. Go, eat and drink your fill. You can take up your duties in my guard again once you've rested."

Eburus frowned and Narina might have laughed at the outraged look on the big man's bearded face, but she noticed Bellicus's similarly black expression and realised this might turn out to be another bone of contention between prince and druid. Things were certainly never easy in Dun Breatann.

Ysfael watched until the men outside all departed and then he stood up to close the door.

"No," said Narina. "Leave it open. I like the sunshine."

He closed it over despite her request, replying, "Don't be silly, it's getting cold and there's a wind blowing. There's always a bloody wind blowing here, that's the problem with living on a rock beside a river." Then he came back across to sit beside the queen on the bed, grasping her hand again and it was clear to Narina that he was establishing ownership of her, the house, the fortress and everything else. Letting Bellicus know he was not just a young man with a wispy beard – he was a prince of the Votadini and wed to the Damnonii queen and should be treated with greater respect than the druid had shown him so far.

Of course, the room was quite dark now, since the door had been shut, which somewhat ruined the scene Ysfael was trying to paint.

"So," Bellicus said. "Where's Catia?"

CHAPTER FIVE

"Where are all the Damnonii warriors?" Duro asked in a low voice. It was evening and Bellicus had joined them at last in the great hall. The cooking fires kept the chill of approaching autumn at bay and the homely orange glow would have made for a much more pleasant atmosphere if they weren't surrounded by Ysfael's men.

"Some of them are guarding the walls – you just haven't seen them yet," Bellicus replied, happily digging into the thick stew a serving girl had placed before him: beef, carrot, cabbage, onion and parsley had all gone into it and the druid couldn't remember ever tasting, or smelling, much better. "The rest went out to deal with some Dalriadan raiders a few days ago. I expect they'll return soon enough."

Duro shook his head almost imperceptibly, glancing around as if spies were eavesdropping although, in truth, the Votadini warriors eating and carousing around them were making more than enough noise to mask what the centurion was saying. None of Ysfael's men were paying them much attention other than to throw them the occasional curious glance. "It's not right," Duro opined. "Narina shouldn't have let Gavo take her men off, leaving her alone with these...outsiders."

Bellicus shrugged. He agreed completely, but Narina was her own woman and did things her way. She clearly trusted Ysfael.

Just then the door opened and Bellicus smiled, jerking his head for Duro to look over his shoulder for he was sitting with his back to the entrance. "What were you saying about Gavo?"

The centurion glanced back, mouth open as he chewed a piece of meat, and broke into a smile as he saw the Damnonii guard captain coming towards them. A bear of a man, Gavo had long hair and a grizzled beard which were both turning from brown to grey now that he was in his fortieth year. He wore red checked trousers, a loose fitting blue tunic, and a bronze torc around his neck which marked his high rank, although it was obvious from his bearing he was a man used to command.

"Did you really think he'd leave Narina's side for long?" Bellicus asked, before Gavo grabbed Duro and they held one another in a rough embrace. Bellicus was next, and then Cai, whining in pleasure and licking the captain's face despite loud protestations and laughter, had his turn to say hello.

"And you're still here?" Gavo said, taking a seat beside Eburus and eyeing him with clear surprise. "I thought you'd have joined your kinsmen at the other benches."

The Votadini shrugged, and said in his heavily accented tones, "These are my friends. I'm used to their company now. Ysfael will no doubt order me to join his ranks again soon enough, but until then I'll sit with who I choose."

"See?" Duro hissed. "Even he doesn't trust the Votadini, and he's one of them!"

Eburus snorted, spoon halfway to his mouth. "Eh? I trust them fine, centurion, I just feel more comfortable around you and Bellicus. My kinsmen are as honourable as any others."

"That's what worries me," Duro said suspiciously. "Soldiers take orders from their leaders, and the likes of him," he looked towards a laughing Ysfael at the high table, apparently enjoying Narina's company, "are always looking for opportunities to expand their borders and their wealth."

Gavo shrugged. "He's already married to the queen," he said, eagerly tucking in to the bowl of food that had just been put before him by a servant. "Why would he need to use his men to take Dun Breatann?"

"You like him?" Duro asked.

"No," Gavo replied, blowing on a spoonful of stew. "He's an arrogant little prick. But I've never had any reason to think he's plotting to seize this place for himself. He and Narina are happy enough with one another, as you can see. He's not who I'd want by her side, but it is what it is." He shoved the food into his mouth and cursed as he realised it was still too hot. A quick mouthful of ale soon sorted him out and ready to do much the same thing all over again.

The centurion was not convinced. "Maybe he's all right now, but he's young yet. His natural arrogance will soon have him wanting more. More than a share in Dun Breatann, and more than Narina."

"Oh, he already wants more than the queen," Gavo said. "It's no secret. He goes with any pretty girl that'll have him." He noticed Bellicus's dark look and waved his spoon in the air, dismissing the druid's fears. "It's not like it was with Coroticus. Narina seems quite content."

"Maybe it stops him from bedding her," Eburus said. "And maybe she's glad of that."

Bellicus thought back, for the hundredth time, to Narina's almost desperate kiss earlier, and her unmistakable lust. Eburus was surely right – Ysfael and Narina did not lie together often, if at all and, while the young prince satisfied himself elsewhere, the queen did not. Bellicus wasn't sure why Narina didn't find some discreet bedmate of her own if she missed such companionship. Of average height, with her slim figure, brown hair, and light green eyes she was very pretty and had a confidence about her that Bellicus had always found attractive. He thought again of the look she'd given him earlier, and the feel of her lips on his...

"Did Aife give you any hint that she was thinking of leaving Dun Breatann?" he asked Gavo, forcing his mind in another direction.

The guard captain shook his head. "Everyone knows how loyal I am to Narina, and, well, the two of them were not close. The Pictish girl rarely spoke to me."

One of the servants dropped a jug of ale on the floor and it shattered noisily, contents spilling all over the rushes as a couple of dogs appeared from the shadows to greedily lap up what they could. Men cheered and the serving girl, an attractive brunette with dark eyes and a narrow waist, did her best to gather the pieces of broken pot.

Bellicus looked at Ysfael. The prince was watching, with obvious pleasure, as the girl worked. The druid turned his eyes on Narina, in the high-backed chair to the prince's left, but she didn't seem interested in anything that was happening, instead staring into the hall thoughtfully. She was wearing a white dress with a slim gold torc around her neck which set off her pale skin perfectly thought the druid.

When Bellicus looked again at Ysfael he realised the tables had been turned and the prince was now watching him as he stared at the queen.

The edge of Ysfael's mouth twitched, as if he was about to smile knowingly, almost mockingly at the druid, but just then a hand clapped down on Bellicus's shoulder and his attention was drawn away.

"You're back!" It was Koriosis, the novice druid who'd been sent from the isle of Iova to help out in Alt Clota during Bellicus's many recent absences. He'd proven an able deputy, much liked and respected by all it seemed, despite his youth. The days of aged, white- or grey-bearded old men being druids were passing, and a younger generation was taking their place, in Alt Clota at least. "I was out tending to my bees all day and just got back to the news that you and Duro had returned. It's good to see you, my lord."

"Here," Gavo used his foot to hook a stool and drag it over for Koriosis. "Sit, druid. You can fill them in on what's been happening here just as well as I could. I've got work to do, checking the guards on the walls and gates are alert." With a final, gruff, farewell, the captain shrugged his cloak around him and strode off out the doors to perform his duties as he'd done in Dun Breatann for two decades. The hall seemed somehow less welcoming when he was gone; for all his gruff demeanour, Gavo was a likeable fellow.

Koriosis's chatter was all about his work as a druid, his interactions with the people of Alt Clota, his bees, which he was immensely proud of, and the herbs and other ingredients he'd managed to find scattered about the land. Duro and Eburus soon lost interest and wandered off to watch some Votadini warriors playing a game of tafl.

Bellicus was more than happy to listen to Koriosis, however. He was supposed to be the younger druid's mentor after all, so they conversed and drank ale together, becoming quite oblivious to all around them.

"Oh, I have a gift for you," Koriosis said, eyes lighting up as he remembered the thing he'd found, right there at the foot of Dun Breatann. "I left it in your house. Honey, from my bees. Medicinal, and delicious too."

"Honey, eh?" Bellicus replied, grinning. "That sounds good, thank you." He swallowed another mouthful of ale, finally feeling at home and more relaxed than he had in a long time. He planned on heading out to join in the search for Catia at first light, but, for now a warm glow had filled him and he meant to enjoy it while he could.

Again he felt a hand press down on his shoulder, looked around, and his pleasant feelings evaporated. Prince Ysfael stood there, eyeing him coolly.

"My lord," Bellicus said.

"How about a friendly contest?"

The druid gazed at him, wondering what kind of competition or game Ysfael thought he might beat him at. Was the man completely drunk and looking for a fight, here, in front of everyone, in hopes of putting Bellicus in his place and proving how strong he was? The prince didn't look that inebriated – his eyes were shining, but more from the firelight than any internal, ale-born glow – and there was a playful cast to his features that did not speak of violence. Competition, aye, but there was nothing murderous about Ysfael's expression.

"What d'you have in mind?" the druid asked.

Others in the hall had noticed their conversation and a hush was beginning to fall.

"Arm wrestling," Ysfael suggested, and this brought laughs and nods from the handful of his closest companions. They were the men in Dun Breatann who knew the prince best and, despite the great difference in size between Ysfael and Bellicus, the Votadini soldiers seemed to think their leader would not be outmatched in such a contest.

Was this some trick? Bellicus wondered if something had been put into his drink to weaken him. As a druid, he knew very well such a thing was possible and, indeed, he'd suffered a similar thing while hunting the Saxons who'd abducted Catia some years before but...He did not feel weak. Bellicus was not an expert at arm-wrestling, but it was a popular pastime among the men of Alt Clota; indeed, of all Britain. Since time immemorial drunk warriors had used the sport as a way to prove how strong and manly they were, so Bellicus had seen many such bouts over the years. One thing always stood out to him: the biggest, strongest man of the two did not always win. Victory in arm-wrestling was as much about technique as it was mere brute strength.

Ysfael's confidence suggested he'd learned these techniques and thought he'd have enough to best the much bigger druid.

Bellicus looked around, noting the eager, smiling faces dotted about the hall, willing him to agree to Ysfael's challenge and provide them with some entertainment on this otherwise regular evening. Could he refuse? Of course not.

While he was away with Arthur's army in the south he and the warlord had been forced into a battle in an old Mithraeum. It had been quite an adventure as the two men, along with a handful of inexperienced warriors, tried to fight off an enemy warband. Then the druid had almost been killed when an attacker slashed his arm and the wound became infected. It had been a long road to recovery and, even now some weeks later he was still not quite fully healed, having lost a fair amount of muscle mass and overall weight while laid up in his sick bed. He should be strong enough for this though, surely?

Even the serving girls, especially the one who Ysfael had been watching clean up the dropped jug earlier, looked excited at the promised contest and, again, Bellicus thought these people had spent the last few months in the prince's company. They'd probably seen him arm-wrestling men bigger than himself and defeating them, hence their interest in this particular battle. The expressions on the audience's faces suggested Ysfael would be no pushover.

"Aye, all right then," Bellicus said, smiling grimly and gesturing towards the stool on the opposite side of the table. "I've never been one for arm-wrestling, but I'll give it a go."

Ysfael sat as Koriosis moved ale mugs and empty trenchers of food aside, the young druid finally pushing himself back, well out of the way. He looked as interested in the contest as anyone, Bellicus noted.

"I thought you druids were experts at everything," Ysfael said as he rolled up his sleeves to reveal slim yet toned arms. Bellicus examined his face, wondering if the question had been meant in a mocking way, but he saw only vague curiosity there. Or perhaps disbelief. Did the prince think Bellicus was lying, playing down his skill in order to throw his opponent off guard?

"Not quite everything," the druid said, taking off his cloak and pushing up his own sleeves, drawing murmurs of appreciation as the watchers took in the size of his heavily muscled arms. He might have lost some of his bulk when he was injured in the summer, but it was returning, and he still cut a powerful figure. "We learn how to fight, unarmed and with weapons, and some of us are better at it than others, as in any discipline. But," he smiled and placed his elbow on the table, flexing his fingers. "Arm-wrestling isn't something my tutors ever taught me."

"Best of three?" Ysfael asked and that seemed to be the cue for everyone in the hall to draw in, encircling the table that they might see what happened as well as possible. Even Narina was there, right in the front rank of onlookers, as interested as anyone to see what would happen but maintaining a neutral expression.

Bellicus could not tell who she wanted to win, but not everyone was so hard to read.

"You better not lose this," Duro called loudly. "You're almost double his size!"

"The prince has beaten bigger men than him!" one of the Votadini soldiers retorted merrily and Bellicus wondered if that was true. He hadn't met many men bigger than himself over the years, so it was unlikely but not impossible.

"Ready?" Koriosis asked, taking the role of referee.

Both men fixed their eyes on one another, locked fists, and gripped the edge of the table with their free hands. The cooking fires crackled, but not as much as the atmosphere, as men and women hurriedly picked a side and placed bets before, at last, Koriosis shouted, "Go!"

They flexed their arms, testing, probing, feeling out one another's strength and technique, Ysfael with the air of a champion about him while Bellicus held his own face in as blank a mask as he could, given the effort he was expending in simply holding his forearm in place. And then the druid felt something change – his hand seemed to be rotated to the right, putting him into a decidedly awkward shape, and then, when Ysfael applied more pressure, Bellicus couldn't stop the downward movement of his arm. He put everything he could into halting Ysfael's momentum, but it was no good, the back of his hand touched the table and Ysfael let go, grinning in triumph as his supporters cheered and Duro groaned.

Even Cai, lying at Bellicus's feet beneath the table, seemed to be eyeing him with disappointment. The druid took a drink of his ale, huffed out a deep breath, and then placed his elbow back on the table for round two.

This went much the same as the first, to start with, as the men seemed stuck in a deadlock for a time, with everyone shouting and cheering about them, but Bellicus had almost fallen into a trance. The hall around him faded away, until all he was focused on was his hand in front of him, and the pressure Ysfael was applying to it. Eventually, the druid felt that same rotating movement as before, but this time, as soon as it started, Bellicus applied the same technique. Without giving Ysfael time to react, the druid pulled on his opponent's hand, bending it back and using his prodigious strength to drag the prince's hand down onto the table.

There were raucous cheers and laughter at the reversal of fortunes, but Ysfael was not smiling now. Instead, he seemed angry, and not at all happy to have lost, but he immediately put his elbow back onto the table for the final round. Not a word passed between the rivals as Bellicus resumed the starting position and they glared at one another, most of the earlier humour now gone, along with Ysfael's arrogant confidence.

Yet Bellicus was tired. He knew he could have won this contest if it had taken place six months ago, but that injury he'd suffered and the fever that followed, had come close to killing him. He'd lost not only weight and muscle, but stamina too, and this unfamiliar battle after the long journey of the past few weeks had really taken a toll on him.

Did it really matter that much if he lost? Ysfael was the queen's husband now, and Bellicus should really want the Damnonii people to respect a man in that position. It benefited everyone, surely, to have a strong man by the queen's side. But then the druid saw Narina in his peripheral vision and all thoughts of giving in fled from his mind.

Koriosis called for the start of this third and final round and immediately Bellicus went on the attack, trying to use the same rotation of Ysfael's wrist that had won him round two. It did not work this time, for the smaller man was expecting it and already moving into a different technique. The prince was turning his hand in another direction, but he was also leaning back on the stool, drawing Bellicus's hand forward, away from his shoulder which had the effect of almost neutering the druid's greater strength.

Bellicus tried to move his fist back to the starting position but he was at a real disadvantage now and the momentum was well and truly with the prince, whose Votadini subordinates were lustily cheering on. Apparently Ysfael wasn't much liked, even by his own men, thanks to his arrogance and dismissive attitude to anyone lower than him on the social scale, but contests like this always brought out the most tribal instincts in people and this was not about two men in a hall anymore. It was about Votadini versus Damnonii, and Bellicus could feel his chances of winning slipping away with every passing moment.

Ysfael's teeth were bared in a savage, lupine grin as he sensed triumph, and the sight of his snarling face enraged Bellicus. Yet what could he do? The prince clearly knew various tricks and techniques to win these matches, whereas all Bellicus had to his advantage was his strength, which was useless right now, and his size...

In a final, desperate attempt to halt Ysfael's momentum, Bellicus shifted all his body weight to the left, putting everything he had into pushing his fist in that direction. It was enough to force another momentary deadlock, and the prince roared, trying to muster every last drop of power from his straining muscles.

The druid had a better idea of the forces in play now, though, and, using his longer reach, he rolled his hand, raising his wrist so it was above Ysfael's, giving Bellicus an immediate advantage. Sure enough, just moments later, Bellicus slammed his opponent's hand down onto the table with savage glee, and stood up with his arms in the air, fists clenched, as he took the acclaim of the few Damnonii who'd been supporting him.

Ysfael stared up at him, a mixture of loathing and disgust on his scarred, yet youthful, face. He didn't even attempt to hide it which simply made Bellicus more amused. The druid had been trained to retain control of himself even in stressful situations, but he was a young man in his late twenties with a few ales inside him and he'd just bested a rival – of course he was going to make the most of it.

The prince stood up, staring balefully at his laughing conqueror, and then, shaking his head, he headed for the doors, half-a-dozen of his most loyal guards going with him, their expressions mostly unreadable. "Eburus. You come with us," he called to the red-headed Votadini champion. "You're one of us, don't forget."

Eburus sat up straight, clearly surprised by Ysfael's order. He looked from Duro to Bellicus, and the druid gave an almost imperceptible nod. With the young prince in such a black mood it would not be wise to begin an argument over Eburus's loyalties. His command was quite plainly a petty way of striking back at Bellicus.

"We'll see you tomorrow," Duro said, standing and clapping Eburus on the shoulder as he pulled his cloak around him and followed his prince and kinsmen from the warmth of the great hall, out into the chilly autumn evening.

A couple of the Damnonii men came over, congratulating Bellicus on his victory, toasting him with overflowing mugs but, as the elation of his hard-fought win began to fade, the druid wondered if he should have just let the young fool win. Ysfael was the kind of arrogant nobleman who'd take this kind of thing badly, harbouring a grudge forever and letting his sense of outrage fester until it manifested in some unpleasant way. Would he take out his temper on Narina? He turned and saw the queen deep in animated conversation with a handmaid. They didn't seem worried or anxious at all, quite the contrary in fact, and that set the druid's mind at ease a little. If Ysfael was in the habit of raising his hands to Narina she would surely not look as relaxed as she did now.

"This is a very strange place to be right now," Duro said, taking the stool recently vacated by the Votadini prince and using the back of his hand to wipe some crumbs onto the floor. Cai nosed at them for a moment before lazily licking them up.

"Aye," Bellicus agreed. "It doesn't feel like home at all. It's not right."

"What can you do about it?" the centurion asked.

"I don't know yet." He exhaled and massaged his aching bicep with his left hand. "But once we find Catia, I'll need to talk with Narina and Gavo."

"You want another drink?" Duro asked, rather half-heartedly. "More meat?"

"Nah." The atmosphere in the hall was subdued now and Bellicus didn't want to spend any more time there. Again, he wondered if he should have just let Ysfael best him, but that simply wasn't his way – he always played to win, and always would. He was Bellicus, Warrior-Druid of Dun Breatann!

He looked sourly around the room, wondering why he felt as though everything was spiralling out of control, as if a whirlwind had swept into Alt Clota and picked him up. The sensation of spinning felt so real, nausea suddenly filled him and he opened his mouth, sucking in a frightened breath as he realised he was pitching sideways, off the stool, and he could do nothing to help himself.

CHAPTER SIX

"So much for a quiet evening with a few ales, some decent hot food, and a real bed."

"Well, to be fair, we did get all of that. Apart from the quiet part."

Bellicus was staring at the ceiling, watching motes of dust play in pale sunshine, wondering where in the Otherworld he was, but, hearing the voices he turned his head to see Duro and Eburus sitting beside him. He was, he realised, in his own small house, and in his own bed, the familiar weight of a large mastiff at his feet.

"The queen was just coming to ask him to sing for everyone too," Duro was telling the Votadini warrior ruefully. "Gave her quite a shock to see him falling off his stool."

Eburus was smiling now, looking at Bellicus with clear relief on his face. "I'll bet it did. I thought you could handle your drink better, druid."

Bellicus closed his eyes, feeling light-headed again although the sensation was mercifully not as powerful as it had been the night before. "So did I," he admitted, bemused by what had happened to him.

Someone else stood up from behind the head of the druid's bed, looked down at him, lifted an eyelid, stared at him, grunted. "You seem fine now," was Koriosis's expert opinion. "A combination of ale, heat, cooking smoke, and unused to physical exertion; nothing more sinister than that, I'm sure, brother. Duro told me about your injury down south – you need to take it easy for a while. Recover your strength properly before you get into any more arm-wrestling matches."

"That's a shame," another voice broke in, followed a heartbeat later by Prince Ysfael coming into the house.

Bellicus blinked and turned away from the sunshine glaring into his protesting eyes through the open door.

"I was hoping for a rematch," the Votadini nobleman said. "I'm sure I could beat you, now I have your measure." He jerked his chin at Eburus, signalling that he should get out of the way and let Ysfael sit in his place.

With an irritated look at Duro, who raised his eyebrows in understanding, Eburus did as he was told, and made his way outside, where he stood, as if guarding the house.

"It's good to see you're all right," Ysfael said and Bellicus searched the young man's face for any sign of duplicity or amusement, finding nothing but sincere concern. He was something of an enigma this prince, the druid thought. Not easy to read, he seemed to act differently to most other men. Bellicus did not mind that – it was good to forge one's own path in life, he believed, and Ysfael certainly seemed like a man who followed a vision all his own. Perhaps they would even be friends, eventually.

"Get out," Ysfael said then, turning to Duro and waving his hand as if to shoo the centurion away, as someone would do with an annoying puppy. "My wife's coming to see the druid, and she'll need that seat."

Duro flushed, and opened his mouth to say something but at that moment Narina appeared, stepping into the house and smiling as she saw Bellicus awake. The centurion threw Ysfael a last, black look, which the young man didn't even notice, and then he went out to stand with Eburus. Two of the best warriors in Dun Breatann at that moment, dismissed as if they were mere slaves by a man yet to earn renown either as a soldier or a leader.

Bellicus took it all in but said nothing as Narina sat down on the stool Duro had just vacated. Ysfael might grow into his new role as the queen's consort, become a good leader and companion, but it seemed unlikely to the druid.

"You're all right then?" Narina asked, concern etched on her pale, tired features. "You gave us a fright when you passed out. Duro filled me in on your recent injury, it sounds as if you've just over-exerted yourself." She arched an eyebrow critically. "You should know how to take care of yourself better, as a druid."

Bellicus smiled wryly. "Blame your husband. I didn't expect him to be as strong as he is."

It was meant as a compliment, to offset the beating Bellicus had given Ysfael, but the prince scowled, clearly offended. "Do I look so weak to you, druid?" he asked coldly.

Narina turned in surprise, but neither she nor the druid said anything. Bellicus simply wasn't sure how to deal with the man, and Narina just looked bemused but unwilling to start an argument which was clearly where things were heading. The atmosphere was icy now, but a voice calling outside soon had the inhabitants of the house on their feet and rushing for the door, even Bellicus, heedless of his previous night's collapse.

"They've been found! Princess Catia's been found!"

"Move!" Narina shoved past anyone who got in her way, almost hysterical as she ran in the direction of the shouting messenger. "Where is she? Where's Catia?"

Ysfael moved slower, and Bellicus looked directly at him as he followed the queen. Ysfael did not appear overly pleased by the news. Of course, the druid thought, Catia was nothing to the Votadini prince, they were not blood kin, yet there still seemed more to Ysfael's expression than mere indifference.

"Catia!"

Bellicus couldn't waste time staring at Ysfael so he raced after the queen, his heart filled with happiness that Catia – his daughter! – had been found. His joy faded, however, as he saw Narina with her hands on a man's arms, shouting at him.

"What do you mean, 'she's not here'? Where is she then, by Taranis?"

"My queen," the man replied, bowing his head as he spoke. "Two of the Votadini trackers, Docimedis and Maccis, came across the princesses near some woods far to the north."

"And?" Bellicus demanded, catching up and standing beside Narina.

"I'm not sure what happened," the man said, breathing heavily for it seemed he'd ran up the stairs ahead of whoever had carried the news to the fortress. "There was a fight, from the looks of the hunters. They're down at the gates, my lord, having their injuries tended to."

Narina cursed and looked up at the druid, fear plainly written on her face.

"What's happened?" Ysfael asked, coming up behind them but receiving no answer or even acknowledgement as both queen and druid hurried off again, this time making their way down the steps towards the gatehouse below, leaving a gathering crowd behind them asking the messenger what he knew. "Those are my men," Ysfael called, hastening down the stairs. "I should be there when you question them!"

It wasn't long before Narina charged into the guardhouse at the foot of the fortress, eyes casting about in the gloom for the men who'd found Catia. Bellicus was right behind her and Ysfael appeared too, just as the queen spotted the men in the corner beside the hearth. Both had blankets around them and mugs of ale in their hands as they reclined on stools, backs against the walls. They quickly figured out who the three newcomers were in the guardhouse and stood up, wide-eyed. Almost nervous, Bellicus thought, wondering if it was just the usual reaction when a common foot-soldier or peasant met the likes of a queen or a prince.

"What happened?" Narina demanded, striding across to stand before the men, barely restraining her nervous energy. It looked as if she wanted to grab the trackers by their collars and shake every last drop of information they held about Catia from them. "Where are they? And why didn't you bring them back?"

The men glanced at one another and there was an almost unnoticeable look from the smaller of the pair, Bellicus saw, as if the bigger man was being told to stay silent. It was only the flash of a look, over in an instant, but it suggested much to the druid and he moved forward, using his full, imposing height as he gazed down at the tracker.

"My lady, we, well, we did try to bring them back," said the small man. "But they, that is, the Pict girl, she didn't want to come." He turned to show them a lump the size of an egg on the base of his skull, then pointed to his taller friend's bound leg. Blood had soaked the makeshift bandage, suggesting whatever had caused the wound had done a fair bit of damage. "She's quite the warrior, that lass," the tracker muttered sourly. "Took us by surprise, nearly killed us before we managed to fight her off."

Narina rolled her eyes but didn't question that last remark although it seemed quite clear these two fools had not fought off anyone. They'd been soundly beaten by Aife, with or without assistance from Catia, and allowed to live because they were no longer a threat to the girls' chances of escape.

"Did you speak with them during the fight, Docimedis?" Narina asked the smaller hunter. "Did they say why they'd run off."

Bellicus was watching the man's face intently, and saw him looking at Ysfael before he said, "No, my lady. The Pict just said she wasn't letting us bring her back here."

"What of Catia?" Bellicus barked, and he addressed the question to Maccis, the taller of the pair. "Was she the Pict's prisoner?"

"Er…"

"We couldn't tell, my lord," Docimedis said quickly. "She wasn't tied up or anything, but she didn't look too happy at being ordered about by the bigger girl."

Narina sighed and muttered an oath. They didn't seem to be learning much at all from these two. "At least," she said in a quiet, defeated voice, "they're still alive. That's some comfort."

"Which direction were they going?" Ysfael asked. "To Dunnottar?"

The little tracker nodded. "Aye, my prince. They were heading north-east. The Pict was going home to her da', no doubt about it. They'll be there now, I'd say."

"Damn it!" Narina shouted, shaking her head in despair before turning and storming from the guardhouse, dashing at her tear-filled eyes as she passed the embarrassed guards at the door.

Bellicus thought Ysfael would go after her, to offer some comfort as a husband might reasonably be expected to do, but the prince stood where he was, looking at his men with an unfathomable expression. The druid couldn't quite tell if the prince was pleased or angered by the trackers' tale. A mixture of both, perhaps.

"How did you get the injuries?" Bellicus asked, again directing his words at Maccis.

"The big princess—" replied the smaller hunter, before the druid cut him off by holding up his hand and glaring at him.

"I was asking your friend. Be silent, and let him speak."

Docimedis's jaw sagged and he looked at Ysfael. The prince simply shrugged, however, and gestured for the big tracker to answer the question.

"She ambushed us," said the man, a hint of venom in his tone. Ashamed to have been so handily bested by a young woman, Bellicus thought. "We didn't want to hurt her, so we were holding back."

"She wasn't though," Docimedis put in.

"No, she wasn't," Maccis agreed. "Stabbed me right in the leg, and knocked him over," he nodded to his companion. "Then knelt on his back and smashed him in the back of the head. Bitch."

"That's enough," Bellicus spat. "She's a princess, and she was defending herself from strangers who were hunting her. Perhaps if you were better with that sword at your waist she wouldn't have been able to beat you so easily, and wander off to Dunnottar."

The man's eyes blazed but, despite his small friend's desire not to let him speak, he was clearly not a complete idiot, for he held his peace despite the druid's insult.

"Before I leave you to have your injuries seen to," Bellicus said coldly. "Was there anything else the girls said, or did, that might be of interest? Anything at all?"

Again, both the trackers looked at Ysfael, obviously taking their cues from him.

"No?" the prince said. "Well, I'll have a healer come and tend to your wounds. We may speak again later, once you're rested from your journey." He did not tell them they'd done well, for they clearly hadn't, but neither did he seem willing to say much more in the brooding, watchful presence of the druid and he nodded farewell to the men and then walked out of the building, pausing only to make sure Bellicus was following him.

When they were outside once more, the druid said, "You should go and comfort Narina. She needs support from her husband right now."

The prince gazed up at him, irritation, outrage and, eventually, sardonic amusement playing across his youthful face before he said, simply, "Aye, I agree. She needs me with her." He emphasised the 'me', making Bellicus wonder if he'd heard the rumours about Narina and the druid's relationship over the years.

If it gave Ysfael a sense of victory over the druid, to know that he shared a bed with the woman Bellicus once coveted, well, it didn't matter. Let the young man have that – they had to have some kind of equality between them if there was to be peace in the coming months and years, after all.

As Ysfael headed for the stairs leading up to the queen's house, he turned back and said with a suggestive smile, "I'll go and *comfort* Narina right now, druid. Tell the men not to disturb us for a while, eh? I think I'll need some comforting of my own…"

The druid watched him go, climbing the steps two at a time, eager to reach the queen's bedchamber, and, not for the first time, Bellicus felt a deep distaste for the young man. There was clearly something going on in Dun Breatann and Ysfael was deeply involved, as the discussion with the trackers had shown.

But what? Bellicus wondered, beginning the ascent himself. And was it somehow connected with Aife and Catia's hurried journey to Dunnottar? Had they uncovered some plot of the Votadini?

Or am I simply jealous of his marriage to Narina, and looking for reasons to judge and despise him?

Druids were trained not to act so childishly, to let jealousy or other base emotions cloud their reason, but Bellicus was still, after all, only human and, as he came at last to his own house, he thought back to the night before and his victory over the Votadini prince, and grinned.

CHAPTER SEVEN

"I'm home!" Aife raised her toned arms to the sky and smiled as the windswept fortress of Dunnottar came into view. It was lashing with rain as it often was in the Picts' coastal lands, and Catia felt quite miserable as they forged onwards towards their destination. Aife's obvious pleasure did make the younger princess happy, but, for her own part, she wished she was in Alt Clota with her mother.

"I'll be glad to get inside and dry off at last," Catia said, pulling her hood tighter and squinting as another gust blew drizzle into her cold face. "Will they have fresh clothes in my size do you think?"

"Of course," Aife said happily. Her hood had blown down a while ago and her long, brown hair was soaked through, yet she seemed to revel in the terrible weather. "Come on," she grinned, lengthening her stride as they reached the road that led to the fortress. "I might even have some old clothes that will fit you."

Catia doubted that, for Aife was almost six-feet tall, as physically imposing as most men, although, she thought, if Bellicus truly was her father, Catia might one day be as tall as the Pictish princess. That was at least a couple of years away, though, and she wondered what kind of clothing she'd be given in Dunnottar. It didn't really matter, as long as she was dry; it seemed like she'd been soaked and blown about forever although, in truth, the rain had been persistent but only really become heavy over the past two or three days. The pair had passed a few steadings and farms, places owned and worked by people loyal to Aife's father, and Catia had suggested getting horses from them, but it became obvious that the warrior-woman was not keen on riding.

Given Aife's prowess with a blade, Catia had not been terribly surprised at that – spending all of one's time becoming an expert at a particular skill often meant others were never learned. And Aife had been a slave-woman's daughter, a bastard who'd not been brought up in the royal household learning the usual things a princess might need to know until her childhood was almost over and her obvious skill with a blade was noticed by the king.

Becoming comfortable on horseback was probably well down on the younger Aife's list of things to do, and so their journey was completed on foot.

As a result, more of their pursuers from Dun Breatann had managed to catch up with them. Thankfully Catia and Aife had heard their hooves pounding in time to get off the road and into the trees before the hunters spotted them, riding past and losing the trail thanks to the sodden, shifting ground and the footprints of other travellers, cattle, and sheep. After that first pair of hunters had attacked them, with the bigger one, Maccis, saying Ysfael would thank them for killing Aife, Catia had realised her friend's fears and reason for escaping Dun Breatann had been valid. Those men had wanted to kill Aife, and probably Catia too. They could not allow themselves to be caught.

"There's a lot of trees in your lands," Catia had said after another pair of mounted hunters had ridden past and disappeared into the distance ahead. "We don't seem to have as many in Alt Clota." Indeed, that made escaping from the place rather harder than it might have been had there been more cover. Birch, rowan, ash, alder, and oak seemed more plentiful the further north they travelled.

Aife had nodded. "That's because the Romans cut them all down to build their forts and walls and so on. The lands of your Damnonii and the Votadini and the other tribes further south will take many years to return to how they were before the legions came. Of course," she'd smiled proudly then, "the Romans never managed to conquer us Picts, so our trees were left in peace."

Catia felt quite sad, to think of all the trees around Dun Breatann being torn down to feed some far-off emperor's war machine. What a waste.

As they approached the first of the gatehouses leading to Dunnottar, however, the thought of a similar tree burning merrily in the King Drest's great hall was irresistible to Catia, who could almost feel the wonderful heat from the imagined blaze drying the rain from her in a glorious haze of steam.

"Just be warned, "Aife said, turning back, her face serious now. "The walk to the fortress isn't supposed to be very pleasant."

Catia frowned, wondering what her companion meant, but then she saw the skulls stuck atop the stakes that had been forced into the ground all the way along the path which led down and then up to the main buildings. Human skulls. "I've seen that kind of thing before," she said. "We do the same in Dun Breatann at times, to warn enemies away."

"Princess!" Two guards appeared from the small gatehouse leading towards the skull-lined path, helmets gleaming, spears readied, but amazed smiles on their faces. "How did you get here?"

Aife returned their grins and walked forward to clasp arms in the warriors greeting. "Well met, lads," she said with an easy familiarity. "I escaped from Dun Breatann, with some help from my friend here." They all turned to look at Catia who returned their stares coolly. "And she's a princess too, so take care to treat her with respect, all right?"

The guards nodded deferentially to Catia and then began firing more questions at Aife, asking how she managed to escape, and had they walked all the way there, and so on, but the princess shook her head, laughing.

"You'll hear all about it soon enough, I'm sure," she told them. "But, for now, we're bloody soaked and starving, and in dire need of some warm ale so let us pass, will you?"

The men stepped aside and Aife waved to them, leading Catia onto the path and past the first of the skulls. She was impressed by her older friend's conversation with the guards, it was clear Aife was seen as a friend and a comrade-in-arms rather than just some royal girl. Catia thought she would like to be seen the same way when she was fully grown.

The wind picked up speed as they were by now right on the coast, walking up a flight of slippery, stone steps towards another, more imposing set of gates. They ran, not even noticing the men on the walls above staring down at them curiously, but they'd either been recognised or the first set of guards had signalled, for they were not forced to stand in the deluge and wait to be admitted. The gates swung open as they reached them, and more soldiers welcomed them inside.

"My lady Aife!" A grizzled veteran with a bulbous nose and a thicker accent than most Picts Catia had ever met, was nodding his head, eyes twinkling. From his bearing and the manner of his dress it was obvious he was in charge of the men guarding the walls and, from the hug Aife bestowed on him, a favourite of hers.

"Denbecan," she said, and Catia imagined she could see tears in her friend's eyes, although it could just have been rain. "I've missed you."

"Come on," the man said, leading the girls away from the gates, towards an imposing three-storeyed building. "Your father'll want to see you, and find out why you're here when you're supposed to be a prisoner of the Damnonii." His stride was long and Catia had to hurry to keep up but there was a delicious smell coming from the building and, as the man led them inside, the wave of heat and sounds of folk chattering struck the young girl like a blow. She staggered, and might have even fallen down if Aife hadn't turned at the right moment and seen her distress.

"Are you all right?" the Pict asked, face a mask of concern. "I'm sorry, Catia, I shouldn't have pushed you so hard to get here."

"I'm fine," Catia replied, standing still for a moment, head bowed as she waited for a bout of dizziness to pass. Mercifully, it did, and she looked up, seeing faces gazing back at her, men, women, children, and then a familiar dark-haired woman of surpassing beauty was coming towards them.

"Come here, child," the woman said, frowning in concern as she placed her arms around Catia and gently led her towards a seat near the fire. "Let's get you some warm clothes. Some of mine should fit."

"Thank you, Ria," the girl said with the dignity expected of a princess, although inside she was mentally cursing the woman. Ria, druidess of the Pictish king, Drest. Small, wonderfully formed, beautiful, a former lover of Bellicus…And the woman who almost allowed Drest's invading army into Dun Breatann to slaughter everyone inside. Only Duro's suspicious mind had saved the Damnonii fortress from being taken that day, but even before that had happened Catia had not liked the woman. There had been a clear rivalry between her mother and Ria, and Catia had obviously taken Narina's side.

It hadn't helped that Ria had defeated Catia when they sparred with wooden practice swords either.

Still, the druidess was doing her best to make Catia comfortable now, calling for a servant to fetch clean, dry clothes and another to bring food from the steaming cauldron hanging over the fire for both Catia and Aife.

Drest himself was sitting at his own high table, looking surprised and not exactly happy to see his daughter standing in the hall. Aife was supposed to be a hostage of the Damnonii after all, held captive as an assurance that the Picts wouldn't try to invade Alt Clota again any time soon. Why had she come home? Had she been set free by Narina? Had she escaped, and if so, what would the Damnonii do about it? All this and more Catia could see in the king's face, but, at last, he stood up and crossed the hall to embrace Aife.

It wasn't the warmest greeting Catia had ever seen, but it was something. She imagined Narina's reaction when they finally saw one another again and tears blurred her vision, knowing that meeting might be a long way off.

"Why are you here?" Drest asked, taking the stool a servant brought across for him. Aife sat on another, while Ria's servant took Catia into another, more private, section of the hall to change into the fresh clothes.

How long would she live here, in the Picts' stronghold? It wasn't so long ago that Catia's people had been at war with the folk of Dunnottar, yet now she was expecting them to feed and clothe her for…the gods knew how long it would be before she could go home. Her decision to run away with Aife seemed foolish now – she should have let the older girl travel alone. She was certainly capable of looking after herself in a fight. Catia had argued that the Damnonii hunters would simply have shot Aife down like any other prey. If they were found, only Catia's presence, and the chance of injuring or killing her, would hold the hunters' missiles at bay and allow the princesses to make it out of Alt Clota alive.

So Catia had reasoned but in truth she'd not really believed it. A good archer would have no trouble hitting Aife. Catia just wanted to go with her friend on this adventure and hadn't really thought through the ramifications. She felt a deep bond with the Pictish girl and wanted to help her escape Ysfael's wrath. She also wanted to prove to herself that she was no longer the impotent, weak child that had been abducted by Horsa's warband not so long ago.

Fear and anxiety threatened to overcome her as she thought of that terrifying journey south with the Saxon raiders and she forced herself to be calm, as Bellicus had shown her. Bellicus. When he returned to Dun Breatann, Catia would be able to go home surely? The giant druid, along with Duro, would sort Ysfael out.

"Are you dressed? Ah, you look beautiful!" Ria's head appeared around the partition and she looked Catia up and down with satisfaction. "Very much a princess. Come on then, lady, let's get some hot food inside you before you fall over."

Catia smiled, as much from the thought of a good meal as from Ria's compliments, and she gladly followed the druidess while also reminding herself that the dark-haired woman was always working for the good of the Picts. Everything she did was to serve her people and her gods, and she would use the likes of Catia if she saw an opportunity to gain from it. Catia would need to be on her guard while she was in Dunnottar, even with Aife whose natural loyalties would also lie with her kinsmen rather than her young friend from the south.

They sat with the king and Aife by the fire, although that pair were locked in a deep discussion, with Drest's complexion seeming redder than it had been earlier. He was angry about something, so Catia guessed Ysfael's behaviour was being discussed. Ria took her attention away by pushing a bowl of steaming stew before her and handing her a spoon.

"Eat," the druidess said kindly. "And drink. Gather your strength, and then you may either rest or enjoy the evening's entertainment."

"Entertainment?" Catia asked, blowing on a spoonful of stew before slurping it in rather an un-princess-like fashion.

"Aye," Ria said. "You're not the only guests in Dunnottar today." She looked past Catia to the front doors. "A trading ship arrived at our docks not long ago. The men in charge of the vessel will need to be hosted and entertained. Drest likes to impress visitors to these lands, so there will be stories and singing and so on. You know, the usual fare." She smiled and Catia found herself warming to the druidess, understanding why Bellicus had been so taken by her. She was charismatic and pleasant, as well as being strikingly pretty.

"Where are they from, these traders?" Catia asked, greedily attacking the stew now that her blowing had rendered it cool enough to swallow without scalding her mouth.

"There they are now," Ria said, nodding towards the doors as they were opened and a gust of cold wind heralded the newcomers' arrival. "You can probably tell where they're from just by looking at them."

Catia turned, curious, and then it felt like a heavy stone had settled in her stomach and she put down the spoon, appetite completely gone. Ria was correct – it was quite obvious where these 'traders' had come from, thanks to their height, the furs they wore, the hammer amulets around their necks, and their light-coloured beards.

They were Saxons.

"No," Catia whispered, and her voice cracked as she stared at the tall men trooping into the hall. "No, no, please, no."

Ria looked at her in surprise. "What's wrong?" she asked, laying her hand on the girl's arm.

"They've come for me," Catia sobbed, and she knew she was close to becoming hysterical. Her body was shaking uncontrollably, and it was difficult to breathe so she gasped, shoulders heaving up and down as she tried desperately to take in air. All she wanted to do was stand and run out of the hall, out of the fortress, and back to Dun Breatann where the Saxons could never reach her.

"Catia." Ria's voice, calm and utterly in control, came to her, and she felt the woman's hands on her, holding firmly to her. "You're safe, Catia. The Saxons are here as guests. Traders. There's only one shipload of them, they're not here for you, and even if they were, I would not let them take you. Breathe, Catia, you're safe with me."

Still, Catia stared at the bearded warriors, her arms shaking, mind whirling with thoughts she couldn't quite take hold of, just random, meaningless impressions of fear and danger and…The night the Saxon witch, Thorbjorg, had been about to carve open her throat as a blood sacrifice to the sea-wolves' vicious gods. These men were here to take her back to Thorbjorg, the *volva* would finish what she'd started that night Bellicus and Duro had come out of the darkness to save her.

"Catia." Ria repeated her name, coolly, levelly, without any hint of alarm or anxiety and, at last, it worked. The fear began to drain from the young princess, replaced by relief, and she threw her arms around Ria, hugging her fiercely as tears spilled down her cheeks and she cried uncontrollably.

"I'm sorry," she said, wiping her face with the back of her hand. "I don't know what happened. The sight of them…"

"Ssshhh," Ria murmured, stroking the girl's hair. "There's nothing to be sorry for. I've seen it before when people are faced with the memory of a traumatic event, or the threat of one occurring again. It happens often in battle, even to the most hardened of warriors. Just breathe deeply and regain control of yourself, Catia, you're safe. Just tell yourself that. No-one will harm you. Look, the big arses aren't interested in you."

It was quite true. One or two of the newcomers had glanced their way, but they were more interested in the beautiful druidess than the red-faced, sobbing eleven-year old.

"Are you all right now? Yes? Good." Ria released her embrace and sat back, smiling. "Have a sip of the ale."

They both took a drink and sat quietly for a time, trying not to stare too much at the Saxons who were chattering noisily amongst themselves, eating and enjoying a large amount of King Drest's ale.

"I've been training," Catia said in a soft, puzzled tone. "You know, with weapons. Teaching myself how to fight, so if I ever did have to defend myself against men like that, I would be ready. You know I'm good, we sparred together before and I almost beat you." She looked at Ria fearfully. "But I'm not ready for a real battle, am I? I'm still just a terrified little girl, as much as I try to act like a warrior."

"I told you," the druidess replied, and her voice was a little harsher now, more insistent. "What happened to you is a natural reaction to danger. It can happen to anyone. But you overcame it and regained mastery of yourself. *That* is what's important. Now, you know how this kind of thing can affect you, and if it happens again, you will be ready for it."

"Has it ever happened to you?" Catia asked.

Ria hesitated for a moment, then shook her head. "No, but I've not been involved in that many battles, and I've won most of them." She winked and patted the dagger at her waist before becoming serious again. "I've seen older men pissing themselves going into a fight, just overcome with fear, remembering…" She trailed off, not wanting to speak too graphically of the horrors of war. "Remembering the friends they'd seen cut down in previous battles, and the terrible injuries warriors suffer in such conflicts."

"But I'm not an old soldier," Catia protested.

"No, like I said, such a reaction can happen to anyone who's suffered a horrific, painful event in their life. Mothers who've lost children can find themselves reliving the moment months or even years later and fall on the floor, crying hysterically. Children who've seen their parents slaughtered by enemy raiders will see it again in their mind's eye, flashing into view months after the event at the sight or sound of an innocent butcher's cleaver at work." She looked away, eyes downcast, almost as if suddenly aware she was giving away too much of herself.

"I was terrified," Catia said, still shocked by the strength of her emotions upon seeing the Saxons entering the hall.

"There's nothing wrong with fear," Ria told her firmly. "It keeps us alert and warns us of danger. The important thing is to not let it master you." She took both Catia's hands in hers and drew her eyes to hers. "Remember who you are. Who your parents are. You are Catia, Princess of Dun Breatann, and you are a warrior now, not the child the Saxons abducted. Never forget that. If you are ever in a fight for your life, put your fear to one side, and let your training take over."

"Go into a trance," Catia said thoughtfully. "Like Bellicus does."

Ria was grinning now. "Aye," she agreed. "Something like that, I suppose. You know I learned how to fight with Bel when we were training as youngsters?"

The comment suddenly reminded Catia who she was talking to, and she leaned back, recalling how the druidess had fooled Bellicus and almost brought about the destruction of the Damnonii people. They sat in silence for a time and then, to Catia's relief, Aife approached and sat down next to her.

"Are you all right?" the older princess asked, features pinched with concern. "I saw you hugging Ria."

"She's fine now," the druidess said, pushing herself up, still smiling. "She's wise beyond her years, that one. But I'll leave her in your care, my lady. I have tasks to attend to."

Aife nodded.

Catia looked up at Ria and, despite the history between them and their two peoples, the princess returned her smile. "Thank you," she said, and that was enough. The druidess disappeared into the crowd, her slim frame mingling amongst the revellers and becoming lost from sight almost as if by magic.

CHAPTER EIGHT

"It's not right," said Aife the next day when she and Catia were out walking in Dunnottar, enjoying the views of the sea, and the bracing, fresh air. "Treating slaves like that I mean. That sea-wolf 'nobleman' is no better than an animal."

Some of the visiting Saxon traders were also out making the most of the clear, sunny weather and one – a jarl, Catia could tell from the way his men deferred to him and the arrogant way he carried himself – was enjoying himself at the expense of a man he led about in chains. Every now and then the Saxon would shout something at his slave and then he'd either laugh at the fellow or kick or slap him.

"That's no farmer either," Aife continued as they walked on, glancing back at the jarl and his smirking entourage. "That man he's got chained up is a mighty warrior. Or he was, once."

"A warrior?" Catia asked, looking at the slave in surprise. "How can you possibly know that? He's not got the muscular arms of a fighter, or the thighs. He's skin and bone. He just looks like any other thrall to me."

A sudden warm gust of wind jarred them and Aife laughed, steadying Catia who wasn't quite used to the strong coastal airstream yet; Dun Breatann was situated on a river, and saw its share of storms and high winds, but Dunnottar was something different. A child could be blown off their feet in an instant here, even on a day that seemed generally calm and sunny.

"Look at the way he carries himself," Aife said, nodding towards the slave just before the princesses rounded the corner of a storehouse and the Saxons were lost to sight, while the view of the sea opened up even more. "Proud. Straight backed, despite his beatings and abuse."

"Maybe he's a nobleman," Catia suggested.

"Oh, he's that," Aife agreed. "But his movements are light and controlled, like a cat's almost. And, even in the short time we saw them there, I noticed his eyes searching our walls for signs of weakness. For some way he might escape, if he could just get those chains off." She turned suddenly thoughtful, grim almost. "I wouldn't want to be one of those sea-wolves if he ever does manage to get out of his shackles."

Catia eyed her older companion almost suspiciously. "Do you like him or something?" she demanded, grinning. "You seem to have taken a great interest in him, considering he's just a slave."

Aife returned her smile, unabashed and obviously enjoying this unusual companionship with someone who was her social peer, or better, perhaps. They might be princesses, but they were two young women, simply talking about things any other girls their age would find terribly important or at least interesting. "He's too dirty and skinny for me," Aife said. "But if he broke free, had a few good meals and a long bathe in the sea, well…Who knows? I might have a tumble with him."

They walked on, revelling in the sea air and the cries of the gulls. The ship which had brought the Saxons to Dunnottar could be seen at the docks below, where men were unloading the goods brought for trade. The ship was not particularly big, nothing like the great trading vessels the Romans must have once sailed to Dun Breatann, Catia thought. The Saxon cargo would probably consist of relatively small, high-value items such as pepper, spices, and finely crafted glassware like jars, beakers and bowls. For such warlike people, the Saxons, Angles, Jutes and so on were skilled craftsmen who enjoyed high culture, or so Catia's tutors had taught her. She found it hard to believe.

"I hope that slave does escape," she said, hooking her arm inside Aife's and smiling grimly. "And teaches his captor a lesson."

They reached the end of the long storehouse and turned back, away from the cliffside, towards the centre of the fortress once more. Another gust of wind propelled them across the well-trodden grass, towards the Saxon jarl with his chained pet. They did not avert their eyes as they approached, as some women might do, instead staring openly at the men.

Some of the Saxons muttered as they looked at them, particularly at Aife, speaking in their own tongue but casting such lascivious glances at the tall princess that there was no need for a translator to understand what they were saying. The jarl himself eyed Aife coolly as they walked by, as if he recognised her and felt as though they were in some way equal, although, now that they were close, Catia could see his right arm had been disfigured. Whatever social rules or scale applied to a Saxon jarl and a Pictish princess, Catia could tell there would be no equality if it came to a fight between Aife and the sea-wolf.

Perhaps the slave had been the one to cause such a devastating injury to the jarl, she thought. That would explain the chains and the constant humiliation: payback.

She found herself staring directly at the thrall, noting his lank, filth-encrusted hair which had perhaps once been as blond and luxurious as any Saxon's. He had a scar on his forehead, yet, in spite of his grimy appearance, there was indeed something quite striking about him. Something noble which set him apart from his captors.

Their eyes met and the slave recoiled very slightly, frowning, before the jarl tugged on his chain and slapped him across the head, shouting something in the Briton's own language but with such a heavy Germanic accent that Catia couldn't quite make it out.

And then they were past and heading for Drest's great hall with its ever-present cooking smells and smoke drifting into the pale blue autumn sky.

"I think he liked you."

Catia glanced at her companion, hearing the quite distinct note of jealousy in Aife's tone. She did not reply, though. Aye, the slave had given her a piercing look, but there was no physical attraction there, it had been something else in the man's eyes: Recognition.

Catia did not think she'd ever met the slave before – he was so striking that she'd surely remember any previous crossing of paths but, as they went into the hall, assailed by the overpowering smell of smoking meat, the young princess could not shake the strange feeling that the slave's gaze had awakened in her.

"I have to speak to him," she said, almost to herself.

"Oh, really?" Aife rolled her eyes and filled a mug with ale, only half-heartedly trying to hide her disappointment at the slave's attention being focused so fully on Catia. She soon rallied, however, and, smiling a little sheepishly said, "All right then, my young friend. Let's see if we can meet this enigmatic thrall."

CHAPTER NINE

In Dun Breatann, the rest of the Pictish prisoners of war – taken after the battle to ensure Drest and his advisors would not try to invade Alt Clota again any time soon – were questioned yet again about Princess Aife's decision to escape to the north. Of course, as soon as Aife and Catia disappeared these noblemen and sons of powerful Pictish leaders had been interrogated but all claimed to know nothing. Narina believed them, because the princess had never seemed close to those particular hostages during the months they'd spent together within the fortress.

Aife's closest ally in Dun Breatann had not been one of her fellow Picts – it had been Catia.

But, with Bellicus there now, and the confirmation from Ysfael's hunters that the two girls had indeed gone to Dunnottar, the queen thought it worthwhile to question the rest of the Pictish hostages another time. The druid could well spot something the rest of them, even the similarly trained mystic Koriosis, had missed.

It proved fruitless, however.

"They know nothing," Bellicus stated flatly, following the queen and Ysfael out of the cell which Lord Gartnaith, one of the Picts' erstwhile commanders, was housed in. Aife had been afforded fairly nice quarters, on account of her being a king's daughter, but the other Picts were kept in simpler, sparsely furnished, less comfortable rooms on the southern side of the rock and treated more like hostages. They were not harmed, but neither were they given all the comforts of welcome guests.

"Then why did Catia leave with her?" Narina muttered. "It makes no sense."

"We're going round in circles again," Ysfael said irritably. "We've been over this, and over it." He strode past, shaking his head as he turned back to address them. "I've had enough of it now. We know Catia is safe and well, so you can stop worrying, Narina. She's clearly just a spoiled, petulant child who wanted to run off on some adventure with her exotic friend. She'll soon grow tired of Drest's court, and the shit weather up there." He made a dismissive gesture. "I'm done with it. Move on, Narina, and start acting like a proper ruler. This place is falling to ruin." And, with that, he strode off, towards the steps leading down.

They watched him go, Narina with an angry, hurt expression, Bellicus merely thoughtful. The druid guessed the Votadini prince would be heading for the stables, where he'd find his favourite horse and take it out hunting or 'patrolling' with some of his own warriors. That seemed to be his pastime of choice, at least so the druid had heard.

It was dry but cloudy, and a south-westerly wind made it uncomfortable to stand still for too long, so Bellicus smiled and said, "Come on. Let's have a proper talk about everything, indoors, where it's not so bloody windy."

The queen looked at him with a piercing stare, and then nodded and started to walk rather quickly up towards her home. Bellicus followed, marshalling his thoughts. Narina was moving so fast that she reached the summit before the druid's long strides could catch up, but she didn't go inside immediately. Instead, she crossed to the wall and looked down, watching for a time in silence. Eventually, four riders passed through the gates and galloped northwards.

Narina watched them go, mouth in a thin line, and then she looked at Bellicus and said, almost imperiously, "Come."

There were no guards on her door at that time, for the house was empty and there was no threat of danger from within the fortress, so Narina opened the door herself and gestured with an open palm for Bellicus to go in.

He did so, and Narina came in at his back, closing the door, pushing the heavy bolt across, and then, silently, put her hand inside the front of his breeches and began to rub his manhood.

"Narina—"

"Don't, Bel," she said, pulling the breeches down so she could get at him properly. "He's gone for a while. I intend to make the most of the time. Unless you're unwilling?"

He gasped in pleasure and shook his head. It had been quite some time since he'd lain with a woman and the memories of that frenzied kiss Narina had given him at their earlier reunion had been playing on his mind ever since. "I'm willing. Oh, by the gods, I'm willing!"

* * *

Afterwards, when they'd washed themselves down with perfumed water and got their clothes back on, they went outside for some air and to enjoy the view of the great River Clota that wound through so much of the countryside. The sun was starting to appear through the clouds, but, although still a little windy out, druid and queen welcomed it, for both needed to cool down and catch their breath again.

"That was…"

"Wonderful?" Narina said, looking up at him and smiling suggestively.

"Foolish," Bellicus replied, then, seeing her frown, added quickly, "And wonderful too."

"I don't regret it for a moment," the queen said, drawing her brown hair back and using a clasp to tie it back.

Bellicus recognised the clasp, for he'd given her it himself as a gift, years before. It was silver and had a depiction of a Roman goddess on it. He'd forgotten about it until now, but felt quite touched to realise she still used the thing after all this time.

"Being caught by Ysfael would be disastrous," he told her, lifting a hand to halt her protestations. "I know he has lovers, but he fears me; sees me as a rival. You're going to have to spend the rest of your days as his partner, Narina. It's madness to turn him against you by sleeping with me."

"It would be better if I slept with some servant? Or some landless warrior from, oh, Dun Buic, or Cardden Ros? Should I do that next time I want to lie with someone? Would you prefer that?"

"Don't be silly," he replied softly, lowering his voice as a woman carrying dirty water from washing clothes came up and emptied it over the side of the wall, nodding respectfully to queen and druid. "You know I would rather you came to me but…" He sighed. "It feels like we've gone back in time, to that period when you took over from Coroticus."

"You thought we shouldn't be together then, too," Narina said.

"And you know I was right. As I'm right now."

"So, it's never to be between us?" She turned to look directly at him, leaning her arms on the wall, the sunshine lighting her pale, almost flawless complexion. "Even though we both want one another? Why must it be so? I'm a queen, and you are a druid! Why should we not do whatever we like, by Taranis? We allowed politics, and common sense, to guide us before, Bel, and look where it's got us."

They eyed one another as a second washerwoman tipped more water over the side of the wall, the dirty liquid splattering noisily against the rocks below, and they said nothing more until the woman returned to her companions who were clearing up for the day. Some previous rulers had banned the washing and drying of clothes up here, thinking it uncouth and unsuited to a royal fortress, but Coroticus hadn't minded. The things dried quicker up here and it was easier on the women who were glad they didn't have to carry the laundry up and down so many stairs. Narina had never even thought to change things when she became queen. She quite enjoyed seeing the ladies hard at work yet chattering and laughing together. It was a nicer sight than warriors standing about on guard or sparring all day long.

"I've been talking with the people," Bellicus said, apparently changing the subject. "About Aife and Catia."

Narina frowned. "And?"

"You were right about Ysfael having lovers."

The queen shrugged, clearly irritated at this unexpected and seemingly unrelated statement. "So what?"

"Well, it made me wonder if that had something to do with the princesses running off."

Narina gazed at him and her expression darkened the longer she looked. It seemed this line of thought had never occurred to her.

"Are you saying he slept with our—" She broke off, glancing around to make sure no more of the washerwomen were nearby before continuing. "That he slept with my daughter?"

"What? No!" Bellicus shook his head, amazed that, considering how closely they'd been aligned just moments ago in the queen's bed, they were now thinking along entirely different lines. "I mean he might have wanted Aife as one of his lovers."

The fury in her eyes died as she thought about what he was saying.

"Did she ever say anything to you about Ysfael?"

Narina shook her head immediately. "No. We were not close. I was her captor, after all, and I don't think she'd allow herself to forget it. And I had other things to worry about than ingratiating myself to a woman who'd wanted to kill all my people just a few months ago."

They stood contemplating things for a time, before Bellicus declared himself hungry and Narina agreed to accompany him to the great hall for something to eat.

"What are we going to do now?" the queen asked as they approached the doors with the guards who, Bellicus was glad to see, were now Damnonii warriors rather than Ysfael's Votadini. "About Catia and the Picts I mean. Aife was a hostage – we really ought to do something about it. Hostages can't just decide to wander off home whenever they feel like it."

Bellicus pursed his lips. "In the old days, we'd have killed a couple of the others. Sent Drest a message." He shook his head firmly. "But until we know exactly why Aife ran off, I think we should hold off on doing anything so violent. She may have felt there was no other choice and, in that case, it's not her fellow prisoners' fault."

"We have to do *something*," Narina argued. "They almost took Dun Breatann, Bel! They'd have killed us all in our beds if Duro hadn't realised something was wrong."

The druid heard the accusation in her tone. She was still upset over his dalliance with the Pict, Ria which allowed the druidess to get inside the fortress, and Drest's forces to follow her through the now sealed-up secret tunnel. It had been a hard lesson for Bellicus who, although a learned and skilled druid, was still a young man who'd allowed his head to be turned by Ria's pretty face and lithe figure. He would be more careful in future.

He couldn't help smiling then, thinking back to what he'd just been doing with Narina in her bed chamber. Of course, he would be careful…

"You find this amusing?" the queen demanded, misreading the reason for his expression.

"No," he replied, straightening his face and his posture. "I agree with you. I think we need to send a delegation to Dunnottar, to find out what's been happening, and to bring Catia back home."

Narina's eyes lit up. "Agreed. I'll go."

"Don't be silly, Narina," Bellicus said, trying not to sound harsh. "You're the queen. You can't just walk into Drest's fortress! He'd take you prisoner and use you to take control of Alt Clota."

"Well, who goes then?" Narina demanded, accepting his words but still disappointed that she'd have to wait even longer to see her beloved daughter. "You, no doubt. You love wandering about the lands, don't you? You're hardly ever here these days."

"Aye," he said. "As much as I hate Dunnottar and would like to never set foot in the place again, I think I would be the best person for the job. Drest at least respects me. Fears me, even. And, as a druid, they'll not kill me."

"He nearly did before," Narina reminded him.

"They were never going to kill me," he said. "Duro perhaps, but not me. You know it was all just a ruse to make us trust Ria when she helped us escape."

"Aye, and it worked."

Bellicus heard her hard tone and refused to meet her eyes. "I don't think Duro will want to come with me," he said, steering the conversation in a less contentious direction. "And that's perhaps a good thing. He'll help you here. Help Gavo."

"And I'd be very happy to have him around," she said, her face softening again. She liked the bluff centurion and greatly respected his leadership skills. He'd been a very young man when he was an officer in the legions, but he had a natural talent for command. "Where is he anyway?"

"Checking the walls and other defences with Cai. He even put on his Roman armour and helmet to make it seem more official!"

"And Eburus?"

"I think he's with some of the Votadini men. I told him it would be a good idea to keep in with them, since Ysfael might insist he rejoins their ranks soon."

"To annoy you."

"Aye, although," he shrugged expansively. "Eburus is one of the Votadini. His place is with them, not following me and Duro about."

"Sometimes friendship can be more important than ties of tribe or even blood," Narina said quietly, almost wistfully but she didn't expand on her thoughts, instead grinning at the druid and saying,

"Let's go and find Duro and Cai and see what our centurion thinks of your plan to go to Dunnottar."

Together they walked down the slope, returning the respectful but cheery nods from the washerwomen who'd by now almost finished their work and were looking forward to a rest and a well-earned meal. Bellicus felt a strange sense of peace, and he knew if Catia was safely there in the fortress with them, all would be right with the world. Well, almost all.

He pushed aside his worries for the future and resisted the urge to take Narina's hand in his own. The gods had their plans for them all, he just had to pray things would turn out right in the end.

"Ah, there he is," the queen cried, laughing as they caught sight of Duro striding up the stairs towards them, crested helmet gleaming, Cai loping along at his side, tongue lolling, eyes shining. "How did you find my sentries, centurion? And my walls? Are they fit for purpose?"

Cai ran to Bellicus, whining softly as if they'd been parted for a month rather than an hour or two, licking the druid's fingers and palms although he knew better than to place his paws on his master's chest and try to kiss his stubbled face.

"Aye, they'll do," Duro said, halting to catch his breath. He was supremely fit for his age, but the steps in Dun Breatann would take a toll on any man. "I'm parched though. Shall we head up to the hall for an ale, and I can give you my report there?"

"Aye," Narina replied, and she slipped her arm into Duro's as they headed back up towards the great hall. "That sounds like a good idea. We have much to discuss, Duro."

"Oh, really?" He looked back over his shoulder at Bellicus, squinting suspiciously, but the wink he received from the druid in reply merely deepened his frown. He was no fool, the centurion – he could tell something had gone on between Narina and his friend, but Bellicus didn't care.

Of all the men in Alt Clota, he knew Duro could keep his mouth shut.

CHAPTER TEN

There had been another feast in Dunnottar the previous night, as Drest tried to show his Saxon visitors how great a lord he was. Many of the Pictish warriors wore clothes which showed off their bare skin, and the tattoos which they were famed for. Serpents, birds, wolves and other animals were drawn on limbs and even faces, along with strange geometrical symbols which Catia could not recognise or decipher. The Pictish king knew how important appearances were, especially to the likes of Jarl Leofdaeg, who clearly thought dragging a man about on a chain made him look dangerous and powerful.

Catia thought it simply made Leofdaeg look ridiculous. She'd watched him continue to strike the skinny slave – always using his left arm – and wished someone would do something to help the captive, who took the beatings stoically.

The other nobleman who'd accompanied Leofdaeg, however...He seemed much smarter than the others. More thoughtful, more restrained, less needlessly cruel. But that probably made the wheezing Sigarr even more dangerous as a result.

Catia sat beside Aife and they'd observed the sea-wolves' behaviour, wondering what the true purpose of their visit might be. Was it purely for trade, as they claimed, or were they scouting the fortress in preparation for a future attack? Or perhaps they wanted to form an alliance with the Picts who, despite their defeat by Queen Narina's forces the previous summer, were still the major power in these far northern lands.

Dunnottar's other druid, Qunavo, an older man with a long, white beard and piercing blue eyes, had entertained the visitors and Drest's own people with tales and songs of old, while much meat and even more ale was consumed. It was a long, loud feast which almost spilled into violence on a couple of occasions as drunk Saxon 'traders' and proud Pictish hearth warriors puffed out their chests and sought to prove their dominance as such men always did.

Cooler heads, and even the intervention of Ria, who simply had to look at unruly men to bring them under her control, had meant the night ended peacefully enough although there were a few aching heads this morning, and the sounds of retching and puking could be heard like a demented chorus outside the hall. Catia would never, she was certain, understand why people drank until they were ill.

"Look, there's the Saxons," Aife said, staring into the gloomy corner of the great hall. "They'll be going down to their ship soon enough. Are you ready?"

Catia nodded. They'd devised a plan during yesterday's feasting, and it was time now to see if it would work.

"Remember," Aife reminded her. "I'll talk to Leofdaeg, try to keep him here in the hall while you go and talk to the slave. Be as fast as you can, all right?"

Catia set her jaw and nodded again. Aife had offered to simply question Leofdaeg outright about the slave, or even have her father, the king, do it, but, for some reason Catia didn't want the jarl to know his captive had aroused this interest. She had no idea why that was important, but Bellicus had told her before how vital it was to trust one's instincts.

They'd noticed on the previous nights that Leofdaeg's slave had been returned to the Saxon ship when the sun went down and the drinking got properly underway. Once he was in his cups, Leofdaeg seemed to grow tired of the thrall's brooding presence and sent him away with a lackey to spend the night on the beached trading vessel.

All Catia had to do was go down to the beach that morning and speak to the slave.

She placed a hand on the short sword sheathed at her waist, took a deep breath, and smiled at Aife. "Keep that idiot busy for as long as you can. I'll be back soon."

The princesses went in their opposite directions, Aife striding across the hall with confidence and poise, drawing eyes towards her like iron filings to a lodestone, while Catia headed out through the door into the pale, morning sunshine.

It was a fair walk from the hall down the steps to the beach and she was given curious looks by the guards at the main gatehouse, but none questioned her. Either Aife had told them to let her move freely about the fortress, or someone else had. She guessed she was as much a prisoner here as Aife had been in Dun Breatann and, if she attempted to leave, to head onto the mainland, she'd be stopped. Letting her wander within the boundaries of the fortress was not an issue to the guards, though, and she soon found herself crossing the pebbled beach as gulls wheeled noisily overhead, and men and women worked on the docks.

A fishing ship had come in and was being unloaded before it would head out into the sea again, and another trading vessel, this one crewed by Votadini sailors from the shouts Catia heard passing between them, was also being emptied of goods. Already the beach was a hive of activity, noise, and smells, and the young princess felt more at home here than she did in the Picts' hall. This seemed more like the docks at Dun Breatann, although she felt a pang when she looked out at the sea and saw only water – at home she could see land on the other side of the Clota but here…It felt like the end of the world.

No-one took any notice of her as she flitted past them in her borrowed dress and cloak. There were other children there on the docks and on the beach, working alongside the adults, earning their keep, so another one was not cause for alarm or even interest.

The Saxon ship hove into view as she passed the Votadini vessel and the sight was a stark contrast to what Catia had just passed. Instead of hustle and bustle, and light-hearted or raucous shouts between the workers, the Saxon craft was silent. The slaves had unloaded their masters' cargo days before, and whatever had been bartered in return loaded onto the ship the following day so now there was nothing for the pitiful captives to do but sit, chained and dead-eyed, on the beached ship.

Two Saxons remained on board to keep watch over the slaves, and they looked almost as fed-up as their charges as they sat gazing out to sea. They whistled to themselves, though, a jaunty shared melody which seemed entirely out of place on the unhappy ship.

"Hey," Catia called as she approached, drawing the attention of the guards and those of the slaves who still had a spark of interest in the world outside their own suffering. Then she said, in the sea-wolves' own tongue, for she'd picked up some of their words during her time as Horsa's captive, "You two. Saxons."

They peered curiously down at her, interested in this disruption to their boring morning, but not interested enough to get up or say anything back to the girl staring imperiously up at them. She placed her hands on her hips, pushing back her cloak to show the sword at her waist, and flicked her hair the way Aife, Ria and her own mother sometimes did.

The guards' eyes widened slightly as they took in the fine sheath which housed Catia's sword and she grew bolder. They were not too stupid to realise she was a person of wealth – of worth – then. She gestured to the slaves sitting glumly where the oars would be when the boat got back into the water. "Why are they doing nothing?" she demanded in a harsh tone, reverting to her own language, knowing the Saxons would most likely not understand her words, especially spoken as fast as she was doing now. "They should be earning their keep even when the ship is not afloat."

The guards eyed one another, and Catia, warily. This angry child was obviously related to the king, or some other highborn Pict, so they did not want to offend her. They'd been well warned by Jarl Sigarr not to do anything that might anger their hosts.

"What are you saying, child?" one of them asked in his own tongue, and the respectful tone the man used gave her confidence. She gestured to the slaves again, noting the blond man who interested her so much. He was watching the scene play out with great interest.

"Weorc," she called back irritably to the guard, who gazed back with a confused expression on his seamed face. "Handweorc," Catia said, pointing to the beach. She believed the phrase meant, "manual labour" in her own Brythonic tongue, which, even if she was correct wouldn't really tell the Saxon much, but she hoped it would be enough.

The two guards spoke to one another, then they laughed and turned back to Catia, nodding and bowing happily, almost mockingly. Whatever message they'd taken from her mangled version of their language had amused them. She stood, hands still on hips, to see what would happen next.

The guards got up and began shouting at the cowering, sullen slaves, who stood up in response. There were eight of them, eyes almost glowing white behind the thick grime on their faces, and all had chains on their ankles and wrists. One of the guards jumped over the side of the ship onto the beach, and waved his hand forward, beckoning the slaves to follow. They did so, one or two of them stumbling and sprawling on the pebbles before hauling themselves onto their feet.

The second Saxon jumped down behind them while the first walked a little way up the beach, lifted a stone, and said something to the slaves, showing it to them. Then he put it down on the ground and collected a few more of the rough pebbles and made a little pile of them. He pointed it at, then to the slaves, then to the beach, and it was enough to get his point across: The slaves were to gather stones and make piles with them.

The guard walked across to the nearest of his charges, a middle-aged man whose loose jowls suggested he'd been heavily overweight before he was taken as a slave and starved half to death. The man looked confused, and the Saxon slapped him hard across the side of the head making Catia wince.

She did not cry out, for she realised the Saxons had taken her for someone as cruel as their Jarl Leofdaeg. They believed she thought slaves should never be allowed to rest when they could be working, so they'd dreamt up this ridiculous task for them.

The guard went through the motions of making a pile of stones again, but the blond slave, along with some of the others, were already following his example, and now the jowly, middle-aged fellow set to work too, eagerly, as if he was actually glad to have something to do other than sitting on the static ship with only his thoughts for company.

The Saxons looked on as the stones were piled uselessly on the beach, grinning at one another and Catia, who smiled demurely back, as if she was pleased by their ingenuity and the sight of the lazy slaves being put to work. She did not leave, though, and, eventually the Saxons grew bored and sat beside one another on a large stone, one of them whittling a piece of wood with his dagger, the other picking dry skin from his weather-beaten fingers.

The blond slave had evidently understood something of what was happening, of Catia's true purpose, and he moved to the far end of the line of slaves, away from the bored guards. He worked steadily, silently, building his pile of stones until it inevitably collapsed and then beginning the task again without comment or complaint.

Catia walked past the slaves, watching them with a frown, as if judging their work, preening a little as if she thought she was the most important girl in the world.

"Be careful," one of the Saxons said to her seriously, tapping his waist. "Weapon." He nodded at the slaves and waved a finger, apparently warning her that one of the manacled men might take her blade from her.

Catia laughed lightly, drawing the sword and spinning it expertly in her hand. It was a flashy move but proved she knew one end of the thing from the other and, in truth, very impressive given how young she was. The guards grinned, appreciating her skill as she thrust the blade back into its sheath and fastened the little strap that stopped it from sliding out of its own accord. She was letting them know she could take care of herself and they either believed her or didn't really care. If she got hurt, that was her business.

None of the slaves appeared the least bit interested in Catia as she paced along the beach, or the Saxon guards; they were too busy going about their tasks with resigned looks on their filthy faces.

The blond man's pile of pebbles collapsed for the fifth time as she drew near, but he simply turned around and walked back to collect another random stone. He was not making any real attempt to build much of a pile, selecting stones which were obviously unsuitable as foundations. He'd been given this task by his masters, but there was no requirement to build some miniature Tower of Babel and he didn't make the attempt, unlike some of the other slaves who cursed when their constructions collapsed after gaining a couple of inches in height.

"How did you come to be here?" Catia asked the blond man when she was close enough to speak without the guards hearing her words. They did look across at her, but her demeanour was haughty, as if she was berating the slave, and they quickly lost interest in the girl.

"The ship brought me," the blond man replied simply. His reply might have been sarcastic or cheeky, but his tone was flat, utterly devoid of emotion, as if his time in captivity and the beatings doled out by Leofdaeg had trained him to speak a certain way.

"I can see that," Catia said. "How were you taken into slavery? You don't move like the rest of these men – you move like a warrior."

He glanced at her, surprised. "I do? Even now, with my muscles wasted and my spirit beaten out of me? Well, I don't suppose it'll last for much longer."

"If I was to hand you my sword, I'd wager you could kill those two guards," she told him. "Aye, even in your present state."

He smiled very slightly. "Maybe. But your blade can't cut through metal, can it?" and he held up his wrists to show the chains.

"What's your name?" she asked, using an irritated tone, still playing the role of a haughty young noblewoman for the Saxons' benefit.

"My real name? Or the one my master calls me?"

"Don't be obtuse," Catia retorted, and now her annoyance did not need to be feigned.

"Lancelot." He continued stacking his stones, never managing to get more than three or four on top of one another before the construction would collapse but the princess fancied he watched her for some sign of recognition when he said his name. It tickled something in her memory, or so she thought, but it might just have been her imagination.

"You are – were – a nobleman?"

"I was," he admitted. "It was me who damaged Leofdaeg's sword arm before his men slaughtered my warband and he took me as his slave."

"Is that why he hates you so much?" she wondered. "I mean, more than any of these others?"

"I also killed his father."

"Oh." Catia watched him work. He really did move with an effortless grace she'd rarely seen in a man before, in spite of his wasted muscles.

"Why did you come here?" the slave asked and for the first time in their conversation he sounded genuinely interested. "Why are you talking to me? If it had been a year ago, when I was tall and strong and my hair was well-combed I'd have thought you were attracted to me, but—"

"Attracted to you?" Catia laughed loudly at the unexpected comment and the slave blushed. So, his spirit had not been completely crushed after all.

"Aye," he growled, glaring at her. "Not so long ago I was considered handsome."

"That may be so," she replied. "But you're old enough to be my father! Even in your finery I'd not have looked at you in *that* way." She could see she'd hurt his feelings and that hadn't been her intention in coming here. "You're too old for me, but my friend Aife certainly thinks you're handsome," she said in a conciliatory tone.

Her words seemed to work as Lancelot snorted with laughter and continued his pointless tower-building task with better humour. "So," he muttered as yet another pile of stones collapsed. "You didn't answer my question: Why are you here talking to me?"

She gazed at him and he met her eyes. "I don't really know," she admitted. "When we saw you that first time, with the Saxon jarl, I felt like …" She trailed off, unable to put her feelings into words.

"I feel like we've met already, somewhere," Lancelot said, turning away from her and walking towards the sea where he found a big stone and carried it up to where the rest of his failed towers lay. "But I've never been here before. I've never met any young Pictish noblewomen."

"Oh, I'm not a Pict," Catia said, feeling insulted that anyone should think her one of these rough, painted northerners. "I'm of the Damnonii tribe. My home is in Dun Breatann, I'm only here…visiting."

The slave stopped in his tracks, still holding the big stone, and he looked at her face again, eyes boring into her as he examined her features. "Dun Breatann," he breathed. "You're Catia."

"I am," she replied, but he continued to speak.

"You're the princess Bellicus was looking for."

"You know Bel?" Catia was dumbfounded but the mention of the big druid made her feel instantly homesick and she broke off, fearing that she might burst into tears.

"Know him?" Lancelot replied, face lighting up for just a moment as he thought of Bellicus. "We're good friends. He was with me when I killed Leofdaeg's father on that raid together, just the two of us. What a day that was!"

The sound of footsteps crunching across the pebbles towards them made Catia turn and look back towards Dunnottar. "Shit," she hissed, immediately wishing her mother was there to scold her for such bad language. "That Saxon bastard is coming."

Leofdaeg appeared confused as he took in the sight of the slaves performing their bizarre and pointless task on the beach, rather than sitting on board his ship. He shouted at the guards and it was obvious he was angry at them.

"He probably wants you lot, the slaves I mean, on board and ready to row at a moment's notice," Catia muttered as the jarl ranted at the two stony-faced guards. "In case there's trouble with the Picts. I better go. It was good talking to you."

"Get a message to Bel for me, Princess," Lancelot hissed after her as she turned to walk back to the fortress. "Please. I can't survive like this for much longer. Please, ask him to help me!"

Catia did not turn to look at him but the pleading tone in Lancelot's voice tore at her. She knew what it was like to be held in thrall by a cruel Saxon master. Bellicus had come to her rescue, but she didn't even know where the druid was now. How could she possibly get a message to him? Let him know his once-proud friend was living like this, beaten and broken down by the jarl who was staring blackly at her now?

"You should feed them more," she said, not stopping or even slowing as she passed Leofdaeg, but gesturing back towards the men who were being shepherded back on board the landed ship. "*Feorm*," she said, remembering the Saxon word for 'food' and waving her pinched fingers at the bemused jarl as she mimed the act of eating. She was beyond him now, and she finished by shouting, in her own tongue, "You'll get more from them if you keep them well fed."

Leofdaeg didn't reply. His face was red and he would surely liked to have questioned what she'd been doing with his slaves, but he was wary of upsetting his hosts and, although he may well have known Catia was not a Pict herself, she was obviously highborn. Whatever his mission was in Dunnottar, disrespecting a noble's child would not help its success, so he held his tongue.

As she climbed back up the steps to the main part of the fortress, Catia could hear the jarl bawling again. Lancelot would probably face the brunt of the man's rage and, eventually, the blond slave who'd once been a proud soldier would be killed by the Saxon.

Aife was watching as she came up the stairs and, together, they walked across to the walls, going up the steps to peer down over the battlements at the docks and beach below.

"Did you manage to talk to your boyfriend?" the warrior-woman asked with a wink as they gazed down at the busy scene.

"His name's Lancelot," Catia replied softly, staring at the blond-headed figure in the ship beneath them and not noticing Aife's start of recognition.

"Lancelot? He's supposed to be one of the greatest fighters in all of Britain," the Pict cried in amazement. "Is that truly him? Why hasn't the warlord, Arthur, come to find him then? The two are said to be the best of friends." She frowned at Catia, as if the girl was pulling her leg. "Are you making a jest or something?" she demanded.

"No," replied Catia, eyes still fixed on Lancelot. "I'm not. But if Arthur isn't coming to help him, and I have no way of sending a message to Bellicus, there's only one thing to do."

Aife watched her, baffled.

"A friend of Bel's is a friend of mine," Catia said firmly. "We'll have to free him ourselves."

CHAPTER ELEVEN

"Kill them. All of them."

Narina looked at her young husband, wondering if he was trying to be darkly humorous, but Bellicus could tell the Votadini prince was serious – he thought the Pictish political prisoners should be put to death as a consequence of Aife's escape.

"You have to send a message, my wife," Ysfael said. "Otherwise you'll appear soft."

They were in the quarters used to house the Picts, who glared back at them in fear or anger. Both the queen and her husband wore gold torcs that day, reminding their captives who held the power in Dun Breatann, as if such a reminder was needed.

"You can't kill us," one said, face flushing almost purple as he spoke. He had a blue fish tattooed on his cheek but it's original vibrant colouring had begun to fade. "It's not our fault the girl buggered off. You can't blame us."

"Maybe not," Ysfael replied with an almost bored flick of his hand. "But you're an expense Dun Breatann can do without. Guarding, and feeding, you all is as good as tossing our wealth into the Clota, and, clearly, as much use."

"If you kill us," said Lord Gartnaith in a calmer tone than his compatriot. "King Drest will have no reason not to come back here and lay siege to your lands again. And this time he might not be as careful as before."

"Are you threatening me?" Ysfael asked, laying a hand on the pommel of his sword.

Bellicus watched the scene play out, noting how the Votadini prince so easily referred to all things Damnonii as being his. Which, the druid supposed, they were now, but Ysfael's manner suggested the prince saw himself as ruler of Alt Clota, rather than just part of it. It was a strange situation for them all to be in, Bellicus thought, wondering if he should be more suspicious of Ysfael, or if the man was acting how anyone would in this situation. The druid's education had not prepared him for this scenario, so all he could do was rely on his own instincts.

"A message must be sent," he said. "Ysfael's right."

The prisoners blanched, for, although not that familiar with the Votadini prince, they knew Bellicus was a man of his word. Gartnaith in particular was fearful, for he'd struck Bellicus when the druid was just a child. The youngster, acting as a serving boy during his druid training, accidentally spilled some ale on Gartnaith and the man slapped his ear so hard it had almost deafened Bellicus. Now, years later, their roles were reversed and the Pict, knowing the druid remembered that earlier attack, swallowed nervously.

Narina, bloodless lips drawn in a thin line, made a shallow nod to show she'd heard their advice, then turned and walked out of the building, the Picts' babbling, pleading, or threatening cries ringing in the air behind her.

Ysfael's eyebrows lifted and he grinned at the druid. "Nothing like a good execution to get the people onside, eh, Bel? And these fools certainly deserve it." With that, he followed his wife outside, leaving the druid alone, looking at the frightened noblemen behind the iron gate that stopped them from following Aife back to Dunnottar.

"You can't do this, druid," Gartnaith shouted, shaking his head in disbelief. "We're not some common criminals, we're highborn warriors. We deserve respect."

Bellicus shrugged. "You're prisoners of war – you're lucky you weren't cut down the night you tried to storm Dun Breatann." He turned away and began walking out of the room, towards the exit. "If I were you, I'd make peace with your gods, lads. If Ysfael has his way you won't be around much longer."

He was not a cruel man, or at least he didn't believe himself to be so, and he took no pleasure in the Picts' fear, but Bellicus could never forget how close those prisoners had come to slaughtering everyone within Dun Breatann and taking control of the fortress. It would have meant the end for the Damnonii people, who would have become Picts within a generation.

If Narina decided to execute them all, well, that was the way of war. When you brought an invading army to another land you could not expect mercy if the war didn't go your way. Their own Princess Aife's actions had forced the queen's hand in this. The gods take them.

Still, the druid did not believe Narina would act so harshly, for it would bring nothing but trouble, and he did not think her so bloodthirsty.

Narina didn't wait for Ysfael or Bellicus as she strode from the prisoners' quarters to the great hall. By the time the druid's strides brought him inside the long building the queen was seated at a table across from Gavo. Ysfael took a place beside her, helping himself to meat from the trencher that had been placed there already, and Bellicus came in and sat next to Gavo. The guard captain nodded to them all.

"What have you decided, my lady?" he asked without preamble.

"Nothing," sighed Narina, drawing a frown from her husband.

"But—"

"I know, Ysfael," she broke in, irritated and plainly stressed by everything that was happening. "I said we had to send a message, but I can't just kill those men."

"You're too soft," the Votadini prince retorted, with just the slightest curl of his lip.

Bellicus did not think the queen soft, but it wasn't his place to defend her.

"Maybe," she said. "But I'm not a murderer, and besides, if we kill them, what will Drest do to Catia? Have you forgotten that she's in Dunnottar, at least as far as we know?"

"What then?" Ysfael asked, sounding bored again as he chewed another slice of roast beef. "Do nothing? That will be seen as a weakness by the likes of the Dalriadans, and you know more of them are coming across from Hibernia every day. Soon they'll be pushing against our border, and our patrols won't be enough to stop them."

Bellicus thought of those patrols. At the moment they were being led by Narina's other captain, Gerallt, an unimaginative man nearing his fifties but still a good leader for missions such as defending Alt Clota's western frontier. The warband he led was necessary to keep the many Dalriadan warlords at bay, but it was a constant drain on resources. Ysfael's point about not appearing weak to their many potential enemies was a fair one.

So was the queen's comment about Catia's safety, though.

"For now, I advise we do nothing with the prisoners," he said. "Leave them where they are and continue to treat them fairly. I'm ready to leave for Dunnottar right now, if you command it, Narina. Darac will carry me there within the week."

"And what will you do when you get there, druid?" Ysfael asked, head tilted on one side, chin resting on his fist as he regarded Bellicus. "Attack the fortress single-handed? Use your magic to kill the Picts inside?"

"I'll speak with Drest," Bellicus replied, again surprised by the prince's words and tone. Why was the young man so hard to read? "I'll remind him of the oaths of peace he made with us when we defeated them last year. He won't harm Catia, I'm certain of that."

Ysfael smiled as he masticated another sliver of meat. It seemed this was all just an entertaining game to him. "Oh, well, if you say so. You are the mighty Bellicus, Warrior-Druid of Dun Breatann, after all."

Narina and Gavo were also eyeing Ysfael curiously, but Duro's gaze was more hostile although he held his tongue.

"Aye, that's true," Bellicus nodded, smiling himself, eyes boring into the prince who held his gaze for a moment before turning away. "The Picts respect me, if nothing else. And besides, we destroyed most of their army. They'll not want us to attack them – it could mean the end for Drest. He'll deal with me sensibly."

Narina was nodding. "All right, Bel. Go. Go now. Bring my daughter back to me."

The druid stood, saluting to Gavo as he did so. "Take care of the place when I'm gone."

Ysfael wasn't looking at him, and he waved dismissively and muttered, "Whatever you say, big fellow."

Duro looked like he might start an argument, call out the prince for his disrespectful and immature behaviour, but Bellicus gestured for the centurion to follow. They went out and headed for the druid's house, Cai noisily lapping at the bowl of water that always sat beside the front door which they bolted behind them.

"By Mithras," Duro exploded once they were inside. "What is wrong with that idiot boy?"

"Keep your voice down," Bellicus said. "The walls are thin and his men are all over Dun Breatann. I don't know what he's playing at, but I hope Gavo keeps a good eye on him while we're away."

"You think he'll make some play for the throne?" Duro asked, voice now a low, worried murmur. "Harm Narina?"

Bellicus shook his head and gathered the provisions and gear they'd packed for the trip to Dunnottar the night before. "No, not really, he doesn't seem that ambitious to me." He frowned. "I just want a cool, wise head around to make sure things don't go belly-up over the next few weeks. Are you sure you want to come with us?"

The centurion blew out a long breath. "The thought of seeing Drest again makes my blood run cold," he admitted. "But my place is beside you, Bel. And I'm no spy."

"You wouldn't be spying if you remained here. You'd be helping Narina keep Dun Breatann and its people safe."

"Shouldn't need to do that against threats from within the place's own walls! Do you not want me with you or something, druid?"

"Of course I do," Bellicus said, smiling and reaching out to pat the centurion's arm. "I just know how much you suffered in Dunnottar, and I wouldn't ask you to go there again if you would rather not." He stood up and checked one final time that his sword was snugly in place, the pockets within his robe were stocked with the herbs, spices and other ingredients he always carried, and then he lifted the eagle-topped staff which marked him as a druid. "And I'm sure Gavo would be glad of your help. As I say, I don't read anything in Ysfael that tells me he covets Narina's throne for his own. I merely think he's rash and could be prone to causing trouble without even knowing it. He's thoughtless, impetuous and filled with the immortality of youth. You remember that?" He grinned, but Duro didn't share his amusement.

"No," said the centurion. "When I was his age I'd already seen dozens of my friends and comrades kill and be killed. I didn't feel immortal at all."

"Perhaps not, my friend," Bellicus said, unbolting the door and letting Cai lead the way outside. "But you know what I mean. So…Are you sure you want to come with us?"

Duro nodded and shook his own bulging pack. "I'm coming, Bel, so stop going on about it. Besides, you'd be better worrying about yourself. Remember what Drest did to us. What Ria did. What the Picts are capable of. We have to be careful, Bel, I mean it."

They looked at one another and the force of Duro's words, the emotion behind them, struck Bellicus deeply.

The silence lasted another moment, and then Duro said, "We better get moving then, druid, Daylight doesn't last very long up here in the frozen North."

"'Frozen North'," Bellicus repeated as they started walking down the stairs to the stables, Cai loping ahead but stopping to look back at them every so often. "It's not even winter yet, but, even so, by the time we get to Dunnottar we'll know all about being frozen. The chill in that place seeps right into the bones of a man."

"I still think we should be taking someone else with us," Duro said as they came to the bottom of the stairs and walked over to the stables. "A small warband. Travelling alone, all that way, is folly, even for us."

Bellicus turned and smiled. "I agree. That's why we're not going alone."

"Eh?" The centurion's brows drew together. "Well, who are we taking then?"

"Are you ready to go then, or what?" The thick Votadini accent filtered out from the stall housing Darac, and Duro's brow furrowed.

"Eburus?"

"Aye, me." The red-haired warrior could be seen beside Darac, readying the animal for the long journey to come, before the door opened and man and horse walked out, both laden with packs of food and survival gear.

Duro was obviously pleased although he tried his best to hide it behind his frown. "What about Ysfael, though?" he asked, turning to the druid. "Eburus is his man, not one of your Damnonii fighters, Bel."

The druid took Darac's reins from Eburus and vaulted up onto the horse's broad back. They headed towards the gates and Eburus went into the next stall, bringing out his own horse and nimbly mounting before following the druid.

"Ysfael?" the Votadini warrior asked mischievously. "Who cares? Now are you coming or not, centurion?"

"Eh? Aye, wait for me you pair of bastards," the centurion called as the guards manning the gates lifted off the heavy beams which held them shut, and opened the way for the riders to move out.

Over his shoulder, Eburus grinned. "Hurry up then, old man!"

Duro ran to fetch his own horse, happy to see it was ready to go and held by one of the stableboys. He quickly attached his pack and, with the lad's help, jumped up onto his mount's back. Kicking his heels gently into the animal's great sides, he hurried after his friends, giving Dun Breatann's soaring, grey rock a last glance as he passed out through the gates and the three men, with the giant dog, began the long journey north.

* * *

"Tonight should be good," said Leofdaeg to Sigarr as they refilled their ale mugs in Dunnottar's hall. "That druidess is going to tell a story about a drunken *Waelisc* prince."

Sigarr grunted. "Not sure why that excites you, Leofdaeg," he said. "We've seen plenty of drunk *Waelisc* since we arrived here."

"Pah, you're too serious," Leofdaeg grumbled. "These druids always tell a good tale, and have you not seen her? Ria, they call her. She's a rare beauty. It'll be a pleasure to sit and drink and watch her."

Even Sigarr smiled then. "Aye, fair enough," he said. "Better than looking at the white-bearded old druid, I'll grant you that. Just remember, don't let your men get into any fights. We want the Picts all nicely drunk and asleep so we can..." He didn't finish the sentence, but his eyes strayed to the young Damnonii princess sitting beside Drest's daughter.

"You're happy to go along with my plan, then?" Leofdaeg muttered, eyes scanning the hall in case anyone should be eavesdropping. "To take the girl with us, back to Hengist?"

Sigarr nodded, mouth set in a firm line. He was not a reckless man, and, when Leofdaeg had first suggested they abduct Princess Catia he'd been dead against it. They were there to try and plant the seeds of a lasting friendship with the Picts and their king – to lay the foundations for an alliance. Hengist's Saxon army had been soundly beaten by Arthur's Britons in the recent battle at Nant Beac, but they'd not been utterly destroyed. Many of them had made it back to Garrianum to regroup and await more of their kinsfolk sailing to join them from Jutland, Saxony, Frisia, and Anglia. There were always more men willing to come from those lands to plunder, or simply settle in, Britain.

In the meantime, Hengist thought it would be a good idea to befriend the northerners. Both Saxons and Picts were similar in many ways, their love of war and raiding being the most obvious. Hengist had grown tired of the settlements he'd taken control of in Britain being attacked by Drest's folk, for it was a distraction he could do without, although there had been noticeably less raids by the Picts this year.

If Sigarr and Leofdaeg could go some way to stopping those raids completely, the Saxons might focus all their energies on expanding further into the territory defended by the Britons' warlord, Arthur. And their talks with Drest had been quite productive in that sense, Sigarr thought. The Pictish king seemed strangely eager to talk of payments – bribes in reality – from the Saxons, to keep his warriors from raiding Hengist's coastal territories come the following spring and summer.

As the days had gone on, though, Sigarr came to realise why Drest was eager to accept payments for peace, and why the Picts had been raiding less this year: Their army had been decimated after a recent war with the Damnonii tribe. What young warriors Drest was still able to call upon had been needed at home this summer, and probably the next one too, to make sure their nearest enemies didn't try to take advantage of their weakness.

Of course, Drest himself had not offered up this valuable intelligence. Instead, Sigarr had questioned the men and women in Dunnottar, teasing out little bits of information here and there, using his cunning and his cleverness. The fact that he was rather a small man, with a ready smile and a marked wheeze, made him seem less of a threat than the other Saxon visitors.

People liked to talk to Sigarr, for he made them feel important. That was why Hengist had sent him here. Leofdaeg and the rest of the crew would play the part of boisterous, uncouth sea-wolves quite naturally, while Sigarr's unassuming manner would discover things the others never could.

When Leofdaeg had discovered who the little, highborn girl strutting around Dunnottar was, one of his sailors had told him all about Horsa's mission to abduct her some two years before, and how it had all gone wrong for the Saxons when the *volva*, Thorbjorg's, plan to sacrifice Catia to the gods was thwarted.

Now, here was the girl again, and Leofdaeg's simple mind had seen a great opportunity to please not only his *bretwalda*, but the witch too. Whoever brought this supposedly magical child to them would surely be richly rewarded by Hengist and Thorbjorg, for they could finally complete that blood sacrifice and win the favour of the gods. He'd suggested all this to Sigarr, who well remembered that failed ritual and saw some merit in Leofdaeg's plan.

The hall was beginning to fill up as night fell outside and Drest's bannermen came in from the cold to make merry. They too knew the Saxons would leave on the morrow and they expected their king to make one final effort to impress the visitors with his wealth and hospitality.

A door slammed as a terrific gust of wind blew through the hall, making the candles and torches flicker, shadows dancing as everyone gathered indoors thanked their gods for the thick walls that separated them from the late-summer elements. It would be a wild night, outside and inside, Sigarr thought. The wind picking up was a good omen; Thunor's rage would help to hide the Saxons' movements as they took the Damnonii princess from Dunnottar and sailed south with her.

Of course, Drest and his druid advisors would be furious when they woke up in the morning and realised what had happened, but it mattered little to Sigarr. He knew now that the Picts were in no position to raid Hengist's lands this year anyway, and, when they finally rebuilt and were the force they had been before, well, another delegation could come with bribes and seek an alliance, or at least a promise of peace.

Sigarr thought of Thorbjorg's belief that Princess Catia's sacrifice would bring complete and total victory to the Saxons' conquest of Britain. Annoying King Drest would be a very small price to pay for that glory.

"There she is," Leofdaeg said, a little louder than he'd spoken before. The ale was already affecting him, Sigarr thought irritably. "Just look at those legs, and her pale skin. Gods, I'd like to—"

Ria strode out in front of the warriors and Pictish noblemen who were lucky enough to be there that evening. It was obvious that she recognised her own beauty and used it to entrance the mostly male audience. A show-woman *and* a druidess, Sigarr thought. Quite the combination. He did not envy any man who tried to make her his own, for she would be nigh-on impossible to tame. He glanced at Leofdaeg, who was practically drooling as he gazed at the dark-haired woman, and stifled a laugh. Certainly that one, with his crippled arm and stunted intellect, would be no match for the druidess.

"I'd like to tell you a tale, this night," said Ria, and her voice was melodious yet strong. "A tale from lands much farther south, in a place known as Maes Gwyddno." She spoke in her own Pictish tongue, which was rather different to that spoken even by the more Romanized Britons hailing from the likes of Dun Breatann or Dun Edin. Sigarr could understand her just well enough to follow the story, but the Saxons had a translator with them who listened to Ria and told Leofdaeg and the others what was being said. It was hardly the ideal way to enjoy a tale from a druidess, but it didn't seem to matter. Ria had enchanted everyone with the combination of her beauty, controlled voice, and the ale that the audience had imbibed that evening.

A pair of serving girls appeared and all the Saxons except Sigarr pushed mugs forward to be refilled from the overflowing jugs they brought. For once, not one of the men grabbed at the girls' backsides or made any crude remarks about them, such was the sway Ria held over them all already.

"In Maes Gwyddno," began the druidess, "ruled the mighty King Gwyddno Garanhir."

As she spoke, the white-bearded druid, Qunavo, sat behind her and played a soft melody on a three-stringed lute, the music forming the perfect accompaniment to the words of the story.

"His lands were fertile," Ria continued. "Much more fertile than any others, thanks to the presence of a faery well which supplied Maes Gwyddno with fresh, clear waters which held magical powers. The well was tended by a priestess named Meredir who made sure the water never overflowed. To provide a further safeguard against the well flooding the lands completely, a dyke was built, and this was guarded by the king's friend, Seithennin. It was a golden age for the people of Maes Gwyddno, whose crops flourished and their animals and children thrived on the waters from Meredir's well."

Qunavo's melodious arpeggios, although picked softly, seemed to fill the room with the same sense of peace and harmony that must have once infused the lands Ria's tale spoke of.

"During the coldest of winters, when other lands' rivers froze over, the faery well of Maes Gwyddno would be as cool as it was in spring." Ria's eyes shone with wonder as she continued. "And, in the driest of summers, when it wouldn't rain for weeks on end and neighbouring kingdoms suffered droughts, Maes Gwyddno would be as rich and lush as ever. The well would continue to fill the lakes and rivers, the crops would grow fat and full, the flowers would burst with life and colour, and King Gwyddno Garanhir's people would sing his praises."

"What's she saying?" one of the Saxons whispered. He was deaf in one ear and unable to follow their translator, but his attention never turned away from Ria who was stalking the great hall like a sleek, dark cat.

"Shush!" Leofdaeg replied irritably and he too spoke in a quiet voice for he was following the story well enough and not merely lusting over its teller.

The lute melody, peaceful and soothing until now, became a little more strident, a little more upbeat, as Ria stopped, took them all in with her gaze, and started the next part of her tale.

"The king often held feasts, for his larders were overflowing and the piled food had to be eaten before it turned rotten."

As if on cue, the servants moved through the hall with more heavily laden trenchers. Roasted beef, pork, duck and swan were all available. The flavours were varied thanks to the meats and exotic spices, including ginger, pepper and cinnamon. It was obvious Drest's Picts traded with merchants from all over the world and probably grew some of their own ingredients such as leeks, onions and garlic. These had been introduced to Britain by the Romans and were used to flavour the dishes on offer to the revellers.

"Remember we want the men clear-headed," Sigarr muttered to Leofdaeg as he saw their crewmen accepting more ale from the serving girls. "If we're to leave in the dead of night, we don't want to be stumbling down the steps, or unable to fight if the Picts try to stop us taking the girl with us."

"Don't worry, the men'll be fine. I've warned them not to get too drunk," Leofdaeg replied off-handedly. "Now, shh. I'm listening to the woman."

"Seithennin, the keeper of the dyke, was a good watchman who rarely left his post. But he was also a man who enjoyed a feast, and who doesn't?" At this Ria lifted a mug of ale from out of a Saxon's hand and took a long pull, spilling much of it down her face before slamming it back on the table before him and grinning. Her comment brought the expected cheers and further slamming of mugs on tables before she went on, wiping her flawless chin. "So, Seithennin had been invited to a feast by Gwyddno Garanhir and, not wishing to offend the king, he went. And he drank." She merely mimed the action this time, once, twice, three times lifting an imaginary mug to her mouth and crossing her eyes at the last as if she were wholly inebriated. "And he became very, very drunk."

Her words were slurred too now, and the audience laughed and cheered again, as the music picked up pace again. Sigarr realised that at some point old Qunavo's simple lute had been joined by the beating of a small drum and some other stringed instrument which offered more of a drone than a melody.

"Eventually," the druidess's voice was as clear as before as she returned to the story, words weaving expertly in and around the musicians' playing, "Seithennin, Keeper of the Dyke, wandered out of the king's hall, roaring drunk, and unsteadily made his way back towards the mighty wall which protected Maes Gwyddno from flooding."

The music took on a jaunty tone and Ria looked down at one of Drest's young warriors. "Seithennin was a very handsome man, rather like you."

The warrior's face flushed red as the translator relayed her compliment and his friends laughed and slapped him on the back as she wandered off, continuing her tale.

"As Seithennin passed the faery well his voice was lifted in song, and it was heard by the keeper of the well, Meredir. She came out of her house to see who was making all the noise. It was a lonely life for the priestess, who had to remain at her post all day and, when she saw the handsome soldier passing by her heart was filled with longing." Ria looked once more at the young Pictish warrior and added, "With lust."

Again, the man's face flushed scarlet and his friends laughed at his discomfort.

"I know how she felt," someone shouted, drawing nods and cheers.

"Don't we all?" said the smiling druidess. "Lust is often the strongest emotion, and Meredir acted upon its impulse now, calling out to Seithennin, who was struck just as powerfully as the Well Maiden. They walked together and, before long found themselves locked in a passionate embrace in a grove of trees."

Ria's expression, of amusement until now, changed to one of profound sadness then, as the music also returned to the softer tones of earlier. It was melancholy and seemed to the audience strangely at odds with the joy Seithennin and Meredir surely must have felt as they made love.

"As they rutted in the grass together," the druidess said in a harsh tone, "the faery well began to overflow. Meredir was not there to stop it and its waters spread, all the way down the hill."

Sigarr frowned. "What about the dyke?" he muttered to himself. "Surely that would stop the flood."

Ria couldn't have heard his question but it was the one on everybody's mind. "Seithennin had left the sluice gates open in the dyke," she said. "They were always left open, to let the well's waters feed the land. But Seithennin should have been at his post to close them now."

She clapped her hands together, mimicking the sound the gates should have made as they were slammed shut against the rising flood waters.

"What happened to Maes Gwyddno?" the handsome young warrior asked as the hall fell into thoughtful silence.

"As the keeper of the dyke and the priestess made love, the waters flooded down into the valley, destroying crops, drowning the animals in the fields, sweeping away houses, and covering the land completely. Everyone except Seithennin and Meredir died that day, and Maes Gwyddno passed into myth and legend, its once great halls submerged beneath the lake which remains in place to this day."

Sigarr sat in silence, wondering at the druidess's choice of story. He'd expected something fun – bawdy and uplifting. Not this cautionary tale about…what? How important it was to always remain alert and on guard?

"As for Seithennin and Meredir," Ria said, the music behind her slowing even further, heralding the end of the performance. "When they saw the devastation they'd caused, they were overcome with grief and threw themselves into the water. Some say their cries can still be heard if you stand on the shores of the vast lake even now, as their spirits were doomed to swim there for all eternity."

With that, Qunavo struck a final, lingering minor chord which rang out over the hushed gathering and Ria, with a last wink at the handsome young warrior, left the hall.

Slowly, the revellers began to talk amongst themselves, and the serving girls went around collecting empty trenchers and offering more ale and, eventually, the strange, subdued atmosphere lifted as more musicians took up the abandoned instruments and struck up a happier tune.

Sigarr made a point of speaking with all his men and warning them again not to drink too much. He reminded them they'd be leaving in the middle of the night and such an exit might cause some consternation amongst the Picts, especially if the princess tried to put up a fight when they took her to their ship and sailed off into the darkness. They all promised to behave and keep their wits about them, but Sigarr knew he didn't have the presence or force of personality his cousins, Horsa and Hengist, had. Still, the men knew he was a clever fellow and generally trusted his leadership, even if they didn't see him as a powerful warrior.

Eventually, when the fire had begun to burn low and the servants stopped bringing out more meat and ale, the king bade his guests good night and retired to his chamber. The heavily inebriated Pictish guests were slowly dozing off themselves, scattered about on the benches they'd been sitting at, or even on the floor beneath in some cases.

Sigarr was always amazed at how quickly a drunken feast, so noisy and bursting with life, could become quiet and still, with only the snoring of men disturbing the peace.

The Saxons pretended to fall asleep themselves, but they remained alert, biding their time until the moon swept across the sky outside and Sigarr thought they could make their move. The blood pounded in his veins and his heart thumped as he nodded to Leofdaeg and, in pairs, the sea-wolves gradually filtered out of the great hall.

It had been decided that Sigarr and three of the men would go ahead to the ship, clearing the path and disabling any Pictish guards that might get in the way. Leofdaeg would go with the other three to the room which Princess Catia had been using as her bedchamber since she'd arrived in Dunnottar. They would quickly bind and gag the girl and carry her down to the ship where Sigarr would be waiting, ready to cast off.

It was an incredibly dangerous plan which could go badly wrong at any moment, and Sigarr felt as if he was standing in a shieldwall, preparing to meet a charging enemy army as he led his companions down the steps to the beach. They moved quietly, and when they reached the gatehouse they saw two guards inside, faces lit by a brazier.

Sigarr waited as a couple of his men slipped inside – the door to the wooden building wasn't even locked since the Picts didn't fear danger from within the fortress – and, when the guards were killed it seemed as if the sounds were deafening. In truth, his men had worked quietly and efficiently, and no alarm was raised. Within moments the four Saxons were moving down the steps again, and on their way to the ship.

"D'you know, I don't think that druidess liked us very much," Sigarr said to the man behind him as they walked. He spoke with a lightness of tone that suggested he was quite relaxed about this whole undertaking but inside he felt on the verge of panic. So much could go so wrong at any moment.

"What do you mean?" the big fellow at his back asked, and his voice was genuinely hard and level. Unafraid.

"That story of hers," said Sigarr, licking his lips for it felt as if they were sticking to his teeth. "This was to be our last night as King Drest's guests. I'd have expected a more rousing, memorable tale, filled with action and excitement."

He stopped suddenly, gazing into the darkness, and his men stumbled into the back of him, muttering curses and demanding to know what he was doing until, soon enough, they too fell silent. As they stood there in the gloom Leofdaeg and the rest of the crew ran down the stairs to join them on the beach.

"The girl isn't there," Leofdaeg hissed as he reached Sigarr. "Her bed's empty and her stuff was gone, even that sword she carries about all the time."

"Aye," one of the men who'd gone to the bedchamber with him agreed. "She must be sleeping in one of the other rooms this night."

"Why are you standing here anyway?" Leofdaeg demanded, staring in bemusement at Sigarr. "What are you doing, man?"

Sigarr laughed and shook his head. "I was just saying that I'd hoped for a more exciting send off from Drest and his folk here in Dunnottar." He turned to Leofdaeg. "Well, it seems we've got it. Look."

He pointed and every eye was aimed along the beach, at their ship. Or, at least, the spot on the beach where their ship had rested just a few hours ago.

Leofdaeg started to run, followed by the others. All except Sigarr who was still laughing and shaking his head in disbelief. He well understood the message of the druidess's strange tale now.

"It's gone!" shouted Leofdaeg. "Some thieving Pictish bastard's stole my ship!"

Thinking of Princess Catia's empty chamber, Sigarr realised with a sickly feeling who that thieving bastard must have been and his laughter faded. "Not a Pict," he said. "A little girl from Alt Clota." And, although he and his men were now stranded in Dunnottar, he couldn't help but admire how cleverly they'd been outwitted.

CHAPTER TWELVE

Catia was starting to think it might not have been the best idea to steal a ship which was manned by a crew of malnourished slaves, in the middle of a storm.

In truth, it was hardly the worst weather anyone had ever sailed in, more rainy than windy, and would have held no fears for Sigarr and his sea-wolves, but to the princess it was quite terrifying. She watched Lancelot and his fellows, still shackled, as they tried to work with the sails and oars in the darkness, feeling utterly impotent for she had no previous experience of sailing such a large boat. Her skill with boats only stretched to rowing up and down the Clota on a calm afternoon. Those halcyon days seemed miles and miles away in both space and time at that moment, but the thought that they'd managed to steal the hated Saxons' ship warmed her even as the icy spray lashed her.

Aife was more useful, having some experience of sailing for, living on the coast as she did, there was ample opportunity to spend time on her father's patrol ships. It was ironic that King Drest's sailors patrolled the sea around Dunnottar mostly searching for Saxon pirates.

A wave buffeted the hull and Catia felt bile rise in her throat as Aife and the men cursed but maintained their course, at least as far as the young princess could tell. On top of the nauseating motion of the ship, she was terrified they'd not be able to navigate properly in the storm and end up smashing into the rocks that must border the entire coastline. She could swim well enough, but a girl's skin and bone would be no match for the razor sharp, stone teeth which she could imagine tearing a hole right through the pitch-sealed wooden hull which was the only thing keeping them alive.

Aife laughed – she had taken the steering oar, her air of competence and command proving exactly what the slaves needed to galvanise them. The Pictish princess was revelling in her new role as helmswoman, and the fact that they'd pulled off this insane plan.

Catia retched but nothing came up and that, along with Aife's obvious lack of fear, started to set her mind at ease, just a little.

Maybe they would be all right. Maybe they would avoid the jagged rocks, and the threat of capsizing, and the morning would see them safe and far from any pursuers.

She heaved a deep breath and allowed her iron grip to loosen on the bench, thinking back to how this all came about…

"You want to steal their ship?" Aife had been utterly incredulous when Catia first suggested the idea to her, on the afternoon she'd first spoken to Lancelot.

"Aye," Catia replied, keeping her voice low as they walked down the stairs leading to the beach once again, this time heading away from the docks. "Why not?"

"Why not?" Aife repeated, laughing in astonishment. "Well, do you know how to sail a ship like that?" She jerked her head backwards and spread out her hands as they approached the glistening waters lapping over the pebbles at their feet. "How to navigate by the stars? Or how to do it if it's cloudy and the stars aren't visible? Do you know how to raise and lower the sail, and when it needs done?"

"No," Catia admitted, only a little perturbed by her friend's arguments. "But surely at least one of the slaves will know how to do all that."

Aife raised an eyebrow doubtfully. "All right, let's say one of them does. Lancelot, perhaps, although he's known for his skills with a sword, not with a steering oar. But let's assume he can sail – by the gods, girl, how are you going to get on board? I know you're a good fighter for your age, but the Saxons will always have at least a couple of guards on board, and I can assure you they will kill anyone who tries to steal their ship. Saxons love their ships!" She shook her head, still astonished at Catia's outlandish plan. "They would see you coming along the beach and be ready for you."

"Even in the dark?" Catia asked, drawing yet another exasperated exhalation from Aife.

"You mean to steal a ship in the dark?" the Pictish princess demanded. "Have you ever tried to sail near the coast in the dark? Even a master sailor would think twice about casting off during the night."

"That's why my plan will work," Catia said, nodding and smiling. "No one will be expecting it. And, when the Saxon guards see me approaching their ship they'll never suspect I'm there to steal it."

"You're just going to walk up and attack – kill – two, possibly more, men? Just like that? All to rescue a man you've never met before now?"

Catia's face did finally betray a hint of doubt then. She had never killed anyone before and, as much as she hated the Saxons in general for what they'd done to her, and were doing to Lancelot and his fellow slaves, the thought of slaughtering unsuspecting men was...

"You couldn't do it, Catia," said Aife, reaching out with her right arm and giving her small friend a quick hug as they continued to walk. "So, I guess that's the end of that idea. We'll need to think of some other way to—"

"Not so fast," Catia broke in. "No, I couldn't just walk up and start stabbing them with my sword, but perhaps we could trick them somehow. Make them leave the ship while we..." She trailed off, realising that wouldn't work either.

Aife took pity on her. "I must admit," she said, "it *is* a bold plan. If you could pull it off."

Catia looked up at her, disappointed but pleased by the praise.

"Maybe I can help."

"How?" Catia brightened again.

"I'll come with you. I'll help you steal the ship."

"But this is your home," Catia replied with a frown. "I'll be returning to Dun Breatann if I can, and, well, you don't want to do that. My mother would make you a prisoner again."

Aife nodded. "I suppose so, but my father was right when he said my escaping put the rest of the prisoners in a dangerous situation. He says I should take you and go back before Narina, or Ysfael more likely, decides to harm them, or comes with an army to lay siege to Dunnottar so...That's what I'll do."

Catia stared at her friend, happy that they wouldn't be parted, but anxious about Aife going back to Dun Breatann, and Ysfael.

"What if he tries again to..."

Aife sighed. "I don't know yet. Maybe Lancelot will speak up for me, if I tell him everything. He was – is – a great lord after all, and he'll owe us something if we give him back his freedom." She shook her head irritably. "If only I knew what it was Ysfael had been talking with his men about. What made him fear me so much that he wanted me dead. If I knew that…"

"I'll speak with my mother," Catia said grimly. "And Gavo. I'll tell them to make sure you're guarded properly, as we should have done in the first place. And Bellicus might be home by now. He'll make sure Ysfael leaves you alone. Him and Duro won't stand for any of that."

Aife smiled broadly and they embraced, a mixture of relief, happiness, excitement, and fear flooding through them.

"So, how should we get the Saxon guards off that ship so we can sail away in it?"

Aife laughed and they walked across the glistening pebbles towards a low hill which rose up from the beach. "Maybe I can ask some of my kinsmen to help us. We'll need to do it soon though; the Saxons will be leaving within the next few days."

"Won't your father be angry with you?" Catia asked as they reached the slope and sat down on the soft grass, gazing out across the sun-spangled, glittering waters. "The Saxons will surely be angry with him when they find out what we've done."

Aife nodded. "Maybe, but he'll probably just gift them one of our ships. So, we'll have to move fast once we're underway, for they'll come right after us." She smiled. "I think my father will be proud of me though, if we manage to escape with the Saxons' ship. It'll make a great story for Ria and Qunavo to tell at his feasts. Besides, he's the one who's told me to go back to Dun Breatann!"

When they returned to the fortress, they heard the news that Jarl Sigarr and his men would be sailing for home the very next morning. The princesses knew they had to act immediately and Catia waited, nerves building inside her, as night drew in and the weather worsened.

She ate a little bread and cheese in the hall with Ria and the druidess commented on her silence. It was obvious the woman knew something was playing on Catia's mind but she did not press her on it, and the princess was relieved when they parted. Still, she got the worrying impression that Ria somehow knew everything that was going on within her head.

Afterwards she managed, somehow, to catch a couple of hours' sleep and awoke as the evening's revelries were just beginning. She returned to the hall with Aife for a little while, then slipped back to the bedchamber she'd been allocated and made sure her meagre belongings were packed and her sword strapped to her waist. Then she waited, nibbling her fingernails and pacing the room until, after what seemed like an age, Aife came for her.

The older princess was dressed in a low-cut tunic which showed off her cleavage, and tight-fitting leggings which displayed her long, muscular legs. Over this she wore a dark cloak, and she carried a sack on her back.

"What's in there?"

"My proper clothes and mail vest," Aife replied, and her earlier jocularity was gone. Now she was calm and focused intently on what they were about to do. "Carry them down for me. One of my father's guards has left food and supplies for our journey hidden on the beach."

"Only one of them?" Catia asked, a little surprised. She'd hoped Aife would have gathered a bigger warband to make their task easier. "Will he help us take the ship?"

"The fewer people who know about this, or can be blamed for it, the better," Aife said, shaking her head. "Jarl Sigarr is a relative of the Saxon war-leaders, Hengist and Horsa. If Sigarr thinks my father was involved in stealing his ship and their slaves, well, it could start a war. They're supposed to be here on a trading and diplomatic mission after all." She opened the door a crack and peered out. The sounds of laughing and carousing filtered along from the nearby hall. "We have to make it look like we did this together, just you and I."

Catia nodded, thinking of Horsa and his character during the time she'd spent as his prisoner. When he found out about this night's work he would mock Sigarr and Leofdaeg mercilessly for being outsmarted by two girls, but, if he thought Drest's soldiers played any part in the ship's theft, he would push Hengist to retaliate in as violent a manner as possible.

Aife was right – this whole thing had to seem like the rash actions of her and Catia alone.

"Everyone's in the hall," Aife whispered. "Apart from the sentries, and the Saxons guarding their ship. Come on."

With a last look at the bed she'd spent the last few nights in, Catia drew herself up, patted her sword hilt, and followed the Pictish warrior-woman out into the corridor. Ria's voice could be heard now, although just as a drone, no words could be picked out. They headed for the outside door, not hesitating when they reached it but going straight out into the darkness and closing the door behind them. There were no guards posted here, and Catia didn't know if that was down to Aife, or if it was just normal procedure. No enemies could reach that part of the fortress from outside anyway, so it would surely be a waste of men to have any stationed here every night.

"It's cold," Aife noted, drawing the ties of her cloak tighter and covering her chest. "It'll be raining soon, no doubt. Let's go as fast as we can." She led the way towards the gatehouse which guarded the steps down to the docks, but, rather than going directly there, she veered off. "I know you can climb, so we'll go this way, and avoid alerting the men in the gatehouse."

Catia spotted a coiled rope when they reached the wall and, as they'd done back in Dun Breatann, Aife tossed it over and they used it to make their way down to the beach. They were hidden from any watchers by the moonless night and Catia was glad she couldn't see the waters or the hard ground far below as they descended. They moved quite slowly, carefully, making sure they had firm hold of the rope as they went. The long hours each of them had spent practising with sword and shield stood them in good stead for their muscles were hard and perfectly suited to this kind of action. Soon they were standing on the beach, smiling and drawing in relieved breaths.

The row of ships stretched away into the near-impenetrable gloom, and without any further conversation, they walked towards the Saxon vessel. It was growing cooler by the moment and Catia fancied she could even feel moisture in the air. It might have been her imagination, but she was sure Aife's prediction of rain would soon come true, especially when a sudden gust whipped at them, blowing Aife's long cloak up. The wind carried with it the scent of the sea, but also a mild and pleasant smell of burning. As they walked, the princesses could see the unmistakable figure of a Saxon man, framed by the orange glow of a brazier on the beach a short distance ahead.

Aife laid a hand on Catia's shoulder, halting their progress, and motioning for the younger girl to wait by some stacked barrels. Then the warrior-princess undid her tunic, the pale skin of her chest showing in the dim light from the nearby brazier, and her teeth flashed white as she smiled reassuringly at Catia.

"Wait here," she muttered, and turned to walk towards the Saxon ship.

The guard heard her feet crunching on the pebbles as she approached, and he squinted into the darkness. Catia could see his eyes widen as Aife neared the brazier and became more visible, and the sight of her cleavage made him instantly sit up straighter. He looked flustered as she came closer and gestured with her hand, winking suggestively as she slipped into the shadows behind a large pile of refuse.

The Saxon guard hesitated, peering back into the interior of his ship, but he didn't say a word as he made his mind up and slipped quietly past the brazier, glancing over his shoulder guiltily as he left his post and padded across to where Aife was waiting for him.

Catia leaned against a barrel, blood pounding as her senses strained to give her some idea of what was happening. Aife was a warrior, but the Saxons were no fools.

Or perhaps they were, for moments later Aife reappeared from the pile of refuse, alone. She glanced along the beach to where Catia was hiding and waved. All was going well, so far. Catia let out a long, heavy breath, relief flooding her, although she knew this was merely the beginning. There was a lot to do yet.

Without slowing, Aife used her powerful arms to haul herself on board the ship. The brazier's light showed her plainly now, and Catia could see the tunic she'd been wearing was gone. Anyone looking at the Pictish princess could now see every curve of her body, barely concealed beneath the low-cut top she'd chosen to wear. Caria heard a man's voice, still low but obviously somewhat alarmed at the sudden appearance of this striking woman.

Aife gave a little laugh and then playfully jumped back down onto the beach, grinning mischievously backwards as she headed towards the same pile of refuse she'd used as cover before. Catia watched, shaking her head at the Saxons' stupidity as the second guard was lured away by the warrior-woman's wiles.

She felt a little more relaxed as the Saxon disappeared into the shadows, for Aife obviously had things well under control, and they'd soon be aboard the—

Catia froze, staring at the ship and the third guard who was stepping past the brazier and clambering down onto the pebbles below.

Gods, there were only supposed to be two!

She was already moving, trying her best not to crunch on the stones which littered the entire beach, but this thought quickly became redundant as she heard a man cry out, and the third Saxon guard began running. So did Catia, drawing her sword as she went.

A man stood up in the ship, his lank, greasy hair framing his face as he stared impotently into the shadows. He pulled and the clanking of iron, and the frustrated grunt which followed, made it clear he was tethered to the hull and had no way to help Aife. The unmistakable sound of sword striking sword followed and Catia sprinted as hard as she could, not an easy task given how slippery the pebbles and seaweed were.

She came around the side of the refuse heap and had no time to think as she saw Aife struggling for her life with the Saxon nearest to her. Their swords had locked together – Taranis knew how he'd managed to figure out he was walking into a trap in time to draw the weapon and defend himself– and now they stood in a vicelike embrace, teeth bared, grunting and gasping as each sought to gain the advantage.

The other Saxon, the one who'd just arrived on the scene, was staring at them, trying to understand what was happening. Why was his kinsman fighting with this scantily clad woman? And why hadn't he already disarmed her?

Catia could imagine the thoughts going through the man's head, but it didn't take long before he drew back his sword and stepped in, spotting an opening. Aife's side was completely undefended and he didn't hesitate, drawing back his sword and—

"No!" Catia lunged, forcing the point of her own short blade into the Saxon's side. He was not wearing armour, just some kind of animal fur which offered little resistance to the honed, oiled steel of the young princess's sword. It tore deep into his body and his own attack faltered as he grunted in shock and turned, eyes seeming to glow in the light from the ship's brazier. Catia couldn't move, she was too stunned, staring into the Saxon's eyes as the radiance faded from them. He dropped to his knees, all the while accusing her with his gaze. Tears rolled down her cheeks and she felt like vomiting. Even the life-or-death struggle between Aife and the remaining guard didn't penetrate the fog that had descended over the youngster's mind.

Thankfully the sudden death of his companion had unnerved the Saxon, who turned slightly to see what was going on behind him. This gave Aife the chance she needed. She slammed her forehead into the man's cheek, and, when he fell back, stunned, she hammered her knee between his legs then struck him on the nape of the neck with her sword's pommel as he bent over in agony.

The princesses stared at one another, gasping for breath and listening for further sounds of danger. Aife quickly took command, taking Catia's sword from her and wiping off the blood on the dead Saxon's furs before pushing it smoothly into its sheath at Catia's waist.

"Take that one's weapon, and his belt and sheath. Come on, we need to move. Get on board the ship, now." Her tone broke the spell that had rooted Catia in place and she nodded, wiping the tears from her cheeks before bending to remove the dead Saxon's things, then running somewhat unsteadily across to the Saxon vessel. Lancelot was there, eyes shining, a broad grin on his grimy features as he reached down and helped the girl climb up onto the deck.

Aife quickly dragged the dead Saxon behind the refuse, and then the man she'd battered unconscious was similarly deposited and harvested for his weapons. A large sack was also hidden there, and this the princess hefted over her shoulder and brought to the ship, the muscles on her arms straining as she lifted it up to Lancelot and a second slave who'd come to help.

"What's this?"

"Food," Aife replied. "Hands off," she growled as the rest of the slaves looked eagerly at the sack, their gaunt faces testament to the near-starvation diet they'd been fed during their captivity. "There's plenty there, but it'll need to be rationed so leave it alone. Anyone I find near that sack will suffer the same fate as the three guards we've just dispatched, all right?" A sudden thought struck her, and she glanced at Lancelot.

"Aye, there were only the three of them," he said reassuringly. "But what now?"

Catia had regained some of her composure and she replied, saying, "You men help us push the ship into the water, and we can get away from here."

Lancelot lifted his hands, showing the chains that held him and the rest of the slaves on board. "That's not happening," he said and there was a frustrated edge to his tone. As if he knew their escape attempt was doomed already.

"Quickly," Catia said to Aife. "We have to free them."

Aife returned her stare. "How? I have tools in the pack but it'll take a long time. Time we don't have. It'll also make a lot of noise."

The young princess felt a wave of fear and disappointment wash over her. To have come so far, done so well, only to be thwarted now.

"Come on then," she said, stepping across to the bow. "The two of us will have to push it into the water."

Lancelot shook his head sadly. "You're not strong enough, lass," he told her. "It'll take a lot more than you two to get us into the sea."

"Well, what do you suggest then?" Catia demanded, rounding on the blond slave furiously.

"What tools do you have?" Lancelot asked Aife then. "A hammer?"

The warrior-woman opened her sack and rummaged about, the light of the brazier allowing her to see well enough and, at last, she pulled out a heavy iron-headed hammer. "Aye, but we don't have time to undo all your chains."

"No need," Lancelot said. "If we were all thinking clearly we'd have realised that straight away." He held out his hand and took the hammer from Aife. "We only need to remove one pin." He walked to the side of the ship and Catia saw a thick metal peg had been driven into one of the boards there. A length of chain was attached to that peg and the princess's eyes followed the trailing links, realising that single pin was what held *all* of the slaves tethered to the ship.

There was a ringing sound accompanied by a shower of sparks as the iron hammer met the peg, but it barely seemed to move.

"Hurry," Catia muttered as Lancelot struck another blow, and another. The noise died away quickly but each hit was loud and the princess thanked the gods for the rising wind and rain which would hopefully dampen the sound even more. A fourth strike saw the peg finally falling onto the deck and the chain thumping down after it.

Lancelot was already moving, clambering over the bow onto the beach, exhorting his comrades to follow, which they did with surprising speed and agility. Presumably the possibility of escaping their hellish lives of slavery was enough to galvanise their exhausted, malnourished bodies for this effort.

The rain was sheeting down now, fat drops hissing as they landed on the merrily burning brazier, but the slaves were pushing the ship and it moved easily across the pebbles. The Saxon vessels were designed to be light and easy to launch and so this one proved now.

"It's in!" Catia said, running to the stern and gazing out into the night, rain dripping down her face.

"We're not safe yet," Aife replied, jumping overboard for one of the slaves, weaker than the rest, had slipped and fallen and was now being dragged along by the momentum of the others. Aife reached down and pulled him onto his feet as the waves soaked him. "Come on, we're almost free," she told him. "Get back onto the ship!"

The man was panting like a dog and his eyes were wide and fearful for it was obvious he wouldn't have the strength to pull himself back onboard and must be left trailing in the water until he drowned or froze to death.

Lancelot and the others were already safely on the ship again, reaching down to the man who tried to catch their hands but couldn't muster the energy.

"Leave me," he sobbed, looking up at Lancelot as the sea rose further up his chest. "I can't do it."

"You *can*, and you *will*," Aife grunted, leaning down as she jogged in the deepening water and put an arm around the slave's almost skeletal waist. "Now, grab his hands!" She put all her strength into lifting the man, who cried out as his feet left the ground, and then he finally managed to take the Lancelot's outstretched hand and was hauled, gasping and crying, onto the deck.

Aife needed no help to follow, nimbly jumping into the ship and, without another word, the slaves who were able hurried to their usual places on the benches and drew out the oars. Aife hastened starboard where she sat down and took hold of the steering oar. When the slaves had dragged them far enough from the beach she pushed against it and the ship turned to the right.

To the south, and, for the slaves, freedom.

Another wave buffeted the ship and Catia came back to the present, shuddering but thankfully not feeling as nauseous as before. The storm had picked up once they'd got under way, meaning there'd been no chance to break the slaves' individual manacles off. There had been little opportunity to do much more than try to keep the ship on course, away from the coastline, and huddle beneath the waterproof skins and furs they found on board.

The man who'd been thoroughly soaked by falling into the water still wasn't able to take his place at the oars. He was shivering, despite being wrapped in the heaviest cloak Catia had been able to find and she prayed he would survive the night. Apart from him, the crew appeared healthy enough.

Catia occasionally caught Lancelot's eye and he would smile at her, looking far more alive than at any time since she'd first met him.

There was hope for him now. For all of them, now that they were free.

She looked at Aife, contentedly guiding the Saxon vessel through the churning sea, and felt a pang of guilt. No, they weren't all free, or at least they wouldn't be for long, since the Pictish warrior-princess had volunteered to return to Dun Breatann and become a hostage there once more. It was a selfless act, and a courageous one, and Catia admired her friend for it.

Bellicus would look after Aife, Catia hoped. Bellicus would look after them all.

Then, amazingly, despite the motion of the ship, and the howling wind, and the rain and spray that continued to drench her, Catia fell fast asleep.

CHAPTER THIRTEEN

Catia awoke to the sound of metal striking metal. She had no idea where she was and, at first, panicked, wondering what the noise was and why she was outside, the sun beating down on her.

Squinting, she opened her eyes, hand falling to her sword and then she remembered where she was and how they'd got there. A grin spread across her face and she relaxed once more, allowing her head to settle back on the rolled up cloak someone had placed there as a pillow. She watched as Aife wielded the hammer, striking the iron pins that held the slaves' manacles in place.

Lancelot was sitting in the bow of the ship, gazing out at the sea ahead and the coast that lay to their right. He had his back to her, but Catia could tell by his posture that the removal of his chains had given him some of his pride back, for his shoulders were held higher than they'd been before. He also wore the sword belt Catia had taken from the Saxon guard she'd killed and that too must have felt like a restoration of Lancelot's manhood.

There was a yelp and all aboard looked at the man whose wrist manacles had just crashed onto the deck. He was rubbing his skin but smiling. Aife's hammer hadn't struck him, but he'd half expected it to. Now, relieved, he thanked her although in some strange unknown tongue Catia didn't recognise – his sentiments were clear, however, and he happily moved out of the way to let the next of his fellows take his place.

"Good morning," Aife called, noticing Catia had awoken. She gestured with the hammer. "Would you like to take a turn?" She wiped sweat from her forehead and breathed deeply. "This is hard going."

"I don't think I'd have the strength," Catia replied uncertainly, standing and shaking out her hair. She had a little comb in a fold of her tunic, a prized gift from her mother, and she took it out now to try and brush through some of the knots in her hair. "I'll give it a go, though."

Lancelot stood up and stepped easily across the swaying deck, holding out his hand to take the tool from Aife. "I'll do it, my lady," he said. "It'll be good to do something other than dragging on an oar for what's seemed like every waking moment these past few weeks or however long it's been."

Aife nodded and handed it to him, moving aside and walking across to Catia just as gracefully as Lancelot had traversed the deck. She sat next to the girl and sighed happily, glad to rest her bones for a time. The previous night's squall had passed while Catia slept and now the sea was calm, glittering in the sunshine as a steady but gentle wind filled the sail and pushed them further from Dunnottar with every moment.

"How are you feeling?" Aife asked, raising her hands as a man, bald on top but with long hair at the back, rummaged in the sack of food at the stern and tossed a chunk of dark bread through the air. The princess caught it and showed it to Catia questioningly. "Up to eating?"

"Am I?" the younger princess demanded, realising only now how ravenous she was. "I feel fine. Last night's sickness has passed and I could eat a horse. That'll do though." She watched greedily as Aife tore the bread into two pieces and handed her the biggest. They fell to their meal in silence, chewing and watching as Lancelot slammed the hammer down against the slave's manacle. The gentle rocking of the ship combined with the rhythmic thudding to lull Catia into an almost hypnotic state.

"What's the plan?" Lancelot asked them once the wrist and ankle manacles were removed and the joyful slave, tears actually streaking his grimy face, made his way over to a bench where he rested in thoughtful solitude as the next man sat before Lancelot and waited his turn for freedom.

"We'll put ashore soon enough – once all the men's chains are off – and then start walking to Dun Breatann. My mother will be glad to welcome you all, especially you, my lord. Bellicus will be happy to see you too, I'm sure."

Lancelot smiled. "'My lord'," he repeated. "Never thought anyone would call me that again, unless in some cruel jest." He smashed the hammer down into the pin holding the next slave's wrists together and the manacle popped open at that first blow. "I'll gladly journey with you to Alt Clota, and I'm sure the rest of the men will too. We all owe you our lives and our freedom, my ladies. We're in your debt."

Neither Catia nor Aife argued with that. They did not know the men on board the ship with them – it would do no harm to remind them that they were beholden to the princesses. One or all of them could be violent criminals after all and they might decide simply to take advantage of the girls and strike out on their own now that they were free of their bonds.

Yet when Catia searched the faces of their shipmates she found she did not believe any of them were monsters. They looked like underfed warriors, aged between twenty and fifty, and they all eyed the two girls with something approaching awe. No, they would not attempt to harm Catia or Aife – quite the opposite. They were indebted to the princesses now, and the men knew it and seemed, at least at the moment, happy to embrace the fact.

They might be my own personal guard, thought Catia cheerfully, watching the men as they lounged about, rubbing raw ankles and wrists but enjoying no longer being tethered to the fabric of the ship, or each other. They already seemed more like men to the young princess, less like the soulless husks they'd been before.

The sunshine, the salt spray, the breeze blowing them along…It all combined to fill the entire crew with possibilities and, when the final slave had been liberated by Lancelot's pounding hammer, Catia felt as if there was nothing else to worry about in the world. They were free, they'd escaped, and all was well.

"We should think about disembarking soon," Aife said, destroying Catia's peaceful reverie.

"Then what?" Lancelot asked, coming to sit on the bench in front of them. He sat with his legs spread wide, palms on his knees, the sword at his waist already seeming like it was a part of his body.

"Then we make the journey to Dun Breatann," Catia said. "As I already told you, my lord."

Lancelot jerked a head at the freed slaves. "What about them? They're not really in any fit state to walk for long. Or fight, should it come to it."

Catia and Aife shared a look. He was right, and he was also probably too weak to do much if it came to a battle with those who were surely pursuing them.

"We have this," Aife said, patting the ship. "We'll trade it for horses."

Lancelot looked dubious.

"Even if we only manage to get four animals," the princess said. "That'll be better than nothing. We can all take turns riding and walking. It'll make things a lot easier and hopefully keep us one step ahead of anyone looking for us."

"Where?"

Aife replied instantly, for she'd been thinking about nothing else since waking that morning. "Mucrois," she said. "It's a fairly big town so we should be able to trade there."

"The people will know this is a Saxon ship," Lancelot warned.

Aife nodded agreement. "Aye, they will, and that means they'll know it's a quality vessel. The Saxons make better ships than anyone. We'll be honest and tell them it's stolen and the owners might come looking for it. Whoever takes it off our hands will be able to hide it for a few days, I'm sure. These ships are designed to be pushed on land you know. How hard would it be to shove it into some nearby woods?"

Lancelot grinned approvingly. "I hope you're right."

"Why can't we just stay on board until we're into Votadini territory?" one of the men piped up. "We could sail right down and into Kinneil. The Roman wall runs all along there, so it would be easier to walk, and a damn sight shorter journey than leaving the ship at Mucrois."

Lancelot looked at Aife. He might not know the geography of the area but, if what the man had said was right, it certainly made sense.

Aife shook her head. "Mucrois is in my father's lands. The people there will recognise me as their princess and be more inclined to help us than any Votadini."

"But my mother is married to a Votadini prince," Catia said. "Surely that would count for something. Our peoples are allied through that marriage."

Aife was still uncertain, looking up at the sky which had already started to cloud over. "We've been lucky so far. First, to escape in the midst of a storm, and second to have had calm weather today. But I'm not a skilled sailor, and I'd not fancy trying to navigate this thing along the peninsula to Kinncil by myself."

"I can help," said the man who'd suggested this new plan. "I'm a sailor."

"Why didn't you say so before now?" Catia demanded. "Poor Aife was left to guide us through that storm while you stayed quiet!"

The man bowed his head respectfully and she saw it was the man who'd thrown her the bread earlier. "Sorry, my lady," he said sheepishly. "But I didn't know what was happening last night. I didn't know who you two ladies were, or what your purpose was in stealing this ship. I wasn't about to offer my help when you might have been even worse masters to us than the Saxons had been. I can see now that's not the case, so...I offer you my service, Princess. I'm Brychan, of the Votadini tribe myself. I know the waters around Kinneil well enough to take us there safely."

Lancelot and Aife were smiling but Catia was irritated. "Is anyone else a sailor?" she asked, standing up and walking across to the freed slaves. They all shook their heads, apart from one man who merely stared blankly at her. Either he was moon-touched or didn't speak the girl's language, but Catia couldn't be bothered trying to make herself understood. "All right," she said, swinging back to Brychan. "Take command, captain. The rest of you men, give him whatever help you can. He's in charge until we reach dry land, when Princess Aife'll take over again."

The 'captain' smiled in relief and stood up. "Thank you, Princess. I honestly don't think my body would have taken a journey as long as Mucrois to Dun Breatann."

"Is she always so bossy?" Lancelot asked Aife, making no attempt to lower his voice.

"Aye," Catia retorted. "I am. And be thankful, *my lord*, for it was my bossiness that got you safely away from your Saxon keepers."

When she turned away, to look out at the sea behind them for signs of any pursuing sails on the horizon, Aife winked at Lancelot and, shaking her head, mouthed, "She's lovely really."

There were no sails coming up behind them, and Catia thought that even if King Drest did give Leofdaeg and Sigarr a ship to chase the fleeing princesses it would not be any faster than the Saxon vessel. And, now that they had a proper sailor in charge, who knew how to work the sail with real skill, capturing every breath of wind and urging the former slaves to pick up oars and row whenever the breeze died to nothing, the fugitives were making better time than ever.

"How long will it take to get there, Brychan?" Catia asked.

The sailor had taken the steering oar and his weather-beaten face turned to her, an expression of contentment on it that none of the slaves had worn for probably many weeks or months. "A few hours, Princess," he said. "If we're where I think we are. We must have escaped from Dunnottar around midnight, eh? So, at the speed we're making I'd reckon we'll reach Kinneil about late afternoon, all being well."

Catia peered up at the sky. Dull grey clouds had obscured the sun but she could still see where it was and she nodded approvingly. Travelling by ship, once she'd got over the initial nausea, was certainly much easier than walking or even riding, if somewhat slower. "All right," she said, facing the rest of the freed slaves. "I'd suggest you all have something to eat." She looked at Aife who moved across to the pack of food she'd brought and began dishing it out to the grateful men. "And then maybe try to get some sleep. We'll have a hard journey to make when we disembark."

Lancelot made his way across to get some of the Aife's provisions, eyeing Catia with respect, but something else the girl couldn't put her finger on.

"What is it?" she asked as the blond man sat down, still looking at her curiously, and began chewing the bread he'd been given.

"You..." he squinted, taking in her features and her bearing. "Remind me of someone," he said.

Catia didn't reply, she just returned his gaze until he turned away. She knew who he was talking about, for she was able to see the resemblance to Bellicus herself more clearly with every passing day now. Or at least, every day when she was able to look in a bronze mirror. There seemed little doubt Coroticus had not been her true father, but she did not want to think about that just now. She had loved the old Alt Clotan king, and it made her feel guilty whenever a sense of pride arose at the thought of Bellicus's blood, not Coroticus's, running through her veins.

But, if Lancelot could see it, she knew others would too, for the swordsman had only just met her yet had remarked upon the resemblance.

It was a problem for another day, if it was a problem at all.

"Get some sleep," she said to Lancelot eventually, once he'd finished his meal. "Aife and I will need your skills and your leadership once we reach Kinneil." Another thought struck her then. "Is there no way you and the others could...You know..."

Lancelot barked a short laugh, realising from her discomfort what she was asking.

"Bathe?" he asked, flashing a smile that, had Catia been just a little older, might have made her heart flutter, despite his grubbiness.

"And shave," she nodded. "Maybe cut your hair too. Not just you," she finished lamely. "All of you."

"You all stink like dogshit," Aife grinned, coming to the younger girl's rescue. Some of the men laughed, some looked embarrassed, others irritated or even angry. "What?" she said, spreading her hands wide. "It's true, but we'll soon have you looking, and smelling, like the noble warriors you surely all are. It's understandable that you've not taken care of your grooming, or not been allowed to, but you're not slaves anymore." Her voice was hard now, insistent. "Even if the Saxons catch us, you'll be able to stand and fight them as free men, not beasts of burden. You should look the part."

"She's right," Lancelot said. "We had no hope, so we let ourselves become almost like animals. These girls – ladies – have given us hope again. Come on." He held out his hand, nodding towards Aife's ankle. She drew out her knife and gave it to him, and he went to the men who'd been his fellow prisoners for the past few weeks and started trimming their hair and beards.

"You should get some sleep too," Catia said to Aife. "You must be exhausted after steering the ship all night. Go on, get your head down. When it's time to disembark you'll open your eyes to a clean, freshly groomed warband which you can lead to Dun Breatann."

The princesses looked at one another, smiling, proud, and filled with optimism for the adventures ahead of them. Then Catia frowned, eyeing the former slaves. "There's only seven of them," she noted. "I thought there were eight when we set out."

Aife sighed. "The one that got soaked last night, he..." She trailed off.

"Where is he?"

"Couldn't have a body on board, Catia," said Aife softly. "Don't worry, we offered prayers to Dis for him."

The younger princess looked away, face twisted in sorrow. They sat quietly for a time, and then Aife nodded and reached into her tunic, drawing out a little vial and giving it to Catia.

"What's this?" the younger girl asked, admiring the workmanship of the bottle.

"Scented oil," replied Aife. "Have Lancelot fill one of the bailing buckets with sea-water and put a few drops of the perfume in. The men can use it to wash their faces and get rid of at least some of the stink."

Brychan laughed from his place at the steering oar. "A fine warband that'll make, all walking about smelling of rose petals."

"Rather that, than smelling of weeks-old sweat and piss and shit," Lancelot shouted back. "Besides, if our enemies think we smell like women, they won't know whether to fight us, or hump us!"

With that, Aife shook her head and made herself as comfortable as possible before taking Catia's advice and, lulled by the sun and the gentle creak and groan of the ship and its ropes, getting some sleep.

CHAPTER FOURTEEN

"Something's happening." Eburus watched as half a dozen Pictish riders galloped past them, clad in full war-gear. The men eyed them suspiciously but were apparently too busy to stop and question the big Votadini with the black shield, or his companions.

The horsemen were soon out of sight and Bellicus shook his head. "You're right," he said. "Something's happened. Those warriors were looking for someone."

"This early in the morning? Who?"

The druid shrugged and kicked Darac into a faster run. "As long as it's not us, who cares?"

They were nearing their destination now. The road was familiar to Bellicus and memories of his last time in Dunnottar came to him as they approached the long, narrow headland that led to the fortress. Memories of being imprisoned alone in a tiny, dark cell while above him Duro was tortured by King Drest, eventually losing two of his fingers in the ordeal. Bellicus gritted his teeth, knuckles whitening around his mount's reins. Drest had never properly been repaid for his actions, but unfortunately this couldn't be the time.

They were there to find Catia and make sure she was brought safely home to Dun Breatann. Everything else could wait for another day, although Bellicus knew he would find it hard to be around the Pictish king without attacking him.

Druids were trained to remain calm, though, and he was there as a diplomat, so he would act rationally rather than allowing his emotions to control him. Duro would struggle even more, but he was a centurion and prided himself in maintaining discipline even in the most stressful situations. One day Drest would suffer for what he'd done to Duro. One day.

"There it is," Eburus said as the impressive fortress of Dunnottar came into sight at last.

Bellicus made a sign in the air, warding off the evil he associated with the place. "Remember," he said to his friends. "We're not here to start trouble, just to find the princess and get out again."

"You'd be better reminding yourself of that, druid," Eburus replied. "You're the one the Picts locked up and starved, not me."

"Aye," Duro agreed irritably. "But you're the one that could start a fight in an empty room with that big mouth of yours."

"Halt!"

There was no need for the shout, delivered with some authority by a young man atop the first set of gates, for the entrance was blocked and there was nowhere for the travellers to go. They halted.

"Who are you, and what d'ye want?" the Pictish warrior demanded in his own language which Bellicus understood quite well.

"I'm Bellicus, Druid of Dun Breatann. And this is Eburus, Champion of the Votadini tribe, and Centurion Duro of Luguvalium. We're here to see your king."

The guard stared down at them and Bellicus could see two more men peering out over the crenelated walls, helmets and spearpoints gleaming.

"Wait there, my lords," the guard called to them respectfully. "A messenger is going to the king."

So they waited, listening to the sound of the nearby sea, enjoying the breeze that blew Eburus's long hair and Bellicus's cloak.

"Nice dog," the guard shouted after some time had passed.

Bellicus looked at Cai who was sitting on the grass at the side of the path, staring out to sea, nose sniffing continuously. Sometimes the hound's attention was taken by a circling gull or some other movement, and the druid smiled. Aye, Cai was a nice dog, he thought, unless you got on the wrong side of him.

"Thanks," he shouted back to the guard, who smiled, and then turned as he heard the running footsteps of the man sent to speak with the king.

The pair conversed for a moment and then the guard shouted, "You can come in. Keep the dog close beside you though, if you would. He looks friendly enough but not everyone loves them as we do, my lord."

The entrance was thrown open and Bellicus nudged Darac ahead, with Duro, Eburus and Cai following him as they went through the building and on towards the second, final set of gates.

"Nice," said the Votadini as they passed the skulls on stakes that lined the narrow road. Bellicus didn't reply, or even look at the grisly ornaments. His eyes were on the buildings ahead, searching for Catia, hoping he might catch sight of her on the walls.

The next set of guards allowed them to pass into the fortress without challenge, although they bowed their heads courteously which somewhat surprised Bellicus. The Picts were no friends to the Damnonii and any alliance they once had with the Votadini had crumbled when Eburus and his men had joined Narina's army the year before. The guards must have been told to show the visitors' respect, Bellicus thought, and took that as a good sign. It hadn't been Drest's idea for his daughter to escape after all, and the king was surely wary of how things might turn out now. The Pictish army had almost been annihilated by Narina's forces after all, and were in no position yet to renew hostilities.

Aife had placed her father in a very dangerous situation, but Bellicus knew he had to be careful here. Drest might be temporarily neutered but this was his home, his lands, and the visitors were surrounded by Drest's loyal men.

"My lord." A groom was waiting to take Darac's reins, and Bellicus jumped down, happy enough to hand the animal over to the lad. Duro's and Eburus's mounts were similarly given into the care of boys about twelve or thirteen years old.

"What about the dog?" Bellicus asked the groom who was leading his horse away. The boy looked at Cai and blanched, making the druid laugh. "I'm only joking, lad. The dog can look after himself."

"I don't understand why the Picts don't just speak the same language as the rest of us," Eburus said as two burly guards approached and they were ushered into the lower part of the main fortress, only stopping to relinquish their swords for safe-keeping, as was the tradition.

Bellicus shrugged expansively, ducking so his head didn't strike the top of the door frame. "Why should the Picts, or anyone else, give up their heritage? Just to make life easier for people? Besides, it's good for the mind to learn more than one language."

Eburus grunted doubtfully. "Seems bloody stupid if you ask me."

It was true that the Picts had their own language, different to all the other tribes north of the Roman wall that ran from Dun Breatann to Veluniate, but the nobles in Drest's inner circle, and most of those connected to the royal family there in Dunnottar, could speak the Brythonic tongue spoken by Bellicus, Eburus and the Britons further south like Duro. Eventually, the languages would either meld together, or one or the other would be lost in time, but, for now, this was how it was, and the druid was quite fluent in either tongue so it made little difference to him. As they were led towards the great hall, though, they were surprised to hear a third language being spoken, and in aggressive tones too.

They continued walking, the Pictish guards not slowing or seeming surprised by the raised voices within the hall, but Bellicus looked at Duro and they both said at the same time, "Saxons?" Eburus's hand dropped to his side, grasping air where his sword hilt should have been, and he muttered an oath.

"At least you've got that," he said, nodding at the druid's weighty staff with its finely cast but heavy bronze eagle on top.

"And him," Bellicus agreed, smiling and looking down at Cai, padding silently along beside them.

"You've nothing to worry about," one of the guards said, looking back as they reached the doors leading to the great hall. "The Saxons are visitors. They've had…" He looked at the second guard and the pair sniggered like naughty boys. "Some bad news. You'll not have any trouble from them, my lords." He pushed open the door on the left and looked inside. Bellicus could see Drest at his high-backed throne, standing, not sitting, as a man shouted at him in the harsh Saxon tongue. The king glanced towards the door and rolled his eyes in exasperation but waved for the guard to let Bellicus and the others inside.

The druid led the way, hand on Cai's neck reassuring the big hound although there wasn't really any need for it. Cai was used to angry shouts and aggressive gestures. Bellicus wondered what was going on, his eyes scanning the large room for Catia or Aife but seeing only men gathered there. What had made the Saxon visitors so furious? For they were certainly furious. Even someone like Eburus with little knowledge of the Germanic tongue could hear that.

There were four of them, three tall, warrior-types with thick beards, thick muscles, and probably thick skulls too, Bellicus thought, expertly sizing them up in a heartbeat. One other man wasn't quite like the others, however. He was smaller, slimmer, and had a shrewd look in his eyes that made him seem the most dangerous of them all to the druid.

The one shouting at King Drest continued with his tirade for a few heartbeats, demanding justice, a ship, a warband to go after the thieves. Bellicus stood listening, taking it all in, until, at last, the Saxon noticed the trio of newcomers staring at him, and the enormous dog placidly sniffing the air in the hall.

"Jarl Leofdaeg," said Drest by way of introduction. "Please forgive me but we have some more visitors to my fortress today. This is—"

The Saxon looked irritably at Eburus, and then the dog, and then Duro, and finally his eyes fixed on Bellicus.

The druid frowned, recognition flaring within his mind, and then, to King Drest's horror, Leofdaeg pulled a knife from his belt and launched himself across the floor at Bellicus, screaming in the Briton tongue, "You! You *Waelisc* bastard!"

"Stop! Stop this!" Drest's command went unheeded, but Bellicus had brought up his staff and knocked aside the knife which was held rather clumsily in the Saxon jarl's left hand. Cai lunged forward, teeth sinking into Leofdaeg's thigh and, as the man howled in pain, Bellicus punched him in the face.

The two other, bigger Saxons, confused but always ready for a fight, came at Eburus and Duro. Like the other visitors in the hall, they had given up their swords, axes, hammers or whatever they usually carried as their main weapon, but they were still dangerous, even unarmed.

So was Eburus.

The Saxon on the left threw a punch but the Votadini was already in motion, landing a thundering right-hand to the man, whose legs buckled as the blow landed.

Meanwhile, Duro had grabbed the other man and they began to wrestle, teeth bared, roaring with rage and battle-lust. Duro was stronger and wilier than his opponent and, although he took an elbow in the eye, soon had the Saxon in a choke-hold, squeezing until the man's face turned purple.

"Stop! By the gods, guards, stop them!"

The Picts were finally spurred into action, the two who'd led Bellicus and Eburus coming to push back the druid who didn't resist. He called Cai to heel and the dog immediately did as he was told, padding calmly back to stand by his master's side, hackles up, a low, fearful growl rumbling in his chest. Eburus grudgingly let go of the man he was now throttling, pushing him back to stumble onto the floor beside his friends.

Leofdaeg was not fit to continue his thwarted attack, he lay stunned and groaning while his beaten companions gaped at Eburus, Duro, and finally the druid who was completely uninjured and not even out of breath.

"What the fuck is going on?" Drest roared, sitting down and slamming the arms of his throne. "In my own hall, by Taranis!"

"The druid," Leofdaeg cried, blood seeping from his nose down his philtrum, lips and chin. "The druid murdered my father."

Recognition flashed across the smallest Saxon's face and he nodded. "This is the man who was with Lancelot when they raided your camp."

"Aye, Sigarr," Leofdaeg muttered, wiping blood and snot from his face and glowering up at Bellicus. "I swore to kill them both."

"Well, you're not making a very good job of it then, are you?" the little Saxon said sarcastically. "The druid's broke your nose, and Lancelot—"

"I'll kill you too, Sigarr, if you don't shut your mouth," Leofdaeg shouted but he cut a pitiful figure, sprawled on the floor, one arm hanging limp by his side, face and beard coated with his own blood, trousers ripped where Cai had fixed his teeth.

"Be silent!" Drest bellowed, slamming his hands on his throne once again. "Are you men, or animals? This is a royal fortress. Conduct yourselves accordingly, or I'll have you all thrown over the wall into the sea."

Bellicus doubted the king would attempt to carry out that threat, but his words had the desired effect, and everyone grew quiet. The beaten Saxons groaned as they dragged themselves to a bench and sat, downing mugs of ale which had been poured earlier. Even Sigarr swallowed a cup for the short but brutal fight had shocked him.

"Bellicus, my lord," Drest said, sighing as he turned and gestured for the druid and his companions to take seats. "I would ask what brings you to my lands, but I'm sure I already know. The princess."

Bellicus sat down and nodded his thanks as a servant brought two cups and a pitcher of ale to their table. "Princess*es*," he said. "Plural, lord King."

Drest visibly paled but a door opened at the other side of the hall and the Pictish druid, Qunavo came in, followed a moment later by Ria. The pair came and sat on either side of the king, the druidess even smiling playfully at Bellicus, who didn't react to her greeting although he did return Qunavo's nod. The older druid had been Bellicus's tutor during his childhood training on the island of Iova and deserved respect, even after the recent troubles between the Picts and the Damnonii.

The presence of his advisors gave Drest confidence and he said, "Aife's escaping from Dun Breatann had nothing to do with me. She felt forced into it but…" He glanced at the Saxons, then back to the druid. "We can talk of that later, Bel. Some rather grave accusations were made by my daughter."

Bellicus frowned but he'd been expecting something like this. Aife must have had some reason for running back to her father's lands after all. "Where is Princess Catia?" he asked, moving on. "Is she safe?"

Before Drest could reply, Jarl Leofdaeg broke in. "The little bitch has sailed off in my ship," he spat. "Taken the ship, my crew of slaves, and killed some of my men just before the storm hit last night." He pointed a finger at the Pictish king. "This is all on you, Drest. The *bretwalda* shall hear of this."

Bellicus sat listening, trying to take it all in. Catia had done all this? No, the Saxon was blaming her, but surely the girl had some help. From whom?

"Where's Aife?"

Drest turned his attention back to the druid and he looked sheepish again.

"She's on my ship too!" Leofdaeg roared.

Eburus burst out laughing, and Bellicus opened his mouth to rebuke him, not particularly wanting to get into another fight with the Saxons, but then he too started to snigger. How could he not?

"Are you telling me two girls, one of them only eleven summers, attacked your warriors, killed some of them, and then stole your ship? While you two mighty jarls sat drinking and enjoying Pictish hospitality?"

"That's what we're telling you," Sigarr said. "But King Drest here is going to lend us one of his own ships so that we can hunt the thieves down." He spread his hands and stared at the king. "My lord? We've tarried here long enough, every moment takes our ship further away. Do what you can to win back our favour. If you give us your fastest vessel we can catch up with them by mid-afternoon, unless they stop before then."

Bellicus almost felt sorry for Drest. Aife had caused him trouble with two different, powerful, factions now, and he'd been left to clean up her mess. Yet he was the princess's father and surely wouldn't want these Saxons actually catching up with the stolen boat and taking retribution on Aife and her fellow thieves.

The king conferred with Qunavo for a few moments as Ria continued to eye Bellicus sardonically. He didn't bother to react, couldn't allow himself to become distracted by her charms again. He was there to find Catia, not rekindle any romantic or sexual relationship with the duplicitous druidess.

She was so pretty though...

"All right," Drest said. "I'll give you a ship, but on the condition that you swear not to harm my daughter."

"Or Catia," Bellicus said, staring hard at the king, and then turning to the Saxons. "If you bastards touch the girl I'll come for you myself, and you'll get more than a bloody nose, Leofdaeg. You'll get what your father got, and worse."

The Saxon stiffened but Sigarr placed a hand on his arm and hissed at him to ignore the druid's threats. "We accept," the jarl said to Drest, standing and bowing respectfully. "Please have one of your men show us to the ship we've to take, and we'll be off as soon as possible. And remember, my lord King: We know a fast ship from a slow one."

"Your word, Sigarr," Drest said, stony-faced. "Give me your word that the girls won't be harmed. Swear it on your gods."

"By Wotan," the jarl replied. "May my balls shrivel and fall off if we harm either of the princesses. Is that good enough?"

Qunavo got to his feet and arched his back, looking up at the roof as if communing with the gods or channelling some mystical power, and then he pointed a long, steady finger at the Saxons. "Bring our ship back to us, with the princesses safe and well. I draw the spirits from the air and send them with you, to ensure you hold to your word, Sigarr." With that he gestured outwards, throwing the invisible energy at the jarls and their men, who shrank back, wide-eyed.

"We won't hurt them, old man," Sigarr said softly. "We just want our ship back, and our slaves."

"Do what you like with the slaves," Drest said. "They mean nothing to me."

Ria was still staring at Bellicus, who was wondering what his next move should be. She said, as if speaking to the druid rather than the Saxons, "Good luck, Jarl Sigarr. You'll have a hard time killing Lancelot if his shackles have been taken off."

Leofdaeg waved a hand dismissively but Sigarr was already walking out of the hall, led by Drest's guard captain, and the rest of the Saxons followed. When they were gone, Bellicus demanded, "Lancelot?"

"He's one of their slaves," Ria told him, grinning at the astonished look on her former lover's face. "A friend of yours? Rather handsome, if utterly filthy and malnourished."

"Come on," the druid said to Eburus and Duro, rising, Cai following his lead without needing to be told. "We have to find that ship before the Saxons do."

Drest was startled by his sudden intention to depart. "I thought you would stay longer, druid," he said. "We have things to discuss."

"Another time, my lord," Bellicus promised. "Do you really think the sea-wolves will spare your daughter if they catch the stolen ship? Sigarr might, but Leofdaeg is a man without honour, blinded by hatred for the *Waelisc* who have the audacity to fight back against their invasion. You ready, Eburus?"

The Votadini nodded. "Always, Bel."

"One last thing, before we go," the druid said, glancing back over his shoulder at the king. "Why *did* Aife leave Dun Breatann?"

"Prince Ysfael," Ria said, and the playful smile was no longer on her face.

Bellicus nodded, gritting his teeth. "I thought it might be," he replied. "Well, that can be dealt with once this is all over."

"What about the rest of my people held prisoner in Dun Breatann?" Drest called. "Will they be harmed in retaliation for Aife's escape?"

"Not if I have anything to do with it," Bellicus replied. "But Ysfael has advised Queen Narina to kill them all."

Drest paled and he shook his head, chewing his lip anxiously. "Do what you can for them, then," he said. "And my daughter too. She's in Damnonii care. You're supposed to keep her safe!"

"Agreed," the druid shouted as they left the great hall. "I'll do what I can to protect her. Any idea where we should begin our search for them?"

Drest glanced at Ria and Qunavo but neither could offer words of advice.

"Lancelot's alive!" Bellicus said excitedly to his friends as they made their way to fetch the horses.

Duro nodded, face alight with hope although it was tempered by the knowledge that the swordsman had been cruelly used by Leofdaeg.

When they reached the stables the grooms were surprised to see them back so soon. Their horses were still being tended to and the men had to wait for them to be made ready to ride. As they lingered a serving girl came hurrying out of the back door of the hall carrying three sacks.

"My lords, the king sent this for you." She handed one to each of them. "Provisions for your journey. There's some for the big dog too."

"My thanks," the druid replied, pleased at the gift and also the fact that Darac was finally ready to travel.

"Let's go, lads," said Eburus, jumping up onto his mount's back and tying the sack safely in place behind him. "The princesses have a big head start on us, and we have no damn idea where they're even going."

They walked the horses towards the gatehouse and, at the second, the guard came out to pet Cai and give him a morsel of dried meat as they waited on the gates being opened. And then they were out and galloping along the road again, heading south, praying to the gods that they'd be able to find the Saxons' ship before Leofdaeg did.

Bellicus knew even Qunavo's threat of Wotan's curse wouldn't be able to protect Catia, Aife, or Lancelot if the vengeful jarl found them first.

CHAPTER FIFTEEN

"It was quite a happy coincidence," Lancelot drawled, leaning back against the hull and basking in the sunshine as the stolen ship neared their destination. "Having one of the men on board be a sailor," he clarified, noting Aife's puzzled frown. "And a local too, who knows the very place we're headed for."

"We're only headed there because he suggested it, remember," Aife said. "I don't think there's anything sinister in it, if that's what you mean."

Lancelot laughed and shifted his weight onto his other side. "Oh no, I wasn't meaning that he'd been planted among us by the Saxons and might betray us. Not at all. I was thinking it was a good sign, a sign from the gods. Our escape was meant to be!"

"Aye," Aife agreed. "Just remember who you have to thank for it, and I'm not talking about the gods. I might need you to repay the favour one day."

Lancelot grinned, and then they both turned at a shout from Brychan who was manning the steering oar. The sailor was pointing.

"There's Kinneil," he called. "Take down the sail and man the oars, lads. We've made it without the bastards catching us!"

The crew moved to follow his orders, but they were not used to dealing with the sail which was whipping about in even the slight breeze and Brychan had to leave the steering oar to help, asking Catia to hold them on a straight course until he was finished.

"She looks like she's enjoying herself," Lancelot noted.

"Aren't you?" Aife asked. "You're free, the sun is shining, and the sea is calm."

"And I'm in the company of a beautiful woman," Lancelot added, but Aife merely rolled her eyes. "I'm curious," he said with a mischievous smile. "Do you have any of those tattoos I saw the warriors wearing in Dunnottar?"

"Are you too important to row, now that you're no longer a slave?" she asked, pointedly ignoring his question and nodding at the two banks of rowers who'd taken up their familiar positions and were beginning to power the ship towards the approaching docks at Kinneil.

Lancelot's grin never faded as he got up, bowed to Aife, and went to pull out the oar which had been his for so many weeks. "You're a strong looking girl," he called as he fell into the rhythm the other rowers had already established. "You could take a turn too."

"She's a king's daughter," called Catia. "Far too important for that. Now, row faster, I'm eager to get back to Dun Breatann."

The mood on board was light and the crew, those who understood their language at least, laughed at Lancelot's dressing down.

"I'd have to agree with the princess," Brychan said, and the serious tone of his voice made everyone look to the stern where he was standing, staring back at the sea behind them, shimmering as the water met the sunlit sky. "Row faster." He turned then and said to Aife, "One of your father's ships is behind us, and I'm betting it's not Picts on board, but Saxons."

"How do you know it's one of our ships?" Aife asked, chewing her lip as she came over to join him, shading her eyes as she too gazed at the glittering sea behind them.

"The sail," Brychan replied, pointing again. "It's got an emblem on it."

"You can make it out from this distance?" Aife asked incredulously.

"Not quite," the sailor admitted. "But I can tell the type of ship it is, it's a Pictish currach, and one of those in Dunnottar's harbour bore a stag emblem on its sail. I'll wager that's it, and your father's let the Saxons borrow it to catch us."

"Not much else he could do," Catia said with insight beyond her years. "He couldn't survive a war with Hengist." She stood up, placing her palm on the pommel of the sword at her waist, an action that, given her youth, might have caused some amusement amongst the men rowing, but Catia had an air of grim determination about her that didn't seem particularly amusing just then. "As we've already said: row faster, if you don't want to face Leofdaeg and his warriors in a fight."

"Can we do anything?" Aife asked Brychan, but the sailor shook his head, a worried frown on his seamed features.

"Pray," he muttered, still eyeing the ship behind them. It was growing bigger with every passing second. "The Saxons are master shipbuilders, but this is a trading vessel, not built for speed. That one coming after us has the advantage, and a nearly full crew who really know how to get the best out of it, even if its construction may be unfamiliar to them. I'd guess they've been able to travel at, on average, double the speed we've been going. That's how they've caught up with us."

"Shouldn't we let the sail out?" Catia asked. "The wind has picked up again."

"These are dangerous waters, this close to land, my lady," Brychan said, dismissing her suggestion. "I want as much control over the ship as possible. We don't have far to go now, and there's a chance the hidden rocks and currents might get our pursuers into trouble."

"Really?"

"Well," he shrugged. "Probably not. If some of the Saxons are really traders they'll know these waters well enough."

Silence fell on the ship then, only the grunts of the rowers and the cries of gulls disturbing the calm. Catia and Aife shared a glance, but what more could be said? All they could do was hope they reached Kinneil in time to disembark and be on the road well ahead of Leofdaeg's pursuit. If it came to a fight there would only be one winner, and things would not go well for Catia or Aife.

The grim silence continued as the land passed with agonizing slowness, for the rowers were flagging now, even the rations Aife had given them not being enough to fuel their withered bodies. Time was needed to build the men back up, but time was running out and the Saxons sailing the Pictish currach behind them grew closer with every heartbeat. The emblem on the pursuers' ship was clearly visible now, and it was indeed a stylized stag, embroidered in a deep green thread, just as Brychan had suggested.

"You must row faster," Catia cried, turning to the men, her voice almost pleading. "They're catching us!"

Aife reached out and put her arm around the younger girl, and Catia did not pull away, instead allowing herself to be drawn into Aife's embrace, sensing the panic from days before returning. "All will be well, my little princess, remember what Ria told you," the warrior-woman said kindly. It was Queen Narina whom Catia really wanted then, but Aife was a good surrogate, and the unexpected show of emotion did spur the men on. Some of them were fathers themselves, but even those who were childless desperately wanted to prove themselves to the girls who'd risked their own lives to save them from slavery.

"They'll need to bring their own sail in soon," Brychan said, trying to make his tone reassuring. "When they do, they'll slow and that'll give us more time."

"Well, that's good," Lancelot called. He was sweating, the muscles on his thin arms cording as he dragged on the oar. "But I fear our chances have just got even worse. Look." He didn't take his hands from the oar, instead jerking his head upwards, indicating a point on the horizon to the right of the chasing currach.

"Another ship," Aife muttered, straining to make out the features of the new vessel which was coming up behind the currach at a much greater speed, its bigger sail straining as a gust which hadn't yet reached the stolen ship propelled it on.

"That's no currach," Lancelot said. "It looks like a bigger version of this one. They're Saxons."

"You must be joking," one of the other rowers gasped, eyes widening as he put all his energy into hauling on the oar. "How could we have such terrible luck? To escape, only to have two enemy ships catching up with us?"

"Where did it come from?" Catia demanded of Brychan, as if this was somehow his fault.

"Your guess is as good as mine, lady," the sailor replied grimly. "Look, they've reached the currach. Leofdaeg and Sigarr will be shouting over to them, telling them what's happened."

"Will the folk on the new ship help them? Why should we assume they'll all be friends?"

"Sigarr is a cousin to the Saxon *bretwalda*," Lancelot grunted. "Whoever is on that second ship will look to court Hengist's favour. Besides, the sea-wolves love a good chase and a fight." He paused, exhausted from their exertions. "We really need to think about what we're going to do when we reach Kinneil."

Catia and Aife shared a glance. Both had their hands on their swords, fearing the weapons would need to be drawn all too soon. Their earlier plans, which had seemed so perfect as they sailed lazily southwards with no sign of pursuit, were in disarray.

"He's right," Catia said quietly. "We thought we'd have time to negotiate with the merchants in Kinneil. Time to trade this ship for horses. But..." She trailed off, shaking her head in frustration as they watched the Saxons coming up behind them. As Brychan had predicted, their pursuers had dropped their sails so they could manoeuvre and that had certainly slowed the currach, which would only have half a crew – the other half being with Lancelot and rowing this ship instead. The second, new vessel, must have had a full complement of rowers, however, for it continued to move rapidly across the glistening waters, majestic in the sunshine. The sound of men's voices raised in song carried to Catia and she bared her teeth, mentally preparing for what would surely be a fight to the death.

"Me, you, and a few underfed slaves," Aife said, but her voice was light, almost playful and she patted Catia on the arm with a grin. "Against two boatloads of goat-humping sea-dogs. I'd say the odds are fairly even."

Catia couldn't help but laugh. "I admire your confidence," she replied. "But I think we need to come up with a better plan than just getting into a fight with them."

"I've a friend in Kinneil," said Brychan.

"Will he help us?" Catia asked hopefully.

"No, that would be suicide," the sailor replied. "If the Saxons found out, they'd kill him. But I'm sure he'll hide me from them."

Catia eyed him in confusion and then finally she understood what he meant, and, although it angered her, she couldn't blame the man for wanting to save his own hide.

"I'm sorry," Brychan said, although he didn't sound like he meant it.

Catia shook her head, waving away his half-heartedly apology and turning to the men at the oars. "What about the rest of you? Will you fight with us, or..."

The men did not slacken their pace but they shared glances. Some had formed friendships of a sort during their time as thralls and said they'd rather make a run for it once the ship docked. That only left two others, and Lancelot.

"If it's only going to be us," one of them said. "Taking on all those Saxons...I think it'd be best if we all just went our separate ways when we reach the town, lady. Leofdaeg is a right bastard, he might let us live, to row the ship for him again, but he'll make us suffer for this. I'd rather take my chances in the countryside."

One of the men, who had not said a single word to anyone since Catia and Aife had taken control of the ship the previous night, stood up then and clambered across the deck, past his fellow rowers. He was tall, with a dark complexion, brown eyes, and black hair. Catia guessed he must hail from some far-off land in the south, and probably could not understand what was being said by the others on the ship.

He stood before the two princesses and clasped his hands, then bowed deeply.

Aife smiled. "There we go," she said to Catia. "We have one loyal warrior, at least. You'll fight at our side?" she asked the man, beaming at him. "Even though you know we have no chance of winning?"

In reply, the tall man raised a hand, and then, still without uttering a word in his language or anyone else's, he stepped quickly across to the side of the ship and jumped over, hitting the water with a splash.

Everyone gasped or cried out and stood to see where the man would surface. The droplets that had been thrown into the air from his impact glistened in the sun like a rainbow for a heartbeat, and then Lancelot pointed.

"There. Gods, look at him go!"

Every eye peered into the dark, rippling waters, watching the swimmer as he headed for land. It was fairly close and the man clearly knew what he was doing for it didn't take him long to come to the beach and he walked out, shaking himself like a dog as he moved onto the grassy headland and up, over it, until he was gone without so much as a wave or a backward glance.

"Maybe he's gone to gather the men and women of Kinneil," someone suggested lamely. "You know, to help us."

"We'll never see him again," Lancelot said, laughing much harder than Catia thought the situation warranted.

"What about you?" she demanded. "Will you be making your way, alone, back to Arthur's lands?"

The blond warrior wiped his eyes and returned to his oar. "Arthur has no lands," he said. "He's no king, merely a warlord."

"Whatever," Catia snapped.

"No, princess, I'll not leave you. I've always wanted to see Alt Clota, and it'll be good to meet my friend Bellicus again." He looked directly at Aife. During their short voyage she had told him about her troubles with Prince Ysfael and fear of returning to Dun Breatann. Lancelot addressed her solemnly now. "You have my sword, lady," he vowed. "And my protection, as long as you need it."

His words made Aife grin, and Catia was greatly cheered too. At least one of the men they'd freed would stay and fight beside them, even if the others all looked as if they were thinking of following the dark fellow over the side and into the sea.

"Come on," said Aife. "We should hand out the Saxons' cargo. The men, and us, will need things to barter with."

At this the rowers' eyes lit up and they grinned at one another, making comments about being rich at last, and, sure enough, there was plenty in the cargo, so each man got a good share. They might not exactly be wealthy, but it would be enough to buy them food and clothing and get them back to wherever had once been their homes.

Assuming the Saxons, or someone else, didn't kill them first.

Catia smiled as she looked at them all, but her heart was heavy. These men had once been strong, muscular, and filled with vitality. Now, after their time as slaves, some were malnourished, toothless, and didn't appear capable of fighting sleep never mind a brutal Saxon warband. Even Lancelot – probably the pick of the bunch, physically – didn't look like he'd last long if he was forced to wield his new sword in anger.

She took a very long, deep breath through her mouth and let it out slowly through her nose, refusing to let herself be overcome by fear. The man might be skinny, but his reputation was immense and must have been well earned. With him and Aife by her side, Catia thought they stood at least a slim chance of making it back to Dun Breatann alive.

"Are we all ready?" Aife said, standing with her hands on her hips and looking every bit the warrior she was. "You men are set on trying to make your own way when we reach land? Aye? All right then, may the gods look after you." She glanced over at Brychan and he nodded, gently pushing the steering oar and bringing the ship into Kinneil.

The men knew this business well enough and slowed the vessel so it didn't collide with the wooden docks before Brychan disembarked and hurriedly tied the ship to a wooden post on the dock. Then everyone else followed him over the side and, with hasty farewells, the former slaves hurried into the town, disappearing amongst the busy workers, traders and locals. Aife took the lead – perhaps in another time Lancelot would have assumed command, being older and more used to being in charge – but now, in his physical condition, it seemed best to let the princess take charge of the situation.

She led them quickly towards the town but was stopped by a small man with only a ring of brown hair on his shining head. They all had an idea of who he was: a bureaucrat, undoubtedly in charge of collecting taxes and keeping records of all the ships that docked in Kinneil.

"Is that your ship?" he demanded, then added, "My lady," as he took in Aife's good quality clothes and weapons.

"Aye," she agreed, then, before he could say anything else, she placed a valuable trinket – taken from the Saxons' stores – into his hand. "That's for you. Keep an eye on the ship for me. You know who I am, don't you?"

The bald man gazed at what she'd given him, delighted with his good fortune. "No, my lady, I don't think so," he admitted somewhat warily.

"Princess Aife of Dunnottar," she told him. "King Drest's daughter." His eyes widened and he opened his mouth to speak but Aife continued. "We need three fast horses, now. Where can we buy them?"

The man thought about it for a moment, absorbing what was happening. He had spotted the other two ships approaching, noted one was clearly Saxon, and was trying to put everything into order in his head.

"Well?" Aife demanded. "Horses?"

"Sorry, Lady," the official stammered, blinking rapidly as he turned and pointed towards the right side of town. "You see that building there?" he asked. "You can just see the top of its roof from here, it's taller than the surrounding ones. Well, that's the nearest stable. Not the finest animals, or the cheapest, but a good place to start if you're in a hurry. May I ask—" he turned back to look at the oncoming Saxon ship which was almost at the docks by now.

"No," Aife replied curtly. "You may not. Both those ships approaching are full of sea-wolves. If you would stall them, I'm sure my father, the King, would be most grateful. Do not tell them where we went." Her tone left little doubt what would happen if he didn't do as she asked. Drest wasn't his king, that was Cunedda, but lots of Pictish ships traded with Kinneil. And raided too, sometimes.

"Of course, Princess," he mumbled, still blinking nervously.

"Thank you," Aife said, bestowing a dazzling smile on the man which bolstered him somewhat. "Come on, then," she said to Catia and Lancelot, long legs carrying her quickly towards the stables and, hopefully, steeds that would take them to Dun Breatann.

CHAPTER SIXTEEN

Bellicus sat cross-legged, eyes closed, hands clasped in his lap, utterly still, his breathing shallow, to the extent Eburus wasn't sure the druid was even still alive.

The big Votadini had made the mistake of stepping on a dry twig earlier, snapping the thing in two and disturbing Bellicus as he was attempting to fall into the trance which would, hopefully, allow him to commune with the gods. The savage insults the irate druid had directed at Eburus had sent him sheepishly off, to sit a distance away against a tree, polishing the blade of his sword with the edge of his cloak and waiting quietly for the ritual to be over. Duro had enjoyed it all immensely.

Cai, for his part, knew exactly what he was supposed to do, and he lay beside his master, just as still and silent as the meditating druid but completely alert. It would be a foolish attacker who tried to sneak up on them with the mastiff on guard.

That was unlikely to happen, of course, since they were in the middle of nowhere, but Cai's presence allowed Bellicus to fully relax, necessary if he was to get into a deep enough trance that he might pass into the Otherlands and converse with the gods.

Eburus had absolutely no doubt the druid could reach the Otherlands. Everything Bellicus did seemed to be infused with the touch of the gods – from lighting their campfire at night, to fighting, to speaking with kings – it all came so naturally to his giant friend that Eburus could only assume some divine presence was guiding him.

There was a low fire burning in front of the druid, carefully contained by stones so it wouldn't spread out of control. It was very rare, but Bellicus had been taught to be careful, as people occasionally slipped out of their trance and into sleep, waking to find the grass, brush, and trees around them ablaze.

The flames had been used to burn the entrails of a hare Eburus had managed to catch. Bellicus examined the guts for...The Votadini didn't really know what his friend actually thought he would see by staring into that small, red pile but he knew it was an ancient tradition the druids had, looking at things and seeing omens or portents or other signs in the shapes and composition laid out before them.

Eburus was amazed that Cai hadn't tried to eat any of the butchered meat, but the dog was so well trained that he simply lay on the grass watching his master go about his messy business, culminating in the entrails being tossed into the fire, consumed by the flames, the plume of smoke reaching into the sky as a sacrifice to the gods.

And then Eburus saw Bellicus staring into those yellow, dancing flames until, soon enough, a blank look came across the druid's face and it seemed he must have passed into the Otherlands. Eburus wondered what it was like there. Did giants roam about? Beautiful goddesses? Were the colours more vivid, the greens deeper, the orange sun more dazzling, the pale moon clearer and brighter? Were the Otherlands even real, or did they simply exist within the druid's own mind?

Considering this entire ritual was using up time that could have been spent on the road, hunting for Catia and Aife, Eburus hoped and prayed that the Otherlands *were* real, and that Cernunnos or Lug the Light-Bringer or some other god would converse with Bellicus and guide them in the right direction to find the princesses. Otherwise, they could ride in the completely wrong direction and things would not turn out well for any of them.

A spot of rain fell on the Votadini champion's hand and he looked up, surprised, for the sky had been mostly empty of heavy, grey clouds all morning and the air did not have that slightly cool feeling that generally heralded a shower on a day like this. Sure enough, however, a single thunderhead scudded across the sky, covering the sun and making Eburus shiver at the sudden drop in temperature. When he looked back, Bellicus's eyes were open and, for a long moment, the two men simply stared at one another in silence.

Then the druid shook his head and blinked before stretching his neck and arms, as one might do when waking from sleep. "Are you ready to move?"

His voice was low and deep, but carried easily across the meadow to Duro, and Eburus who jumped to his feet, sheathing his blade and starting across the bluebell strewn grass towards the rising druid. "Aye. D'ye know which direction we should go? Did you speak with...anyone?"

Bellicus smiled at the uncertainty of Eburus's question. "Aye," he said, walking across to the nearby stream and thoroughly washing the hare's blood from his hands. The little carcass had been spitted and left to roast gently over the fire while Bellicus was in his trance, so it was quite nicely cooked now, either to be eaten then or wrapped in leaves and packed for later. In truth, there wasn't much eating in it, especially for three large men and a mastiff, and, since no-one had been turning the spit, it was unevenly cooked. So, when the fire had been stamped out and the meat was cool, Bellicus grinned. "Here," he said to Cai. "For being such a good boy."

The dog, who'd been staring intently at the food in his master's hand, bounded across to him, tail wagging furiously as he took it and ate it in a heartbeat.

"That's a good boy," Bellicus repeated, stroking Cai's head lovingly before looking at Eburus and Duro with a confident smile. "We go south, to Kinneil."

"The gods told you that?" The Votadini was already mounted on his horse, eager to resume their journey, while Duro brought Bellicus's animal across and held out the reins for him.

"Aye," the druid confirmed, but he did not elaborate further and that was good enough for Eburus who waited until Bellicus and Duro were seated atop their mounts and they began to move. Eburus knew where Kinneil was, being a Votadini town and a port he'd visited more than once in his life. Cai, hunger sated for a time, happily loped along at their side, as focused as they were on the path ahead.

As they rode, picking their way across the damp grass and through the trees until they reached the main road again, Eburus thought about what Bellicus had said. Clearly, the plan was for them to ride as hard as possible for Kinneil, making it there just in time to find Catia and Aife, or at least meeting them on the road before the Saxons caught up with them.

"You do realise," he said to the druid, "that the princesses will reach Kinneil probably this afternoon? Whereas we still have a couple of days riding before we reach the town, and that's if we push the horses, and Cai."

Bellicus glared at him. "I know," he replied. "But there's nothing else we can do but head there and see what we can do. I'm a druid, but I can't fly, or just magic us there."

They continued riding in silence after that. The rain cloud had passed without emptying its contents all over them, and the day remained sunny and windless, ideal for travelling. Eburus knew Bellicus was right – they couldn't do anything but head for Kinneil and...hope things would turn out for the best. Pray, even. He thought about their destination, wondering if the druid had perhaps been steered in the wrong direction by the gods, or if the druid's decision had even been, truly, inspired by those gods.

There were other places the stolen ship might head for. Closer places, easier for an inexperienced captain to sail to, like Mucrois for example. That would mean more travelling for the girls and their new companions on foot, though, and be much slower than sailing. If there was someone on board who knew what they were doing it would make perfect sense to sail for Kinneil.

So, the gods most likely had steered the druid in the right direction, which was good news.

The fact that they would arrive there a day or two after the stolen ship, however, was not. Eburus looked at his friend, noting the tight frown on Bellicus's face, and realised the giant druid knew very well that their journey was doomed to be a waste of time.

He had heard the stories, from Bel, Duro, and others, about their recent adventures. Indeed, Eburus had been a part of some of them and things had always turned out in the druid's favour. Almost as if the gods were guiding things. Moving Bellicus and his companions, and their enemies, like game-pieces on a Tafl board.

Things just *turned out right* for Bellicus, Warrior Druid of Dun Breatann.

Duro, for his part, seemed content to follow wherever the druid led. There were no questions from the centurion who rode in silence, eyes searching all around for signs of friend or foe in the lands around them.

Eburus turned back to the road ahead, a tight feeling in the pit of his stomach. When they rode from Dunnottar he fully expected to play a major part in the next exciting tale about the druid's adventures – turning up at just the right moment to rescue the girls from danger. Just as Duro had turned up to save Bellicus when he was fighting Horsa, or when druid and centurion had arrived in the nick of time to save Catia from being sacrificed by the crazed *volva,* Thorbjorg. Stories that were told around campfires throughout Britain now, embellished and growing with every retelling. And Eburus had thought his own name would be immortalised in this latest adventure.

Things would not be turning out like that this time though.

Catia, Aife, and Lancelot if he was with them, were on their own.

* * *

"Are you travelling alone?"

Aife raised an eyebrow quizzically at the horse trader's question. "What d'you mean?" she asked. He was leading them, rather too slowly for the princess's liking, around from the front of his stables to a long section at the side where most of his animals were housed.

"Well," the man, who was in his fifties, with a neatly combed beard and bowl-cut brown hair, eyed Lancelot and Catia with a dismissive expression. "It's dangerous travelling without at least a guard. I mean," he continued to walk but looked Aife up and down, and his gaze was now much more appreciative. "An attractive young woman will draw attention from the wrong sort of people, especially out there in the wilderness." He gestured vaguely to the west. "There's a lot of thieves and cut-throats hiding along the old Roman roads, just waiting for folk like you to come by."

Aife rolled her eyes but didn't bother to reply. His words spoke volumes about the state Lancelot was in though. Even a middle-aged horse trader didn't think the swordsman looked much of a threat.

"Well," Catia spoke up as they came to the stalls housing the trader's best animals. Or so he'd claimed anyway. "You'd better make sure and sell us your fastest horses, eh? So we can outrun all those robbers you're talking about." She did not smile, in fact her eyes were hard and so was her tone, and the trader looked at her somewhat nervously, surprised to hear such a young girl speaking both freely and confidently. There was an undertone of threat in her words, as if she was warning him there would be repercussions should he try to cheat them in any way.

The man nodded, looking from Catia to Lancelot, who remained silent, and back to Aife. "Don't worry. I have just the right mounts for you three. Fast and strong—"

"And expensive, no doubt," Aife muttered, opening the stall door they were standing outside and hurrying in to examine the animal within. She checked it over quickly, knowing that every moment wasted meant their pursuers grew closer to catching them. The horse looked powerful and its coat was smooth and glossy. She nodded. "This one will do. Have your stablehands make her ready to leave immediately, we're in a great hurry. Show me the next one."

The trader grinned, knowing he had three sales virtually guaranteed now. Lancelot might be dressed like a beggar while smelling oddly like a woman, but the two girls wore fine clothing and surely had plenty of valuable goods to barter with. "Of course, my lady," the man nodded, walking quickly along to the third stall where a black pony stood watching them placidly. "For the young one," said the trader, smiling at Catia, who pushed past him and inspected the animal as the others moved on again to see the horse earmarked for Lancelot.

"Looks like a tired old thing," growled the swordsman, not even opening the stall door to come to his conclusion.

"True," the trader agreed readily enough. "This one is not as sturdy, or as expensive as the others. I assumed," looking slightly puzzled, he said to Aife, "that you would want a less expensive animal to carry your slave, my lady."

"We don't have time for this," Catia shouted. She was mounted on her horse and staring back towards the docks, her higher vantage point allowing her to see that their Saxon pursuers had come ashore and were actively searching for them amongst the workers and locals. "Get him a horse as good as the other two, now!"

The horse-trader blanched for, although Catia was only eleven years old, she carried the authority of a princess in her voice and demeanour. Still, the man looked to Aife for confirmation. She nodded irritably and the trader hurried on, gesturing for Lancelot to follow. The next horse he showed them was chestnut brown, tall, sturdy, and clearly perfect for their needs.

"We'll take it," Aife said as Lancelot went into the stall and began to prepare his new mount for departure.

Soon enough all three horses were in the yard and ready to ride, the trader's eyes gleaming as he waited to be paid. Catia and Lancelot were mounted, their horses feeling their riders' anxiety and standing somewhat skittishly as Aife rummaged in the sack of goods they'd stolen from the Saxon ship.

"Hurry up," Catia muttered, eyes wide, hand touching the hilt of her sword. The trader frowned, eyeing her, then Lancelot who was also staring towards the docks.

"Don't ask," Aife told him in a hard tone as she drew out an exquisite golden fish from the sack of items she'd taken from the Saxons' ship. "Aye, there are men coming after us. Sea-wolves." He stepped back, as if to distance himself from them, but then his desire to take the princess's payment overcame his fear of the Saxons and he reached out, taking the heavy fish and examining it closely. Aife did not wait for him to complete his assessment of the piece – it had likely decorated a very powerful nobleman's saddle at some point and she knew it more than covered the three horses. She jumped easily up onto her horse's back and stroked the animal's neck, leaning forward to speak softly to it, trying to form a bond as quickly as possible. "All right?" she asked, eyes boring into the trader.

Although he was plainly nervous now that he knew there were Saxons in Kinneil, he was more than happy with the golden fish ornament and he nodded in satisfaction. "Aye, lady, this will do nicely."

"Good," said Aife, looking at Catia and Lancelot who nudged their mounts into a walk towards the yard's exit. "You should know, that fish came from the Saxon ship, so you might want to hide it before the bastards turn up looking for us."

"What?" he exploded, glaring from her to the valuable trinket in his hands. "Wait, I—"

"We're not returning the horses to you," Aife called over her shoulder. "It would be a death sentence for us. Just you hide that ornament and, when the sea-wolves come here, tell them we stole your animals and rode off to the south, back to Lancelot's homeland."

"But..." The man's deflated cry trailed off as he realised that, if he wanted paid for his steeds he'd need to hang onto the stolen fish and make sure the Saxons didn't take it back from him. And then his frown turned to amazement as he recognised the name of Lancelot.

"They're here!" Catia was at the front of the mounted trio, and the first to spot armoured men, helmets and naked sword blades glinting in the sunlight as they ran towards the stables. Someone in town had told the Saxons where to find the girls and their skinny companion. "What do we do?"

"Remain calm," Lancelot called, urging his horse into a trot and taking up a position slightly ahead of Catia, drawing his sword as he did so. "We'll need to get through them to reach the town gates and on to the road. Stay behind me, both of you."

Catia's face was deathly white but she gripped her reins and followed Lancelot's command, allowing him to take point as they approached the screaming, grinning, Saxon warriors. There were at least five or six heading in their direction, with two out in front, ahead of their comrades.

Lancelot held his horse in a controlled gallop and Aife came up just behind him on his left side. Both had their swords drawn, both had their eyes fixed on the threat on the road in front of them.

The closest Saxon was a slim man, lithe and young, and he slowed his run, moving into a more defensive stance as the horses came towards him. His eyes shone as he pictured the glory this battle would bring him, and he opened his mouth to roar a battle-cry, lifting his arms wide and shaking the vicious-looking axes he held in either hand.

"Don't let him hit the horse," Aife shouted. "If he does, we'll never get away."

Lancelot didn't reply but, as he galloped forward, he transferred his sword to his left hand and, in a smooth, practised motion, drew out a knife from somewhere near his ankle and, taking less than a heartbeat to aim, threw it at the grinning Saxon.

It wasn't the greatest throw for the knife was unfamiliar to Lancelot, having been given to him by Aife, but the enemy warrior was forced to turn and dodge to the side, the missile harmlessly clattering against the blade of one of his axes. And then Lancelot's horse was beside him and the blond rider's sword licked out, drawing a long, deep slice across the Saxon's neck and up across his bearded face.

There was a terrible scream and the man dropped one of his axes, reaching up to his ruined neck to try and hold the skin together. Catia stared as she rode past, amazed at the amount of blood that was already coursing down the enemy's hand and arm.

Lancelot and Catia, both on the right side of the road, raced past the dying Saxon but Aife, on the left, was forced to pull back on her mount's reins, halting the animal abruptly. She had a knife, but she knew, in the instant she had to think about it, that copying Lancelot's trick would be both incredibly difficult, and probably futile. Even if she managed to strike the warrior facing her, he was holding a shield and clad in thick leather armour. His helmet would surely turn a thrown knife too.

The warrior's spear was pointed directly at her and she knew her horse would shy away from it so, faced with no real choices, she slowed almost to a stop, then threw her leg across the animal's back and jumped onto the road, letting go of the reins as she walked steadily towards the Saxon.

He stared at her, wary after watching his companion cut down so easily by Lancelot, but his confidence grew as Aife shook out her long, lustrous hair. This simple emphasis on her femininity seemed to make the Saxon relax somewhat, as if she was suddenly much less of a threat. The point of his spear lowered and he watched her approach, unwilling to attack yet, and wary of the two riders who were behind him now.

"You think you're a warrior?" Aife spat as she walked, reaching up to pull her hair back again. It was an old trick the druidess Ria had taught her, and it usually worked well. Men could be so easily distracted at times. "Draw your sword and fight me like one then, Saxon scum."

"Hurry!" Catia shouted, and Aife well understood the girl's anxiety, for the rest of the sea-wolves were closing now.

"I am a warrior," the Saxon facing Aife said in the tongue of the Britons. "And I will take you back to the ship as my slave." He was angered by the princess's insult, but attracted to her at the same time and he dropped his spear, drawing his sword expertly from its brown leather sheath.

Aife was upon him in that instant, hammering her blade sideways at his torso. He wasn't just bigger and older than his slashed comrade though, he was faster too, and he managed to parry the Pictish woman's attack easily.

"Come and be my—" He broke off his sentence and lunged forward with his left hand, aiming a haymaker at Aife, but she nimbly swayed out of the way of his meaty fist, cutting downwards with her sword, into the side of his calf. The blade bit deep and he screamed, falling onto his belly, eyes staring at her in horror but not quite beaten yet as he lashed out in a fury, trying to catch his opponent's feet with his sword.

She expected that, however, and jumped over the wild attack before plunging her blade down through his back and into the road beneath. The Saxon shuddered for a time, a horrible gurgling coming from his mouth as blood filled it and pooled out beneath his face.

"Come on!" Catia screamed, gesturing wildly and Aife didn't even stop to catch her breath, simply dragged her blood-soaked sword out of his body and thrust it into its scabbard before running back to jump onto her horse.

"Go," Lancelot said to Catia, gesturing towards the road which led to the west. The girl, seeing her friend galloping towards them, did as she was ordered. Lancelot, sword still in his hand, waited for Aife to ride past him, nodding in response to her wide, relieved smile.

"*Waelisc hund*!" Four or more of the enemy were sprinting along the road now, almost upon them, faces twisted in rage as they saw their kinsmen lying dead on the ground. "Fight us," they cried at Lancelot as he turned his horse, watching them over his shoulder. "Fight us, you dog!"

Lancelot merely stared at them, not recognising a single one of them and realising they must be the crew of the second ship, not the one captained by Leofdaeg and Sigarr. That pair, and their crew, would surely be along soon enough however, demanding mounts from the unfortunate horse-trader that they might continue the chase.

A hand-axe whistled past Lancelot's head, making him duck and curse in shock, but it missed its target and his horse was running like the wind, carrying him to safety behind Catia and Aife and, for now, they were free.

"We must ride as hard as we can," he shouted over the thundering of hooves as he edged closer to the two princesses. "At least some of those bastards will find horses and be after us soon enough."

Catia did not reply, her mouth was set in a tight line, and she stared straight ahead as if willing Dun Breatann to come to them.

"Nice throw," Aife shouted to Lancelot, still pleased by their victory.

"Aye," he agreed, and now that they were clear for at least a time he allowed himself a small smile. "But that was my only knife. I won't be using that trick the next time they catch us."

Aife's grin faded and she eyed Catia with a more worried expression. "There won't be any next time," she said grimly, trying to soothe the younger girl's obvious fear. "By the time they get horses we'll be long gone and past tracking. We're free, my friends. Free!"

They were not, though, and all three of them knew it.

CHAPTER SEVENTEEN

The miles passed quickly for the three riders. The horse-trader had been fair with them, and sold them healthy animals which were, so far at least, able to maintain a good, steady pace without trouble. They actually saw two of Lancelot's fellow ex-slaves ahead on the road, but on hearing the thundering hooves the men sprinted into the trees in a panic and were lost to view.

"How long will it take to get to Dun Breatann?" Lancelot asked. His skin was flushed from the air rushing past them but it made him look more healthy, more alive, than at any point since the princesses had met him.

"We'll need to slow our pace soon," Catia said. "Or risk injuring or wearing out our horses." She reached out and patted her mount's neck. "After that, er…" She looked at Aife, realising she had no idea how far Kinneil was from her home.

"We should get there tomorrow night, or the following morning," Aife said. "I worked it out when we were on the ship. I'm not certain how far it is, but the Roman wall will guide us and provide better terrain to travel on than fields."

Catia's eyes lit up at the mention of the wall. "Ah, I know where we are now then, my tutor gave me lessons on the wall and the forts along it. You're right, it should only be a couple of day's ride back to Dun Breatann, and the Saxons might not want to come after us for the people in the settlements along the way will be hostile to them."

"What's your tutor like?" Lancelot asked, seeing an opportunity to divert the girl's attention from their predicament. "I bet you hate him, eh? I know I didn't like mine at your age, although, when I got older I realised he was not that bad really. Some of my friends had much worse teachers to deal with when they were little."

Aife, who was at the front of the group, took this as the cue to slow their pace, from a canter to more of a walk. It was too hard trying to have a conversation over the stamping of hooves and whistling wind and she, like Lancelot, felt chatting would do Catia good. If it had been any other group of people chasing them – Dalriadans, Picts, Selgovae, whatever – Aife believed her young friend would have dealt with things more stoically. The Saxons seemed to trigger such an intense, uncontrollable fear within the girl though.

"No, he's all right," Catia said, screwing up her face, the expression belying her words. "Most of the time." Something caught her attention and she glanced back in the direction of Kinneil, face growing pale as she saw five dark shapes behind them. "They're still coming after us," she mumbled, looking at Aife in horror. "How? How can they have caught up with us already? That trader told us these were his fastest horses!"

Aife shrugged, shading her eyes with her hand and straining to make out details of the riders coming along the road behind them. "Merchants lie," she said. "That's how they make a profit. Never trust them. Don't panic, Catia, we have a head start and not that far to go. Besides," she stared at the girl grimly, "there's only five of them."

Catia smiled nervously at that, for, although it was surely supposed to be a jest, Aife and Lancelot would be at least somewhat of a match for the men coming after them, despite the difference in numbers. She fixed her gaze on the Saxons – she was quite sure that's who the riders were – and tried to pick out details, perhaps see if she recognised any of them from their brief time in Dunnottar.

"Is that a woman?" It was Lancelot who asked the question. "In the middle, with the grey. Look how she sits on her mount, more like, well," he nodded in the direction of Aife and Catia, "you two, than the rest of the folk there. A woman, with four men."

There was a sudden cry from the riders behind them and it seemed to confirm Lancelot's suggestion that one of them was not a man. The cry rose in volume, changing from a simple long, held screech, to an ululating sound that made the hairs rise on the back of Aife's neck.

"Lug protect me," Catia said with a shudder, gripping the reins so hard that Aife half-expected the whitening skin to split on the girl's knuckles. "It's Thorbjorg!"

Lancelot frowned. "The *volva*?"

"Aye," Catia said. "You know her?"

"We burned an effigy of her during the Battle of Nant Beac," he replied, mouth twitching in amusement at the memory. "Merlin made it out of wood and clay. One of Horsa too. Quite good likenesses. We burned them! It really frightened the Saxon army and helped us beat them." He looked away from the following riders, back at Catia. "Why would she be chasing us? Why would she even be here?"

"She wants to sacrifice me," the girl whispered, eyes still fixed on the grey-cloaked figure coming after them who started her eerie, ululating screeching again.

"How would she have found you?" Aife demanded, becoming annoyed at her friend now. "Enough is enough, Catia. You're frightening yourself for no reason."

"I am not," the girl retorted, angered herself by Aife's hard tone. "Listen to her, she's casting a spell. Why else would the warriors have brought her with them?"

"Maybe she's a good fighter," Lancelot suggested coolly. "Like you two."

"Maybe she is," Catia nodded, still irritated. "But she's a witch. It's Thorbjorg and if she catches us we'll all suffer much worse than simply being run through by a sword or having our heads smashed in with an axe in the fight."

Lancelot shrugged. "You're right. I saw her slaughtering some of our prisoners before that battle. We just need to make sure they don't catch up with us then."

On they rode, not pushing the horses too hard, knowing it could be a death sentence for them all if one of the animals was injured or driven to exhaustion. The Saxons closed the gap but, as night began to fall there was nothing to do other than stop and rest.

"We can't sleep," Catia said fearfully, constantly checking back to see how far away their pursuers were although the terrain had long since hidden the Saxons and the road behind. "They'll sneak up on us."

"Listen," Aife said, shaking her head and dismounting. "We need to let the horses rest. Drink, and eat something. The Saxons will have to do the same, and one of us will keep watch all through the night."

Catia still sat atop her mount, staring backwards, but all they could see were trees.

"Were there any dogs with them?" Lancelot asked, his voice gentle and reassuring. "I didn't notice any. So, even if they continue to ride after us while we're camped here, they won't know where we are and they'll go right past. You don't need to worry. Come on." He jumped down and his legs gave way as he landed.

Catia stared at him, then she hastily dismounted and ran to him. "Are you all right? What's wrong?"

"He's tired," Aife said, also coming to help Lancelot back to his feet. "This is why we have to rest. We're all at the point of exhaustion, and he's not in the best physical condition so he's feeling it worse than us. Follow me, there's a stream we can use for water just over there, and hopefully somewhere decent to shelter for the night. It'll rain soon."

Lancelot was on his feet now, shaking his head and sucking in long breaths. He gave Catia a smile but his face was drawn and it was obvious he couldn't go on without at least a few hours' sleep and some food.

On foot, they led their horses off the main track and into the trees to the south. The ground sloped gently upwards here and, as they came to the top of the rise, they were glad to see there was a shallow depression on the other side where they could camp and be completely hidden from anyone on the road.

"This'll do nicely," said Aife and her smile was not a pretence, she was genuinely happy with their campsite and the thought of some time off her mount's swaying back. "The trees make a natural canopy to keep the worst of the rain off and the ground is soft. Not as soft as your mattress in Dun Breatann, Catia, but not too bad, eh?"

Catia's mouth rose at the edges but it was more of a grimace than a smile. She did set about making her horse comfortable though, letting it drink from the stream and then rubbing her down before tethering her securely to a tree for the night. The horse happily nibbled on the short grass while Catia went to take care of Lancelot's horse. He was so tired he'd just sat down on a boulder and began polishing off a chunk of bread and some cheese from the pack Aife had brought.

When the horses were settled the princesses joined Lancelot and helped themselves to some of the food, eating with gusto for they were both starving. Catia had filled an empty skin with the water from the stream which they found to be clear and refreshing and, sated, the three just sat or lay back on the grass and let their aches and stresses of the day fade away as much as possible. Aife's prediction of rain proved correct and it started not long after their meal, both a blessing – for it would hamper those coming after them and make their trail even harder to follow – and a curse, for the leaves on the trees didn't do all that much to stop it coming down on them.

Lancelot soon fell asleep beneath the branches of a large beech and the girls set about finding long sticks and grass to fashion a hasty and very makeshift shelter over him. There was little doubt he would, in normal circumstances, be mortified to lie resting while two princesses did their best to keep him warm and dry, but the three of them would enjoy the benefits of the shelter for they could all take a turn to sleep beneath it.

It took longer than expected because they didn't want to use their swords and knives to hack at the branches, or to make too much noise snapping them in case the Saxons, who must surely be fairly close, heard them. Eventually, however, they had tied plenty together and set them on a frame over Lancelot before using mud to fill the gaps and make the simple roof waterproof.

"I'm quite proud of that," Aife grinned, and Catia was happier too, the task having helped take her mind off things. "You get under there beside him, there's enough room, and get some sleep, all right? I'll keep watch."

"If you hear anything you wake us, Aife, promise?"

"I promise," the warrior-woman nodded. "No-one will sneak up on us, especially in this weather. Just you pull that cloak of yours around you as a blanket and get to sleep. I'll wake Lancelot after a couple of hours, and then he'll wake you for your turn. Make sure you stay alert."

"Oh, don't worry, I will," Catia replied grimly. "I'm so on edge I doubt I'll get any sleep at all."

Aife nodded and, once she was sure the girl was comfortable, she walked away, hand on the hilt of her sword, to patrol the perimeter of their camp and make sure she didn't also nod off. Catia was soon fast asleep, proving just how much of a toll recent events had taken on her, and Aife was glad. Strangely, despite the proximity of a Saxon warband who wanted to capture or kill them, the princess felt very alive. In fact, had Lancelot been in decent condition, she might even have suggested going out to hunt down their enemies.

The rain continued, lessening slightly after a time, and Aife, hood down so she could hear better, stalked in a circle around the camp, alert but quite content. They might reach the safety of Dun Breatann tomorrow, and then…The gods knew what would happen after that, but at least they'd be alive.

CHAPTER EIGHTEEN

Lancelot felt surprisingly strong, given his recent lifestyle and the events of the past couple of days. The food Aife had brought for their escape from Dunnottar was far better quality than his Saxon captors had been feeding him and, along with that and the couple of hours sleep he'd managed to grab beneath the hastily constructed shelter, he was feeling fitter than he had in a long time. Of course, the psychological boost that being a free man brought probably played a big part in his current state of wellbeing.

And the sword at his waist truly made the blond warrior feel like he was back in charge of his own destiny, rather than being pushed hither and thither by whatever wyrd Jarl Leofdaeg decided to weave for him.

Still, he did not *look* like the noble warrior he'd been before. Not yet. If he did, maybe they could stop at some nearby settlement and ask the people there for aid in fighting their pursuers. As it was, with him looking like a bedraggled thrall, and Catia just a child, he knew no-one would want to support them against a group of marauding Saxons. They would just have to take their chances on the road.

He smiled as he looked at the two princesses fast asleep in their shelter. They were quite different in some ways, but both had a similar desire to succeed in whatever task they put their minds to, a trait of their royal bloodlines perhaps. Certainly, they'd come together to make a rather ramshackle-looking shelter, but it was proving to be more than adequate for its task, keeping the rain from those resting underneath. Lancelot had been amazed, and pleased, to find himself dry when Aife woke him up for his turn to stand guard. He'd known it would rain and fully expected to be quite sodden when roused from his slumber, but the girls had taken good care of him. He'd already felt very protective of them both, and his admiration for them grew with every passing hour he spent in their company.

The rain had eased, but it was still quite chilly and he would have liked to set a small fire, both for warmth and to heat some food for himself but the Saxons were out there somewhere. He stood up, staring out into the dark woods around them, senses straining for any hint of danger. A fox had come past earlier, hoping for food, but it had slunk off when it saw the man watching it.

There was a sudden, shrill cry from somewhere to the east, and not too far away. Lancelot's sword was out in an instant, although he was sure it was merely the earlier fox, or perhaps its mate, for the sound was feral and wild. He looked at the shelter and saw Catia staring at him. Aife was also awake but unmoving, lying in the gloom listening for whatever had roused them. No-one spoke, although the horses snorted, ears tipped forward stiffly, clearly frightened by the eerie noise.

It came again, shattering the darkness, and now they all knew this was no fox, for there was a word – unknown to any of them, harsh and eldritch in nature – within the sound.

"It's Thorbjorg," Catia said, jumping to her feet and grasping the pommel of her sword spasmodically. "She's near. We have to go. Now!"

"Wait," murmured Aife, placing a hand on the younger girl's arm as she started walking towards the spooked horses. "Just listen, and think about what's happening before we react."

The breeze stirring the leaves was the only sound apart from the occasional snort or soft stamp from one of the horses, and, as they stood listening, Lancelot saw the tension visibly ease from Catia as the youngster forced herself to be calm.

"They don't know where we are," Aife said softly but quite firmly, as if she knew her words to be true. "It's a trick. They want us back on the road, riding hard for Dun Breatann, so they can ambush us. The *volva* is behind us, driving us forward, like boys drive game towards a party of hunters waiting with their spears and bows."

Lancelot came closer so he could keep his own voice low, unheard by anyone nearby. "I'd say she's right," he said. "And that means some of the Saxons are ahead of us. They'll have kept going after we stopped, and overtaken us in order to lay this trap."

"What do we do, then?" Catia asked in clipped tones.

The woman screeched again, now even closer, but to the south, proving to Lancelot that they were right, and their pursuers had only a vague idea of where they were camping and wanted to smoke them out with their witch's cries.

"All we have to do is avoid them," Aife said quietly, scanning the shadows all around. "I say we head north for a bit, stay off the road, and then turn back west. They'll be waiting for us to pass, but we'll be miles away."

Catia thought about that, frowning. "Maybe that's their plan," she said. "They *want* us to think they've laid an ambush on the road, so we avoid it."

"We could second-guess them all night," Lancelot growled. "From the screeching, we know the *volva* is to the south, so I agree with Aife: we head north."

"The moon is up," Catia argued. "If there's no trees to the north, we'll show up to anyone watching."

"What, then?" Aife asked, patience wearing thin as evidenced by her clipped tones. "Sit here all night, frightened? Pray?"

"No," Catia said, in a similar harsh voice, drawing her sword and stooping to smear the blade with mud and moss so it wouldn't glint in the moonlight and give away her position. "I say we go south and find the Saxon witch. We all agree her screaming is to drive us towards something. So why don't we head for her, and deal with her once and for all."

Lancelot and Aife turned to one another uncertainly.

"Not so long ago you were terrified of her," the warrior-woman said.

"Aye," Catia nodded fervently, and her teeth were bared. "But, like you told me, we all have to face our fears at some point, instead of trying to run from them. If we kill the *volva* the Saxons might lose heart."

"That's probably true," said Lancelot. "At least to an extent. They do place a lot of stock in their wise women, just as we do our druids, and the Christians their priests."

"You're willing to do this?" Aife asked the younger girl. "Kill a *volva*? You're not worried about the bad luck it might bring? I would be."

"Bad luck?" Catia spat. "That bitch would have cut my throat if Bel and Duro hadn't turned up. Her gods aren't mine, and I don't fear them. Yes, harming a witch can make one fate-marked. My own father, King Coroticus, killed a druid and, well, things didn't turn out well for him. But, as I say, the Saxons' gods and goddesses aren't mine, and they haven't any power in our lands, other than what we allow them. Well, I won't let Thorbjorg hold any power over me."

As if on cue the high-pitched, unearthly shriek split the night air again, this time back to the east, behind them.

"All right," Lancelot shrugged, taking out his sword and dulling the metal's shine as Catia had done. "I'm always ready for a mission like this."

"Any warrior should be," Aife agreed. "And killing the Saxon warleader's own personal seer, the most powerful of all their *volur*, will bring us much glory if we survive."

"Leave the horses," Catia said, somehow taking charge despite her youth, inexperience, and earlier nervousness. "We'll move much more quietly on foot, and we can come back to get them once the witch is dealt with."

"Listen," Lancelot said, all jocularity gone from his demeanour. He gestured with his fingers, drawing his two companions in close. "This is going to be dangerous. The *volva* is experienced with a blade, she knows where to cut someone to do the most damage – all these types do. And whatever we might think of Thunor, and Wotan, and Frigg, and the rest of the Saxon gods, we all understand the power people like Thorbjorg can wield."

"I'll be careful," Catia said.

"Good, but I'm not just talking to you. I will lead," he held up his left hand, silencing any protests. "I'm the most experienced by far. I've taken part in raids like this before, and always come out them alive." He didn't mention his last raid, the one on Garrianum, which had seen his entire warband wiped out and him taken into slavery.

Catia did not argue – she was but eleven summers old after all, and knew she was not the right person to lead – and Aife, although she seemed inclined to speak out at first, quickly decided this wasn't worth wasting time over. Lancelot's name was known throughout Britain, from one end to the other. He was the right-hand man, champion and closest advisor, after the Merlin, to Arthur, war-leader of the Britons.

"Lead on then," the warrior-woman said with a small smile, and Lancelot nodded gladly, turning and moving east, in the last direction they'd last heard the witch's blood-curdling scream come from.

In response to his gestures Catia went a few paces to his left while Aife took a position on the right. They moved at a steady pace, looking out for dry branches that might snap and warn Thorbjorg of their approach, and, soon enough they reached the end of the treeline, looking out onto the moonlit remains of the cobbled Roman road. All three crouched, staring into the gloom, eyes, noses, and ears probing the night for any sign of their quarry.

The *volva* must have been growing impatient for there soon came another of her weird, throaty screeches. As before, silence seemed to swallow the land when the cry faded away, as if the animals and insects, even the trees, had been terrified into silence by the bizarre sound.

She was close. Very close.

Lancelot pointed into the trees and nodded, moving towards the spot in a crouch, sword held ready as his companions followed his lead, maintaining the distance between themselves as they went.

The cry had come from a spot very near to where they'd been camping, and where the horses yet remained. Lancelot wondered if this was a really bad idea. Surely Thorbjorg wasn't just blundering about in the dark here, moving in and out of the trees, all by herself. She would need a guard at least. There was nothing else to do now, though, they had set their plan in motion and—

"Hai!" A guttural, Germanic cry tore the silence into tatters and Lancelot instinctively raised his sword in the direction of the shout, grunting as a shockwave ran through the blade and into his arm. Sparks lit the darkness for just a moment and then there was a thump and the dark shape that had accosted Lancelot was thrown sideways, against a tree trunk. Aife had kicked the attacker, but she was beset herself now by some other enemy. Lancelot thrust the point of his sword into the man by the tree, feeling it bite home, not deeply but enough to elicit an anguished scream.

Before the stabbed Saxon could right himself Lancelot saw the small figure of Catia dart behind the man and the tip of the girl's sword poked against the front of the enemy's chainmail vest. She'd cut right through the enemy's back and torso, the metal armour only doing enough to stop it erupting out the other side.

Lancelot sprang away, towards Aife who was trading blows with another Saxon. She was holding her own but the darkness made everything a confused blur. Lancelot ran at the man, thundering into him and sending him sprawling. The Saxon rolled and was on his feet in an instant but Aife's foot lashed out, catching him square in the face and, again, the man fell onto the ground. This time Lancelot hacked down, once, twice, three times, each time cutting deeply into the downed warrior until at last he knew the Saxon would not be getting up again.

"No!" Catia appeared again, flitting between Lancelot and Aife like a white-faced wood-spirit, slashing her sword through the air at yet another foe.

Lancelot turned to see a woman, eyes blazing like some nocturnal fire, facing them. She was clad in a hooded robe which might once have been white but was now grey and encrusted with what looked like bloodstains. Not her blood though: Lancelot's racing mind told him it was blood from a myriad of victims, human sacrifices the *volva* had made to her gods. How disgusting, thought the swordsman, that she wore the filth as a matter of pride.

"In the name of Wotan," screeched the Saxon witch, pointing her weapon – the stone-bladed knife which Catia's searching sword had just managed to divert from Lancelot's back. "I—"

"You will do nothing!" Aife bellowed, sword-hand flashing out, fist slamming into the *volva*'s temple and sending her reeling back. Again the witch opened her mouth, although she looked dazed. "Shut up, woman," Aife said, this time in a more controlled tone, but the next blow she landed was, if anything, even more brutal than the first one. The *volva* collapsed like a dropped sack of flour and didn't move or try to cast any more spells.

"Leave her, Catia," Aife said, touching the younger girl lightly on the arm. "She's no threat to us now. Killing anyone when they're unconscious would be dishonourable, but even more so when the victim's the Saxon equivalent of a druidess. I know this woman, Thorbjorg, did you great evil, but…"

"It's not her," came the soft, almost disappointed reply. "Thorbjorg, I mean. It's just someone that looks like her. One of the other *volur*. A younger one."

Lancelot breathed deeply, finally feeling as though the danger had passed, for a moment at least. "That's a shame," he said. "I'd have liked to see Thorbjorg being put on her arse for what she did to the prisoners at Nant Beac. But, no matter, we have to go. Remember there were at least five of them behind us, and we've only dealt with three here. Two more are still out there, possibly more if others from their ships found horses, so remain alert."

Aife had stripped the two dead Saxons of any valuables, but she hesitated at the unconscious *volva*. Catia, mouth set in a line, stepped past her friend and knelt on the ground, watching the witch for any signs of movement, hands rummaging in the woman's cloak.

"Bellicus keeps valuable spices and things in—" She broke off, finding what she was looking for in a pouch tied around the *volva*'s waist. She untied it and tossed it to Aife who, rather gingerly, as if the thing might contain the stolen souls of dead victims, looped it around her own sword-belt for later examination. Then Catia lifted the dropped stone knife and shuddered. "How many lives has this abomination taken?" she muttered. "How many men, women, and children?" Her teeth came together and she put the wicked, grey blade up against the *volva*'s neck.

Aife did not say anything. They might be doing the world a service by killing the witch, but it would surely bring bad luck on them all.

"May your powers die along with this accursed weapon," Catia spat, getting up and walking over to one of the dead men. There was an axe looped through his belt and the girl pulled it out, then she found a flat rock, placed the stone dagger on it, and smashed the axe-blade down into it. The metal proved stronger and the dagger shattered in two. For good measure, Catia bent over, took one section, and hurled it deep into the trees. The other piece she left for the *volva* to find when she came back from her trip to the Otherlands.

"Done?" Lancelot asked in a neutral tone.

Catia wiped sweat from her forehead and nodded.

"Let's go then. Back to the horses."

They headed west again, returning to their earlier camp. Another shock awaited them there, for two of the animals they'd bought from the horse-trader were gone, and only one remained.

"Shit," Lancelot exclaimed as he stared at the empty patch of grass where his mount had been. "The sounds of fighting must have spooked them and they ran off, probably back to the stables in Kinneil." He inspected the tree which his horse had been tethered to, noting a recently snapped branch. "I wouldn't be surprised if the merchant had trained the beasts to return to him any chance they got!"

Catia's horse was the only one remaining, for it seemed Aife's had similarly escaped from where she'd tethered it. "This is going to make our journey home even longer," said the young princess dully.

Aife reached out and put her arm around Catia's shoulders, squeezing her affectionately for just a moment. The smaller girl looked up and smiled gratefully but there was something different in her eyes now. Another part of her childhood had been burned away this night, another layer of innocence evaporating along with the souls of the men they'd killed.

Lancelot watched them sadly for it was always a painful thing to see a child suffering. One thing was certain, though: Catia had proved herself tonight – not to Lancelot, or Aife, but to herself. The next time the girl faced an enemy she would not panic.

Taranis help the other Saxons if they stumbled across them that night, or anywhere else on the road back to Dun Breatann.

"Well," he said. "Since you're apparently the only one who knows how to tether a horse properly, it's only right you get first ride on it. Come on, we'll have to make do as best we can."

CHAPTER NINETEEN

"Look, we have to be careful. The people won't take much more of your aggression, Leofdaeg. They'll snap eventually and then we'll be in trouble." Sigarr snorted mirthlessly and took another sip of his ale. "As if we weren't in enough already."

Leofdaeg's lip curled. "Pah, these folk are nothing more than sailors and dock-workers. There's not a warrior amongst them."

"Don't be foolish," Sigarr warned. "They might not have stood up to us yet, but that's not through fear of fighting us. It's more from fear of others of our kin turning up and destroying their town."

"And they *should* be fearful of that happening," Leofdaeg growled, but his boast was cut-off before he could say anymore.

"Should they?" Sigarr demanded of his fellow jarl. "And who will command these armies of Jutes, and Saxons, and Angles, who will come here? You?" For once the little man was visibly furious and he slammed his hand down on the table. "Hengist and Horsa are so far above you, Leofdaeg, that they might as well sit amongst the gods." His ire would have been more impressive if he hadn't started to wheeze as he became more stressed, but he continued on, forcing out the words as he hammered home his point. "*I* am leading this mission, Leofdaeg, never forget it. I am cousin to Hengist, and I have his authority to make the alliance with Drest, or to offer him mercenaries for his army. You are along as a mere courtesy, and because you and your men needed experience. I've let you act as you pleased until now, but I'm warning you: Stop goading the people of Kinneil, and, once the men return from hunting the princesses, we pay for what we've taken, and leave in peace. Do you understand?"

Leofdaeg scowled at him. He believed himself more of a warrior, even with the arm that Lancelot had ruined, than Sigarr, and it rankled that he was forced to bow to the smaller man's wishes. But it was true, Sigarr was closely related to the *bretwalda* and Leofdaeg feared their war-leader's wrath. Not to mention Horsa…

"Aye, fine," Leofdaeg muttered, looking away and shoving another piece of burnt fish into his mouth. "Whatever you say. I just want to return south with my ship, my trade profits, and Lancelot in irons again. The girls will merely be a nice extra."

"Good," Sigarr said, his wheeze noticeably improving. "Then remain here in this hovel, and do not abuse the locals. I'll go and see if there's any sign of our men returning."

Leofdaeg nodded sourly, but then he smirked and said, "You should see the *volva* about those breathing problems of yours. It's quite bad. Must really hinder you in a fight."

"Not as much as that bent arm of yours," Sigarr retorted, uncharacteristically angry at the other jarl's jibe. He lifted his cloak from where it lay over the back of a chair, threw it on, tying it around his neck, then, without another word, went outside.

It was sunny, although clouds periodically scudded past, throwing the town into shadow and lowering the temperature. It hadn't rained yet, however, and Sigarr looked around, breathing deeply of the fresh, river air with its mingled scents of fish and wood-smoke. It seemed to do his lungs good and he allowed himself to become calm after the confrontation with Leofdaeg. The barb about his wheezing had struck home, for it had been an issue all of Sigarr's life and there seemed to be no cure for it. Some days it was worse than others and, when he had asked a *volva* about it – Thorbjorg herself, no less – all she could suggest was some crazy old Roman remedy which involved drinking owl's blood mixed with wine.

He'd rather suffocate than force a concoction like that down his neck, although Thorbjorg had gleefully offered to mix it for him.

Sigarr pushed those memories aside and thought about their current predicament. They'd been in the town for two days now and it was wearing, spending so much time with Leofdaeg. They'd been met by the other Saxon ship during the chase and shouted across to its captain, telling him what was happening. The man, a grizzled old sea-wolf named Tata, had laughed at them for losing their own ship to a couple of girls, but he'd gladly joined the chase. Tata's faster vessel had come to the docks ahead of Siggar and Leofdaeg, and some of the crew had immediately started the hunt for Catia, Aife, Lancelot and the other escaped slaves.

When two of Tata's men were killed in the initial fight outside the stables, the captain had been furious, taking the rest of the horse-trader's animals, five of them, and giving them to his crew members to continue the chase. He himself returned to his ship with the remainder of his crew and waited to tell Sigarr what had transpired once his borrowed Pictish currach had docked.

Sigarr sighed as he thought of it. Two more Saxons dead at the hands of these *Waelisc* troublemakers. Were they worth the hassle? Lancelot certainly was not, to Sigarr anyway, but Leofdaeg would not rest until his pet was returned to him, and he could once again abuse his father's killer – the man who'd also ruined his sword-arm. The princesses were far more valuable prizes in Sigarr's eyes, and so he'd been happy to send three of Leofdaeg's crew out to also join in the hunt. It had taken a while to find another three horses and threaten their owners into giving the Saxons the animals, but, eventually, those warriors had been able to ride westwards, following Tata's five crewmates along the course of the wall built by the Roman, Antoninus.

Sigarr did not go, for he was not as good a fighter as the other men, and Leofdaeg could barely ride these days thanks to his arm. They'd remained in Kinneil with Tata although, while Sigarr and Leofdaeg had demanded use of a house near the docks from the local headman, Tata preferred to spend his nights on board his ship.

So the time had passed, with Tata and his skeleton crew doing repairs to their vessel during daylight hours, and sleeping on board at night. Sigarr wandered about the town, talking to those who could understand his version of their tongue, trying to change Votadini views of Saxons as vicious, violent fools.

Leofdaeg, of course, had done his best to live up to that reputation, strutting around as if he was some mighty jarl, taking what food and drink he wanted from the vendors around the docks and threatening to bring an army to burn the town to the ground. With only a handful of men to back him up, however, Sigarr knew the Votadini townsfolk would soon tire of Leofdaeg's nonsense and stand up to him. That would not end well for the Saxons…

"Good morning," Sigarr smiled at an old lady selling pieces of roast meat in some kind of pastry. He was fed up eating fish, and nodded at the woman's wares. She glared at him and barked something he couldn't understand. When he brought out a handful of hacksilver she reached out, as fast as any expert swordsman, and snatched one of the pieces. It disappeared in the blink of an eye and she handed one of the savouries to him which he took with a grin and a deep bow of thanks. She didn't seem to care for his politeness, but Sigarr believed it was always prudent to have good manners, especially when not in one's own lands. And even more so when potential enemies outnumbered your own allies by twenty to one or more...

"Good day." A man nodded to Sigarr and he returned the greeting as they passed by and continued on their way. It cheered him that some people did seem to appreciate his respectful demeanour, it being a pleasant contrast to Leofdaeg's scowling about the place.

Where were the men that had gone after the escaped princesses? Two days, with no word from any of them, it was worrying. And Tata had told him that a *volva* had been on board his ship and gone with the warriors on their hunt. Surely her magic would bring luck to the endeavour so...where were they? Why had they not returned to Kinneil with their prisoners, or at least a report on how they'd managed to kill the three fugitives?

His wandering brought Sigarr to the edge of town, near the horse-trader's establishment. The jarl had visited the man after his stables had been cleared out and promised to pay for the animals, whether they were returned to him or not. There was no point in turning the townspeople against them, for the Saxons had to co-exist with the various tribes of Britain and the Votadini, being on the eastern coast as they were, offered many good trading opportunities. The trader was grateful, for Tata's men – after seeing their two slaughtered comrades' bodies on the road – had been in no mood for haggling over fair prices for the mounts. They'd simply told the trader they were taking them and, when he'd tried to argue, to demand payment, the *volva* had spat in his face and punched him in the eye while the men laughed at him.

Sigarr's promise of payment was better than nothing and the horse-trader had been embarrassingly happy to speak with him.

Stopping, the jarl gazed at the land around the town. There were no walls here, as any threats usually came from the sea, so he had a good view. There were some travellers on the road, but no sign of his erstwhile comrades. "Where are you all, by Wotan?" he asked softly. Surely they hadn't all been killed by those they were supposed to be hunting. Aye, the Pictish woman was obviously a skilled fighter, and even the younger lass, Catia, was said to be able to wield the short sword she carried with some skill. Lancelot too, well, his prowess was legendary. But they were only three, the rest of the slaves that had manned Leofdaeg's ship were nowhere to be seen when Tata's men came to the stables, it was just the girls and the blond Briton who rode off to the east. It was impossible that those three had been able to defeat the combined efforts of two sets of Saxon pursuers. Wasn't it?

His eyes searched the land for any clue to his companions' fate but all he saw was grass, the old Roman road, and lots of trees. He shook his head and looked towards the stables.

Now something did catch his eye and, frowning, he walked briskly into the yard and towards the main house, loosening his sword in its scabbard as he went. He might have breathing problems at times, and not be as tall or broad as Horsa, but he'd been in his share of battles, and killed enough enemies to feel little fear at the thought of facing whoever he might find here in the stables.

"Hail, friend!" A voice came to him and the horse-trader hurried out of the house, so quickly that Sigarr knew the man had been watching him on the road. "What can I do for you, my lord?"

Sigarr walked past him, towards one of the stalls, not bothering to offer a greeting. His lips were pinched in a thin line as he nodded into the gloomy little chamber. "Where did this come from?" The trader's mouth worked nervously as if he was searching for words, and Sigarr snapped angrily at him. "Where did it come from, idiot?"

"My lord, it returned home during the night. Last night. It's one of the animals your comrades took a few days ago."

"I know it is," Sigarr growled, staring at the horse which eyed him placidly in return. "I remember the colouring on its head. Why didn't you tell me—" He broke off, shaking his head. Why would the man tell him one of his own horses had returned home? What did the trader have to gain by doing so? What did it mean, though? That was what bothered Sigarr. Where was the horse's rider? Had it simply thrown the man off and headed back here, to the place where it knew it would be fed and cared for? "Have any others returned?" he asked.

The trader thought about his answer and must have decided there was no point in lying for he nodded, licking his lips nervously. "Aye, lord," he began walking quickly to another stall two doors along, opening his palm and gesturing with it at the horse staring back at them. "This one. And that one." He motioned again, at the very next stall. "Those two belonged to the people your men were chasing, though."

Sigarr felt a thrill run down his back at the implication. "If any more return, come and tell me, all right?"

The trader nodded furiously but the jarl had already turned away and was walking slowly, thoughtfully, towards the docks. He had to let Leofdaeg know about this, and Tata as well, before they decided what their next move should be. His mind raced at the possibilities. Had all three of the riders been killed? Was Lancelot dead then? The princesses? But how had the horses been allowed to simply wander off and find their way home?

Sigarr wondered if the animals had perhaps run off while their riders had been asleep. Maybe the horse trader had *trained* his beasts to do that? The idea didn't make sense, however, for the man had made no attempt to hide the returned horses. They were clearly visible from the road.

Selfishly, Sigarr was glad he'd not gone with the hunting party, for he felt certain some ill fate had overtaken the riders of those horses. There had been eight of his Saxon kinfolk in total though, so, if there had been a battle with Lancelot and his companions, there must surely have been only one outcome. The Saxons' numbers were too great, even for the fabled swordsman who was, after all, a shadow of the figure he'd been just six months ago.

By the time the hovel Leofdaeg and he had been staying in came into view again, Sigarr felt much happier. There *had* been a fight, he was sure of it, and the fugitives must have been either killed or captured. The victorious Saxons would ride into town soon, bringing, Thunor willing, Princess Catia alive and well. Gifting the girl to Hengist and Thorbjorg, a 'magical child' according to the *volva*, would make all the troubles of the past few days worthwhile.

The jarl was actually smiling as he approached the hovel, imagining how pleased Hengist would be with him when they returned to Garrianum with their young prisoner. Even Horsa, notoriously sour-faced and perpetually hostile, would be impressed with Sigarr's success.

He turned to look back along the road, hoping to catch some glimpse of his kinsmen coming back safely to the town, and another thrill ran down his back for there, passing the stables, were warriors on horseback. Sigarr stared at them, trying to figure out if they were from Leofdaeg's crew or Tata's but, as they grew ever closer his smile faded and fear made a knot in his guts.

The riders were not Sigarr's Saxon kinsmen. They were Britons, and, loping along at their side was an enormous dog.

"By Wotan's bollocks," he gasped, throwing open the door to the hovel and grabbing the small pack he'd brought from the borrowed Pictish ship. "Get your stuff, Leofdaeg," he shouted. "Hurry up man, for goodness' sake! We have to go, now!"

The other jarl stared at him as if he'd gone mad but the alarm in Sigarr's voice had the desired effect and Leofdaeg got up, gathering his few belongings and an amphora of wine he'd taken from a local merchant. "What's going on?" he demanded. "What's the rush?"

Sigarr stuck his head out the door and stared along the road before stepping out and walking briskly towards the docked ships. "Come on," he hissed out of the side of his mouth, glaring at Leofdaeg. "That giant *Waelisc* druid and his war-dog have just come into town so, unless you think you can best them in a fight, we have to get to Tata's ship and sail far away from Kinneil!"

CHAPTER TWENTY

Bellicus looked at the town, eyes searching for some sign of anything out of the ordinary. "Everything seems normal," he said, lips pursed pensively. The place was busy, as expected in a port like Kinneil, as ships were unloaded, cargoes traded and transported to neighbouring settlements, and sailors looked to enjoy themselves after hours or days at sea. "Notice anything unusual?"

Duro didn't answer at first for he too was scanning the bustling place for signs of danger or unrest. They were moving slower now, guiding their horses past travellers, workers, and wagons filled with goods, shouts all around as merchants hawked their wares, dogs barked, gulls screeched overhead, and two men ran towards the docks while looking back nervously over their shoulders.

"There," Bellicus cried at the same moment as Duro spotted the fleeing figures. "Saxons!"

The man at the front of the pair, whom Bellicus recognised as Hengist's cousin, Jarl Siggar, had reached the ship he'd been running towards, and he jumped on board, calling out to the crew.

"Go carefully, Bel," shouted Duro as they dismounted and began to shove their way through the milling, astonished locals. "We've no idea what we're getting into here, or how many of the bastards are on that ship."

"You people," the druid was shouting, his enormous frame towering above the townsfolk who couldn't help but stop and take in what he was saying. "Those Saxons have abducted the Princess of Dun Breatann, and also Princess Aife of Dunnottar. Help us stop them from escaping and both Queen Narina and King Drest will see you well rewarded."

Eburus was grinning at the thought of a good fight, and Cai's hackles were up as he sensed the volatile atmosphere all around them. The sight of his master gesturing with his huge staff only made the dog more skittish and the people of Kinneil shrank back from the dangerous-looking group as they hurried towards the row of ships ahead.

"Come on!" Bellicus called again, looking at the local men and women and raising his staff in one hand, sword in the other. "Your own Prince Ysfael is married to Queen Narina. You're duty bound to help us stop those Saxons from escaping."

"I don't know about that," a portly fishmonger replied loudly, coming round from behind his stall, tearing off his sticky apron and lifting the knife he used to gut his wares. "But that one" – he pointed his blade at Leofdaeg who was on board the Saxon ship now – "has been an absolute prick for the past two days, walking about town as if he was our lord. I'll gladly help you kick his arse."

There were cries of agreement and more of the locals found weapons and fell in behind Bellicus, Duro, Eburus, and Cai as they approached the docks. The druid was smiling grimly, but he was surprised to see their enemies weren't even attempting to cast off. In fact, the older man he assumed must be the captain of the vessel, was remonstrating with Jarl Sigarr. Their words were in the Germanic tongue, and they were angry, but Bellicus was able to understand the gist of their argument: The ship's crew was not prepared to flee.

"Typical sea-wolves," Eburus said, laughing as he saw half-a-dozen of the Saxons jump off their ship to stand on the wooden docks, swords and axes in hand, shields firmly locked in place, side by side. "Too stupid to run away when they're outnumbered."

Bellicus could only agree with his friend's assessment of the situation, but, then again, their enemies' courage, or confidence in their own martial prowess, had surprised the locals. Their earlier rush to attack Sigarr and Leofdaeg had faltered as they realised they would have to face a shieldwall. The fishmonger, so full of bravado just moments before, seemed to melt back into the crowd, which had noticeably slowed, leaving a widening gap between them and the druid's group.

Even Leofdaeg was emboldened by the sudden shift in momentum, drawing his seax awkwardly with his left hand and coming over to stand on the edge of the shieldwall.

"Come and get us then, druid," the jarl bellowed, waving his blade defiantly although with a clear lack of skill.

"What happened to you anyway?" Bellicus asked, nodding at Leofdaeg's bent right arm. "Your *volur* not know how to set a broken bone properly? You're as much of a danger to your own men, waving that thing about in your left hand with all the skill of a five-year-old."

Even some of the Saxons smirked at that, but Leofdaeg just hawked and spat a glob of phlegm onto the docks.

And that was it. Somehow everything exploded into motion, and Cai's terrifying bark turned into a horrific snarl, accompanied by the shrieks of pain from the man who'd found himself unfortunate enough to find his ankle being crushed between the mastiff's jaws.

Leofdaeg, who'd positioned himself on the wrong end of the shieldwall to fight left-handed, found himself jostled by the Saxon next to him and the jarl stumbled, falling back into Tata's ship like a sack of grain, groaning as his head struck one of the benches and almost knocked him unconscious.

"Attack!" Bellicus was shouting, as he swung his staff and parried a thrust from the centre of the shieldwall. To his right, Eburus had his black shield in hand and was chopping his sword brutally down into the linden boards of their enemies, moving so fast and with such ferocity that very little came back from the Saxons.

The man whom Cai was mauling tried to smash the pommel of his sword into the dog's forehead, but Bellicus's staff lashed out, the heavy bronze eagle shattering bone and teeth. As Cai's jaws released, the Saxon stumbled back, face a bloody mess, before losing his footing and ending up on board the ship, sprawled over Leofdaeg.

With two of the sea-wolves out of the fight, the townsfolk were filled with courage once more and stamped forward, weapons of all kinds smashing against the Saxon shields, wood splintering and metal ringing as blades struck the rounded bosses.

"Stop them!" Bellicus was forced to defend both himself and Cai, grabbing the dog by the nape of his neck and hauling him back for the fighting was too confused now. The Saxon ship had cast off though, and Sigarr and the captain were trying their best to get the thing moving by shoving against the docks with oars. "Stop them! The princesses might be hidden on board!"

"They're not!"

Bellicus froze, the fighting continuing around him, screams and bellows of pain washing over him as the locals, unskilled in this kind of battle, began to take casualties.

"We never found them!"

Bellicus realised it was Jarl Sigarr shouting at him now, and he focused his attention on the man as the ship began to move away.

"You're wasting the lives of those townsfolk, druid. For nothing! The princesses, and Lancelot, rode west."

Bellicus's eyes took in the hull of the Saxon ship. Could the bodies of three people, dead or alive, be concealed there? It didn't look like it, and on reflection, why would the Saxons still be in Kinneil if they'd managed to capture their prey?

"Let them go!" he bellowed, powerful voice carrying over the din of the fighting. "Let them go, Eburus," he repeated, grabbing his friend who seemed unwilling to stop hammering at the men and their shields before him.

"Let them go?" the Votadini warrior demanded incredulously. "I haven't even properly bloodied my blade yet, druid!"

"Maybe not, but some of our enemies have bloodied theirs. No more townsfolk need to die needlessly." He hauled Eburus back and looked at the men and women of Kinneil who'd come to join the fight. They were happy enough to retreat, helping their wounded as they went. The Saxons, teeth bared, jumped into their ship as it moved off, quickly putting distance between themselves and the docks.

By now, Leofdaeg had managed to disentangle himself from the man who'd fallen on top of him, and he sat on one of the rowers' benches, shaking his fist at Bellicus. "One day, you big bastard. One day I'll kill you!"

"You'd better get practising with that left arm then, little man," the druid called back dismissively, turning away to help tend to the wounded. As the Saxon ship was rowed away to the east, seawards, Leofdaeg continued to rant and threaten Bellicus, Duro, Eburus, Cai, the people of Kinneil, and anyone else he could think of. Eventually, Jarl Sigarr could be heard, ordering the noisy fool to shut up and give them all peace.

Two of the men from Kinneil had been mortally wounded in the battle and were beyond even a druid's healing, but Bellicus spoke some words over their bodies, commending them to the gods and praising their valour. Then he moved on to assist Duro in cleaning and bandaging the wounds of another two men and a woman, again praising their bravery and skill. The fishmonger, who didn't have a scratch on him or his blade, merely received a cold look.

When the injured locals were seen to, Bellicus led the way back towards the buildings along the docks in search of food and drink.

"My lords, I'm the owner of the stables there," a man called to them, pointing at the buildings beside the road near the town entrance. "I'll take care of your horses if you want?"

"My thanks," Bellicus shouted over the babbling townspeople. "We'll be along in a little while to pay you for your services. Make sure to rub them down and feed them well, they've earned it."

The horse-trader nodded vigorously and, already holding Darac and Eburus's mount by the reins, nodded to a young lad who ran to get Duro's horse which had wandered off a short distance and the pair led the animals away from the crowd.

Many of the locals had followed the druid, some of whom seemed to be important figures in Kinneil, given the respect they were afforded from their peers. Questions were asked, and answered by the druid as best he could. One man led the way to an alehouse, opening the door and ushering the visitors in, pressing himself against the wall as Cai sauntered past. Then he waved most of the other curious townsfolk away, although a handful pushed past, professing their own thirst.

"I'm Mandacus," said the man, showing Bellicus and Eburus to a table while simultaneously shouting to the serving girl for food and three ales. "I'm the headman here in Kinneil."

"Glad to meet you, my lord," Bellicus replied, telling Mandacus who he was, and introducing Duro and then Eburus.

"You're King Cunedda's Champion?" Mandacus asked, eyes wide.

"Aye," Eburus confirmed. "Although I've not seen him in months. Been adventuring around Britain with the druid here."

The drinks were brought by a young woman who smiled and walked off, returning moments later with a bowl of water for Cai, and some scraps of gristly meat. She went off to serve the other patrons without asking for payment, and Bellicus assumed Mandacus would take care of it later.

"Well, I'm glad you adventured here today," Mandacus told them. "That Saxon with the bent arm has made a complete nuisance of himself since they arrived here a couple of days ago. It was only a matter of time before the people got sick of him and started a fight."

"Your folk gave a decent account of themselves," Bellicus said, drinking deeply of his ale and sighing happily as it went down.

"Aye," Mandacus agreed. "But we took casualties, and that's what I was worried about." He shook his head. "Well, at least they're gone now."

"Why were they here?" Duro asked.

"They were after some escaped slaves, according to the smaller Jarl. Sigarr, he was named, a decent sort, as far as sea-wolves go. He said they'd sent riders to track the fugitives and would wait here in town until the hunters returned." He shrugged, lips pursed thoughtfully. "But none of their men have come back yet. It's strange. And those 'escaped slaves' managed to kill two of them, right here in town."

"Indeed?" Bellicus smiled, picturing Aife and Lancelot forming an unlikely yet quite deadly partnership and taking down their surprised attackers.

"Aye," said Mandacus. "Outside the stables. I wasn't around but the whole town was full of talk afterwards. A skinny man with blond hair, a woman, and a child. Yet they managed to best two Saxon raiders and escape along the old Roman road." He smiled and raised his ale mug in salute. "Gods go with them. I hope they've not been captured by the bastards tracking them."

Or killed, thought Bellicus darkly, although he felt sure he'd know if Catia was dead. They were bonded by blood after all. No, the girl was alive, she had to be.

"We should really get on the road after them," Eburus said once his ale was drained and he was chewing on some freshly roasted fish the serving girl had brought over. "They can't be too far ahead and, for all we know, the Saxons are still on their trail."

"I could send some of our men with you," Mandacus suggested.

"Why didn't you help the girls before?" Bellicus asked, trying hard to keep any criticism from his tone before he knew the facts.

"Like I say," Mandacus replied a little testily. "I wasn't here when they arrived and, from all accounts, they neither asked for help nor waited around to see if they'd get any. They came off their ship, ran to the stables, and rode off. The Saxons were right on their tail from the moment they docked." He blew out a heavy breath, shaking his head. "You know what those men are like. We've been lucky here in Kinneil; we've avoided the wrath of the sea-wolves so far. They trade with us, and it benefits both sides. But we've heard what they've done all throughout the southern lands." He was still shaking his head. "Raping, burning, killing…It's best to try and stay on good terms with them."

Bellicus tipped the last of his ale into his mouth. "True. You've done well by your people, Mandacus, and by us. If you can gather, say … two?" He looked at Duro who jerked his head upwards. "Three, then, of your men to come on the road with us for a short distance, just in case we run into more trouble, I'd appreciate it. Hopefully we can discover what's happened to our friends and to the rest of the Saxons."

"Shouldn't be hard to find men to travel with you," said Mandacus, getting to his feet and leading them back out into the daylight, the fresh, sea air a welcome relief from the warm, smoky interior of the alehouse. "Why don't you go to the stables and check on your horses? I'll find hardy men to join you as quickly as I can." He put out his arm and Bellicus took it in the warrior's grip.

"My thanks, lord," said the druid. "Your hospitality will not be forgotten."

They parted, Bellicus leading Eburus and Cai along the road to the stables, while Mandacus was already shouting on someone to come and talk with him.

It was a stroke of good fortune that three horses had returned home to the stables, for Kinneil's headman was as good as his word and within the hour men had come to join Bellicus's party. They were all mounted and on their way in short order, suitably armed and on the lookout for signs of other travellers, the plan being that Mandacus's men would ride with them for a day or so until they reached Alt Clota's border, and then return to Kinneil.

"Darac looks as fit as when we set out from Dun Breatann," Eburus noted, eyeing the druid's big black. "Mine isn't from quite as good stock, although he's holding up well enough, given how much we've been riding."

"Aye, Darac is from a long line of noble animals," Bellicus said, stroking his mount's neck affectionately. "That horse-trader has taken good care of them too so hopefully we can get all this sorted quickly and be home in Dun Breatann within the next couple of days."

"Agreed," said Duro. "This has been a strange few weeks. It'll be good to get back to some kind of normality."

"*Normality?*" Eburus burst out laughing, drawing odd looks from the men of Kinneil. "I don't know what that means any more!"

Bellicus could only agree. He didn't need to be a druid to know their future would likely prove to be anything but normal.

CHAPTER TWENTY-ONE

"They came this way anyway, we can be sure of that," said Eburus, kneeling and examining the ground.

"Your tracking skills amaze me, my friend," Bellicus drawled, sliding down from Darac's back and nudging the corpse beside the road onto its back with his foot so he could see its face.

"Hoofprints," the Votadini went on, oblivious to the druid's sarcastic tone. "And I'd say it's obvious Lancelot and the girls were responsible for those bodies."

"And I'd agree with you," Bellicus said, moving to the second body which lay further off the road, beneath the trees. It was, like the other corpse, a dead Saxon warrior, with wounds to his back and his front, as if attacked by two separate enemies. The injury to the back was low down, as if someone smaller had inflicted it. The idea of Catia stabbing someone to death...It was not a pleasant thought and Bellicus pushed it away. He knew better than most how cruel, how hard, life was, and how one must fight to preserve it when faced with danger, but Catia was still just a child. How the druid wished he could have been a proper father to her, or at least that Coroticus had been allowed to continue in that role without the Saxon interference that had turned all their worlds upside down and brought them at last to this place.

"We're not all that far from Kinneil," one of the local men said. "They must have stopped to camp and somehow ended up in a fight. Should we look around? There might be more of the sea-wolves in the trees."

Bellicus thought about it. They'd been riding for a while now so it would do them all good to have a rest. "Aye," he said. "Let the horses graze for a bit and have something to eat yourselves. I'll scout in the trees. Duro, Eburus, you two check the other side of the road, and be careful." He headed into the canopy of trees, eyes searching the moss, leaves, and broken branches that lay strewn around. He hadn't gone far when Cai picked up a scent and led him to the broken blade of a *volur's* stone knife. He bent, recognising it immediately for many of his own druid brothers and the Pictish druidess, Ria, carried similar magical weapons, mainly for ritual purposes.

Two dead men, and a Saxon witch who must have been incapacitated to allow her knife to end up broken and tossed aside amongst the rotting mulch of the forest floor. Bellicus grinned. Aife, and even Catia despite her youth, were very handy with their swords, but meeting Lancelot had added an extra dimension to their group. The Saxons must have got a rude awakening when the fighting started here.

Leaving the ill-fated blade where it lay, to be swallowed up by the earth, he quickly finished checking the area and returned to the others. Eburus and the centurion were already there, having found nothing on their own search. Duro handed Bellicus some dried meat which he took and chewed gratefully, washing it down with a long drink from his ale-skin. He sat on a boulder and Cai lay next to him, allowing the druid to absentmindedly stroke his smooth coat.

The travellers finished their meal in thoughtful silence, the sounds of a nearby stream, and the horses munching the grass beside them, proving so relaxing that Bellicus found himself beginning to nod off. He came to with a sudden start, to see Eburus grinning at him.

"Tired?"

"Aye," Bellicus said sheepishly. "I think we've rested enough, let's get moving again. But keep an eye out for riders coming towards us. Catia and the others must be almost at the next settlement, they'll be getting closer to Damnonii territory, and the Saxons won't want to follow them I'd imagine."

A carrion crow, so big Bellicus thought at first it might be a raven, landed on the road beside them, staring balefully at him. The druid watched it, wondering what it meant. Was the bird a good omen, or ill? He did not know, but the crow would dine well on the Saxon corpses once they rode off. Perhaps that would make their fate more favourable; one could never tell whether they were looking at a bird, or a god, after all.

"There's a village not far from here," said Loubus, who was one of the men from Kinneil. "Mayhap your friends will ask the people there to help them."

"What village?" Bellicus asked, picturing the area in his mind. They had passed what, two, old Roman fortlets? Ruins now, but once quite formidable defensive structures that helped the Wall function efficiently, or at least that had been the Emperor Antoninus's plan. In reality, his wall had proved fairly needless, which was why it had been abandoned long before the one further south that was built by the earlier Emperor Hadrianus. So, the druid mused, if they had ridden past two fortlets, that must mean they were approaching Medio Nemeton. The very place where he and Duro had first met Eburus, who'd been with King Cunedda's Votadini army marching on Dun Breatann.

"Shivra," said Loubus. "And we'll take our leave here, my lord, if that's all right? You're not too far from Alt Clota now. If you find whoever killed Caitotus before we do, make them pay, will you?"

The druid nodded and the men from Kinneil waved farewell as they headed back along the road, hoping to make it home before night fell.

Bellicus and his friends rode harder now, fear settling in the druid's guts like a heavy stone. These were not Saxon lands, but neither were Catia, Aife, or Lancelot from here. The people who lived near Medio Nemeton – the highest fortification along the wall but abandoned many generations ago – might not want to take sides if forced into it. Britons, Picts, Saxons: what difference did tribal allegiance make to folk living in a village miles away from the main centres of civilisation, or at least what still remained of it?

There was also the *volva* to consider, casting gods-knew what magic and mischief. The woman had seemingly been bested in a fight, but whoever had defeated her had not wanted to kill her. Bellicus hoped that respect for the life of a representative of the gods would extend to him if he ever needed it in enemy territory, but part of him wished Lancelot or Aife had just run the witch through, for he'd seen first-hand how much trouble the Saxon *volur* could cause.

Eburus commented on his pensive expression and Bellicus explained his fears.

"Ach, I wouldn't worry about one mad woman going around the place," the Votadini warrior said, waving a hand dismissively. "She's a Saxon. The folk about here won't listen to her nonsense, trust me."

CHAPTER TWENTY-TWO

Aife was exhausted and, when she looked at Lancelot she wasn't sure if he would be able to walk for much longer. Catia was the only one who seemed to have any energy left but then the young girl had spent more time than the others riding their sole remaining horse that day.

Before it had broken its leg.

Aife shook her head. It was terrible luck. Everyone knew the Romans made the best roads; no-one else had ever even attempted to cross the country with such a useful mass transport system. Designed to allow Roman troops and all their war equipment to move quickly from once place to another, their engineering skill was such that the roads – hundreds of years old now – were still in decent condition, at least along this stretch of the Wall. Neither the local Votadini, nor the Damnonii people whom Catia belonged to, could ever have constructed such a road, and both those tribes felt great respect for the Romans who'd managed it. Aife had certainly been impressed when she saw it, as she always was when she saw the things the legions had built.

So it was a nasty shock when a loose stone in the road had given way beneath their horse's hoof, turning the ankle and breaking the leg. The image of the animal, falling in pain and throwing Catia onto the grass beside the accursed road, came back to Aife. The horse's nostrils flaring, eyes wide, as if it knew what such an injury meant…

Aife had taken Catia on ahead, walking along the road without looking back as Lancelot put the poor animal out of its misery. Considering how valuable the horse had been to them in allowing them to escape certain death at the hands of their pursuers in Kinneil, it had been a sad end for the noble beast and Aife could not help but shed a tear for it.

They had since passed two tiny settlements, visible from the road, but they were so small that Lancelot deemed it a waste of time seeking another horse in either of them. Such places were hardly well stocked with magnificent examples of the equine species, and it was more likely those steadings had nothing more than an ox to pull carts to market, if even that.

"It's getting dark," Lancelot said, and his voice was little more than a grunt. He looked at the sky which was cloudy with a touch of red. "It'll stay dry until tomorrow I'll wager, but we should find somewhere safe to rest up."

"That's true," Aife said heavily. "We still have no idea how many of the sea-wolves are after us."

"Maybe they've given up," Catia smiled. "We did thin their numbers after all."

"Maybe," Aife replied.

They continued to walk, forcing one foot in front of the other, until, at last they saw, in the deepening gloom, a dark shape on a hill to the north.

"What's that?" Lancelot muttered, waving his hand towards the shadowy edifice.

"Must be one of the old Roman forts," Aife said, squinting up at the hill, trying to make out any details or if there were any lights visible within the structure. "As good a place as any to camp. There might be buildings we can shelter in, if it does rain."

"It won't," Lancelot said dully, and he was already making his way up the slope towards the old fort, the girls at his back. Aife forced herself to look at the road and the lands around them, to make sure they weren't being observed, although it had grown dark quickly and she felt sure no-one would be able to pick them out traversing the inky hump of the hill.

It felt like an age before they reached the summit, but Aife was happy to see some structures still standing when they finally made it and passed through the remnants of the old timber walls. Lancelot didn't stop, continuing his slow progress towards the least ruined of the buildings.

Aife didn't object, for it was as good a place as any to spend the night. She followed the blond warrior inside, looking about and wondering what the structure had originally been. It was hard to tell for the Romans seemed to make everything bigger and grander than it needed to be. The building could have been a decent sized home for a Pictish family, but to the Romans it might have been nothing more than a storage area for grain or wine.

"Should we light a fire?" Aife wondered, but Lancelot was already snoring from somewhere in the darkness nearby.

"I don't think we should," said Catia, and she too was hidden by the darkness.

It was absolutely pitch-black inside the building and Aife felt a shiver run down her back as her imagination populated the gloom with Saxon warriors and a furious *volva*. There were no sounds though, other than Lancelot's breathing, and she forced herself to be calm. If there were enemies here they would have been attacked already. Still, Catia was right, a fire, even with the majority of its light hidden by the building's walls, could draw their pursuers right to them, like moths to a flame.

* * *

Aife awoke with a start, wondering where she was. It seemed to be almost dawn, for light was streaming through the door. What door? Yesterday's memories flooded back in an instant – the lamed horse, the exhausting walk, the Roman fort, and…She realised then that they had all fallen asleep as soon as they were within the building, without setting a watch, and that made a thrill of fear and shame run through her. What kind of warrior was she? At least Lancelot had an excuse, he was badly weakened from his weeks as a slave and unfit for their forced march. Catia too, she was just a child after all. What excuse did Aife have, other than simple tiredness?

All this ran through the princess's mind in that waking instant, but then, as sleep fled and wakefulness took over, she heard a noise beside her and opened her eyes, squinting against the sudden light. A strong, sweet smell of stale sweat pervaded the air and confusion momentarily blurred Aife's thoughts.

A man was bending over Lancelot. No, two men. Shit, there were at least three of them! One had his hand clamped firmly over the blond warrior's mouth, the other two had already bound his arms and legs, and now Aife did react, reaching down in a fluid, practised motion, and drawing out the dagger she kept strapped to her leg.

A heavy weight fell on her other arm as yet another man appeared, and she lashed out, hammering her blade into his side. He screamed, an oddly high-pitched sound for such a large person, and she stabbed him again, feeling the iron bite deep into his flabby torso, the flesh yielding beneath her fist. The man fell with a heavy thud onto the floor but as Aife tried to roll and stand up, something dropped onto her legs and light exploded in her head as she was brutally kicked.

The room was filled with angry shouting, men bellowing in anger, barking commands at one another, and the princess flailed with her dagger, trying desperately to cut one of them. They were speaking the same tongue as the people in Kinneil, with the same clipped accent, so they weren't Saxons, that was something. Or was it? The attackers had managed to knock her weapon out of her hand, and now they forced her onto her face, their superior numbers giving her no chance. She felt rope being twisted around her wrists and pulled taut while another man did the same to her legs, above the knees.

"Do you know who I am, you bastards?" she gasped, squealing as the rope caught a fold of skin, nipping agonisingly. "I'm King Drest's daughter!"

The men finished binding her and, finally, everything came to a rest within the old Roman building. Lancelot was staring at her with an unreadable expression, limbs secured like hers. She managed to turn her head and saw Catia, not only bound, but with a strip of linen tied around her face, effectively gagging her.

For a time the only sound within the room was the heavy, ragged breathing of everyone in it, until one of the men snarled, "He's dead. She's fucking killed Elpin!"

Everyone looked at the fat man on the ground next to Aife. A pool of blood was spreading from his body and his face was already a strange colour, eyes open but no longer able to see anything, in this world at least.

"You were supposed to tie her hands, Broccomaglos." The same man who'd already spoken pointed a finger at the man kneeling beside the Pictish princess. His face was twisted and his eyes were filled with tears. "What will I tell our ma?"

"I did! It's not my fault, Kunaris," Broccomaglos whined. "She's as fast as lightning. Your brother should have been more careful. We were warned that they'd be dangerous."

"Dangerous? You have no idea," Aife said, and spat at Broccomaglos. "You'll all be sorry for your work here, I swear it."

"Shut up, bitch!" Kunaris, the dead man's brother and apparent leader of the group of attackers, kicked out, catching Aife in the thigh. He glared at her, teeth bared, eyes and mouth glistening in the sunshine filling the building.

Lancelot had not spoken a word, but Aife saw him sizing up their captors, examining weapons and armour, what little of it the men wore. Catia was in a worse state, whimpering through her gag, a terrified expression on her face. Rage filled Aife and she strained against the ropes around her wrists as she was lifted forcibly onto her feet. The bonds were much too firm, however, tied by men who knew what they were doing, perhaps from tethering farm animals. They all had the weather-beaten faces of men who spent their days doing manual labour outdoors.

"If you harm the girl," Aife said, addressing Kunaris. "I will make your death much slower, and much more painful than the one I gave your fat brother."

The man's face twisted and he raised his arm to strike her, but a voice came from the open door and all eyes turned to the speaker.

"Leave her, for now. We want them to walk, it'll be easier than carrying them. Gag her and the man, though."

Kunaris took a deep breath and lowered his arm before nodding deferentially. Then he reached out and grasped Aife by the hair and pulled her forward, tying a linen strip around her face and mouth before leading her outside like a cow being taken to market.

Or to slaughter.

The Pictish warrior-princess tried to ignore the pain in her scalp, fearing Kunaris would tear the hair from its very roots if she didn't move fast enough for his liking.

As they passed the person standing in the doorway, real terror threatened to overcome her as she recognised the *volva,* Yngvildr. Somehow the witch had not only managed to track them down, but persuaded the men of some nearby settlement to do her bidding. What strange, dark power did the woman wield?

They were forced to walk to the nearby village of Shirva, Yngvildr smiling triumphantly the whole way down the hill.

"Put them in there," Kunaris commanded when they reached their destination. He pointed towards an old barn and turned to the *volva*, bowing his head to her. His obsequious demeanour made

Aife feel nauseous as he said, "We'll guard them until we know what's to become of them, lady."

Yngvildr watched as the prisoners were dragged away to the barn and shoved roughly onto the hay inside. There were walls on three sides, and a roof, so it would provide protection from the elements should the weather turn, and everyone could see them from outside so there'd be little chance of them removing their bonds unnoticed.

"Perfect," said the *volva*, flashing her smile at the men of Shirva. "You've all done well. I think you've earned a good drink, eh?" Her strangely accented speech combined with her exotic looks seemed to have cast a spell over the fools, Aife observed from her place in the rickety barn. "I already know what's to happen to them, though."

Kunaris nodded. "What's that?" he asked.

"Tomorrow," Ynvildr replied, and her expression became hard. "I will sacrifice them to the gods."

CHAPTER TWENTY-THREE

Yngvildr was young, yet wise beyond her years. The gods had gifted her with beauty, and a quick mind, and the ability to read omens in many things. All these qualities had been recognised when she was in her fifteenth year and one of the wise women, the *volur*, visited her village. Until then, Yngvildr had spent her days doing menial tasks such as weaving baskets, mending and washing clothes, cooking meals and, at night, singing for her fellow villagers. It had been a boring life, and the girl hoped she was destined for other, better things. The other children had never appreciated her intelligence and been frightened by the strange trances that would often come over her unbidden. So, despite her undeniable physical beauty, no young man wanted to wed her, and the women resented her looks.

The arrival of the *volva*, one middle-aged woman carrying a sturdy staff carved from an ash branch, changed everything for Yngvildr. She sang that night in the mead hall, and the next morning she left her village with the *volva*, who'd been so impressed by the girl that she paid Yngvildr's parents and adopted the youngster. It was an incredible honour, to be taken into the care of a wise-woman, learning how to commune with the gods and serve the great lords of Jutland and beyond.

Five years later, Yngvildr sailed to Britain with a shipload of warriors, singing to protect them from storms and rogue waves. She had learned much in the intervening years, from languages to magic and more, surpassing her teacher in every way and, when the chance came to travel to these new lands, she jumped at it. She spent time around Hengist's army, even met the man himself, and his own personal *volva,* Thorbjorg.

That woman was impressive, Yngvildr thought. Well, obviously she was, that was why she'd ascended to such a lofty position, chief among all the *volur*.

Thorbjorg was not a young woman any more, however, despite her long, slim legs, and striking features. Soon Hengist, or perhaps his successor should the war with the Britons not go as he planned, might be looking for another *volva* to replace Thorbjorg.

Yngvildr knew she was destined to take over that mantle one day, she just had to bide her time and impress the most important jarls in Hengist's army. That meant travelling with warbands and, as she'd done most recently, venturing north on trading missions to Votadini lands. When they'd come across Hengist's cousin, Jarl Sigarr, sailing a borrowed Pictish currach while pursuing two princesses and the famed swordsman Lancelot, well, Yngvildr knew this was her chance. She would finish the job Thorbjorg had failed to do, and offer the magical child, Princess Catia, as a blood sacrifice to the gods. If she could add the Pictish noblewoman and Lancelot to the ritual, all the better.

Hengist would recognise her as the true chief *volva,* there would be no other choice for him.

Yngvildr told all this to Kunaris as he stood over her within the dimly lit room and his face twisted in bemusement. "How could the men in your village have not wanted you? Did they prefer the company of goats?" He shook his head, astonished that anyone could be so stupid. "I would do anything for a woman as beautiful as you. Anything!"

Yngvildr flashed her white teeth and took hold of his erect manhood once again, stroking it expertly and drawing a groan from him. "Thank you, Kunaris," she murmured. "You and your people will be well rewarded for your service today. Capturing those criminals was a very good deed, and you deserve much in return."

Kunaris groaned again, almost on the point of ejaculation. Fleeting thoughts of his dead brother, and of the three prisoners who would die on the morrow flitted through his head like sparrows hunting midges. The man, a scraggy slave who'd probably spent his whole life thieving, and the woman who'd murdered his brother, they both undoubtedly deserved what was in store. But the third? She was just a young girl…

Yngvildr stood up then, and at the sight of her firm, naked breasts he forgot everything except the Saxon *volva.* "Let me bed you," he gasped. "I must!"

"Tomorrow," she whispered. "It will add to the magic of the ritual and bring us both the gods' favour."

"Please," he whispered, but she thrust her tongue into his mouth and his body began to convulse, waves of intense pleasure shaking him more violently than any orgasm he had ever before experienced. When she stepped away, wiping her hand on his own discarded cloak, Kunaris had to sit down, so light-headed was he.

The *volva* quickly re-dressed, pulling on her blue dress and grey cloak and smiling at him. "Did you feel the power of the gods?" she asked.

Seriously, Kunaris nodded, still breathing heavily. "Aye," he said. "I've never known anything like it."

"Would you like to feel even more pleasure?"

Somehow, despite being fully clothed once more, she managed to look as alluring as ever and Kunaris found himself becoming aroused again, much to his amazement. The thought of sliding his—

"Tomorrow," Yngvildr said. "I will let you do whatever you want to me... Now, I must spend the night in preparation for the ritual. Do not disappoint me, Kunaris. And do not allow anyone to disturb me tonight – I must prepare for tomorrow, and my guards will not look kindly on anyone ruining my preparations."

With that the *volva* left, retiring to the small house which had lain empty since its last occupant died during the previous winter. After the villagers had captured the criminals and brought them back to Shirva, three Saxon warriors had turned up looking for supplies and directions back to Kinneil. As it happened, they were companions of Yngvildr who'd become separated from her and were glad to rejoin her company. No-one would dare to disturb the *volva* with those three guarding her for they were well-armed and looked dangerous.

"I won't disappoint you," Kunaris muttered, staring at the door Yngvildr had left through, fully erect again at the thoughts of the coming day's incredible pleasures. "By the gods, I would kill everyone in the world just to feel myself inside you, woman!"

His ardour left along with the *volva* though, and feeling cold as the sweat cooled on his body, he pulled up his trousers and threw on his cloak, oblivious to the sticky mess on the fabric at the back. Through the door he could hear his fellow villagers talking, laughing and even singing, although the songs were melancholy rather than triumphant. They had lost one of their own that day, and Elpin had been a popular man. His death would be felt keenly, and not just by his brother, Kunaris, and their mother.

A pang of guilt hit him then, and Kunaris went out into the night, making towards the building everyone called the great hall although it only held twenty or so people comfortably. Hardly the biggest, grandest of feasting places, but enough for the small settlement. He knew his mother was in there, drinking ale along with the rest of the folk, and trying to come to terms with the death of her firstborn son.

The doors were open, letting out the stench of stale drink, sweat, and vomit, and smoke from the fire that burned practically all year round, even in summer, providing warmth and light to the settlement. Kunaris walked in, squinting as the smoke assailed his eyes. There were no armed guards at the doors, there never was, but some of the villagers saw him coming and nodded respectfully to him, in recognition of his grief. A dog approached, sniffing at his cloak, and he aimed a blow with the back of his hand but the animal was too fast and dodged aside, wandering off in pursuit of scraps.

"Ma," said Kunaris, taking a stool at the long bench to the right of his mother. "I'm so sorry." He had already apologised for not protecting Elpin earlier in the day when they'd first returned from the Roman ruins with the prisoners, but he felt the need to repeat it now.

"Don't," the woman replied. She was in her early fifties, and portly, like her dead son, and her eyes were red from crying and the smoke in the hall. She waved Kunaris's words away and lifted a wooden mug to her lips. She was in no mood to talk that night for her pain was still too raw.

"Here." The man seated on Kunaris's other side tapped him on the arm and slid an overflowing cup along the bench to him. "Drink. Celebrate Elpin's life, as he'd have liked."

Nodding his thanks, Kunaris took the ale and downed it in two long draughts, standing and leaning over to grasp the jug near the centre of the bench for a refill. It wasn't long before he was onto his third cup – and that on top of the good skinful he'd had in the afternoon – and things were beginning to become blurred. Just as he wanted.

"I saw the Saxon witch coming out of your house a little while ago," said Kunaris's companion on the right. It was a man of about twenty-five, very thin, with a sparse blond beard. Dagvalda was his name, and he'd been Kunaris's friend for many years. "What was she there for?" He was grinning, or perhaps his expression would better have been described as leering. His question was rhetorical, for he'd guessed what had been happening within his friend's house, and he was jealous. "D'ye think she'd let me have a go too?" he asked seriously.

Kunaris couldn't help laughing, although he made sure his mother didn't see him. "You keep away from her," he said. "She has magic powers. She chose me, and she'll curse you if you bother her. Maybe make your cock fall off, or boils break out on your face, covering it all over. That might be an improvement, actually."

Dagvalda's smile faded as he thought of that, but it wasn't long before his mood lifted again. Shirva was a small village, with only a few inhabitants and very few visitors since the Romans had abandoned the nearby fort. Nothing exciting ever happened there, and no-one interesting ever passed through, at least not since Dagvalda or Kunaris had been alive. The people lived in peace and they were content with it, for the most part, but the arrival of the beautiful, exotic Saxon woman had thrown the place into turmoil.

The violent death of one of their own as they'd tried to capture the criminals had only added to the sense of excitement.

"What do you think she'll do tomorrow? To those three prisoners I mean?"

Kunaris scowled, lip curling as he remembered the sight of his older brother's lifeless body and the defiant eyes of the woman who'd killed him. "I don't know exactly, but I hope that bitch pays for what she did to my brother."

Dagvalda looked away, eyes darting around the hall at the people gathered to drink and sing and dance the night away in remembrance of Elpin. They were normal people, hard workers who did what they could to eke out an existence from the land, trading what they could, and finding happiness where they might. They were not murderers. Dagvalda looked back at his friend and said, "Are you sure about this? We don't know anything about the prisoners, or why they were sleeping in the ruins. One of them's a little girl, by Cernunnos. And that big one said she was a princess!"

Kunaris didn't reply immediately. He was still frowning into his ale cup, but he sighed deeply, as if wrestling with everything that had happened and was yet to come.

"Maybe you're right," he admitted sadly. "I've never killed anyone. I thought we'd just go to the fort and help to capture the criminals Yngvildr told us about. I didn't think anyone would die, either today or tomorrow."

His mother, Totia, overheard them and slammed her mug down on the table, the crack reverberating around the hall and turning many eyes towards them.

"They killed your brother," she shouted, face twisted in fury. "They must pay for that! Don't you worry," she stood up, shaking her head, lip twisted at Kunaris's weakness. "You won't have to kill them. The witch will do it, and if anyone tries to stop her, her guards will deal with you." She looked around at the villagers and most avoided her gaze for Totia was well-known to have a tongue sharper than any warrior's blade. "Their blood will be spilled just as the druids used to do in order to appease the gods and ensure a good harvest and luck for us all in the coming year. You heard what the witch said – the prisoners deserve what's coming to them."

Indeed, Yngvildr's tale about Lancelot, Aife and Catia had been a dark and lurid one – a complete fabrication which painted the three in a terrible light. The *volva* knew how to tell a story, and how to persuade people to believe her words. When she'd ridden into the village that morning – more striking than any woman the villagers had ever seen, and more confident too – claiming to be on the trail of three dangerous outlaws, every ear had listened. The men in particular had watched, open-mouthed, as the *volva* dismounted and stalked about the village centre, pleading for the people of Shirva to go the ruined fort and capture the three fugitives before they did any more harm. Very quickly, Yngvildr had recognised Kunaris as the most influential of the men, and just as quickly he had fallen under her spell.

How could he not? He'd been married when he was twenty, but his wife died not long after and, given how few people lived in Shirva, he'd never found another bride.

"That man," Totia pointed towards the doors in the direction of the barn that was being used to hold the three prisoners until the morrow. "Raped the Saxon woman, and killed five innocent men in Kinneil, while the big woman and the little girl helped him. You've all seen the bloodstains on them! They are criminals, and they murdered my son." She shook her head and seemed to regain some composure as she went on in a cold, hard voice. "You all knew Elpin. He was a gentle soul. He never deserved to have that bitch's knife stuck in him until he was—" She broke off and fell onto her stool, face buried in her arms on the bench as her body was racked with sobs.

Kunaris reached out to comfort her but she shrugged him off angrily and he got up, downing the last of his ale and walking out of the hall and back towards his house. Behind him the villagers were chattering, voices raised in angry support of Totia's words. As Kunaris closed his door behind him and lay down on his bed, head spinning, he closed his eyes and steeled himself to do what must be done the next day.

The criminals would die, aye even the girl, and it may be a hard thing to watch and be part of, but it would be justice, and...His thoughts returned to the firm, naked breasts of the Saxon *volva,* the slim legs, the probing tongue, the blazing blue eyes, and the rapturous orgasm as he finally pushed himself as deep inside her as he could.

Gods! Tomorrow could not come fast enough!

CHAPTER TWENTY-FOUR

It was a cold night, but Bellicus and his companions had made it at last to the old Roman fort of Medio Nemeton. They'd taken a very quick look around the place in the moonlight, Cai's keen nose searching for any hidden enemies within the mostly mouldering buildings but finding no-one, and then they'd set up the tent and made themselves and the horses comfortable.

They ate a cold supper and drank some of their ale and then sat together, gazing up at the stars and the clouds that sailed past the moon. It felt good to rest for a time for the past few days had been hard going.

"How about a song, druid?" said Eburus, smiling. "You know plenty, I'm sure."

Duro nodded. "Aye, good idea. A tune is always good for raising the spirits."

"You got your flute?"

The centurion nodded and fished around in his pack, drawing out the wooden instrument with a grin of anticipation. "Ever since Drest cut off those two fingers," he held up his hand, "I've had to relearn how to play this. It's been a while since we performed a song together, Bel."

"It is," the druid agreed. "What should we do then?" He looked at Eburus. "Any requests?"

"When we were in the south with Arthur's army," the red-haired warrior replied, "I heard some of his folk singing about men with golden torcs. Do you know that one?"

Bellicus glanced at Duro and they both said, "The Lay of Caer Ebbas," at the same time.

"We know it," the centurion confirmed, humming the tune softly to remind himself how it went, visualising on the flute where his fingerings would be. "Ready?"

Bellicus nodded and the first notes from Duro's instrument filled the night air, soft and wavering at first but becoming more confident as the centurion warmed to the task. There was something otherworldly about the music here in this moonlit old Roman fort, but it was not sinister. It was magical, and Eburus's eyes twinkled like the stars overhead as Bellicus started to sing.

"The warriors went to Caer Ebbas,
Their fame spread far and wide,
With golden torcs and arm-rings,
To war and death they'd ride

The fortress was besieged by men,
With spear and sword and shield,
But warriors forged in battle,
Would never think to yield

Bellicus's voice became more strident as Duro's flute picked up the pace, and Eburus laughed, hitting his hand on his thigh in time with the song.

As sunlight shone on spear-points,
The battle cries were roared,
And the grass was turned to crimson,
As their enemies died in scores,
Their enemies died in scores

The tune came to a stop, before druid and centurion took up the original melody again, although much slower this time, more mournful than its earlier joyous nature.

The warriors went to Caer Ebbas,
Their fame spread far and wide,
With golden torcs and arm-rings,
To war and death they'd ride,
And on that day they died...

Bellicus nodded at Eburus to join in, for the song was coming to its end, and the tune became more celebratory again, faster, and perfect for a crowd to sing together in a mead hall or in a ruined old fort.

Caer Ebbas, Caer Ebbas,
For those warriors we pray,
Caer Ebbas, Caer Ebbas,

Oh, the crows fed well that day."

Their voices faded along with the last sweet note from Duro's flute and Eburus, grinning, clapped his hands in appreciation, although none of the men spoke. They simply looked at one another, glad to be alive and in one another's company there on the hilltop with food and ale and clear skies. The words to the song were not joyful, but the way druid and centurion had performed it was uplifting and, strangely, it filled them all with hope for the coming day.

Later, Bellicus took first watch, leaving Cai to guard the sleeping forms of Duro and Eburus while the druid patrolled the fort on his own. He was sure they were alone, for Cai would surely have smelled anyone hiding within what remained of the timber walls, and the moonlight would reveal anyone travelling along the road or approaching up the hill, so Bellicus felt quite safe. He idly examined the old structures, appreciating the skilled construction and engineering that allowed a place so long abandoned to remain standing; a silent, if crumbling, sentinel by the road. Finding a section of wall which looked sturdy, he climbed the creaking stairs and looked out over the crenelated battlements towards the lands in the south.

There were tiny steadings and settlements dotted all around here, places even the druids probably had never visited, so small and insignificant were they. One of those villages was apparently having some kind of celebration that night for Bellicus could hear singing drifting through the darkness, carried on the cool breeze that seemed to blow continuously in these parts. He couldn't make out any words, just a general raucous babble that only occasionally flirted with melody and, at those times, the druid recognised some of the tunes. To him, there seemed no obvious reason for a celebration for this was not the time of the equinox or any other well-known feast, but he could hear enough to guess the villagers were mourning a death. Their songs alternated between fast and jaunty, and slow and melancholy.

A momentary thrill of fear ran through him as he wondered if it was possibly Catia the people were mourning. Lancelot, or Aife, perhaps? But he knew that was impossible – although he couldn't make out individual words within the songs, they were charged with emotion. The singers were lamenting the loss of someone they knew, not some random traveller.

Bellicus closed his eyes and quietly offered a blessing for the departed villager, commending his shade to the gods and requesting safe passage to the Otherlands. Life was hard enough for the folk out here in the middle of nowhere, he knew. Hopefully death would be a little easier for whoever the villagers mourned.

He looked up at the moon, surprised to see how far it had travelled across the sky while he'd been contemplating the almost ethereal singing drifting on the wind to his lofty vantage point in the centuried fortlet. It was time to wake Eburus for the next watch. Time for Bellicus to catch some well-deserved sleep.

He came gingerly down the groaning stairs and crossed to the tent, smiling at Cai who, alert as ever, was watching him from his place at the entrance flaps. He gently shook Eburus, the Votadini warrior coming to with little fuss and little noise, so as not to wake Duro who snored contentedly on as the other two swapped positions.

Within moments, sleep claimed the druid and he passed into the dreamless, healing slumber that a hard day's ride often seemed to bring.

* * *

Bellicus awoke with a start, feeling something touching his face. Instinctively he moved to strike whatever was attacking him, but he immediately realised that it was soft, and warm, and unmistakeably Cai's tongue.

"Gah, get off, you big oaf," he laughed, rolling onto his side and putting an arm up to defeat the dog's affectionate awakening. "It's not morning already, is it?"

"Aye, it is, you lazy bastard," came Duro's voice through the leather folds of the tent. "Come on, we need to get moving. Here." His craggy features appeared at the entrance and he handed Bellicus a cup filled with water. "Get that down you. We've got some food on the go here too."

"You made a fire?" The druid sipped the cool water, smelling woodsmoke filtering into the stuffy interior of the tent.

"Aye," Eburus called. "We're in no real danger up here. There can't be many Saxons about, and the smoke might even bring Catia and that to us, if they spot it."

Duro nodded and disappeared outside again as Bellicus began packing up his things. The smell of cooking meat made his mouth water and his belly rumbled jarringly loudly. They were right, he knew – the Saxons wouldn't light a fire for they were in enemy territory and would be looking to travel without attracting attention. Only someone who felt as though they belonged there would be comfortable enough to cook their breakfast.

It didn't take the druid long to gather everything into his pack and, by the time he came out and began loading it onto Darac's back Duro was already tearing down the tent. Eburus was intent on the bacon that was sizzling over the fire in the folding pan. He'd cooked his own portion first and was chewing with obvious relish. The smell was strong and almost maddening for Bellicus who felt like he'd not eaten a good, warm meal in ages.

"Is that nearly ready?" the druid asked, coming across to the fire and staring longingly into the pan.

"Aye," said Eburus. "But this is Duro's. You'll have to wait."

"Bollocks," the druid muttered, scowling at the centurion's cackle.

"Why don't you and Cai take a look about, see if there's anything interesting here?" Duro suggested, reaching out to take the plate Eburus was tipping his breakfast into. "It was too dark to do it last night, but who knows? Maybe Catia and the others camped here before us." He lifted a piece of bacon and bit into it, cursing as the hot juices burned his mouth.

"Ha, hope that hurt," the druid said, grinning at the obscene gesture his friend made in reply. "Fine, you two fill your bellies. I'll go and do all the work, as usual. Come on, Cai. We'll have to wait to eat."

"The dog's already had his," Eburus called. "He got a big slice of fat before you woke up."

"By the gods," Bellicus muttered as they wandered away towards the nearest buildings. "Even the animals get fed before I do." The dog wasn't listening to him, instead it was stalking towards one of the buildings that was in better repair than the ones surrounding it. The druid followed, remembering Cai had headed straight for this particular structure the night before but only sniffed curiously at a spot not too far inside. Since the hound had shown no sign of alarm, Bellicus had called him back and they'd set about preparing the camp. Now, with the sun casting plenty of light even within the low building, they both went inside for a better look.

Cai headed straight for the spot he'd been nosing about the previous night, and Bellicus, frowning, bent to look. "What's that?" he asked the dog, although it was quite obviously blood. The familiar brown stain, and the interest Cai was showing, made it very clear that it was also fairly fresh.

Instantly, Melltgwyn was drawn and in the druid's hand. He was sure they were alone inside the building, but the signs pointed to a violent confrontation there not too long ago, and it was only wise to be careful. "Lads," he called over his shoulder, directing his voice through the open doorway. "Come here."

Duro arrived first, noting the drawn sword in his friend's fist and pulling his own spatha free as Eburus, a puzzled look on his bearded face, walked in through the doors and handed a plate of bacon to the druid.

"What's the matter?" asked the Votadini, looking about and, at last, noticing the brown stain on the ground. "Blood?"

Bellicus nodded. His initial alarm had passed and he sheathed Melltgwyn, kneeling and examining the dried blood more closely. For a moment he said nothing, and Duro walked past to do his own investigating.

"Someone was here, on the floor," the centurion noted, pointing the tip of his sword at the dust, which had been disturbed recently. "There was a struggle."

"Here too," said Bellicus, indicating a spot right next to the bloodstain.

"And here," Eburus growled, standing by a third area to the right. "You can see where their feet were. They've struggled but…" He stared at the spot, where the gathered dust of decades had been disturbed. "Their feet must have been tied together or something. The dust is only spread about here, over a narrow area."

"Three people," Bellicus said, looking up to meet the eyes of Duro. "And enough blood to suggest someone was severely, if not mortally, wounded."

They remained in silence for a time, minds racing, wondering what had happened in that old building and, more importantly, where the three people that had once been here were now.

"Can the dog track them?" Eburus asked. "Get the scent of the blood? It must have been dripping down so there'll be a trail surely."

Bellicus rose up to his full height, head almost touching the ceiling. "No need. I know where we have to go. Come on!"

He ran from the structure, almost forgetting his bacon in the alarm although he ate it as they broke down the cooking tripod and pan and kicked dirt over the fire to extinguish it. The flavour of the meat he'd been so looking forward to didn't even register with the druid as he chewed and swallowed it as quickly as possible.

"Where are we going?" Duro asked as their gear was packed and split between the three horses.

"And why?" Eburus put in as he jumped up onto his mount's broad back. "How can you possibly know where they went without tracking them?"

All three were mounted now, and Cai was gazing up at Bellicus, ready, as ever, to follow him into the Otherlands if needed. The druid nodded in satisfaction and gently kicked his heels into Darac's flanks, leading the way out through the remnants of the gatehouse. "During my watch last night," he said, staring to the west, noting the distant cooking fires rising into the sky above the woods that separated their party from what had to be a village. "I heard people singing. Lamenting the death of one of their own. That is where we must go, and, if they've harmed my…Princess," he growled, more to himself than his companions. "By the bones of Dis Pater, they'll be mourning a lot more of their people this night!"

CHAPTER TWENTY-FIVE

"I thought druid magic worked best at night, under a full moon and in an oak grove," said Kunaris, looking up at the sky which, although filled with clouds of varying shades of grey, was bright. "Or beside pools of water or something. Not in our little, out of the way village."

Yngvildr shot him a dark look. "What do you know of magic? Do you even have a druid here in this village? No? Well, how did you come to be an expert in their ways?"

Kunaris's face flushed. "Well, I'm not, but I've heard things. Just because Shirva is off the beaten path doesn't mean we're all idiots. I thought it was best to work your spells at night because that's when the gods, or spirits, whatever, are abroad." He shrugged petulantly. "Everyone knows that."

"Do they now?" Yngvildr's earlier frown had changed to the kind of smile one would bestow on a child, but she fluttered her eyelashes at the man, cleaning one of her upper, very white, teeth with her tongue. He grinned back at her and she almost laughed. "Well, the druids have their ways, we *volur* have ours. Magic is not something that's fixed and rigid. It has to be used carefully, and with respect, but, if the *volva* is powerful enough, the gods can be invoked at any time, and anywhere."

Kunaris nodded thoughtfully, accepting her words as if he understood.

He did not, and, in truth, Yngvildr would much rather have sacrificed the three prisoners under a full moon, and on a more propitious date, in a more suitable location than the wheat fields beside this pitiful settlement. Ideally, she would have taken the prisoners to Hengist in Garrianum and conducted her blood ritual before him and Thorbjorg, but the distance was too great. There was a real danger of someone in these enemy lands stopping them on the road and freeing her captives, so…They would die here, in this village when the sun came up, and she would take fingers from each of the victims as proof of her deed.

She feared the villagers might change their minds though, and refuse to allow the ritual to go ahead. Already she'd seen some of the people giving her frightened, uncertain looks and she knew that, if they delayed, things might not go as she wanted them to. The villagers might have already tried to stand up to her had it not been for the three Saxons from Jarl Leofdaeg's ship who'd become lost while searching for Lancelot and the princesses and come to Shirva looking for supplies. That was a stroke of good fortune that only the gods could have arranged.

No, the prisoners must die today, their blood being used to nourish the ground and ensuring a bountiful harvest for the villagers that year. Or at least that's what Yngvildr had promised the simple folk of Shirva – in fact, her ritual would be designed to bring victory to Hengist and the rest of the Saxon army in Britain. Not to mention the success of Yngvildr's own dream of supplanting Thorbjorg as chief *volva* in all Britain.

It was a lot to ask of the gods, but they would be receiving much in return for the sacrifices were people of noble, even magical, blood. This would surely be the greatest ritual celebrated on these shores for many generations, and Yngvildr would be the one to conduct proceedings.

"Do you really believe our harvest will be helped by their deaths?" Kunaris asked, watching as Yngvildr's guards dragged the prisoners out of the low hovel where they'd spent the night. The Pictish woman's head hit the thatch that came down over the doorway although she never showed any sign of pain.

The *volva* looked sidelong at Kunaris, hearing the uncertainty in his voice and knowing the fierce resolution of the night before was fading in his mind with every passing moment.

"Of course," she replied. "How could it not? Thunor already circles – look at the gathering clouds. And Freyja, goddess of fertility, is beneath, waiting to feel the blood nourishing her. Just close your eyes and feel their power flowing through you. Do you feel it?"

Kunaris did as he was told, but his expression remained blank. Yngvildr knew the dense man would need something more tangible to think about. Something much more visceral to take his mind off the deaths of the three bound captives.

"When the ritual is over," she said, voice becoming low, husky, as she straightened her back, her firm, heavy breasts pressing against her dark cloak. "We will make our own offerings to the gods."

"What do you mean?" Kunaris whispered, and already his trousers were showing clear signs of his arousal.

"You shall spill your seed inside me," she muttered. "Every last drop. And then I will take you in my hand, making you hard once more, and we'll do it again. And again." She was facing him, staring deep into his eyes. "I will show you things you've never dreamt of, Kunaris. Pleasures so intense you'll never want them to stop." She had her back turned to the gathering villagers in the field and she reached up to cup one breast. Her woollen cloak did little to conceal the shape and only seemed to inflame Kunaris even more as his mind began to work, imagining what Yngvildr would let him do as soon as this ritual was over.

"Let's do it now," he begged. "I—"

"No," said Yngvildr firmly. "First, we offer the gods death, and then, afterwards, love. Now, I must begin the ritual." She turned and began walking towards the prisoners who had been forced onto their knees amidst a cleared circle of long wheat stalks. As she walked, her distaste for Kunaris faded. The man was an idiot, but he was necessary to make sure the villagers carried out her wishes. Still, his doubting the power of her magic rankled – she was a *volva* and communed daily with the gods and goddesses! She did their bidding and, occasionally, they did hers. Kunaris and his people had no real sense of magic, they spent every day working, with no idea of the hidden worlds surrounding them. How could they? The shovel and the scythe were their tools, to nurture and grow the things that kept them alive. They had no ambition, other than to fill their bellies every day and, perhaps, to fight or fornicate if the mood took them.

Yngvildr was proud that her own people, specifically her kinsmen and women from Jutland, wanted to push out into the world, mould it to their own ends. Hengist and Yngvildr were not content to let the world wash over them – they would grasp fate by the neck and force it do their bidding!

A villager walked past her and she heard him say to Kunaris, "I'm not sure this is a good idea. We don't even know who those prisoners are. What if—"

"They're criminals," Kunaris snarled, his sexual frustration coming out in his harsh tone. "Do you want our harvest to be as bad as it was the last two years? We were lucky to survive the recent winter. Yngvildr's magic, and the blood of those criminals, will ensure we have plenty to eat for many months, so be grateful she's here to help us."

"Help you, more like," the man retorted. "You just want to empty your balls, Kunaris, don't think I haven't seen how you bow and scrape to her. She's treating you like a fool, man. Our fields are overflowing with wheat already, look at them!"

There was a clicking sound, and then a thump. Yngvildr did not need to look back to know Kunaris had punched the man, snapping his teeth together and putting him onto his arse. The *volva* smirked – she had chosen well. Kunaris would do anything to make sure this ritual was completed. He might not really understand her magic, but he was utterly enthralled by her looks and the pleasures she promised him.

She halted before the prisoners, staring down at them, one hand on her hip, the other gripping her wand. They looked back at her from their knees and she saw both the man and the woman had bruises on their faces. Still, they appeared defiant, but her Saxon guards had beaten them into silence and they knelt on the crushed wheat ready to accept their fate. Even the child did not seem particularly frightened by the prospect of death and, again, Yngvildr felt a surge of elation. These people were truly of noble blood, it was obvious in their demeanour and their features, and their deaths would surely bring the *volva* all the power she craved.

"Do you remember this?" she said to the captives, drawing the broken stone dagger from the folds of her cloak. "You snapped it in half. Now, I will use it to slice your skin, tearing it open so your blood soaks this land."

The child stared at the stone blade and her face was deathly pale. Perhaps she was not so brave after all. Yngvildr's supposition was confirmed a heartbeat later as the girl looked to the gathered villagers and blurted, "Don't let her kill us!" She would have said more, much more, but one of the Saxon warriors slapped her across the ear, knocking her onto her side.

"Shut up," the guard muttered in his own language, dragging the sobbing girl back upright. His blow had been painful enough that she didn't cry out again, although both her male and female companions called out threats, promising vengeance on everyone gathered there. They too received heavy blows from the guards at their backs. When Lancelot tried once again to remonstrate he was smashed so hard across the back of the head by a Saxon fist that he retched and did not say any more once he was finally hauled onto his knees again.

Yngvildr stared out at the fields, focusing her mind. She raised her hands, closed her eyes and turned her face to the sky. A gentle breeze caressed her skin, bringing the scent of wildflowers to her, and the sounds of some small birds hidden amongst the wheat. It might not have been the ideal time to work magic, but it was a wonderful day and that would surely count for something. She stood like that for a long time, until her arms grew heavy and she let them fall, turning once more to look at the villagers. Some were watching her with a mixture of fear and anticipation, others were fidgeting, unused to standing quietly for so long.

She looked at the guard standing behind Catia and nodded. He lifted a wineskin from the ground beside him and stepped across to hand it to Yngvildr, who took it, unstoppered it, and raised it to her nose. She breathed deeply, inhaling the strong, bitter scent, her eyes almost watering at its potency. And then she put it to her mouth and took a long draught, feeling the liquid burning her throat all the way down into her stomach. She gazed out into the middle-distance, a heady glow already working its way through her limbs, and then took another drink. She coughed, eyes stinging, but, as she looked at the gathered audience she was grinning wildly.

"What's she drinking?" an elderly man in the front row asked Kunaris but he shrugged. Yngvildr had asked him for the wine, and told him she would use it to make a powerful concoction that would allow her to commune freely with the gods, but she hadn't told him what the other ingredients were. Every *volva* had their own recipes for such draughts, and carried the necessary herbs and such everywhere they went.

She could taste the belladonna despite the sour wine Kunaris had given her to mix it with, proudly assuring her it was 'good stuff'. If that was the best this village had to offer she did not want to try the worst, and she had tasted many vile things in her life.

As the effects of the magical brew became stronger, she undid her grey cloak and let it fall to the ground. Below, she wore a blue dress, with white sleeves and red cuffs. She removed her shoes and there were murmurs of surprise and appreciation mainly from the female villagers as they spotted the silver rings Yngvildr wore on her toes. Such trinkets were incredibly valuable and showed how successful the *volva* must have been in her life to be able to afford them. Beneath her clothes, she had smeared an ointment made from an exotic plant known as Belene on her armpits.

Power flowed through her, growing in intensity with every passing moment, and she could see the crowd responding to it. Her pupils would be greatly enlarged by now, and elation filled her as she took in the looks on the faces of the villagers. They had never seen anything like this before, and their doubts had been pushed aside for surely the gods were circling nearby, drawn by the magic of this beautiful, exotic priestess from far across the sea.

It was not just the gods being drawn to the fields though; carrion crows, a pair of magpies, and many jackdaws flew overhead, some even being brave enough to land on the flattened circle of wheat which held the prisoners, guards and Yngvildr. The birds knew people gathering like this often meant a feast, with scraps and crumbs for the corvids, but, when they realised there was no food involved in this particular event most of them flew off. Their sleek, dark shapes, and the screeching and chattering that accompanied them, added to the weird spectacle in Shirva that morning.

Some *volur* would sacrifice a small animal to begin a ritual such as this, smearing themselves in the blood of the animal. The sight of that was guaranteed to command attention but it seemed unwise to Yngvildr to do it on this day. The villagers were already under her spell, she was sure of it. There was no need to waste time on such theatrics. The sooner the three people cowering at her feet were dead, the sooner she could hack off their fingers as trophies, return to the ship in Kinneil, and sail south to Hengist with the news of her triumph. Even if the *bretwalda* doubted her story at first, word of the sacrifices would quickly spread throughout Britain, given the noble blood and prominence of the victims. She would make sure the people of Shirva knew *exactly* who they'd allowed her to slaughter once the deed was done…

Her body felt light now, as if the gods were drawing her skywards, and she looked up at the clouds. She pointed, wordlessly, eyes shining, and the villagers followed her gaze.

Some cried out, seeing a face within the shifting grey vapours, others, seeing nothing unusual, pretended they did so as not to feel left out.

Joy filled Yngvildr as she looked at the blond man kneeling on the flattened stalks of wheat. His jaw was clenched, as were his fists, but he was still bound and helpless to stop what was coming. The *volva* thought back to her childhood, the life she'd led in her own small settlement back in Jutland, and the things she'd endured in the intervening years. Not all of it had been pleasant, indeed images of the horrific suffering and pain she'd gone through as part of her learning flooded her mind now, but it had all led to this point.

She raised her cracked stone dagger to the sky and screamed to Thunor and Freyja, beseeching them to bear witness to Lancelot's death. Her body became weightless and she laughed as she thrust out her blade and began the ritual.

CHAPTER TWENTY-SIX

Bellicus was first to reach the wide-eyed *volva*, his long legs eating up the ground between them until he was beside her, reaching out and lifting her slim figure into the air. She stabbed with her knife, but Lancelot was safely behind her as the druid's momentum carried them forward, and then Bellicus let her go and she went flying, hitting the ground with a thump and rolling into tall stalks of wheat.

The villagers stared in amazement at the biggest man they'd ever seen, but, before anyone could react to his arrival, a similarly enormous dog was launching itself at the Saxon warrior behind Lancelot. The man was holding Lancelot in place with both hands so had no weapon ready to defend himself and he screamed, stumbling backwards into the field with the war-dog's jaws crushing his forearm.

"What are you doing?" Kunaris shouted at the druid, stepping forward, an expression of utter bemusement on his face. He watched as two more men – one dressed like a Roman officer, the other a younger warrior with long red hair and beard – also appeared from the tall stalks of wheat. The centurion engaged the Saxon guarding the child while the red-haired warrior went for the man holding Aife. Both the Saxons had reacted to the druid's attack, drawing their swords in time to fend off the newcomers. Swords came together, the sound reverberating around the flattened circle as each pair traded blows, trying to gain the upper hand and victory.

Bellicus had taken his staff from its place on his back and ran into the wheat, towards the screaming man who was still trying, without success, to make the dog leave him alone. The druid's staff snaked out, the brass eagle on its top striking the Saxon's forehead and dropping him instantly. "Cai, come," Bellicus commanded and the dog appeared a heartbeat later by his side, eyes bright, muzzle bloody.

"Who are you, and how dare you come to our home and attack us?" Kunaris strode right up to Bellicus, showing tremendous bravery even if he did flinch and step backwards at the sight of Cai. "This is an important ceremony!" He looked over at Yngvildr who was on her feet but still looked as if she had one foot in the Otherlands.

Duro and Eburus had pushed back their opponents, safely away from Aife and Catia who had wriggled across the ground and placed themselves back-to-back. Their fingers worked, trying to undo one another's bonds although it was proving a tough task.

"I am Bellicus of Dun Breatann," the druid said, not shouting yet his voice was so powerful that it carried over the villagers, most of whom were frightened, but thoroughly enjoying the day's entertainment. Bellicus stood more than a head higher than Kunaris, who wasn't a small man, yet seemed like a child next to the towering druid.

"You!" The *volva* had come, somewhat, to her senses and she quickly retrieved her wand, which had been sent tumbling into the wheat when Bellicus threw her. She pointed it at him now, pupils so dilated that her eyes appeared almost completely black. "I challenge you."

"Are you insane?" Kunaris demanded, running across to the *volva* and grasping her arm. She lashed out, striking his mouth and splitting his lip.

"I challenge you," she repeated to the druid. "To a magical battle."

Eburus and Duro's fights came to a halt, all four combatants breathing heavily but no longer attacking one another as they heard the *volva*'s words.

"Never mind that shite," Eburus called to Bellicus. "Just kill the witch and let us be on our way."

"My magic is stronger than yours, *druid*," Yngvildr spat. "Even here, on your own little island. Face me, and we shall see."

Kunaris's expression was one of relief as he realised the woman wasn't challenging the druid to a physical fight. There could be only one winner in that kind of battle, but this? "Aye," he shouted, wiping the blood from his lip. "Let's see whose magic is the greatest. Whoever wins gets the prisoners to do with as they please."

"Don't be stupid, Bel," Eburus said. "All we have to do is cut their bonds and walk out of here. None of them are going to stop us." He turned his attention to the people of Shirva. "I'm Eburus,

Champion of the Votadini. *You are Votadini*! Now, do as your king would ask, and help us."

Some of the villagers looked like they wanted to do as he said, but the two remaining Saxon warriors had slowly worked their way from where they'd been fighting Eburus and Duro, to stand behind the confused crowd. Their presence, and Kunaris's dark look, were just enough to hold them in position.

"Come, druid," Yngvildr said, stalking forwards to stare up into Bellicus's eyes. "Meet me in the Otherlands. We will settle this there, unless you fear my magic will be too much for yours?" She laughed and spun away with her arms outstretched, like a child playing in a spring meadow.

"Don't rise to her taunts, lad," Duro cautioned. "Eburus is right, we can just take our friends and get out of here." He was on one knee having placed his spatha on the ground and he was using his dagger to slice Catia's bonds apart. Eburus had done the same for Aife and was moving on to Lancelot.

"That bitch killed my son," a woman shouted suddenly, stepping out of the crowd and facing Bellicus as she pointed at Aife. "She must face justice. You can't just walk away, druid, even we know that's not how justice works, in Dun Breatann or Dun Edin. King Cunedda" – she glared at Eburus, who ignored her as he finally freed Lancelot and helped him sit up to rub life back into his reddened wrists and thighs – "King Cunedda would demand justice be served, would he not?"

"What would you have us do?" Bellicus asked her softly.

"Accept her challenge," the woman said, turning to Yngvildr. "Let the gods decide who has the right of it."

"Get back into the crowd, woman," Eburus shouted, striding forward to stand next to Bellicus. "You have no more authority than those jackdaws to tell us how to settle this."

Catia had not run to Bellicus, sensing that would not help the situation, but she was hugging Duro, while Aife and Lancelot had also got unsteadily to their feet and were armed with the daggers used by Eburus and the centurion to free them. Neither of them would be much use in a fight with the villagers he could see, not yet.

He searched the faces of those villagers, sure that at least half of them, while enjoying the drama, did not want to commit to taking a side. The other half, however, were on the side of the man, Kunaris, and the middle-aged woman. Aye, Bellicus could call their bluff and simply walk out of the settlement – there was a good chance he and his companions would win any ensuing battle.

But Bellicus had no desire to slaughter simple farmers who were understandably angered by Aife's killing of their kinsman. More would die, on both sides, if the druid refused Yngvildr's contest.

Were his gods stronger than those of the *volva*? Part of him wanted to find out. Had to find out.

"I accept your challenge."

"What?" Eburus cried in disbelief.

Duro merely squeezed Catia's arm and rolled his eyes, as if he'd known all along it would come to this. "Oh, here we go again," he muttered.

CHAPTER TWENTY-SEVEN

"'Here we go again'? What d'you mean?" Bellicus asked Duro as the two sides faced off against one another, the villagers forming up on three sides, the field of high, golden brown wheat stalks behind them all. "When's the last time I had a magical battle with someone? I believe this is the first time since we've known one another."

"Aye, maybe," Duro muttered, eyeing the *volva* who was wandering about on her tiptoes now, which should have been amusing but somehow seemed deeply disturbing. "But it's not the first time you've agreed to some stupid contest."

"It's either this, or we fight to the death," the druid said, rolling his neck muscles as if it was a physical fight he was about to enter.

"We'd win," Duro replied instantly, and Eburus nodded beside him.

"No doubt," Bellicus said. "But some of us might die, and so might some of those innocent villagers who only seek justice for the death of their comrade."

"Fat bastard deserved it," Aife spat. She looked much more like her old self now, tall and proud despite the bruises on her face.

"I'm sure he did," said the druid. "But everything isn't black and white. All sides have valid points and opinions. I'll defeat the Saxon witch and we'll be on our way without any further bloodshed."

"And the *volva* just walks away? To cause more havoc another day?" Catia looked anxious and upset but her tone was filled with anger. "She's dangerous, Bel. Really dangerous. Just look what she's done here in a couple of days."

"And what if she beats you?" Duro asked, brow furrowed.

"She won't," the druid growled. He was confident in his own abilities, but he knew the coming contest would not be a *true* magical battle. There was no time to call up a storm, or a mist, or to read the future from an animal's entrails, or turn the wind, or any of the grand feats mystics were famed for. That sort of thing was what Bellicus thought of as Greater Magic, and it took a lot of time, preparation, dedication, and help from the gods. In truth, the gods would play little part in this battle between druid and *volva*. It would boil down to a test of Lesser Magic. An invaluable tool in a druid's arsenal, of course, but victory this day would prove nothing in terms of which pantheon of deities – Briton or Saxon – held most power.

That would not stop Bellicus, or indeed Yngvildr, claiming so, however.

The *volva* approached the crowd and held something out to one of the men. "A normal coin, isn't it?" she asked in her strangely accented version of the Britons' tongue. The man, and those beside him, peered at it, noting its shape, the silver it was made from, and even the emperor's profile, who Yngvildr claimed was Constantine. The man nodded, as did those gathered nearest to him, and then their curiosity was replaced with utter amazement as the *volva* held up the coin and, with her other hand, *stretched* the metal with seemingly little effort. It was quite a small coin and no longer in use in these lands, but the people who'd touched it were convinced it was genuine, so, to see it somehow expand before their eyes at Yngvildr's touch was not just astonishing, it was terrifying.

"By Mithras!" Duro gasped, turning to gape at Bellicus. "How did she do that?"

"Never mind how she did it," Lancelot muttered, speaking for the first time since his would-be saviours had turned up. "Can you do something better, Bel? That's all that matters." His face was purple, his lips and eyes swollen, and he was almost skeletally thin compared to the last time the druid had seen him, but Bellicus smiled reassuringly at him.

"Watch this," he said with a wink, striding across to the people in the crowd just along from the man who'd tested the magic coin. The people leaned backward, staring up at the huge, shaven-headed man before them. "This is my dagger," he said, reaching down and pulling a knife with a bone handle from somewhere within his clothing. "See it?"

A woman, more interested in the show than fearful of what might happen, reached out. Bellicus let her take it, and she turned it this way and that, to muttered appreciation from those beside her for it was an extremely nice weapon. Far superior to anything the villagers were used to. And yet, for all that, it was merely a dagger, of metal and bone, and the woman handed it back to Bellicus, careful not to cut herself on the finely honed blade.

The druid placed it flat in his hand, and it slowly *floated* up into the air, seemingly without anyone touching it.

The woman before Bellicus burst out laughing almost hysterically then turned and ran backwards, seeking the safety of her kinsfolk for this was surely the work of some dangerous, and possibly evil, force. Everyone around her was also laughing, some fearfully, some in amazement, but all in pleasure. As the dagger slowly floated back down and came to rest once more in Bellicus's great palm he held it out and, nervously, still sniggering, the woman pushed back through the crowd to stand at the front again. She took the knife gingerly, eyeing it as if it might shatter, or turn into a serpent at any moment, but it was just a normal, if rather fancy, dagger, and this she proclaimed as she gave it back to the druid and he sheathed it within his garments again.

"Was that better than a coin getting a little bigger?" Bellicus asked loudly as he turned back to his friends. Eburus grinned and shouted agreement, as did most of the villagers.

The first round had been close, but probably went to the Briton.

Yngvildr was far from done though.

"Is that it?" she cackled, coming to within touching distance of Bellicus, so he could smell her. He recognised the scent of the ointment she used but it was combined with something else, designed to inflame the senses. No wonder the men of this village had been taken in by her, at this distance the woman had an aura of great power about her.

Or perhaps it was just that he couldn't help but find her physically attractive.

She spun away from him and walked along the front row of the audience, smiling confidently at them. As she reached the end of the semi-circle she clapped her hands together and faced the stalks of wheat growing beside them. "Freyja! Mother!" She held out her right hand, gesturing with her fingers as if beckoning someone within the field.

"Who's she talking to?"

"Is there someone in there?"

"She's bloody mad."

The villagers didn't know what to make of the display for, at first, nothing happened. The *volva* did not seem worried, however, and continued to beckon towards the field.

"Look! Look at the flattened wheat!"

All eyes turned to the edge of the circle, where the last stalks of wheat had been trampled. As Yngvildr moved her fingers the stalks, crushed flat into the ground hours before, slowly began to straighten and become upright once more, as if time was somehow reversing.

Again, the people of Shirva reacted with a mixture of joy and terror, laughing, screaming, cursing, and shoving one another as they attempted to put some distance between themselves and the invisible agency that was seemingly raising the wheat from the dead.

Truthfully, not that much wheat stood up again, but it was enough for the crowd to think Yngvildr must be the winner of this round, and she stumbled back from her handiwork as if exhausted by her efforts, as Bellicus looked on, lip curled.

"Wheat?" he called, gesturing at the recently-raised stalks, moving his arm to encompass the rest of the field with its harvest of golden stems. "Truly a gift from Cernunnos, and," he looked upwards to the sun, "Belenus. Without wheat we would have no bread, and we would all likely starve." He walked across to the audience, choosing another section to place himself in front of this time.

An older man, almost completely toothless, gurned at him, as if demanding the druid show him something impressive.

"Wheat," Bellicus repeated, raising his hands so that the old man and those gathered about him could see they were empty. And then he tilted his palms and, as if from nowhere, ears of wheat began to fall, from the druid's hands into the old man's as he stretched them out to catch the falling bounty which quickly turned from a trickle to a torrent.

And then it stopped, and this time the people did not laugh, or cry out, they simply stared in wonder at the pile of materialised wheat.

"Can you do that with beer as well?" the old man demanded, craning his neck to peer up at the druid, who laughed, as did everyone else.

"Pah!" Yngvildr shouted, walking across and pushing in front of the druid. She took the elderly man's hand, still with the wheat in it, and closed the fingers into a fist. Then she stood back and, staring intently at him, commanded, "Open it!"

The old man took a moment to process the *volva*'s accent, but then he did allow his fingers to release, like the petals of a flower opening to the sun's warmth, his palm was revealed. A mouse sat there, tail trailing over the edge of the man's wrinkled hand, nose twitching as it looked about.

The man shouted something unintelligible, grabbing his wrist with his other hand and shaking it in fright. The little mouse jumped off and disappeared into the stalks of wheat Yngvildr had raised moments before. "How?" the greybeard shouted. "How is it possible?"

The villagers were all babbling now, as those who were close enough to witness the impossible feats told those further back all about it. Arms were raised as people gesticulated wildly, shouting and laughing, and others bellowed back in disbelief.

Bellicus looked down at the *volva,* staring into her massive, dilated pupils. She returned his gaze but a muscle in her neck twitched, and the druid knew she was contemplating attacking him. Undoubtedly, she had more than just mice and expanding coins hidden within the folds of her blue dress. That stone blade of hers could appear at any moment.

No-one saw how he did it, but Bellicus's knife suddenly appeared, unsheathed, in his hand. The *volva*, to her credit, did not flinch as he held it up, sunlight glinting off it, but he meant her no harm. He stepped back, away from Yngvildr, and put the handle of the knife in his mouth, so the blade was pointing outwards, towards the villagers. He stood there for a moment, looking rather foolish, and then began to turn widdershins, quickly, his arms never moving from his side.

When he once more faced the crowd, knife still held between his teeth, they eyed him curiously for a few breathless heartbeats, and then someone noticed what had happened.

"It's in its sheath!" a young lad cried. "Look, it's sheathed itself without moving from his mouth!"

The audience surged forward for a closer look but the youngster was correct. Somehow, without him moving his arms, Bellicus had brought the sheath up and put it onto the dagger as he turned in a circle. Even Yngvildr looked surprised and the druid guessed it was a trick she'd never seen before. He couldn't help a small smile forming on the edges of his mouth as he removed the knife and tucked it back into his robe .

The *volva,* face flushing, stepped lightly across to the stalks of wheat she'd raised and plucked two near their base. Then her fingers worked nimbly as she stared at them, as if the wheat was the only thing in the world. Soon enough she was finished and brought her creations over to the watching people.

"It's a little man," a child shouted from atop his father's shoulders. "Two of them!" He was laughing, and his parents joined in, wondering what the woman would do with her straw men.

"Watch," Yngvildr said, reaching out and placing one figure into the little boy's hand. "Now, hearken." She began to sing a soft melody, haunting and beautiful for she had a well-trained, sweet voice which greatly affected the villagers, although in different ways. They did not understand the words of her song, which was in the tongue of her native Jutland, but when she finished she was gazing at the child perched atop his father. "Look," she said.

Everyone looked at the boy, seeing the straw figure in his small hand, unchanged. And then they noticed the *second* figure in his other hand. A dozen pairs of eyes swept across to look at Yngvildr, and her hands were now empty.

"She made it jump from her hand over to little Inam's. Hold it up, boy!"

The child did so, raising both his arms above his head to show everyone the two figures Yngvildr had crafted from wheat. He was laughing and kicking his feet against his father's chest in delight, much to the man's dismay. "It's magic!" screeched the boy, making his father wince even more.

The *volva* wasn't done yet, though. She gave no chance for Bellicus to respond to her trick, instead weaving through the villagers like a wood-spirit, the people parting to let her through. She went inside the feasting hall and returned a moment later, carrying a sturdy iron ladle.

"She's going to magic us up some broth," a man with bushy eyebrows laughed.

"Aye, you'd like that wouldn't you, Tamm, you fat old goat."

The people cheered and laughed at the insult but Tamm didn't mind, he joined in with them, rubbing his bulging belly and licking his lips.

There was to be no soup, however – the ladle was not for food. Yngvildr stood in the circle of wheat and held up the utensil, and then she began to rub its neck. Everyone watched, silence settling over them, wondering what she was doing. Her thumb and forefinger rubbed and then those of the villagers with the best eyesight began to murmur and mutter for the bowl of the ladle seemed to be tilting while the rest of it remained in place. Soon there could be no doubt about it: the top of the utensil was no longer in line with the handle, and then there was a clatter as the top snapped completely off and landed on the crushed wheat.

Yngvildr still held the handle.

"What dark magic is this?" the man whom Kunaris had put on his backside earlier that day shouted. "What kind of demon can snap the head from an iron ladle without even touching it?"

"She was touching it," Kunaris replied, although he sounded uncertain himself.

"Only rubbing it a bit," the other man said hotly. "It would take a lot of force to break something as sturdy as that."

"It's just magic," shouted the little boy on his father's shoulders, and that seemed to explain it all well enough for everyone else, who cheered once again and called for Bellicus to do something too.

The druid had not been impressed with Yngvildr's last two feats. He knew very well how they were done, and they did not take much skill. He could do both within his first year of training on Iova with Qunavo and the other druid tutors. Yet the *volva*'s strange, dance-like movements around the circle of wheat, combined with her sweet voice and natural beauty, made her tricks appear more impressive than they really were.

He needed to do something impressive now. Something to make the people realise his magic was far greater than the interloper's. He looked along the line of people, searching for the type of man every settlement – no matter how small – had at least one of: the handyman. The person who everyone went to when something broke and they didn't know how to fix it. The man who had a tool for every job, and knew how to use them. Bellicus spotted such a man easily enough, for he was standing at the very front of the villagers, arms folded, a collection of small tools hanging from his belt.

"You," the druid said to Kunaris. "Do you have a sturdy cord? Or a narrow chain, even?"

"What for?" the man replied, eyes hooded.

"He does," cried the little boy. "Eisu's got everything in his workshop."

The man didn't look best pleased at the child volunteering such information to the druid but Bellicus's stare was enough to make him stalk off through his fellows, towards a barn-like structure that looked better built than most of the houses in the village. The druid winked at the child, who grinned back, and they waited until Eisu returned, shoving people out of his way.

"Here," the man grunted, thrusting out a length of leather cord about four feet in length. The druid took it without a word, and spun away, striding towards the centre of the flattened wheat circle.

When he turned back he raised the cord and pulled it hard. He was clearly putting great effort into it but the leather held firm. "You," he said to another burly villager. "Come here."

The fellow looked mortified at the thought of standing in front of the audience, but he came forward as commanded, smiling nervously and looking back over his shoulder at a woman who must surely be his wife. She waved jerkily, as if this was the most exciting thing that had ever happened to either of them, which, Bellicus thought, it probably was.

"And you," the druid said, pointing at Kunaris, who was still frowning as if someone had shat in his porridge that morning. "Come."

The villager blew out a heavy, exasperated sigh, and looked at Yngvildr who made no response as she was doing some strange dance and appeared to be completely caught up in her trance now.

"Come on," Bellicus said. "I'm going to place this cord in a knot around my neck, and you two are going to pull it as hard as you can."

Kunaris's eyes lit up as he thought about that, a fierce grin replacing his frown, and he strode forward, hand outstretched as if he couldn't wait to throttle the giant druid who was holding him back from Yngvildr's promises of pleasure.

"Check it," Bellicus said, handing the cord back to Kunaris. "Make sure it's strong. Go on. Show the people how tough it is."

The man took the cord and did as Bellicus had done before him, pulling it as hard as he could. The leather, again, held firm.

"Now you," said the druid, nodding to the other villager. "Check it."

Kunaris handed it over and the burly man took it, straining to try and snap it, his face turning scarlet with the effort. At last, he puffed out a long breath, shaking his head as he gave the cord back to Bellicus.

"It's not going to break," he said. "I'm as strong as an ox."

"So he is!" bellowed his wife from the front of the crowd. "That's my man!"

Bellicus nodded at her, but his smile appeared less confident now. As he lifted the leather cord and looped it around his neck there was clear anxiety on his face. Duro and Eburus shared a glance. Even they had rarely, if ever, seen such an expression cross Bellicus's features for the druid was trained to deal with any kind of dangerous situation without showing trepidation. Yet now he looked unsure of himself, as if he feared the two sturdy villagers might pull the cord so hard it would snap his neck, or crush his windpipe.

"What's he playing at?" Eburus asked in a harsh whisper. "If he gets hurt, we're finished. And this looks like it'll do some damage if it doesn't work as he hopes."

Duro didn't answer, just shook his head, lips set in a thin, tight line.

Bellicus refused to meet their eyes, instead he looked up at the sky and took a long, deep breath before holding each end of the cord out to the villagers. They took it, Kunaris eyeing the druid with fierce determination.

"Are you ready?" Bellicus asked, and there was a tremor in his voice that was so out of character that even the crowd noticed it and felt his fear. The child on his father's shoulders was not smiling now, he was looking down at his mother for reassurance. Many more of the villagers were muttering to one another. This whole ritual was supposed to ensure a good harvest this year; it could hardly be beneficial to their settlement for a druid to be killed there.

Yngvildr had stopped her strange dance and stood watching Bellicus as intently as anyone. Whatever the druid was planning, she did not seem to know what to expect.

He took one more long breath, exhaled slowly, jaw tightening as he steeled himself, then he shouted, "Pull!"

The villagers didn't need to be told twice, both dragged on their end of the cord, Kunaris even clenching his teeth with a savage, hateful grimace. The cord tightened, the druid flinched, and…

Kunaris and the other villager stumbled back as the cord seemed to lose all tension and they were left still holding the leather while Bellicus grinned and raised his hands over his head in triumph.

The crowd exploded in uproar, crying out in amazement and disbelief. Duro and Eburus turned to one another and shared relieved smiles, as did Aife and Lancelot. Only Catia seemed unsurprised. Either she had more faith in the druid's powers than anyone else, or she'd seen him do this particular trick before and knew all along that it would end well.

"You're not beating that, witch!" shouted Eburus, moving towards Yngvildr and the two remaining Saxon warriors. "We've won, and we're leaving now. You'd better get to your ship and sail back to Hengist and the rest of your filthy sea-wolf friends before word reaches King Cunedda that you're here, and he sends his warband to deal with you."

His words had no effect on the *volva*, or her guards, but the villagers, now that Yngvildr had been bested by Bellicus, seemed to remember where their loyalties lay. And the fact that Cunedda was also their king.

"There must be a blood sacrifice," Yngvildr stated flatly, her voice strong enough to be heard over the murmurs of the audience. "The gods expect it, and they must be appeased, or things will not go well for this settlement."

"Sacrifice a sheep, then," Bellicus retorted. "Or one of your guards. We'll help you, if you like." He drew his sword, Melltgwyn, and the earlier anxiety that had been on his face was gone, replaced with his usual confidence. He also seemed to have grown in stature since the trick with the cord, so that he once more towered above everyone there, even Eburus.

"A sheep is no use," said Yngvildr, sidling towards the centre of the flattened wheat. She still seemed to be in an altered state, eyes rolling as she moved, sometimes on tip-toes, sometimes bending her limbs as if she did not have full control over them. It might have been comical if she wasn't exhorting the people to slaughter someone. "Only a human sacrifice will sate the gods' desire for blood."

Although defeated by the druid, she yet held an aura of mystical power that affected almost everyone gathered there, holding them in place as she came to stand in front of Aife.

"You want my blood?" the Pictish princess asked coolly. "Come and take it."

Even Kunaris knew this had to end now, before all their lives changed forever. "Come, Yngvildr. We can find some animal suitable for your ritual."

As he spoke, the *volva* lunged, her broken stone dagger appearing as if magically in her hand. Aife flinched, but she was not Yngvildr's target, the Pictish princess had been yet more misdirection in a morning filled with it.

Catia was the target.

The grey blade, dull in colour yet as sharp as a razor, sliced through the air towards the child's neck. Yngvildr knew the jugular vein would mean certain death for Catia, and plenty of blood to soak the field below, but Eburus moved faster than anyone. Although as surprised as the rest of the audience by the sudden attack, he instinctively raised his sword, the blade managing to knock aside the stone dagger and Catia fell back, safely out of range.

Yngvildr screamed in rage as Eburus, off balance, stumbled. And again the stone blade, robbed of half its length but not its lethal power, plunged forward, this time sliding between the Votadini champion's ribs. It bit deeply and Eburus grunted, but Yngvildr stabbed again, and again, in three different parts of his torso. Each time it slid home, and, by the time he fell onto the crushed wheat the *volva*'s hand was slick with rich, dark blood.

CHAPTER TWENTY-EIGHT

"Yngvildr!" Kunaris roared in shock as the big, red-headed giant lay down, eyes wide, unmoving. The villagers were screaming, some were crying, and the two Saxons had run forward to defend their *volva*, swords drawn although they appeared as stunned as everyone else.

"You bitch!" Aife shouted, trying to land a thrust of her own borrowed knife into the witch, but Yngvildr was fast, and darted back a step, just out of reach, grinning triumphantly.

There could be no escape for her, though. Duro, roaring a war-cry, took on one of the Saxon men, rage making him fight with a ferocity that was unusual even for the centurion. He smashed his spatha against his opponent's sword, once, twice, but on the third strike the Saxon's arm twisted back painfully and he cried out, lowering his guard and allowing Duro's blade to tear through his windpipe.

Blood gouted, but Duro was already moving onto the second enemy warrior who'd placed himself in front of Yngvildr. Both Aife and Lancelot were before him, the long knives they'd been given by Eburus and the druid held out, probing for an opening as the Saxon held them off.

"Eburus." Bellicus knelt beside his fallen friend. He pulled up the Votadini champion's shirt, knowing it would not have offered any protection against the stone knife. Had Eburus been wearing even a simple mail shirt it would likely have turned the blade for it was wide and, although it had a wicked edge, the point was fairly dull. But Eburus was not wearing any armour for it was warm and the Votadini had not thought there was any need for it. Perhaps if they'd had time to prepare for this day's events they would all have worn their mail and the Votadini might have run here with his prized black shield instead of leaving it with their horses.

"Am I dying?"

The druid was jolted back to reality as he heard his friend speak. The wounds were deep and pulsing blood and at least one of them, Bellicus knew, had been a mortal blow. There was no way, no magic, to reverse such an injury.

"Aye," he whispered, unwilling to lie.

"Is Catia all right?"

Tears rolled down Bellicus's cheeks and he nodded, smiling. "Aye," he repeated. "You saved her, brother. Thank you."

A peaceful expression came over Eburus's face as he accepted the druid's words. "Make sure I reach the Otherlands, please, Bel."

"I will. You'll be welcomed by the gods at their feasting table, I've no doubt of it." He sobbed, unable to stop himself. "Save me a place beside you, my friend."

The Votadini champion's fingers jerked and Bellicus looked, seeing his friend's hand was empty. He reached out and lifted the sword that had fallen onto the flattened wheat and placed the grip into Eburus's palm, closing his fingers around it.

And then, with a final gasp, Eburus went still, and a terrible fury replaced Bellicus's sorrow.

The remaining Saxon was still holding off Duro and the badly weakened Aife and Lancelot. The ringing clatter of blades meeting carried out over the life-giving, golden wheat as Bellicus jumped up and took his place beside the centurion. They knew one another like brothers by this point and fought with an understanding that was rare on the battlefield. As Bellicus swung Melltgwyn the Saxon desperately parried it, eyes wide with the knowledge that death was mere moments away. And he was right, for Duro took advantage of the opening and hacked his spatha down into the enemy's wrist. It cut deep and the sword fell from the Saxon's grip before Bellicus, screaming in rage, thrust the point of his weapon right through the man's torso in a spray of crimson.

Yngvildr was already running, sprinting away through the field of wheat, calling for her gods to accept the blood sacrifices.

"After her," Lancelot shouted, although it was clear he was in no shape to do much running, and neither was Aife, bruised and beaten beside him. They set off after her however, pushing their way through the wheat and finding it more of an obstacle than expected.

Bellicus was not so easily stopped. He ordered Cai to stay with the others then charged into the field, long legs thrashing through the plants, leaves and kernels flying in the sun. Duro wasn't sure whether to follow his friend or help Eburus, but Catia was already kneeling beside the downed Votadini. Her tear-filled eyes did not do much for the centurion's humour, and he raced into the wheat, following the path Bellicus had already cleared.

"Come back, witch," the druid was shouting. "Our battle is not over!"

Yngvildr was not tall and she could only just be seen forcing her way through the field for, with the wheat overdue to be harvested, the golden stalks came up to, or even beyond, the *volva*'s chin. She was no longer interested in putting on a performance or impressing anyone. Perhaps her trance had worn off, or been nothing more than part of her act, but, as she glanced across her shoulder at her pursuers, her eyes were clear, her demeanour lucid. She wanted to escape and live to see the fruits of her ritual. It might not have been the princesses who'd spilled their blood for the gods, but three powerful warriors, and the violent nature of their deaths, would count for much.

Much more than a sheep or a chicken anyway.

She looked back again, tiring now for it was hard going in the field. Fear was written plainly on her face as Bellicus was easily narrowing the distance between them.

And then, as they ran the druid noticed his quarry was suddenly moving faster now. She must have cleared the field and be running on more level ground. He cursed, but still felt confident of catching her, for where could she go? He had another trick, of sorts, that might help, he thought. Throwing knives at a target – a person, usually – was considered fine entertainment by most kings and lords, and Bellicus had learned the skill as part of his druid training. Of course, the idea in those displays was to *miss* the target and leave them unscathed, but the technique could just as easily be applied in a more lethal fashion.

He reached down, barely breaking his stride, and took out his knife. The *volva* was still a fair distance away, but he knew he would be able to close the gap between them once he too was free of the field, and then it would be simple enough matter to hammer the blade into the small of her back. Even if the throw wasn't enough to kill Yngvildr, it would stop her in her tracks and allow the druid to catch her. Then justice would be done, Eburus would be avenged, and the gods would have yet another sacrifice to revel in.

And then the *volva* disappeared.

Bellicus almost stopped running, so amazed was he. Had the *volva* managed to perform one last feat of magic, travelling not just in spirit to the Otherlands, but in body as well? He slowed, hearing Duro shouting behind him, wondering what had happened, but then he came over a crest in the field and the land sloped downwards, revealing a river.

"The Celefyn," he said. "I forgot that was so nearby." *Celefyn* meant stem, or stalk, and the name seemed fitting, given how close it was to the fields of wheat. No doubt that was what had given the river its name back in the mists of time. His meandering thoughts, mirrored in the passage of the water through the land, were quickly jolted back to more pressing matters as the druid now discovered how Yngvildr had disappeared from his sight.

Either by the gods' design, or by sheer chance, the *volva* had reached the river right at the spot where a small boat had been left. Its owner was shouting, shaking his fist in the air as the Saxon woman used the single oar to push the vessel into the centre of the fast-flowing river. She was already a good distance away from them and, as Bellicus came up behind the enraged owner of the boat, Yngvildr laughed and made a crude gesture towards them.

"That's my bloody boat," shouted the man at Bellicus, as if the druid had stolen the thing himself.

"Are there any more of them nearby?"

"More of what? Women?" The man was either too stupid, or too stunned by the theft of his property, to understand the question and he shook his head, frowning.

"No, boats, you fool!" Bellicus retorted, eyes scanning the riverbank left and right but seeing nothing that could help him.

"No. That's the only one, and it's mine."

He ran off along the bank as Duro ran breathlessly up to join Bellicus. Neither of them continued the chase, for it was obviously futile. Yngvildr was already a long way away as the waters were flowing fast. Already quite tired after running through the field, the thought of trying to keep pace with the Celefyn's currents, perhaps for miles, was not a realistic one for the druid.

"She's getting away," the centurion spat. "What the hell was that fool even doing here in a boat?" He looked around, seeing a small camp site, with a smouldering fire and a tripod setup over it for cooking.

"Just a traveller," Bellicus muttered. "Who happened to be here just as the witch needed a boat to save her."

There was nothing more to be said to that and they continued to stare at the water even after Yngvildr was carried around a bend and disappeared, along with the enraged owner of the boat. Neither druid nor centurion wanted to face the prospect of returning to the village and dealing with the aftermath of the magical battle and the *volva*'s blood ritual.

The druid sighed at last and turned to his friend, placing a hand on his arm. "Come on," he said heavily. "Let's get back and… see to Eburus."

CHAPTER TWENTY-NINE

When Bellicus and Duro returned to Shirva they found the crowd had mostly dispersed. Aife, Lancelot and Catia were sitting on the wheat, dull-eyed and drained of energy. The corpses of the Saxons had been removed.

"You're back." Kunaris, seeing the black expression on the druid's face, had enough sense not to ask after Yngvildr. "That's good. You'll need to call your dog away so the women can tend to your friend."

Duro's face lit up at the man's words. "Tend to him? Eburus is still alive?" He saw Cai lying beside their fallen friend, a low growl in his throat as one of the village women tried to approach. And then he saw what the woman, and her companions, carried: Water to wash the blood from his wounds, and oils to anoint his body.

"No, he's dead," Kunaris replied bluntly. "The women need to prepare him for his journey to the Otherlands though, and the hound won't let anyone near."

Bellicus looked sadly at Cai and walked over, kneeling beside his canine friend, who whined as they touched heads together and the druid placed an arm around the dog, burying his face in the soft, smooth fur. Catia, face twisted and tear-streaked, ran across and joined their embrace. They remained in the same position for a long time until, at last, the druid gave both Cai and Catia pats on their heads and stood up. His expression was blank but his eyes were rimmed with red as he stared down at the young man he'd met as an enemy roughly eighteen months before but ended up classing as one of his best, and closest companions.

"Call the dog away, druid," Kunaris mumbled. "Let the women do their jobs."

Bellicus turned, lip curled in fury but, before he could move, Duro's fist shot out, striking the headman full in the mouth and sending him crashing to the ground.

"This is all down to you," the druid said, coming to stand over the dazed Kunaris. "You were so desperate to spill your seed in the Saxon witch that you were willing to allow the murder of three innocents."

"And that's led to the death of your own Votadini champion!" bellowed Duro. "This village is Votadini too, isn't it, Bel? Cunedda is king to these folk?"

"Aye," the druid confirmed.

"I wonder what he'll do when he finds out what's happened here today then. And that's not to mention King Drest, when he hears word from his daughter, who you were ready to sacrifice." He pointed towards Aife and Kunaris, hand held to his bloodied teeth and lips, blanched.

"Or *her* mother, Queen Narina of Alt Clota," put in Bellicus, nodding towards Catia. "Or Arthur, Bear of Britain, whose friend and companion Lancelot, would also have been one of your blood sacrifices here."

"I never knew any of that," shouted Kunaris in a tremulous voice. "My own brother was killed too. We were all taken in by the Saxon woman's magic, not just me. You saw how powerful she was. She fooled every one of us."

"All I saw was a pretty face, a nice figure, and a weak man whose intelligence is in his cock!" Duro kicked out at the fallen man, aiming between his legs, but Kunaris flinched to the side and took the brunt of the blow in his leg.

Catia stood up and walked across to Duro, taking his hand in hers. He looked down at her and the rage and loss that were so evident on his face seemed to drain away, replaced by a heavy, deep sorrow.

"Leave him be," she said. "Please, Duro. This isn't you, attacking a defenceless man. You're better than that. The gods will deal with him."

"She's right, centurion." Aife also joined them, staring hard at Kunaris, but her touch was gentle as she gripped Duro's other hand. "Eburus died bravely, as a true warrior. He saved Catia's life. Now we should honour him."

The centurion's face twisted and he turned away, looking into the distance as tears rolled down his cheeks. "Death is never far away," he said in a choked tone. "Especially for a soldier. But it never gets any easier to lose a friend."

"I'm sorry," Kunaris said, getting to his feet and facing Bellicus. "I truly am. I feel like…like my head was deep in the clouds and only now have they drifted away. I don't understand what came over me. I just wanted justice for my brother, and the Saxons offered it to me."

The druid stared at him wordlessly. He was not in the mood for forgiveness. "I don't want to upset Princess Catia," he growled. "So, I won't take your face off. Have someone find and take care of our horses – three of them, tethered over to the east, all right? Good, now get out of my sight, and make sure your people look after Eburus, or I'll leave your village a smoking ruin."

The man paled but recognised this was his chance to save himself from the punishment he probably deserved. "I will, my lord," he said, bowing his head and practically running from the field towards the village centre. Eburus's body had already been carried in that direction by the local women, to be prepared for whatever funerary rites the druid wished to carry out.

Duro gently freed his hands from the princesses' grips and walked into the centre of the flattened wheat. There, he sat down, put his hands around his knees, and stared soundlessly ahead, lost in his own thoughts. Cai padded over and lay down against him as the centurion laid his hand on the dog's broad back.

"I didn't realise you and Duro were so close to Eburus," said Catia, watching the centurion.

Bellicus nodded, the hint of a smile touching his lips. "Aye, it took a while, but we grew to love the big fool. He was good company, and a loyal, brave friend. None of this should have happened, but at least he saved you." He reached out and put his arm around the girl, hugging her in tight.

"What now?" asked Lancelot in a dull, exhausted tone. "I can't face much more excitement."

"Agreed," the druid nodded. "It's good to see you again but, by the gods, man, you look like shit."

Lancelot didn't smile, for the druid hadn't been making a joke. "I know."

"Eburus needs to be properly sent on his way to the Otherlands," Bellicus said, louder so that all of his friends could hear, not just the swordsman. "And then we'll get on our way, back to Dun Breatann. We can talk things over properly on the road."

"We're staying here tonight?" Duro asked unhappily.

"Aye, I think that's for the best. We'll celebrate Eburus's life, and allow Lancelot, Aife, and Catia to recover as best they can from what they've been through. The villagers will be keen to win our favour after all this, so we'll take advantage of their food and drink and get a decent night's rest."

"What if Yngvildr returns?" Duro said, turning to look in the direction her stolen boat had taken her. "There might be more Saxons around that she can enlist. There's at least a couple of them unaccounted for, if the headman in Kinneil was right, and eight of them came from the ships to chase Lancelot and the princesses."

"They won't bother us," the druid said with conviction although how he could be so sure no-one could say. "They're long gone. We can sleep soundly tonight."

"And if the witch does come back," put in Aife, eyes as cold the stone of the *volva*'s sacrificial knife, "she won't escape death a third time. By Taranis, I'll finish the job properly, like we should have done when we had the chance that first night."

There were men and women from the village coming towards them and, instinctively, Bellicus gripped his sword hilt, and Duro swiftly got to his feet. Perhaps these people had decided removing all witnesses to what had happened here would be the best solution to their problems…But they were merely coming to offer food and drink to the companions.

"You all go with them," the druid suggested. "Rest, and fill your bellies. I'll go and make sure Eburus is ready for his final journey. Can one of you take me to him?"

"I'll do it," said a middle-aged woman, and Bellicus recognised her. She'd been speaking to Kunaris earlier and the similarity in their features told him she must be the man's mother.

"Lead the way," the druid said, holding his palm out towards the settlement.

"Would you…" She broke off, looking awkwardly about. "Would you…My son was killed yesterday too." She drew in a ragged breath, the strength seeming to empty from her as she tried to tell the druid what she wanted from him.

"You want me to perform the funerary rites for your son? Of course, I can do that."

She released her breath, sobbing in relief as Bellicus took her arm to steady her and they began walking towards the village, escorted by Cai.

Her son had been part of the group that had started all this trouble, but the fight was over. Now it was time to heal and to say farewell to loved ones, and both of those were as much the druid's tasks as wielding Melltgwyn in battle.

As they walked, Bellicus was already planning what he would say during the funeral but the reality of the situation only seemed to hit him as they came to the windowless building where Eburus's body had been taken for cleaning and preparation. The sight of the tall, muscular Votadini champion – so strong and brash and energetic in life yet now silent and utterly still within that shadowy hovel – made the druid pause and, for a terrible, brief moment, he felt as though he could not go on.

Kunaris's mother felt him hesitate and they looked at one another, sharing a moment of deep understanding before she touched his arm reassuringly and Bellicus felt his resolve returning. He gave a slight nod, and they went inside to make Eburus ready for his final journey.

CHAPTER THIRTY

It felt strange for Bellicus to be the one conducting the cremation rites for, although it was a druid's task and he'd done it many times over the years, the pain he was feeling made it harder than usual. Of course, he knew the Votadini warrior would make his way to the Otherlands and then be reborn in some other place and time where they might even meet as friends once more. That did not take away the sense of loss. Or the knowledge that the journey back to Dun Breatann would be that much quieter and less enjoyable without the presence of the man who'd become such a welcome addition to the druid's inner circle.

The fact that Eburus was so young, still only in his mid-twenties, only made it harder to take. He had so much yet to do, and would never have the chance now, thanks to the Saxon *volva*. Gods! Hengist's sea-wolves had caused so much pain since the Roman legions had departed. Where would it all end?

All of this had come out as Bellicus lamented his companion's death, before the fires were lit and the bier containing the body had been consumed by the flames. The image of the red-haired, tall warrior with the black shield which he'd taken from a defeated Saxon resting on his chest would live forever in Bellicus's memory. One day he would avenge Eburus, but for now they had to return to Dun Breatann and set things right there.

"You did him great honour. I think he would have been very pleased by your words, and the obvious respect and love you held for him."

Bellicus looked to the side and nodded at Aife. Her bruises were even more livid today, but she would heal quickly enough. It was, the druid had to admit, something of a miracle that only one of their group had been lost during these past few weeks adventuring around the country.

"I know you're the druid, and it's *your* job to help people come to terms with loss and grief but...If you ever want to talk, I'm here."

Bellicus felt a lump in his throat at the princess's words and forced a smile. He didn't know Aife all that well, having only spent a little time together in Dun Breatann before he'd journeyed south with Duro and their warband to join Arthur and Lancelot, but he liked her a great deal. The fact that she'd protected Catia all through their travels, and now offered to listen to his troubles, only raised his opinion even higher.

"Thank you," he said. "Maybe we can talk more when we're in Dun Breatann and everything is sorted out." He saw her frown and sighed. "I know," he said. "There's been enough trouble and upset recently, but we need to start thinking about how to deal with things in the fortress. You'll have to explain to me why you ran off, and took Catia with you on such a dangerous trip."

"Ysfael," she replied without hesitation.

"Tell me," he said.

* * *

"Are you all right?"

The centurion smiled at Catia, his face lighting up for the first time since they'd started riding west from Shirva that morning. "I should be asking you that, princess," he said. "After everything you've been through. You'll need to tell us all about it sometime. I bet Bel can make it into a great legend, one that'll be told all throughout these lands."

"It won't take much," she laughed. "I still can't believe all the things that led to us coming here today." Her face fell then. "I wonder if the men who were slaves beside Lancelot got away, or if they were caught."

Duro remained silent. Although they'd all spent the previous day together no-one had said much, for Eburus's sudden death made everything else seem unimportant, so he had no idea what Catia meant when she talked about other slaves. The princess's tale could wait for another day to be properly told though. The centurion could see Bellicus and Aife chatting earnestly and guessed what the topic of conversation must be. He wondered if he should get Catia's side of the tale but he felt it was better if the druid gathered the information he needed himself, without Duro possibly confusing things.

"How do you like Lancelot?" he asked, shifting the subject away to something he hoped would be happier for them all.

"Better, since he had a bath," she replied, smirking.

"Come on," Lancelot said in a hurt tone. "I didn't smell that bad."

"Aye, you did," the girl said, wafting her hand in front of her face as if the noxious fumes were still lingering in the air around them. "But," she spoke to Duro again, "he helped protect us and kept us alive so, I suppose he's not too bad."

"You two kept me alive, more like," the swordsman averred and there was no humour in his words, just gratitude.

"Well, it seems everyone is a hero today then." Duro laughed. "All saving one another and becoming the best of friends, that's what I like to hear."

The three of them smiled at one another and, thankfully, no-one mentioned Eburus.

"Whatever happened to that fancy helmet?" Duro asked Lancelot. "The one Arthur gifted you?"

The blond rider shook his head sorrowfully. "Leofdaeg stole it from me. One day I'll take it back." He trailed off, gazing into the distance as if imagining that future meeting with the Saxon jarl, and then, looking over his shoulder for the tenth time that hour he said, "When will we be safely in the fortress? I keep expecting someone else to come chasing along the road after us."

"Frightened, eh?" Duro said, shaking his head.

"Of course," Lancelot agreed happily. "As you know, old man, I'm the greatest blademaster in all Britain when I'm fully fit and healthy. Brave, deadly, and irresistible to women."

"Oh, aye," Duro growled in reply, looking sidelong at Catia who seemed unsure what to make of Lancelot's boasts. Was he serious?

His eyes were sparkling beneath his blond fringe, however, as he continued. "But in the state I'm in now, centurion, I'd rather avoid another fight. So – when will we reach Dun Breatann?"

"You're safe," Catia told him, pointing up at a nearby hill. "That old fort is in my mother's lands. We're in Alt Clota and we'll reach the fortress very soon."

"Not that soon."

She turned and eyed the druid curiously. "What do you mean, Bel?"

"Aife's told me everything that's been happening with Prince Ysfael." He looked grimly at Duro and Lancelot. "We'll stop here now. Rest the horses, and have something to eat and drink ourselves while we prepare for our return to Dun Breatann. Have no fears, though. Everything will turn out right in the end." He smiled, and it was a genuine, hopeful expression. "Dun Breatann is my home, and Catia's. We'll make sure you're all safe."

"I hope you'll also make sure I get a proper feed," Lancelot said wryly, rubbing his shrunken belly. "Those village folk did their best, but their feast was frugal, even for a man who's barely eaten in weeks. I'm looking forward to plenty of fresh bread, butter, cheese, roast beef and pork, ale…" He trailed off, visibly salivating at the images he was conjuring in his mind.

"Stop it," Duro muttered. "You're just making everyone hungry."

"Here," Bellicus said, reaching into his pack and tossing the centurion some dried beef. "Just pretend that's freshly cooked and dripping with juices. We'll fill our bellies properly in just a few short hours. Oh, it's going to be good to finally go home, I can hardly wait to see the walls of Dun Breatann again!"

CHAPTER THIRTY-ONE

"By Mithras's cock! What's happened here?" Duro stared up at the massive volcanic rock which Dun Breatann was built upon and shook his head in disbelief. "Bel, what is this madness?"

The druid was also gazing upwards at the walls, mouth set in a tight line. "Ysfael," he growled.

Aife had not spoken yet, but when Catia reached out to her the Pictish princess moved away, looking up and grasping the hilt of her sword. She was mouthing something, a prayer perhaps, or a promise. "Why?" she demanded, rounding on Bellicus as if this had something to do with him. "Because I escaped? What kind of monster would do something like…that!"

She flung her hand out, indicating the bodies that were hanging, black and bloated, from the fortress's high walls. They'd been too small to see as the group came towards the fortress, but, as they drew closer everyone had fallen silent. In the lands north of the Roman walls it was an old tradition to hang the bodies, or body parts of vanquished enemies, around a fortress in order to warn others about the brutality of the victors and to glory in their own triumph, so this display was not entirely strange. When Aife had recognised one of the bodies, a man, swinging slowly in the breeze, eyes gone thanks to the questing beaks of jackdaws, surprise had turned to fear. He was a Pict, the son of a very powerful nobleman, left to rot in the open along with all the rest of the prisoners taken after the battle with King Drest's army. What had gone on here?

"Let's find out," the druid said, voice level. There was no point in jumping to conclusions – perhaps there had been trouble with the prisoners and hanging was their punishment. Maybe the deaths had nothing to do with Ysfael.

They approached the gates and the guards there immediately recognised the giant druid on his black steed. "You're home," they cried, grinning and calling down to their comrades beneath the walkway to unbar the outer gates. "And Princess Catia too! But where's Eburus?" There was great excitement and the travellers could hear running feet as a messenger was dispatched to make his way up to the main part of the fortress. Their arrival would soon be the talk of the place. Ysfael and Narina would undoubtedly be ready to greet them in the great hall. That is, unless the queen couldn't wait to see her daughter and ran down the many steps to see her as soon as possible.

The gates swung inwards and the small party passed through, dismounting and handing their horses over to the stablehands. Duro's face was set in a frown and he said in a low voice to Bellicus, "Some of those soldiers aren't Damnonii. Ysfael still has his men on guard duty."

The druid didn't reply, just gave a barely imperceptible nod of agreement. Things had not changed much in their absence, it seemed.

"I have a bad feeling about all this," the centurion murmured, loosening his spatha in its sheath. "Are you sure we should just walk into whatever is being prepared for us up there? It's like the time when we came back from Dalriada and the king tried to kill you all over again."

"What do you mean?" Catia had noticed their surreptitious conversation and came to stand with them. "Is my mother all right? What's happening, Bel?" There was a note of panic in the girl's voice but her face changed in an instant, lighting up as if the summer sun had just come out from behind a cloud and shone full upon her.

"Catia! Oh, you're home, my girl. Oh, praise be to Lug!"

Narina came flying down the stairs just as Bellicus and his companions reached them. The queen was wearing a white dress and had her hair tied up in a tight bun. She looked pretty, if slightly dishevelled, but he had little time to ponder the queen's appearance before he found himself in her embrace.

"Thank you, Bel," she was sobbing, having already practically squeezed the breath from Catia before moving onto him. "You've brought her back safely to me again." She grinned through her tears of joy and relief, then quickly hugged Duro before returning to Catia and taking her hand as if she would never let it go. "Oh, I'm so happy to have you back, my love."

"Happy to have her back?"

Narina flinched and turned to look at Aife, whose venom-filled question had caught the attention of everyone nearby.

"How nice for you, *my lady*." The epithet seemed more of an insult than a term of respect and the Damnonii guards shuffled closer nervously, realising the Pictish warrior-princess had a sword strapped to her belt. None of them had thought to check on her status: Was she still a prisoner? Should they have disarmed her? It was too late now, for she was standing right before the queen, face twisted in fury, hand resting on the pommel of her weapon. "It's a pity the mothers and fathers of my kinsmen who are hanging, rotting, from your walls won't enjoy a similar, happy reunion. *How dare you?*"

"That's enough." A new voice, calm and commanding, filled the air and Dun Breatann's grizzled guard captain, Gavo, strode down the stairs, coming to stand protectively in front of Narina and Catia, who looked like she didn't know which way to turn, her loyalty to Aife tugging at her despite the love she felt for her mother.

"Enough?"

"Aye, enough, Princess," Gavo replied firmly. "This isn't the time or the place for a discussion. I don't know why you've come back here, or what led you to leave in the first place, but you are still a prisoner of war. Our prisoner." He held out his hand. "Give me the sword." He glanced at Bellicus. "I'm amazed you let her walk in here armed, druid."

Aife stood, jaw clenched, while those around her waited awkwardly to see how the situation would resolve itself. Lancelot was at her back but he remained silent for now.

"Aife, give me the sword or the guards will have to disarm you and more people will get hurt." Gavo remained standing with his hand out, but his tone seemed more like that of a kindly father-figure than a threatening soldier, despite his words.

The princess looked at Bellicus and he nodded. "I'll make sure you're not harmed," he said, loudly enough that everyone could hear, letting them all know that they'd face his wrath if anything happened to her. "We'll sort this, Aife. Give him the blade, just for now."

She glared at Narina, eyes blazing with the desire to avenge the dead Picts, but she drew out the sword and held it out, hilt-first, to Gavo, and a collective sigh of relief could be heard as everyone allowed themselves to relax.

"What's happening down here?" More footsteps and another shape appeared on the stairs. "Is Catia back? Is the Pictish bitch with her? She can hang with her kinsmen if she is."

"You bastard!" Aife's mouth twisted in a snarl and she pulled back her hand, then, before anyone could react, threw the sword at Ysfael. Every ounce of strength, all her rage and pain, were channelled into the missile and it flashed through the air, a blur of wood and steel.

It missed the Votadini prince by a finger-width, passing his face and striking the living rock behind him. There was a metallic clatter as the energy dissipated in that breathless instant, and then it fell, spent, on the ground as Ysfael yelled in fear.

"Enough!" Bellicus lunged forward and put his massive arms around Aife, lifting her clear off the ground as she tried to break free of his grasp. She was incandescent with rage, however, throwing her head back in an attempt to break the druid's nose and he was forced to put her down, kicking her feet away and dropping on top of her as she continued to thrash and scream.

Duro and Lancelot scowled as the gate guards ran over and helped Bellicus subdue Aife, rope being produced to bind the princess's arms and legs behind her back. Of course, given her recent ordeal in Shirva, this produced a predictable, even more ferocious reaction as she tried to bite her captors.

Catia ran forward and Narina tried to pull her back but the girl broke free and went to the older princess's side. "Please, Aife, stop fighting them, you're going to get hurt! I won't let anyone harm you, please just stop fighting!" She was crying, the tears and panicked expression a stark contrast to her usual maturity and self-control.

Aife was also crying but it was clear she would never be able to break free and, at last, she ceased her struggles and just lay still on the ground, looking at Catia.

"Take her up and get a rope around her neck!" Ysfael shoved past Gavo and called to those of his own men who were amongst the guards. "Crazy bitch almost killed me with that sword! Come on, what are you waiting for? She can share the same fate as the rest of the Picts, that's what we agreed, Narina."

"Shut up, Ysfael," the queen shouted. She was shaking and walked up behind Catia, gently drawing her into a hug which seemed designed more to comfort Narina than her daughter who looked like she'd rather stand with Aife.

"Shut up?" the prince demanded and now it was his turn to shriek with rage. "Did you not see what she did? She tried to murder me!" He turned back to look at his men who still hadn't moved to follow his order to take Aife up the rock. "What are you waiting for? You, druid, lift her up and—"

For such a giant man, Bellicus could move with astonishing speed when he wanted and suddenly he was on his feet and had his hands on Ysfael's rich, blue tunic. He gripped the material and lifted the prince right off the ground, teeth bared in a lupine snarl as Cai began to bark viciously at the Votadini warriors who had now made a move to run forward and help their lord. The druid threw Ysfael against the stone wall that marked the beginning of the stairs and stared into his eyes.

"I'm warning you now, you fool," he growled. "If you try to harm the Princess *again* I will call down the wrath of Taranis and make your balls swell until they burst, and then I'll lift you like this, and throw you over the wall up there myself, do you hear me?" He punctuated the question by slamming Ysfael against the wall again and raising his voice to a deafening roar. "Do you?"

The Votadini men had no way to help their prince as Cai, Duro, Lancelot, Gavo and the Damnonii guards formed a cordon around the druid.

"I'll have your head for this," Ysfael grunted breathlessly. "I swear it, druid. You can't treat me like this in my own home. I am the queen's consort."

Bellicus, still holding him aloft as if he weighed no more than a sparrow, stared at him in thoughtful silence. At length, as Cai continued to growl and Duro warned Ysfael's men to stay back or feel his 'spatha up their arses', the druid dropped him onto his feet but, instead of letting him go, he grabbed the prince's arm and bent it up his back then pushed him forward, towards the gates.

"What are you doing?" Ysfael shouted, face twisting as Bellicus nudged his arm and sent a shock of pain through it. "Get your hands off me, you big oaf." He stumbled and Cai lunged forward, snapping, but Bellicus quickly hauled him back up and they continued walking as everyone stared, wondering what would happen next.

"Open the gates," the druid shouted to the men who were still manning the outer walls. He didn't need to tell them twice; the main bar was removed, deadbolts clattering as the great entrance was swung open once again.

"Narina! Command this idiot to leave me go. Tell your men to stop him! Ow!"

They passed beneath the gatehouse's walkway, watched by the stunned yet greatly entertained guards, and then Bellicus released the prince's arm, shoving him hard. Ysfael stumbled forwards and the druid turned, walking back through the gates. "Bar them," he said.

The Votadini Prince, husband to Alt Clota's Queen, gaped as the mighty wooden gates were pushed shut and barred against him. He was apparently too astonished to protest, or perhaps just happy not to have suffered a more thorough beating at Bellicus's hands.

"Don't open those gates until I tell you to," the druid said to the guards, who nodded, eyes shining with merriment, and then he strode back, through the second, inner gates, and commanded those be shut too.

Every eye was on him as he returned to reach down and lift Aife gently to her feet. He apologised for her rough treatment, and for the welcome she'd received at Dun Breatann, but he did not remove her bonds. That seemed unwise, for now.

"What are you doing, Bel?" the queen asked in a low voice. "Ysfael might be…well," she glanced at the Votadini warriors and decided she'd said enough about their prince. "But he's my husband and deserves more respect than you've shown him."

"And Aife is a princess and deserved more respect than anyone here has shown her." He spoke levelly but his tone was hard. No-one rebuked him – Narina was queen of the Damnonii tribe but, in their culture the druid was just as powerful, in his own way. In some ways even more so. The fact that he was almost seven feet tall and had an enormous brute of a wardog by his side also held any would-be opponents in check.

"Let him stew outside the gates for a while," said Duro. "You two, along with Gavo, need to discuss what's happened here, and what's going to be happening going forward."

Narina sighed but nodded. "Fine," she said, pulling Catia towards the stairs. "Not here though. Come on, we'll go to the hall.

You, and you." She pointed at two of the Votadini warriors, close companions of the absent prince. "Follow me. The rest of you do as Bellicus commanded and keep the gates locked for now."

The two Votadini that she'd indicated seemed reluctant to go with her but a look from the druid made their minds up and they fell in behind the queen and Catia as they made their way up towards the central portion of the fortress where the main living quarters were.

Bellicus bent and removed the rope from Aife's legs, allowing her to walk, then they, along with Duro, Gavo, Lancelot and Cai, followed them up the dozens of stairs to the flat section of the fortress. They passed Bellicus's own house and he looked at it longingly, wishing he could go in, drink some ale, and sleep, but that would have to wait. He would need to stay alert for now, for lots of different things were at play here in Dun Breatann's internal politics.

He looked at Gavo and received a small but firm nod. The guard captain was on his side anyway, as expected.

"Catia," said the druid when they were finally standing outside the great hall, its chimney hole belching sweet-swelling cooking smoke that made more than one person's belly rumble in anticipation. "You go with Aife to her quarters. Are they still empty, my Queen? Good, then one of you two"—he pointed at the Votadini guards— "escort them up, along with one of Gavo's men, and stand guard outside." He smiled at both princesses. "Please just be patient, we'll not take long. Nothing will happen to you." That last comment was gravid with meaning and the two warriors delegated to take care of Catia and Aife knew it. The girls were led away and Bellicus held out his hand towards the hall's doors. "Shall we?"

Narina's fingers were fidgeting and she didn't appear at all happy to be parted from her beloved daughter again, but she knew her duty and this was her fortress after all. "Aye," she nodded, and the pair of Damnonii guards already standing by the doors pulled them open. "You wait with them," she told the second Votadini, one of Ysfael's most loyal men and perhaps a spy. From out here he would not hear anything that was said inside the hall.

She walked in, followed by Gavo, Bellicus, Duro, and Lancelot. Cai had already made his way to the fire, sniffing amongst the freshly laid rushes on the floor for some scraps but the other dogs that lived within Dun Breatann had already finished them off. The massive hound lay down beside the table in the centre of the hall, eyeing Bellicus as always, ready to move if trouble started.

"Stupid dog," the queen smiled almost sadly. "We're safe in here."

Cai merely eyed her balefully for a moment before turning his attention back to the druid and resting his head on his paws.

Narina called to a serving girl, asking her to take food and drink up for Aife and Catia, and then she turned back to the men before her. "Do you want something to eat? I can have the servants bring some. You must all be tired from the road." She looked at the men, her eyes finally settling on Lancelot. "Who's this?" she asked, as if she'd only just noticed him.

The blond swordsman stood up and bent from the waist respectfully. "Lancelot, my lady," he said. "I'm one of Arthur's companions, although I was captured and held as a slave until recently by a Saxon jarl. Your daughter, along with Princess Aife, and Bel and Duro, helped me regain my freedom."

Narina welcomed him warmly and asked again if anyone wanted refreshments.

"I'd like food, ale, a bath, and...many other things," Bellicus replied coolly. "But it'll have to wait. By the gods, Narina, Gavo, what's been happening here? Why are the Pictish prisoners all dead?"

The queen looked away, staring into the hearth, biting her lip.

"That was Ysfael's idea," Gavo muttered, and he looked embarrassed, but he spread his hands wide. "Look, Bel, to be fair, Aife did escape, and she abducted Catia from what we could tell. There *had* to be repercussions when neither of them came back after so long. What kind of message would we be sending out to our enemies if we let that go?"

"We are surrounded by enemies, never forget that, Bel," Narina put in. "The Dalriadans in the east, Picts to the north. The Selgovae in the south are not at war with us, but they'd love to get their hands on this fortress. And it wasn't that long ago Ysfael's father King Cunedda was on his way to lay siege to Dun Breatann alongside the Picts. You must step more lightly around my husband, druid, or we'll have to deal with that threat from the east again." She shook her head and pressed her eyes with her fingers. "Lug knows what he'll be doing outside the walls right now."

"Wenching, probably," Gavo groused.

"That's enough," Narina scolded but only half-heartedly. "You all need to respect him. Like it or not, he's a prince, and my husband."

"Well, I don't like it," Duro said frankly, surprising everyone for the centurion usually only spoke up when his opinion was asked for. "I know – Dun Breatann, Alt Clota as a whole, this is not my home, you Damnonii are not my people, but it has to be said, my lady. Ysfael is trouble."

Narina's face had paled and she was biting her lip again, a tic Bellicus had only rarely seen in the queen before. "What d'you mean by that?" she asked in a low, husky tone.

"Aife," Bellicus said. "Ysfael and his men were planning to kill her."

Narina's face remained grim. "If true, that might explain why the girl left in such a hurry," she muttered through gritted teeth. "But why would he harm her? And why did she take Catia?"

"Catia insisted on going with her," Bellicus said. "She knew Aife would be cut down by our, or Ysfael's, men if they caught her on the way back to Dunnottar. Catia's presence would offer at least some protection." He shrugged. "They're friends, Narina, and they're young. They wanted to stay with one another. You can't blame them – this is all down to your husband."

They sat in silence for a time but the druid's mind was churning like one of the fast moving rivers that dotted Alt Clota. He'd blamed Ysfael, and it was true the impetuous, and clearly vicious, young prince had acted foolishly. Hanging the Picts would bring nothing but trouble for the Damnonii people, Bellicus was sure of that. But, on another level, he felt shocked that Narina had allowed it to happen. She was queen here, and ever since her previous husband, Coroticus, had died at the druid's hands and Narina took the throne, she'd been a strong ruler. Killing the prisoners was on her too, and the sheer inhumanity of it made Bellicus feel sick. He still loved Narina, and always would, but this…

It was true, he'd killed men himself. He'd even tortured them when he felt the situation warranted such brutal behaviour, but hanging defenceless hostages who had nothing to do with Aife's escape from Dun Breatann? This was a side to Narina that Bellicus had not seen before, and he did not like it. Aye, a strong ruler was essential in these dark times, but those bloated, swinging bodies were an affront to the druid's sensibilities. Their deaths were undeserved. What the gods would make of it even Bellicus did not know.

He stared at the queen. She was looking into the fire again, and the druid tried to read her expression, to gauge her feelings just from her posture and her features. Was she going mad, as Coroticus had done when Catia was taken from them that first time and it pushed the old king to lose himself in mugs of ale and acts of violence? This was the second time the queen had lost her daughter in such a fashion, it was understandable that it would take a toll on her.

She slowly turned and their eyes met and there was a deep sadness within her gaze that told of her guilt and sorrow and Bellicus felt some measure of relief. She was not glorying in her part in the Picts' deaths, unlike Ysfael. That was good. He could still support her as queen for she had apparently not lost her humanity.

And yet she could not be absolved of all blame. Alt Clota would suffer for this, unless something was done.

"We must make reparations," he said firmly, staring at Narina before turning to Gavo to guage the captain's response.

"To whom?" asked the queen and she seemed genuinely surprised by his statement.

"Drest," Bellicus replied. "The Picts."

"What?" Gavo was also frowning. "I admit, killing the prisoners was a step too far, but it was justified, Bel. One of their number abducted our princess and took her to Dunnottar, by Taranis!"

"No," the druid said coldly. "You *thought* that's what happened, but now you know that was wrong. Catia went willingly, because Ysfael was undoubtedly going to attack Aife. You cannot blame either of them for scaling the wall and running away. You killed those men for nothing, and Drest will rightly be furious about it. Their families will be furious!" He sighed. "We've only just beaten them in battle and won an uneasy peace. This will rekindle their war with us."

"Let them come," Narina retorted defiantly. "We beat them once; we'll beat them again. Besides, they lost a generation of warriors in that last battle, why should we fear them now? All they have left is greybeards and boys, while we have our army and the army of Ysfael's father to call upon." She waved at one of the servants who were standing in the shadows at the back of the hall. "Bring us wine and ale," she called before facing the druid again. "I agree it was a mistake to hang the prisoners, but, given the situation, even Drest must see it was somewhat justified."

"Maybe," Bellicus said, gladly accepting the mug of ale that was placed before him by the pretty serving girl. She caught his eye as she placed it down, making what he thought was an unspoken plea, but she quickly moved on to hand out the rest of the drinks and the druid was left to wonder if he'd imagined it. When she was standing in the shadows once more, however, she continued to look at him and he knew he would have to talk with her once this meeting was over.

"If you were to offer Drest your apologies," said Duro, and his hatred for the Pictish king was evident in his harsh tone, "and maybe some reparations as Bellicus suggested..." He shrugged. "Cattle, sheep, wine, whatever. It might placate him." He held up a hand before Narina or Gavo could protest. "Aye, it's true their army was smashed and they're not as strong as they once were, at least until their younger warriors grow a little older. But when we arrived in Dunnottar the Picts were playing host to a shipful of Saxons. Their leader was Hengist's cousin."

No-one said anything for a time, digesting the centurion's words and the ale that they were all thirstily downing. Then Gavo growled, "Are you suggesting they might form an alliance? Picts and Saxons together against us?"

"The Saxons will ally themselves with anyone who'll pay them," Lancelot noted, and no-one could dispute that. "I could hear Sigarr and Leofdaeg talking during the voyage to Dunnottar, and they were indeed hoping to form some kind of alliance with the Picts. What form it might take, whether it was purely for trade or more of a military venture, I have no idea, but that's why Sigarr was there."

"Drest even let the Saxons borrow one of his own ships, a currach," Bellicus added. "To chase Catia, Aife and Lancelot when they left Dunnottar in the Saxons' own vessel. That's not the action of a man who sees the sea-wolves as an enemy."

"How long have the prisoners' bodies been hanging up there?" Duro asked.

"A week."

"Then Drest will know about it soon enough," the centurion said. "Someone will carry word to him."

"Aye, they will," Bellicus agreed. "If not a trader, or a spy, or some other random person, then his daughter, Aife."

Narina sat upright on her stool. "What?"

"We need to release her," Bellicus said flatly. "She saved Catia's life, Narina. The Saxons wanted to take her to Hengist and Thorbjorg, that they might finish that blood ritual they started down at the Hanging Stones when me and Duro disturbed them."

"It's true," Duro confirmed. "Aife has taken care of Catia. She escorted the princess back here, keeping her safe all the way, knowing she herself would be returning to the life of a prisoner."

"You – *we* – owe her, Narina. The least we can do is let her go home to her people." Bellicus's tone was hard and his eyes full of accusation. "It might go some way to placating Drest."

Gavo still looked unsure. "I'm a soldier," he said, stating the obvious. "And it never sits right with me when a man is killed in cold blood. Everyone should have the chance to defend themselves, unless they've committed some crime—"

"They *did* commit a crime," Narina objected irritably. "The prisoners attacked us. They waged an unprovoked war against us. They were lucky we didn't just kill them all when the battle was over and we had them at our mercy!"

Gavo nodded, but everyone could tell the queen's argument was half-hearted. "Well, anyway," the captain went on. "I think we need to have a proper discussion about all this, not act hastily."

Bellicus almost smiled. Gavo was as loyal a guard captain as Narina could ever wish for, and had been for many years. It hurt the man to see the queen's actions being questioned by the druid. "Let's sleep on it then," he said, downing the remainder of his ale. "We could all do with some time to rest and gather our thoughts, eh?"

Lancelot heaved a deep sigh and muttered agreement. He'd remained mostly silent since it wasn't his place to offer advice, but he'd listened intently and Bellicus knew he would be happy to share his opinion later.

"My lord," the queen said to the blond warrior. "I'm sorry that you found us in this state, we should have offered you a better welcome. I'll have the servants make quarters ready for you and—"

"Lancelot will be staying at my house," Bellicus said, much to Duro's surprise. The centurion muttered his disapproval for it would be a tight squeeze in the druid's low house with the three of them, and Cai, but the druid nodded firmly.

"If you're sure," said Narina, somewhat surprised. "Well, eat and drink your fill, Lord Lancelot. You too, Duro. And my fine big boy, Cai," she finished, leaving her stool and bending to kiss and caress the great hound who lay there, revelling in the attention. "Let me know what you want to do about Ysfael," she said at last to Bellicus. "We can't leave him out there all night."

"Why not?" asked the druid.

The queen stared at him, deep in thought, and then she shrugged. "Maybe it'll do him good to learn his place. Think on it, druid, and come see me after, when we might discuss everything in more depth."

Bellicus stood and bowed, wondering if she might try to bed him later. It would certainly be easier with Ysfael locked outside the gates. The memory of what she'd done to the Pictish prisoners cooled his ardour however, and he waited until she left the hall before approaching the serving girl in the shadows. Her clothes were drab and ill-fitting – a grey skirt and brown tunic with a similarly coloured, undecorated belt at the waist – yet, even so it was clear she had an attractive, voluptuous figure. She also wore a pretty, bronze brooch which seemed oddly out of place with the rest of her attire.

"My lord," she muttered as he came to stand before her.

"Did you want to say something to me?" he asked kindly. There were two other servants nearby but they were too far away to hear their conversation.

"I just..." Her voice trailed off and she seemed nervous.

"Go on," Bellicus urged softly. "You know me. You've lived here for a while now. You know you've nothing to fear from me."

"It's the prince," she said, eyes fixed on the floor. Behind them, Duro and Lancelot were greedily tucking into bread and meat the other servants had delivered to the table, and Cai was sitting beside the centurion looking for scraps. "He's been sleeping with some of us too, my lord."

Her statement came as no surprise to the druid. Ysfael would not be the first man to take advantage of his position in such a manner, and nor would he be the last. Besides, this was not news to him – even Narina knew her husband was bedding other women in and around Dun Breatann.

"Not all of us are happy about his attention," she said. "But he never hurts us and gives us nice things so..." She trailed off and the druid nodded encouragingly at her as she absently touched her brooch. "I heard him speaking with his friends, my lord, one of the nights I shared a bed with him," she stopped again, as if scared to go on.

"Tell me," Bellicus said.

"It was before Princess Aife ran away," the servant whispered, wringing her hands. "Ysfael told his friends they had to...take care of her."

"Hurt her, you mean?"

"Aye. Maybe something worse, the way they were speaking. Ysfael said the princess had overheard some plan of his, and he had to shut her up before she told anyone about it. He seemed very worried about it."

Bellicus could imagine the young man, drunk on ale and power, blabbering to his followers, taking no more notice of the girl he'd just bedded than he would a stool or other piece of furniture. And it wasn't hard to believe that Ysfael would think he could treat Aife this way – look what he'd done to the other prisoners after all.

The druid opened his mouth to ask if the servant had told anyone about this, and, if not, why not, but he stopped himself. Of course she wouldn't tell anyone – she was a servant. Who would she tell? Ysfael was a prince, and married to Alt Clota's queen. Opening her mouth without real proof would only mean trouble for the serving girl.

"Thank you for trusting me with this," he said to her, smiling. "I'll see you're rewarded for it, and I'll see what can be done about the prince to protect you and your companions. Don't worry, you won't get into any trouble. If anything like this ever happens again, come to me, Duro, or Gavo, all right? We know what Ysfael is like now."

He walked back to his friends and neither of them made any comment on where he'd been. Both men knew how to be discreet, especially at a time like this.

"Why did you say Lancelot was staying with us?" Duro asked when the druid sat down again and was buttering a thick slice of bread. "No offence, but it's not a very big house!"

"I just thought he'd enjoy our company," Bellicus replied with a disarming smile, and said no more.

They finished the meal, both Duro and Lancelot accepting the serving girl's offer of more although Bellicus refused. He knew he had to see Narina, and it would be easier to have a proper conversation now, when Ysfael wasn't around. He was not looking forward to talking with the queen and his heart was heavy at that, for he'd always enjoyed her company. Could things ever be the same between them, knowing what she'd done to the defenceless Picts?

Sighing, he stood up and muttered something about having things to do. Duro nodded, understanding where the druid was going, while Lancelot had the good manners not to enquire further.

CHAPTER THIRTY-TWO

When Bellicus went outside the sun was high in a sky heavy with grey clouds and a breeze occasionally lowered the temperature as he made his way up the curving path. He passed the familiar spring, giving thanks to the gods for the life-giving water as he always did when he came this way, but his thoughts were churning. He walked by the house which Aife had been given when first taken as a prisoner, seeing the guards standing tall outside. He saluted them but couldn't help wondering if those men could be trusted to protect the Pictish girl. Ysfael certainly seemed unpleasantly surprised to see Aife back here, undoubtedly fearing what she'd accuse him of.

The druid sighed yet again. Ysfael was not like most other men, he was an enigma and Bellicus hated the fact he couldn't read the Votadini prince. Who knew what the man was capable of?

The path came to an end, bringing Bellicus to the queen's house near the summit of the lower peak. He hesitated, wondering what sort of welcome he'd get, remembering the time not so long ago when Narina had been so happy to take him inside and…

There were no guards around as he tapped on the door. It was opened and Narina's pale face looked out at him. "Oh, Bel, come in." She was smiling broadly and the druid went in. The window shutters were open to let in light and air so they could see one another well enough. She reached out to embrace him but he pulled back and she frowned. "What's wrong?"

"Wrong?" he echoed. "I thought I knew you, Narina. I can't believe I judged you so badly. How could you murder those prisoners? Apart from the trouble you must have known it would cause with Drest's people, just the fact that you could stand by and watch defenceless men die like that…" He trailed off, turning to look out through one of the windows. "Have you gone mad, like Coroticus?"

Narina didn't reply for a few heartbeats but, when she did, she was sobbing. "I wasn't here, Bel," she admitted. "I was out riding, looking for some sign of Catia on the road. Ysfael took it upon himself to hang the prisoners in my absence."

The druid let her words sink in and then turned to her, feeling as if a heavy weight had been lifted from his body. "You were not part of it?"

"No. We discussed the possibility of it, as you know. But I always told him I'd not harm the Picts unless we heard bad news about Catia."

"Why did he do it?" the druid asked, genuinely baffled. "I cannot follow his reasoning at all."

"Neither can I," Narina said heavily. "He's not a..." she searched for the word and then went on, "wicked, man. He's thoughtless rather than cruel. So, I don't believe he took any great pleasure in hanging the prisoners, I think he just felt like Aife's escape was an insult and should be punished." She came to him and took both of his hands in hers. "Honestly, he seems to think much like a child does. It can be wearing at times but . . ." She shook her head. "He's not the worst man I could have picked as a husband."

Bellicus stared at her and his heart felt like it might sail away into the air so great was his relief that Narina was innocent of the crime he'd laid at her door. She raised herself on her toes and pulled him down and they shared a long kiss that was more loving than lustful.

"I'm sorry I doubted you," he said when they finally pulled apart, both mindful of the fact anyone passing might look in the open windows and see them. "Why didn't you tell me when we met earlier?"

Narina flung up her arms in exasperation. "I don't know. It's so hard to know what to do all the time now. If I distance myself from Ysfael's behaviour it makes me look weak, as if he's the one in charge here. Spouses are also supposed to respect one another and it's never sat right with me to publicly decry either Ysfael or Coroticus, even when I've felt like they were acting like bloody fools." Tears filled her eyes and she sat down on the bed, looking at her hands. "Catia is still with the Pictish girl. All this time apart, Bel, and she finally comes home and would rather be with Aife than me."

Bellicus sat down and put his arm around her, drawing her in close. "It's been a confusing, and hard, time for all of us," he said. "Catia missed you terribly, I know that to be true. But she also feels loyalty to her friend and, given what's happened here, I understand her decision to stay with Aife."

"Did he rape her?"

Bellicus thought about the question before answering. "No, I don't believe so," he said at last. "Maybe he would have done it eventually but..." He shook his head in consternation. "Aife believed he wanted her dead for some reason, although I still don't know what that reason might have been. His behaviour today suggests she was right to fear him though."

They sat like that for a time, enjoying being close to one another as the insects worked outside and the gulls screeched over the river.

"Where's your friend?" Narina asked at last, standing and walking towards the door. "The loud Votadini warrior."

"He died saving Catia from a Saxon *volva*," Bellicus said, getting up and following her as she went outside.

"What? Another witch? Here in these lands?"

"It's a long story," Bellicus sighed. "I'll explain it all later. For now, I think we should speak with Gavo and decide how things are going to be here in Dun Breatann from now on."

Narina nodded and wiped her face one final time, making sure all her tears were gone. "All right, let's do that." She forced a smile and for a moment looked more like the happy young woman the druid had known a decade ago. "I'm very sorry for Eburus, but I'm so glad you're home again, Bel. This place always feels empty without you."

CHAPTER THIRTY-THREE

"How dare you?" Prince Ysfael's eyes blazed like the torches in the walls nearby and he clenched his fists, glaring murderously at Bellicus. "Do you think I'm an idiot?"

"Well…" Duro muttered but Ysfael didn't hear him, which was probably for the best.

"I know what's behind your actions, druid," the prince forged on, spittle flecking his lips in his anger. "You want to bed my wife, and think removing any power I have here will make it easier. My father, King Cunedda, won't stand for it, d'ye hear me? He sanctioned our marriage in the belief I would be treated here with respect!"

The great hall was dark for night had fallen and the hearthfire cast numerous shadows on the walls which were decorated with tapestries depicting hunting scenes and battles. There were also weapons – swords, spears, long-handled axes – hooked to the walls as display pieces although many of them were still in useable condition. In all, it was an intimidating location but the prince, who'd turned up at the outer gates a short time ago with a bellyful of ale and demanding entry, didn't seem cowed by the gloom, or the people gathered there.

"Your father will take nothing to do with it," Bellicus replied coldly, staring down at the younger man. "You're not a child any more, Ysfael. You're supposed to be a man, a husband, and a queen's consort. I can't see Cunedda having any complaints when he hears what's been going on here. In fact," – the druid poked a finger at the Votadini prince – "he'll probably wash his hands of you completely, when he knows what you've done. The lands north of the Roman wall have only just come to some sort of peace, as uneasy as it was, and your actions have more than likely undone all that. So, spare me your threats, boy."

Ysfael took in the druid's words and then, like a spoiled child who was too used to getting his own way, resorted to the thing that had always seemed to work in his own lands: he had a violent tantrum.

Bellicus saw the bared teeth and knew what they presaged, easily swaying to the side as Ysfael's fist flew through the air. The druid's palm shot out, catching the prince under the jaw and there was a clacking of teeth before Bellicus kneed Ysfael between the legs. As the prince folded, Bellicus slapped him on the side of the head.

"Enough, Bel, that'll do," Narina shouted. Her face was pale and she looked distraught at the continued violence within her fortress. She was right anyway, it *was* enough, for Ysfael was completely senseless. Bellicus hadn't held back with his blows, feeling like it was time for the prince to learn once and for all not to attack him, or anyone else within Alt Clota's borders.

"Lift him," he said to Duro and Gavo while rubbing his hand gingerly, "Put him on that stool."

Without hesitation the two men did as they were told while Ysfael moaned and drooled. Already a lump was forming on his face and it seemed he might pass out completely or vomit. Duro looked at the table next to them and found a cup which he filled with water from a jug and held it to the prince who allowed the liquid to pass his lips. It seemed to revive him somewhat although the fight was gone from him as he finally turned tear-filled eyes on the druid towering over him.

"Your father must have let you saunter around Dun Edin doing what you liked as a child," Bellicus growled. "Every whim, every wish catered for. Queen Narina tells me that you're not a vicious man, and I trust her judgement, but I find it hard to believe."

Ysfael remained silent, as if he'd finally realised that he was completely at the mercy of the people in the hall. None of his own men were there – they'd not been allowed to gather ever since the druid and his companions had returned with the princesses. Then a thought struck him and he wiped his nose and said, "Where's Eburus?"

Bellicus looked at Duro and the pair shook their heads sourly. "At last, you've noticed he's not here," said the druid. "Eburus, Champion of your own Votadini tribe, and a fine friend to those who deserved it. He's dead."

Ysfael frowned. "Dead?"

"Aye," Bellicus spat. "He died saving Princess Catia's life. You could learn something from him. He was a hero."

The prince opened his mouth but decided silence was prudent and closed it again, allowing the druid to speak again.

"From now on, Lord Prince, you will conduct yourself as the consort of a queen should. If you must wet your cock, you'll do it with willing, unmarried women, and you'll do it discreetly, so the queen isn't shamed. You will have no authority over the garrison, and you will have no guards of your own." He paused to let that sink in. "The Votadini warriors who've been here since you arrived will be sent home."

Ysfael's eyes flashed and the old anger returned, but he hesitated and then said, "Wait. That's it? You're going to let me continue as Narina's husband?"

Bellicus shrugged. "We don't see much else to do. King Cunedda *would* be upset if Narina were to cast you off or, as I suggested, killed you." His eyes bored into the Votadini prince and somehow his look was enough to tell Ysfael how close he'd come to being disposed of here, miles away from the protection of his father.

"All right," the prince said hoarsely. "Whatever you say, druid." He looked at Narina and she was nodding too. A smile even seemed to touch the edges of her mouth, encouraging and apologising at the same time.

"Good," Bellicus said, turning away and helping himself to some ale. The tension had gone from him and he no longer looked like he might explode into violence at any moment. "Our alliance with your people will continue, you can live here as a nobleman, and the rest of us can get on with things."

"Things," Ysfael said, lip curling sarcastically.

"Aye, *things,*" Duro retorted. "Clearing up the mess you've left here."

"Why are you so bothered, centurion," Ysfael asked. "You're not of the Damnonii. You're a southerner. A Roman. I thought your argument was with the Saxons. Why should you care about Picts, or...any of this?"

"Duro has proven himself an astute advisor, and put his life in danger numerous times for us," Narina said, reaching out and touching the centurion on the arm. "He's another one you could learn from, husband."

There was no real rebuke in her words, no venom, and it seemed to mollify the prince. He sighed and held up his hands. "Fine. What now."

Bellicus filled another cup with ale and walked across to hand it to Ysfael, who took it gladly. He didn't drink from it yet, though, sensing it had been given to him for a reason other than wetting his dry mouth.

"Now, Prince Ysfael," the druid said, holding his own cup aloft. "We drink a toast, and you swear an oath. An oath that binds you to the terms we've agreed here this night."

The younger man smiled and glanced at his wife. "You all think I'm stupid," he said. "Or a monster. Maybe I am both of those things." He jerked his chin upwards, and met Bellicus's stony gaze. "All right. You have my word."

* * *

"That went better than I expected," Gavo said once the solemn swearing of oaths concluded and Ysfael had left with Narina, to retire for the night to their house near Dun Breatann's summit.

"Aye," Duro agreed. "Well, once Bel had slapped him about a bit anyway. It was simple enough after that." He looked to the druid. "You think he'll hold to his word?"

Bellicus was staring into the fire, perhaps hoping to see some vision of the future within the flickering flames. It seemed like he hadn't heard the centurion's question but, at last, he huffed out a long breath and turned on his stool to face Duro and Gavo. "I can't say," he muttered. "He's an odd character, hard to fathom. But, if we remove his supporters and have our own men keep a close eye on him, I don't see how he can cause any more trouble." He threw back his cup and downed the remaining dregs before reaching out to refill it. "Maybe we'll need to deal with Ysfael in a more…severe…manner eventually but, for now, we just bide our time and try to get things back on an even keel here in Alt Clota."

They drank in silence then, although none of them felt much like getting drunk and soon tired of the ale. It was just nice to relax in the great hall, safe and warm, with no enemies nearby to threaten them that night. Talk turned to Eburus, and the three men shared memories of him, but they were not maudlin, they were celebratory tales and Bellicus found himself laughing and feeling glad he'd spent time with the Votadini champion.

"Right, I need some sleep," the druid announced once the servants had let the fire burn low and the moon could be seen through the chimney hole. "It's been a long day. Gods, it's been a long few weeks! It'll be good to get a full night's rest in my own bed."

Lancelot and Duro got to their feet as well. "Aye, we'll come too," said the centurion. "Any more of that ale and I'll not be able to get up come the morrow. 'Night, Gavo."

The guard captain waved. "'Night, lads. I'll see you in the morning."

The three men, with Cai padding silently ahead, reached the doors and pushed them open, glad of the cool, evening air which felt good after the stuffy, smoky heat of the hall.

"I'll be having a dip in the Clota tomorrow," said Bellicus, grinning at the thought. "Then a proper bath and have my head shaved. Maybe after that I'll feel like a normal person again."

They were soon at the druid's house and Duro went inside, gingerly feeling his way for it was almost pitch-black inside. Bellicus waited for Cai, and Lancelot, to empty their bladders before they too came in and settled down for the night.

CHAPTER THIRTY-FOUR

The night was dark for clouds had obscured the moon and only a few torches and braziers were dotted around Dun Breatann dimly lighting the walls and paths for the guards to patrol.

"Watch where you're going, by Lug!" A hooded, limping man berated his companion softly as they made their way past the great hall and almost stumbled over one another in the gloom.

"Keep your voice down," the other, smaller figure hissed, pointing at a building a little way back along the path. "That's the druid's house. We don't want to wake him and his mates. If they knew what was happening..." The voice trailed off, swallowed by the night.

"Well, they don't," the other man muttered, and he also sounded tense. It seemed like he was speaking merely to fill the oppressive silence as he went on. "We do this as quickly as possible, all right, Docimedis? We don't have time to enjoy ourselves. That bitch knows what the prince plans, so we shut her up before she tells the queen, and get out of here."

"Does she know though, Maccis?" the small man replied in low, clipped tones, glancing up at his companion. "I'm not so sure. She'd have told someone by now. Ysfael worries too much. Besides, it hardly matters. Drest's people are hanging from the walls and there'll be war between the Picts and Damnonii again. King Cunedda just has to wait for their armies to slaughter one another, and then he can invade and take control of all their lands."

"Maybe," Maccis replied. They were almost at their destination now. "But this night's work will make certain Drest goes to war with Narina. We have to do it right this time if we want Ysfael to grant us those promised lands and titles here once Cunedda gives him Alt Clota."

They continued up past the gently gurgling spring towards the small dwelling on the left of the slope. There they glanced at one another, silently preparing for what they were about to do.

This house was not quite at the summit, but behind it one could see right out across much of Alt Clota. Tiny lights burned on a hilltop far off to the east although neither man knew why for these were not their lands. Perhaps they would be, soon.

"All right, lads?" Docimedis greeted the pair of Damnonii warriors who were on guard outside Aife's house. "Change of watch. All quiet?"

"Aye," one of the guards said, teeth showing in the dim light cast by a brazier further up the rock. "Fast asleep in there. Who'd have thought a princess would snore so loud?"

The four men shared a laugh and Docimedis said, "Go and get some kip yourselves, we'll take over here."

The Damnonii soldiers, yawning in unison, wandered off down the slope without a backward glance and soon disappeared from sight.

"Right," Docimedis growled. "Secure that rope. We don't have long before those two get back to the barracks and realise we're not the real relief watch."

Maccis threw off his cloak, revealing a long coil of rope across his shoulder. They knew this was how the princesses had escaped Dun Breatann before so the men had decided they might as well use the same, proven, route. Maccis hurried to the rear of the house and looked over the wall. The ground seemed an awfully long way away, but this section of the rock wasn't as steep as others. He tied the rope around one of the thick wooden posts which supported that section of wall and threw it down. Checking the knot was firm, he nodded in satisfaction. It would hold.

He made his way back to the front of the house, where Docimedis had his ear pressed against the door, listening intently. The small man nodded in grim satisfaction. The princess was silently dozing within – all they had to do was creep inside, silence her forever, and then climb down the rope to safety. They knew there were horses waiting for them at a farmhouse nearby, ready to carry them to King Cunedda in Dun Edin.

"Ready to start a war?" Docimedis hissed, pulling a dagger from his belt.

Maccis grinned, and lifted the latch to Princess Aife's door.

* * *

The blade glinted in the feeble light as the two figures stepped into the single-small dwelling that had been allocated to Princess Aife during her time as a political hostage. A musty smell filled the air from the sweating men who knew this should be an easy task but remembered the last time they'd faced the Pictish warrior-woman in combat. Maccis's limp was testament to that defeat, and, Docimedis stepped straight to the low bed, ready to strike as soon as his eyes adjusted to the dark interior and he could make out his target.

Maccis came behind him, the larger man's clumsier footsteps seeming deafening in the small room. He was there to make sure Aife didn't somehow evade Docimedis's dagger. He was also there to deal with anyone else that might be inside the house.

Like Princess Catia.

Docimedis stood beside the bed, leaning down, staring, wishing they'd brought an oil lamp with them for it was too dark to make out any features on the dark shape lying beneath him. He strained to see, and then gasped.

He couldn't make out Aife's face because she was not in the bed. No one was.

"What's this?" asked a voice in the corner.

"A couple of rats sneaking about in the dark, I think, Duro," said someone else in amused tones.

"Shit," Maccis shouted. "Get out! Over the wall!"

Docimedis threw his dagger into the corner and grinned in satisfaction as he heard a cry of pain before he turned and followed his friend out into the night. Behind them came the pounding footsteps of their pursuers, and the angry bellowing of whoever his blade had struck.

The small man reared back in shock as an enormous black shape suddenly filled the space before him and then he was falling, tripped by something on the ground. As he crashed down he realised it was Maccis he'd fallen over. The big warrior was groaning, trying to pull himself onto his feet although his eyes were watery and unfocused.

Instinctively rolling to the side, Docimedis dragged his axe from his belt and lashed out at the great, dark shape that seemed to have swallowed what meagre light there was.

"Give up," a voice commanded, and Docimedis recognised it instantly.

The druid, Bellicus.

Two men were coming out of the princess's house now and Maccis finally got up, flailing his arms. He held a knife in one hand and an axe in the other, but he was staggering and Docimedis guessed the druid must have struck his friend in the head as he exited the building, probably with that bronze eagle-topped staff.

It was clear they could not win this fight, not against three men. A sudden thrill of cold fear ran through him as he remembered the mastiff that always accompanied Bellicus. What if that monster appeared?

"We can't win," he shouted, stabbing at Bellicus as the druid tried to come for him. "Get over the wall, Maccis!"

"No, don't leave yet." The centurion, Duro shouted and his spatha tore through the darkness, its long, steel blade slicing into Maccis's right arm. There was a horrific, tortured cry, and then a thump.

In the darkness Docimedis couldn't tell if it was just his friend's axe that had fallen to the ground, or his hand, but he couldn't stop to find out as the other man who'd been hiding within the house attacked, plunging the point of his sword into the screaming Maccis's torso. The big hunter fell and made no more sound.

"Get back!" Docimedis roared, dodging out of the way of the druid's probing staff and running along the side of the building towards the rope. He came to the wall, almost sobbing in relief as he reached out, and then he realised the rope was missing.

"You've got two choices."

Docimedis turned to see Bellicus gazing at him. The enormous druid no longer held a staff – instead he'd drawn his sword and raised his left arm, beckoning for the Votadini warrior to come towards him.

"You can tell us why you were trying to kill the princess," Bellicus said. "And live. Or you can take your chances climbing down the rock without a rope, and certainly die."

Other people were coming to see what all the commotion was now. Docimedis could see the girl Catia, and the Pictish woman he'd been supposed to kill carrying a torch, its reddish light casting flickering shadows over Maccis's body. He could also see Prince Ysfael picking his lip as he watched the scene play out.

"My lord," Docimedis cried, reaching out towards the prince.

Bellicus stepped in front of Ysfael and called out, "Tell us who put you up to this. Tell us why you were sent to kill Aife, and you can go free."

Docimedis walked away from the wall, towards the people gathered on the slope at the front of the house and his eyes flickered again to Ysfael, but the prince merely stared back silently.

The druid suddenly exploded into motion, his sword slashing out in a shallow arc. Docimedis parried the blow, allowing it to move across his blade and away before he lunged forward himself, trying to stab Bellicus in the guts. The attack was much too slow, however, and easily dodged before the druid was coming at him again. Docimedis knew he was outmatched, but his attacker was not trying to kill him. Bellicus wanted him alive, to question him. The knowledge made him fight even more ferociously. He did not want to be tortured by the druid and, at that moment, all that mattered was survival. If he could just take advantage of Bellicus's reticence to end his life…

"Boo."

He spun in sudden shock as he heard a voice behind him. It was the centurion! The man must have slipped around the back of the house and crept up behind him. The realisation dawned on him just as the former Roman officer's helmet smashed into his face. Blood spilled from his nose but before he could regain his senses he felt his wrist grabbed and twisted up behind his back. The sword fell from his fingers as they lost all power and then the druid's knee slammed into the back of his and he was lying face down on the ground.

CHAPTER THIRTY-FIVE

"Who put you up to this?" the druid demanded.

Docimedis's face was set hard as he replied, "No one."

"Then why are you here? Why try to kill the princess?"

The captive winced as his arm was pushed further up his back, muscles and tendons protesting agonisingly, and he cried out, "She dishonoured my prince! We were duty bound to deal with her and restore his good name."

"By killing a young woman as she lay sleeping?" Gavo demanded. The guard captain came forward now. His bearded face was scarlet and it was obvious he was furious that this crime had taken place in his fortress. "You're a coward, and you'll suffer the same fate as that other bastard you came here with. What have you got to say to that, *my lord?*" He rounded on Ysfael who stared back with detached calmness.

"I say," said the prince, "that it's only just that he should pay for his actions."

Docimedis gaped in shock at his lord. "What? No. You—"

"Take him away then," said Ysfael, waving a hand dismissively at a couple of Damnonii guards who stood nearby with their spears levelled, ready to finally do what they were supposed to do.

"Wait," Bellicus commanded, addressing his prisoner again. "Did Ysfael put you up to this? Were you working on his orders?" The druid lifted his left hand and placed it on Docimedis's head. "In the name of Lug the Light-Bringer, I command you to speak truly, or suffer the eternal consequences." His voice was level, almost monotonous as he intoned those words, but now his demeanour changed again and his neutral expression became more threatening. "Tell me the truth, or I'll curse you, so you return here in your next life as a *real* scurrying rat."

The hunter blanched, and the defiance was gone completely from his face now, replaced by naked fear. "The prince didn't command us to come here," he said. "We decided to do it ourselves."

Bellicus stared at him and didn't need his years of druid training to know the man was being honest. He mentally kicked himself for allowing Ysfael this escape – obviously there had been some unspoken wish from the prince that his men would deal with Aife but, without an explicit order, Ysfael could not be blamed for their actions.

"This," said the druid, straightening and looking around at everyone gathered there. "This has all gone far enough. It ends now." He shoved Docimedis towards the two Damnonii spearmen. "Take him, lads. Hang him beside the Picts."

The defeated Votadini panicked at this and tried to run off, pushing past some of the onlookers, but he didn't get far and, when he launched himself at one of the pursuing guards, trying to bite the man's face, he was rewarded with a spear thrust to the side. He did not survive long enough to be hanged.

"It ends here," Bellicus repeated, moving to tower over Ysfael. "Your men, those that remain, will return to King Cunedda at first light tomorrow. And I am warning you now, *my lord*," he leaned down and pressed his forehead against the prince's. "Taranis be my witness: If you cause any more trouble in Alt Clota, either directly or indirectly, you will suffer all the torments the gods can bestow upon one mortal man. Now," he straightened, slamming the butt of his great staff onto the ground. "Get out of my sight."

Despite this very public attack on his honour, Ysfael appeared relieved to still be breathing and, rather than railing against his treatment, turned and stalked up the hill. As he went, Aife stepped in front of him, blocking his way. She was taller than him, and she glared down into his eyes as everyone watched, wondering if there would be more bloodshed before the night was over.

"You want me dead?" she asked. "Kill me, then."

Ysfael held her gaze for a moment, but then he gave a short laugh and stepped around the princess and continued to walk up the hill. The sound of the door to his and the queen's home could be heard slamming moments later.

"I don't blame him for refusing your challenge," said Lancelot with a grin. "I'd not want to fight you either."

Neither Narina nor Gavo, the two highest-ranking people apart from Bellicus in Dun Breatann, commented.

The druid nodded, jaw tight. "All right. Gavo, make sure there are good men here to guard Princess Aife." He smiled slightly, just to offset any criticism the captain might hear in his words. It wasn't Gavo's fault this had happened, any more than it was the druid's. "Then round up the rest of the Votadini warriors, disarm them, and keep them in the garrison between the gates. You want me to come with you?"

Gavo shook his head. "No, Bel, I'll deal with it. There'll be no more trouble this night, you can trust me on that. What about Ysfael?"

"Put three men on the house, make sure he doesn't go anywhere. Once his soldiers are on their way back to Dun Edin he can move about more freely but, for tonight at least, he stays where he is."

The guard captain looked at Narina who confirmed the orders with a shallow nod, and Gavo began issuing commands to the guards who were nearby.

Soon the crowd had dispersed and only Bellicus, Duro, Lancelot, Aife, Catia and Narina remained on the grass outside the house which had seen so much violence and death in the past hour.

"How did you know this would happen?" the queen asked. She looked exhausted, which was only natural Bellicus admitted. It was the middle of the night after all. "That they would try to murder Aife, I mean."

"We knew Ysfael feared some knowledge he thought the princess had of his plans," the druid replied. "Feared her enough that he wanted her dead." He shrugged. "I didn't think he would allow her time to use that information. It seemed sensible for the three of us," he nodded at Duro and Lancelot, who had a shallow injury on his forearm from the dagger Docimedis had thrown at him, "to come and guard her."

"We told the real watchmen to act like everything was normal when their relief arrived," Duro said. "Even if they thought something wasn't right."

"Played their part perfectly," Lancelot noted.

Narina sighed gloomily. "Aife," she said, meeting the princesses haughty gaze. "*Do* you have any idea what my husband's plans are? What is this secret he would kill to preserve?"

"I don't know," the princess replied angrily. "He's your bedmate. Why don't you use your charms to get it out of him? Or beat him until he tells you." She was still plainly furious with the queen and made no attempt to hide it.

"Then we're no further forward," Narina said, throwing up her hands. "Those two idiots died for nothing, and we still don't know what Ysfael's secret is. If he even has one." She suddenly turned and looked again at Aife, suspicion in her eyes now. "Maybe…"

"I know what he planned," Bellicus broke in, halting the queen's words before they sent Aife into an even worse rage. "I was in the bushes there," he pointed down the slope to a spot between his own house and the great hall, "when Docimedis and Maccis passed on their way here. I could hear them talking."

"And?" Narina demanded. "Does Ysfael plan to kill me and take my throne? I won't believe that."

Bellicus was shaking his head. "No. We could not read his intentions because he always seems unambitious and, well, lazy. He lacks the motivation to lead a coup against you."

"So, what did you hear his men saying then?" Catia asked. "What's he up to?"

He told them what he'd overheard. That Ysfael had wanted to start another war between the Picts and the Damnonii so that his father, King Cunedda, could take advantage of the warring factions' weakness and invade both territories with his Votadini armies. He would become High King of all the lands north of the Romans' wall.

"So that's why he ordered the Pictish hostages to be hanged," Narina said. "And why he wanted Aife to be killed here too, so Drest would blame us for it all."

"Yes. Ultimately, it didn't matter whether you knew this secret scheme or not," Bellicus said to Aife. "I think he probably knew you didn't when you returned after escaping and he had time to think about it. You could have just told me, or your father, about his plans, and yet, you didn't." He shrugged. "Killing you would simply be the final push, the thing that would tip Drest back into war with us."

"By the gods," Narina cried. "I'll have that bastard killed. Let's go up and do it now, Bel. Come on." She started to walk towards her own house, but the druid shouted for her to stop.

"We can't kill him," he argued. "The only proof we have are the words of a dead man, overheard from within a bush. If we harm Ysfael without more evidence of his duplicity it will only start a conflict with the Votadini."

She stared at him in disbelief, as did everyone else. "So, what? Do you expect me to just carry on living as his wife?"

"Yes," Bellicus replied firmly. "In name, if nothing else. His men will all be sent away in the morning, and we will watch over him closely to make sure he has no more little schemes up his sleeve. Ysfael no longer holds any power here." He held up his palms. "Besides, an accident can happen to anyone, at any time. Maybe something like that will befall Ysfael once this has all blown over and peace is assured."

She digested his words and nodded at last. "You always offer wise counsel, Bel," she said. "It shall be as you say, but I'll no longer share a bed, or even my house, with him." As she said this their eyes locked and it seemed as if a weight was suddenly lifted from her shoulders. Her whole expression changed and, for the first time in months she seemed happy. Hopeful even.

"Will you be all right in there all by yourself for the rest of the night?" Lancelot asked Aife, nodding towards her little house. "Want me to stay with you and make sure you're safe?"

Aife laughed but shook her head and punched him on the arm where Docimedis's dagger had cut him, ignoring his yelp of pain. "I'm sure I'll be fine, my lord." She waved to Catia and went inside, closing the door behind her.

"Brave young woman," Duro said admiringly.

Lancelot nodded, eyeing the door to the house as if hoping Aife would change her mind and ask him to come in and take care of her.

"Where are we going to sleep, mother?" Catia said. "Ysfael is in our house, remember?"

Narina smiled and reached out to draw the girl into an embrace. "We can sleep in the great hall for what's left of the night, my love. Wouldn't be the first time. Come on."

Soon enough Bellicus was in his own bed, in his own house, with Cai at his side. The dog had been left behind there, since Docimedis and Maccis would have known something wasn't right had they caught sight, or scent, of the great hound.

They were both happy to see one another again.

Duro was already snoring in his bed on the other side of the room, while Lancelot, having seen just how cramped the house was earlier in the night, had decided, like the queen, to find a bench within the great hall to bed down on.

Bellicus lay awake, staring up at the roof, pondering everything that had happened and thanking the gods that they'd managed to thwart Ysfael's plans. All was well in Dun Breatann and, once Aife smoothed things over with her fellow Picts, who knew what the coming weeks might bring? Perhaps he and Narina could finally be together, and he could be more of a father to Catia.

His thoughts cheered him greatly and he drifted off to sleep with a smile on his face and high hopes for his future, and the future of the Damnonii people.

EPILOGUE

Aife stared out at the water, waves sparkling in the sunshine, gulls wheeling overhead, their raucous cries filling the air as they looked for scraps or spilled bounty from one of the fishing boats that were gently bobbing on the waves that morning. She felt lonely, and drew her knees up to her chest as a cool breeze ruffled her long hair.

A young man, one of the king's retinue, was walking on the beach and he looked up, waving to her. She returned the wave and sighed. It was time.

She turned and walked back towards the great hall, nodding an absent-minded greeting to the guards as she went into the building and made her way to the main room where the king conducted all his important business. Aife had been allowed to return here, to Dunnottar, and even been given an escort of half a dozen Damnonii warriors and Lancelot, who still felt like he owed her a great debt for saving his life. They'd met a group of Pictish riders out patrolling the land not far from the seaside fortress and, after a moment's tense standoff, their leader recognised Aife and she joined their party. Lancelot and the rest of her escort said their farewells and headed back to Dun Breatann while Aife went on to Dunnottar and another reunion with King Drest.

That had been yesterday evening and her father hadn't asked her many questions for she was clearly exhausted from her time on the road. She'd been taken by the servants for a bath and some fresh clothes and then, after a quick meal, she'd fallen into a deep, dreamless sleep. Drest had told her before she left for bed, however, that he'd expect a full report from her the next morning after he'd broken his fast, and now that time was upon them.

It felt cool, almost cold, within the tower that housed Dunnottar's main feasting hall. The kitchen was located in a separate, small building, so the heat from the cooking fires, along with the smoke, was absent from the room in which she found herself now, looking at her father sipping a mug of watered wine, an empty trencher on the table before him.

Aife stood tall before him but she was dreading this meeting. The old druid, Qunavo, was seated to the king's right, and the young druidess, Ria, to his left. They formed an imposing triumvirate, even to the warrior-princess.

Drest smiled reassuringly at her, though, and said, "Good morning, daughter. Would you like something to eat? Drink?"

Aife shook her head, swallowing nervously. She was not used to formally addressing an audience, even a small one headed by her father, and she wished she was going into battle instead. Being part of a shieldwall might be dangerous, but any time she'd stood in one she'd had companions on either side to support her, and a spear to fight off anything dangerous.

Speaking of support, there was no chair for her, she would deliver her report as any normal scout, or spy, or nobleman would do. There would be time to sit and relax soon enough.

"I'm very happy to see you again, Aife," the king said, although he was frowning. "I'm surprised, though. I didn't think Queen Narina would allow you to leave Alt Clota. We heard that they'd executed all our people they'd been holding as hostages."

The princess looked at Ria and Qunavo and the old druid said, "It's an outrage, and yet, here you stand. Perhaps the rumours were not true. How many of our people are still alive?"

"Father," Aife said, turning back to Drest. "They hanged all of our people. I'm the only one who remains alive of those that were held in Dun Breatann."

"So, it's true?" Drest slammed his fist on the table making his wine cup fall over, spilling the red liquid onto his lap although he took no notice. "But why?" He trailed off, taking in Aife's sorrowful expression.

"It wasn't Queen Narina," she said. "It was her husband, the Votadini prince, Ysfael."

"Wait, he's the reason you escaped and came here with Catia in the first place, wasn't he?" Ria asked.

"Aye," Aife agreed. "I believed he wanted me dead for some personal reason. As it turns out he wanted *all* the Pictish hostages dead."

"For what purpose?" Qunavo demanded. "Is he mad? Cruel?"

Aife explained to them what Bellicus had figured out. How Ysfael had wanted to start a war between the Picts and the Damnonii so his father, Cunedda, could invade both Drest's and Narina's lands and set himself up as High King.

Drest looked angrier than Aife had ever seen him before. "What will we do?" she asked.

His reply shocked her.

"Do?" Frowning, he shook his head. "Is Ysfael not married to Narina? Were our people not Damnonii hostages?"

"Aye, but—"

"But nothing!" Drest shouted and his face was scarlet. "Whether that Votadini whelp gave the order for our people to be hanged is neither here nor there. They were in Damnonii care. They were murdered without provocation within Dun Breatann, presumably by Damnonii warriors. It is an act of war." He shrugged, still shaking his head. "Well, if they want a war, we'll give them one."

Aife listened in silence, trying to digest his words. Her emotions were roiling inside her, for she liked many of the Damnonii, especially young Catia. The thought of fighting them again was not a pleasant one – there were better enemies to fight out there, and yet...Was her father right? Narina might claim to have been away from the fortress when the hangings took place, but she had certainly spoken with Ysfael about the possibility of killing the hostages. If Catia had not returned to Dun Breatann the queen would undoubtedly have hanged them herself.

"But they decimated our army, father," she reminded him. "Would we be strong enough to attack them again? It's not turned out well the last couple of times we've tried."

A servant appeared, righting the king's fallen cup and pouring more wine into it from a large amphora. The sound of the liquid sloshing into the receptacle seemed almost deafening in the outraged silence that had settled upon the hall, as did the sound of the serving girl's sandals slapping on the wooden floor as she retreated back down the stairs to the kitchen.

Drest turned and looked at Qunavo and their hard expressions sent a shiver down Aife's back.

"I still don't think it was wise, my lord," the druid said, shaking his head. "But I agree, the Damnonii rats must pay for what they've done."

Drest glanced at Ria next.

"I also think it might turn out to be a huge mistake but...I can see no other option, lord King." She leaned back and crossed her legs, steepling her fingers on the table. "It allows us more time to rebuild our own army, at least."

"What is it?" Aife asked, frowning. "What have you done, father?"

"When you were here before, when you and the Damnonii princess stole the Saxon ship," replied Drest in grim tones. "The sea-wolves proposed an alliance between our peoples."

"An alliance with the Saxons? But they can't be trusted, you know that! They'll take our wealth, our goods, and, when it suits them, they'll turn their backs on us, or worse." She set her outraged gaze on Qunavo, and then Ria. "You two must know this. The Saxons are only out for themselves."

Qunavo frowned at her, as if surprised to be spoken to by the young woman so forwardly. She was, after all, merely a bastard who'd only been taken into Drest's court in recent years. He respected her abilities as a warrior, however, and replied to her coolly. "We know all that, of course. But we need warriors, and the Saxons are willing to provide them, for a price."

"It's either that," said Ria in a friendlier tone. "Or we wait for our next generation of warriors to fill out the ranks of our depleted army, which will take time." She shrugged. "The only other option is to do nothing, and ignore the fact good Pictish folk were murdered in Dun Breatann, where they should have been safe."

"Which is unacceptable," Drest said. "Those bastards in Alt Clota have caused us enough trouble. This latest outrage is too much to go unanswered." He sighed deeply, lifting his wine cup and looking at it before deciding he needed no more of the stuff and put it back down. "I know you're friendly with their princess, but what Narina's folk have done must be addressed. My noblemen, especially those whose family members have been murdered in cold blood, will demand it."

"They've offered reparations," said Aife, half-expecting her audience to dismiss such talk out of hand, but all three sat up just a little bit straighter. Perhaps another war was not quite as inevitable as it seemed...

"What offer?" growled Drest.

Aife outlined what Queen Narina had agreed to. A certain number of cattle, sheep, and even a few horses would be sent to Dunnottar, along with a chest of treasure. Bellicus argued that they should offer more but Narina and Gavo had not wanted to leave Dun Breatann's coffers completely empty. Especially knowing Drest did not have much of an army to attack them with. Of course, the idea of an alliance with Hengist's Saxons had never seemed realistic to Narina, and Aife watched sadly as her father and the druid advisors reacted angrily to the suggested reparations.

"That's it?" Qunavo demanded, as if it was Aife who'd drawn up the list of goods herself.

"It's not enough," Drest agreed, shaking his head and taking up his wine again. "They'd have had to double that amount to make it worth our while. Do they not realise that 'wealth' would have to be split between those nobles who lost a son? A brother? Would a couple of sheep make up for that kind of loss?"

"It's too late anyway," Qunavo said to the princess.

Drest muttered agreement with his druid. "When you were last here, Jarl Sigarr suggested his *bretwalda,* Hengist, might pay us to stop raiding the lands they'd taken in the south. But they quickly realised we were in no position to raid them this year, or the next, since our army had been smashed by the Damnonii. That was when Sigarr suggested an alliance between us and them instead. Essentially, he wanted us to hire Saxon warriors. Pay them, as mercenaries. They left without an answer, for I was not sure that was a path I wanted to go down at the time." He raised his chin almost defiantly as he fixed Aife with his gaze and told her, "When we heard that the hostages had been killed in Dun Breatann, however, I sent a delegation south, pledging myself to Hengist and his sea-wolves, and making a payment to them. Their army will come to Mucrois in the spring and we will join them there to march on Dun Breatann."

"Again," murmured Aife.

"Aye. Again," Drest said, voice rising as he lifted the wine cup to his mouth. "It took me long years to lead our army against the Damnonii stronghold, far longer than it should have. But after this, I won't hesitate again. Queen Narina, and her arseling consort, Ysfael of the Votadini, will face the wrath of the Picts, even if I have to pay the Saxons a fortune to ride with us!"

Qunavo thumped his own wine cup on the table, calling for vengeance. "And once we have Dun Breatann," he said grimly. "We should take Hengist's sea-wolves and deal with that bastard

King Cunedda, since it was his plotting that ultimately led to the death of the hostages and all this trouble."

Drest grinned. "I like your thinking, druid. With the Saxons under our command we can remove Narina and Cunedda and take all their lands for our own. Only the Dalriadans will remain in the west, and we can deal with them once our own army returns to full strength!" His eyes were shining with excitement as the prospect of seizing control of all the lands north of Antoninus's Wall came alive in his mind.

Ria looked less excited by the prospect of another expensive conflict. "Yet another war started by the actions of a foolish man," said the druidess sourly.

"Aye," Aife agreed, but her hand was resting on the pommel of her sword and she knew she'd be in the front rank when it came to the first clash of shieldwalls. For all she'd grown to love the company of Catia, and deeply respected the druid, Bellicus, Aife was a commander in Drest's army and she would fight for her people with all she had.

She just prayed that she'd never have to face either of those Damnonii when the battle came.

The wrath of the Picts. There was death and suffering to come, Aife mused as her father beckoned her to take a seat at their table and called for meat and drink for her. Death and suffering, aye. Yet, even if they should win, and defeat Narina's people, she feared the Saxons. They may be allies now, but, with both Damnonii and Pictish armies depleted by their recent and coming conflicts, what would stop Hengist from taking advantage of that weakness?

The course had been set, though, and there was nothing she could do to stop it. Nodding her thanks, she accepted a wooden plate laden with bread, crumbly cheese, and cold meat and dug in with gusto. War was coming, and Aife would be ready when the time came to ride out, as was her duty.

AUTHOR'S NOTE

I really hope you enjoyed *Wrath of the Picts*! It was my first novel as a full-time writer and I had a great time coming up with all the different sections. My editor noted that it went along at breakneck pace and perhaps that was down to the fact I was able to write almost every day, rather than simply fitting it around my old job. The story seemed to come together quickly, almost writing itself, although the editing process was fairly lengthy as I had to add some deeper elements (like Ysfael's reasoning for wanting Aife dead) to go with all the action.

Probably my favourite scene was the 'magical battle' between Bellicus and Yngvildr. Druid vs *volva*! I spent some time watching videos of street magicians in action, coming up with interesting tricks that our combatants could perform. Seeing the reactions of real audiences to those 'simple' sleight-of-hand proved to me that such a battle could be very exciting and really get a crowd going. In my books I don't have fantasy magic, with bolts of lightning shooting from wizard's fingers, but we know the druids from rival tribes would have their own face-off before a real battle so I wanted to come up with a realistic, yet exciting, version of that. Some might see such 'magic' as mere parlour tricks, but learning these skills takes an insane amount of dedication and skill. Even now in our supposedly enlightened age, with all our technology and knowledge of how things are done, a really good magician or mentalist like David Blaine or Derren Brown can blow our minds with the things they do. So I greatly enjoyed researching and writing that scene and I hope you thought it was fun to read.

Another element in the novel that might raise eyebrows is my description of Pictish tattoos. Certain Roman writers, including Julius Caesar, Martial, and Herodian, make mention of certain northern Britons tattooing or painting designs on their bodies. It forms a vivid image in one's mind, of naked, hairy, blue-painted warriors, screaming defiance at the legions. Nowadays, it seems historians doubt this was actually true for the methods used at that time for such tattoos might have faded quickly, or even been poisonous! Yet, those Roman writers do mention it, and mummified bodies of Iron Age nomads have been found in Siberia bearing intricate, mysterious tattoos. So it was possible, and besides, the Picts might have simply painted on their designs, allowing them to fade quickly or even wash off, much like the Native Americans' 'war paint'. I thought it would add some colour and interest to a few scenes so that's why I've included the Pictish tattoos, make up your own mind on whether it's historically accurate or not!

Next up from me will be another Forest Lord novelette starring Little John and Will Scaflock. Titled *The Pedlar's Promise*, it'll be out sometime around December 2022 and, as is usual now, has a suitable winter/Christmas setting! After that, well, I am planning a new series, with all new characters and a brand-new period for me. I've no idea when that will be published though as, at this point, I've not even started writing it yet! I'm really excited about the project though, so do look out for it. I think anyone who's enjoyed my books so far will enjoy this next adventure too.

As I said at the start of this note, I'm now writing full-time and I have you, the readers, to thank for that. I truly appreciate all your support, buying the books, reviewing them, and spreading the word. 2013, when I published my first novel, *Wolf's Head*, was a very hard year for me on a personal level so to reach this point now, less than ten years later, is a dream come true. Thank you all so much, and I hope I can continue to entertain you for many decades to come!

Steven A. McKay
Old Kilpatrick,
21 August 2022

ALSO BY STEVEN A. McKAY

The Forest Lord Series:
Wolf's Head
The Wolf and the Raven
Rise of the Wolf
Blood of the Wolf

Knight of the Cross*
Friar Tuck and the Christmas Devil*
The Prisoner*
The Escape*
The Abbey of Death*
Faces of Darkness*
Sworn To God
The House In The Marsh*

The Warrior Druid of Britain Chronicles
The Druid
Song of the Centurion
The Northern Throne
The Bear of Britain
Over The Wall*

LUCIA – A Roman Slave's Tale

Titles marked * are spin-off novellas, novelettes, or short stories. All others are full length novels.

Printed in Great Britain
by Amazon